Holding the Future

Carey

God Bless and Keep you!

Kara M

Enjoy :)

1

1

Josh trembled as he faced his father. Fear ripped through him. He looked up into his father's angry eyes and his blood seemed to freeze. When was this going to stop. Would he never escape. He wanted to plead for his father to stop, but he knew it would only make the pain that much worse.

His father's eyes flashed with anger again.

Josh dropped his head and waited knowing what was coming.

His father raised his belt. "Don't you dare behave that way in church ever again, boy. Am I clear?"

Josh bit his lip. Was his father ever going to stop? He heard the belt as it whipped through the air -

Josh jumped out of bed. His eyes were wide with fright and his body soaked with sweat. The nightmare that had awakened him was more real than the reality that he was safe. He looked around the room almost expecting to see his dad there, even though his father had been sent to prison. He shook his head and sat back on his bed, still gasping for breath and trembling in fear.

Taking a deep breath and letting it out he tried to relax. It had been a long time since he had been faced with nightmares of his old life. Why now? Why did he even think about his dad? Why did he have to have any memories of what his life use to be like? He wished he could just erase them all, but he could still hear his father's voice. He could still see his angry eyes, and feel the hate that had ruled his life.

He shook his head trying to rid himself of the unhappy memories. That was all in the past. It was over. His father was in prison where he belonged, and he wouldn't be getting out for a long time. At least he hoped it would be a long time. He tried to think back to what the judge had said, but he couldn't remember, after all he had only been eight.

His mind raced back to the courtroom. His father's angry glare had held him too scared to even speak. Even when the judge had been asking him questions, he had been to frightened to answer.

Then came the verdict. His father had been found guilty of child abuse and sentenced to five years in prison. His rights were revoked from Joshua, meaning that even if he did get out, unless a judge ruled otherwise, Josh would never have to live with his father again, or see him again.

He could still see the hate in his father's eyes as he had been lead out of the courtroom in handcuffs. "I'll get you for this, boy. You will pay for what you have done!" he screamed as he walked away.

Josh took a deep breath, shaking his head to rid himself of the memories, slowly he stood. Fear still held his heart. He walked to the mirror and looked at the frightened eyes of the boy starting back at him. He shook his head again. "It's going to be fine. No one is going to hurt you. He is long gone and out of your life. You have a good life here. It's all going to be just fine," he whispered to himself in the mirror.

Tears blinded him for a moment. He shook his head and blinked hard, trying to rid them from his eyes. He still felt shaken. His hands rested on the top of the dresser as he bowed his head. "Please, Lord, help. I don't understand why I am having these dreams. This is the third one in just as many days. Please help me to stop having them, unless you are giving them to me for a reason. I really don't understand, Lord. Is there something that you are trying to tell me?

What is it, Lord? What do you want me to know? Please help me. Help me not to be afraid."

He shook his head and walked back to the bed. Slowly he sat down on the edge and rested his head in his hands. What was going on? What was wrong with him? This wasn't like him. He didn't just have nightmares, not any more. Why all of the sudden were they coming back, and why so strongly?

He glanced out the window and could just see the sun beginning to rise above the trees.

No point in trying to get back to sleep. It would soon be time to get up anyway. Besides, if he tried to sleep, he just would have more nightmares, at least, that is what had seemed to happen the last two nights. He shook his head. He didn't want to remember his past, at least not that part of it. He really didn't want to remember any of it. He just wanted to be thankful that he was out of it.

God had delivered him out of his past and after many months and years of fear. He had helped him to live an almost normal life for the last seven, almost eight years. Why was this happening now? He didn't understand.

Again he bowed his head. "I can't shake the feeling that you are preparing me for something, God. What is it?" He paused in his prayer and looked up at the lighting sky through his window. He waited hoping to hear God answer.

Again he bowed his head, "What ever it is, please give me the grace and strength to make it through it. I am afraid of him, God. Please take away my fears."

As he lifted his head, his gaze rested on his Bible. Lying back on his bed he picked it up and opened it. His gaze roamed the pages, but, for some reason, this morning he couldn't seem to get his mind to read. He couldn't focus on the words. He still felt jittery and jumpy. Why? It was a question he couldn't answer.

Suddenly he stopped. It was as if the words jumped off the pages at him. "Fear not; for I am with thee: be not dismayed; for I am thy God: I will strengthen thee; yea, I will help thee; yea, I will uphold thee with the right hand of my righteousness." He looked up at the top of he page, Isaiah 41:10. He read the words again. "Be not afraid." Is that really what God meant? He sighed. Of course that is what God meant. He always says what he means, but was it really possible to live without fear? Was God warning him, or was he trying

4

to tell him something? How was he suppose to live without fear?

He closed his Bible and lay down again, letting the Bible rest on his stomach. He closed his eyes. "God, I am afraid. Are you trying to tell me something? I don't understand. What are you trying to tell me? What are you preparing me for? I just don't get it. If I am not suppose to be afraid, why did you make me live through what I have?"

He sat up quickly and let his Bible fall open on is lap. He glanced down and started to read. This time it had fallen open to Psalm 118. His eyes focused on verse 6, and as he read it tears ran down his cheeks. "The Lord is on my side; I will not fear: What can man do unto me."

His mind went to the scars on his back and the pain he still felt in his heart when he thought of his dad. Man could do a lot to a body, but he can't take away the soul. Only that person can throw away their soul.

Slowly he closed his Bible and bowed his head again. "Lord, I am afraid, but I know I don't need to be. You are taking care of me, just like you always have. I don't need to be afraid. Please help me. Give me the strength I need to make it through whatever it is that you are preparing me for. Help me to trust you."

Slowly he stood. It was time to get ready for the day. He hoped he could keep his foster parents from seeing just how tired he was. What if they did notice? Should he tell them he had been having nightmares again if they asked? Or maybe he should tell them anyway. A lot of times it helped him when he talked to Luke about things.

As he began to get dressed, he thought about it. Soon he determined he was keeping his nightmares secret. He didn't want to worry his foster parents. They had enough to worry about without worrying about him. Besides, there wasn't anything wrong. It was just nightmares. That was all. They couldn't do anything to change it. And if he told them, that would mean talking about his past; and he didn't want to remember anything about his past, and having to talk about it made him remember too much.

He heard the other kids running down the stairs and he smiled. He was so blessed to have been put in this family. He knew he was blessed. God cared about him. He didn't need to fear. God was with him.

He heard Joy singing in the bathroom and smiled again. Mom and Dad, that was what he called his foster parents, had named her right. She was full of joy, and she bathed the rest of the house in it as well. There never was a moment, it seemed, that there wasn't a song on her lips, a smile on her face, and a shine in her eyes.

Josh sighed as he looked in the mirror again. He tried to hide the fear he saw in his eyes. "Please help me, God. You promised, you are my strength. I trust you. Please, help me to stop being afraid, and please don't let them see. Please, help them not to see or ask. Please."

Slowly he made his way down stairs, hoping that most of the younger ones would have made it down stairs before he got there. He smiled as he sat down at the table and watched the kids scramble for their seats. As he watched he thought about what his life was like before he came here, which in turn brought back his nightmares. He shivered as he saw his father's angry eyes in his mind. He closed his eyes and tried to forget, but the look of anger and hate in his father's eyes still haunted him.

He jumped when Joy poked him, bringing his mind slamming back into the present. He looked at her quickly.

Joy could see the Josh had his mind on other things, but she didn't want him getting in trouble. She glanced toward her dad and hoped that Josh got the message.

Josh got it. Slowly he looked at Mr. Dawson, the man who had been a father to him the last seven years of his life, and way more of a father than his own had ever been. He realized that the man must have spoken to him, because all the kids were watching him. Nervously he cleared his throat. "I am sorry, sir, I wasn't listening." He flinched when he said it, but then made himself relax. He had no reason to be afraid. Mr. Dawson wasn't anything like his father.

Mr. Dawson's eyes twinkled, reminding Josh of fireflies on a summer night. "I asked you to pray, son. It's your turn."

Josh glanced away. He felt too frightened to pray, and that feeling was a new one for him. Even in all the things he had lived through, he had never been afraid to pray. What was wrong with him? He took a deep breath trying to shake himself of the fear in his heart. "Yes, sir."

He cleared his throat nervously as he bowed his head. "Dear God, bless this food and help us to have a good day. Amen."

He raised his head to see Mrs. Dawson watching him. He

looked down quickly, but not before he saw a look pass between Mr. and Mrs. Dawson. What did it mean?

Luke Dawson watched his children as they ate breakfast. He noted that all of them seemed to have a good appetite except Josh. The boy usually laughed and joked with his siblings, but this morning he seemed preoccupied with his own thoughts. As the rest of the kids hurriedly ate what was before them and asked to be excused, trying to get in the last few minutes of play time before their mom called them to start school, Josh had simply pushed his food around.

Luke smiled as he watched the children run from the table as soon as they were excused. He heard them chase each other up the stairs and then he heard them again, screaming as they ran.

Josh and Joy were the only ones left at the table with their parents in a matter of a few minutes

Joy, full of life as ever, offered to help her mom clear the table and quickly grabbed the dishes and took them to the sink. Josh stood and picked up his own dishes. His father had taught him long ago to help with the work and to clean up after himself. He shivered and quickly pushed away the thoughts of his father, but the shiver had not gone unnoticed by Luke as he watched Josh.

Luke stood and followed him across the room. He waited silently behind the boy as he put his dishes in the sink.

Josh turned from the sink and nearly crashed into Luke. He jumped seeing Luke standing there. Fear rippled through him. What was Luke going to say to him? He could tell by his stance that he wasn't happy about something. He dropped his head and would have backed up a step if he could have, but there was nowhere to go.

"Son, I am going to be needing your help help this afternoon. The yard needs cleaned up and the grass needs cut. Be done with your school work by the time I get home this afternoon, please."

Josh felt his body start to tremble. He quickly clamped down on his emotions and nodded. "Yes, sir, I will." As he spoke his mind flitted back to his nightmares earlier that morning and the previous mornings. Were they a warning, he wondered again?

He became aware that Luke was staring at him and he froze.

What if God was warning him that Luke was going to start hitting him like his dad had! He looked up into Luke's face. Then trembled and looked away. Were his thoughts evident?

Luke cleared his throat and waited till Josh looked up at him again. Then he looked the boy in the eye. "Josh, you seem to be lost in thought this morning. I want you to concentrate on school and not be a problem for your mom. You have a lot to do today in school and a lot to do after it, so no daydreaming. Do you understand?" He looked at Josh closer, noting the dark circles under his eyes and the fear that seemed to snap in them, "Do you want to talk to me about what seems to be bothering you? You have been a little out of sorts for a few days now."

Josh fought down his fear. He didn't want to talk about anything that was bothering him, but he was afraid, if Luke saw how scared he felt, he would make him talk about it. "Yes, sir. I mean no, sir. I mean, I will be done, and I won't waste time. I promise."

He wondered if he would be able to keep that promise, but quickly pushed the thought out of his mind. He could ignore his fear. He was sure of it. He just had to focus on his school, and his nightmares would fade away. Even as that thought entered his mind he knew it was crazy. There was no way he was going to be able to forget his nightmares, no way at all.

Luke shook his head slightly and turned away. He knew something was bothering Josh, but in the years that Josh had lived with them, the boy had never been able to talk much about what was bothering him until he was ready to talk about it. He wished the boy would be a little more open, but he knew he couldn't force him to be.

Josh relaxed a little as Luke turned away from him. "If you are sure that you don't want to talk about it, son, you had better get yourself up stairs and get ready for the day before your mom is ready for all of you to get started."

Luke watched as Josh walked away. *Dear God,* he prayed in his heart, *please take care of him. Please wash away his fear. Help him to trust me enough to talk to me. Help him to trust you. Please, God, let us know what is going on. Please help me to understand.*

Josh felt himself relax even more as he walked up to his room.

"Thank you, Lord, that he didn't make me talk to him. I know I should be able to, and he wants me to talk to him when I have a problem, but I can't talk about this. If I talk about it, it will make it even more real. I don't want to have to live through this again, God. Please help me. Please take away my fears. Please."

He stepped into his room and shut the door. He just needed to be alone for a little while and sort through everything he was feeling. He sighed again. Why did all these nightmares plague him, and why now? He hadn't seen his father in years. Why all of the sudden did all of these thoughts and feelings have to come barging in? He wasn't ready to deal with them. He didn't want to ever deal with them. *Please, God, take them away.*

Then the thought struck him. Maybe that was why this was happening to him. Maybe God was telling him it was time to deal with his feelings. Maybe it was time to forgive his dad. Maybe it was time to let all the hurt from the past go and trust Luke and Annie, but he still wasn't sure he was ready.

He sighed as he dropped onto his bed. He glanced at the clock and quickly stood back up. Annie was going to be calling up in just a few minutes for him to head down for school. It was time to stop thinking about all the dreams of the last few nights. It was time to live the here and now and forget about his past - that is, if he could.

2

Around four that afternoon Luke entered the house and found his wife at the kitchen counter working on supper. Josh sat at the table staring at a book, but, from what Luke could see, it didn't look like the boy was really looking at it. He frowned slightly. Why was Josh still sitting at the table? Was he working ahead again today?

He walked up behind his wife and wrapped his arms around her. "How is the most beautiful woman in the world this afternoon?" He leaned his head around hers and kissed her lovingly.

Josh looked up as he heard Annie giggle. He saw his mom and dad, and his breath caught in his throat. Had his real dad ever showed that kind of affection for his mom? He wished he could remember. Luke and Annie were always smiling at each other, always holding each other's hands, or giving one another a look of love. Had his dad ever looked at anyone with a look of love?

Tears sprang to his eyes unexpectedly, and he looked away. He didn't want to think about his real dad. He didn't want anything to do with him. Why did all of these thoughts keep coming to him? He tried to push his thoughts away as he looked back down at his book, but tears clouded his vision. He lay his head on his arm resting on the table and fought back more tears.

Luke turned from his wife and looked at Josh. He was surprised to see the boy lay his head down on the table. Was he not feeling well? He shook his head. The boy knew to tell them if he wasn't feeling well, and if he told Annie he wasn't feeling well she would have sent him to bed, not made him stay up and continue to do school. He felt even more puzzled as he glanced at Annie and all she did was shrug.

"Well, son, come on and let's get that yard cleaned up. I want to have it done before dark. We have a lot of work to do in a few hours. Maybe we can have a cook out if we get it done soon enough. I am sure we can find some others to help us out."

Josh jumped and jerked his head up to look at his dad.

Luke smiled as a loud shout rose up from around the corner as the other five kids ran in. "Really, Daddy! Can we really have a cook out? Can we!"

He laughed. "If we can get the yard cleaned up in time to get a fire going and have everything ready by supper time. I am already famished. I don't know if I want to wait till we are done with the big mess in our yard to have supper. So if we are having a cook out we better work hard and fast."

The kids all let out squeals of delight and ran out the door, pulling on their jackets as they ran, for though it was late in April, winter had been late that year and a cold still held in the air.

Five year old Chelsey, the youngest of all the kids, looked up at Josh, then looked at her dad, "Does Josh get to come out and help too, Daddy? Mommy said he has to stay there till he is all done with school, cause he wasn't behaving. Does he have to come help or does he have to finish his school?"

Josh stiffened, but he didn't dare look up at Luke to see what he was thinking.

"Chelsey." Annie's voice was soft, but held a warning.

Luke put Chelsey down and turned to his wife. "Annie, what's going on?" He looked over at Josh, "Joshua, what is going on? What is all this about?"

Annie touched Luke's arm and shook her head slightly.

Luke got the message and nodded, but his curiosity was peaked. He started to say something else, but at that moments the kids all came running back in.

"Come on, Dad. Let's go!" they cried in unison.

Luke laughed. "All right all of you, get out there and get all the sticks picked up and gathered into the biggest bonfire you have ever seen. I will be out shortly."

The kids raced out the door with more hollers and yells.

Josh felt Luke's eyes on him as he stared at his book. He tried hard to make his mind focus on the page, but try as he might he couldn't even hardly see what was on it. He trembled. He could almost feel Luke's eyes burning into him. A shiver ran down his spine. He felt, more then heard, Luke walk over to him. Slowly he lifted his head and looked the man in the eyes. He knew he was in trouble. He felt his whole body tremble. Then he felt himself start shaking.

Luke's deep blue eyes looked concerned, but Josh knew that he was also upset, by the way the muscles of the man's jaw were working. He didn't want to let Luke down, or disappoint him, but he knew he was going to. Luke had told him to be done with his school before he got home and he hadn't even been able to finish one subject today. He just couldn't get his mind to focus. He had stared at the book all day, but he hadn't really seen a thing.

He looked down not wanting to see the disappointment he knew he was going to see in Luke's eyes.

Luke cleared his throat and the noise sounded loud in the silence of the room. "Josh?"

Josh trembled visibly this time, but slowly looked back into Luke's eyes. "Yes, sir?" Even his voice shook.

"How much school have you gotten done today?"

Josh looked away. His stomach twisted into a knot. He didn't know what to do. He knew he couldn't lie, but with everything in him he didn't want to tell the truth. He swallowed around the lump that had formed in his throat.

Annie saw the fear in Josh's eyes and her heart went out to him. What ever was wrong with him today she knew in that moment it must have something to do with his dad or he wouldn't be so afraid of Luke. "It's okay, Josh, go ahead and answer your dad."

Josh looked up slowly, "None, sir." His voice was quiet and sounded as unsure and afraid as he was. He felt shame wash over him. This had never happened to him before. He had always been quick in his studies and good at concentrating and getting things done quickly and efficiently. His father had taught him that.

Abruptly he pushed that thought away. He didn't want to think about his father at all. He looked up at Luke again, wondering what the man going to do to him?

Luke frowned then looked up at Annie. "What is going on?

Why hasn't he done any school today?"

Annie shrugged. She had seen Josh looking off into space for the majority of the day. Every time she had spoken to him, she had to repeat herself. He just hadn't been focused. It was very out of character for him. He was usually very attentive and well behaved. But when she had asked him what was wrong he had insisted that everything was fine, and he didn't need anything. She had told him to stop daydreaming and start working if that was the case. This had happened several times over the morning.

Finally, when the other kids were done with their school and Josh still hadn't completed anything, she asked him again what was wrong, and again he had insisted that everything was fine. She knew he was lying and that something was very wrong for him to be like this, but, since he wouldn't give her a truthful answer, she had told him if nothing was wrong and he was just wasting time today, he would remain seated at the table till he had completed all his school for the day.

Luke again looked from Joshua to Annie. "Why hasn't he completed any school today?" he asked again. "Josh, what have you been doing all day that you haven't gotten any school done?"

Annie glanced at Josh to see if he would admit yet to something being wrong.

Josh bit his lip and looked down. He felt tears sting his eyes as his fear mounted. He shook his head hoping to rid his eyes of the tears and to escape telling Luke the truth.

Annie sighed and looked her husband in the eye when she saw Josh shake his head. "He hasn't gotten any school done today because he hasn't focused on it. He has sat right here ever since we started here this morning. He has been offered help, he has been asked to talk about what is distracting him, he has been offered opportunity to talk about what is wrong. He insists that everything is fine, so I told him he could stay here till he was completely done with school for today if he wanted to lie to me and tell me nothing was wrong." She motioned toward him, "This is how far he has gotten."

Luke stood up. He walked over to Joshua's chair and turned it so the boy was looking directly at him.

Josh felt his skin start to crawl. His father would have whipped him bad for something like this. Would Luke?

He shook his head. Luke might be angry, but he wasn't going

to hit him. He had made him stand in a corner, or go to bed without supper a few times, but that was all. No, surely he wasn't going to hit him.

Slowly Josh raised his gaze to meet his foster father's. "Yes, sir?" He tried desperately to keep his voice from shaking so Luke wouldn't know how scared he was.

"Joshua, is this true?"

Josh felt his mind jump along with his heartbeat. "What part are you wondering if it is true, sir?"

Luke felt weird, Josh calling him sir. It had been a long time since he had called him that. "Are you just wool gathering over here?" Luke felt his temper rise. Silently he prayed for the Lord to help him deal with this situation the right way. It was obvious something was on the boy's mind. But how was he suppose to get him to talk about it? "Is that true?"

Josh looked down. "Yes, sir. I recon it is."

Luke placed his fist on the table and leaned closer to Josh. "Why?"

Josh gulped. He recognized a voice of threat all too well. Seeing Luke's fist on the table sent another wave a fear over him. "No reason, sir," he tried to not sound scared, but he knew he was failing. He dropped his gaze.

Luke gripped Josh's shoulder tightly. "You are lying to me, son?"

Josh trembled as he sank lower into the chair. "Yes, sir," he whispered. Suddenly he realized what he had said, and his head shot up. "I mean – I – mean- no, s-s-sir. I j-j-just – I didn't mean to – I just can't- it's just that-"

Luke nodded. "What's on you mind, son?" He sat down across the table. "Come on, out with it. Now."

Josh looked away again as his stomach knotted in pain. He couldn't do this, he didn't want to do this. He didn't want to worry them. Besides, he wasn't even sure what to say. It was all stupid. He was letting his stupid nightmares affect his whole day. He had to stop. He had to just get over it. And the best way to do that was to not tell anyone he was having nightmares. He looked up at Luke. "I just can't focus." *Truth*, he thought, *just not all of it.*

Luke bit his lip and looked away for a moment. He silently prayed for God to show him what to do. He was at a loss this time.

14

Finally he turned back. "Joshua, I don't know what for sure to say. I asked you to get your work done earlier today. I told you I was going to need you this afternoon. I got home late, and you still aren't done."

Josh looked down. He felt ashamed. "Yes, sir, you did. I am sorry that I-"

Luke cut him off. "Joshua, I am not finished."

Josh snapped his mouth shut and looked down. *If you would have been talking to your dad your lips would be bleeding by now. What is wrong with you?* he chided himself. He knew better than to try and make excuses.

"I don't know what to do now, Son. I need you outside, and your mother told you that you are going to stay here till you are done." He looked him in the eye. "I want the honest truth out of you, son, how much school have you gotten done today?"

Josh gulped. He looked up at Luke with fear in his heart, though he hoped it wasn't shining in his eyes. What was Luke going to do to him when he told him nothing? He opened his mouth to speak, but he couldn't get the words out. He swallowed again. The tremble that had started in his body earlier became even more visible. "Nothing," he finally managed to whisper. His voice trembled when he said it, giving away his horrible fear. He dropped his head in shame and waited for Luke to start screaming at him the way his dad would have done. He felt himself shrink away from him, and his whole being tensed, bracing itself for the whipping he was fearing was coming.

Luke stood up and walked to the other end of the room and back. "You will get that work done today, son. I am going to have the other kids help me in the yard. You are going to sit in this seat and not move till you have captivated your mind enough to get this work done. Do I make myself clear? And you will have it done by supper time. Got it?"

Josh looked away. "Yes, sir," he muttered. He hated being indoors. It made his memories that much worse. He didn't want to sit still. He wanted to get up and move. He wanted to do something to clear his mind.

As Luke and Annie walked out of the room and then the house to join the other kids he let himself relax a little. At least he was alone. Now, why wasn't he able to think straight? "God, help me. Help me to trust you. You said you have all the plans worked out for

15

my life. You said that you will take care of me. Please help that to be true. Help me to trust you."

Finally he turned his attention back to math. "Help me get done with this, God," he whispered as he set to work getting his mind around some of the problems. He heard the family outside laughing and his heart twisted. He knew he wasn't the only one who wasn't Luke and Annie's by birth, but today it was hard not to feel like and outsider.

In all truth, Joy, the one closest in age to him, was the only one who was actually Luke and Annie's. The rest of the kids were either foster, or they had been adopted at birth.

Those kids had no idea Josh wasn't their real brother. Or that Luke and Annie weren't their real parents. Josh thought about that for a bit and shivered.

Why? He asked again. Why? Why did he have to remember his past when the other kids never had to put up with a parent who hated them, or at least, acted like he did. Why did he have to have nightmares about how things were? Why did he have to remember?

Tears burned the back of his eyes. Angrily he pushed his feelings away. He looked down at his math book and forced his mind to focus. He had to get through this.

The problem wasn't school, the problem was his past; and that was more so what he had to get through. The problem was he had to get through it all alone. There was no one who could help him through it. There was nothing anyone could or would do to help.

He rested his head on his hands. "God, you said that you would lead me and protect me; please help Dad not to hit me for today. I am scared. I really am. Please don't tell anyone. And don't let anyone know. Please help me!" He bit his lip when he realized he had been praying out loud.

His mind went back to the ninety-first psalm. "They shall mount up with wings as eagles." He lifted his head and looked back down at his book. "I wish I could mount up on those eagles wings and fly away. But since I can't, God, would you please help me get through this day. Please help me to focus on my school and get it done. Please don't let me disappoint Luke again. "

About half an hour later Josh sensed someone behind him. He jerked around in fear and found Luke watching him. Fear pricked his skin. He trembled as he backed away slightly.

Luke cleared his throat. "How far along are you now, son?"

Josh looked down at his book and ducked his head. He had tried, but he hadn't been able to get anything done, he just couldn't get his mind to understand it. He trembled.

Luke gripped his shoulder. "Son, how far along are you?"

Josh whimpered as he turned away from him.

Luke stepped up behind him and looked down at his paper. He felt his anger rise. What was wrong with his son, and why was he refusing to talk about it? "How many more subjects do you have?"

Josh lowered his gaze. "A lot, sir."

Luke rested his hand on the boys shoulder and felt him tremble. He sighed but forced himself to sound stern. "I asked you a question, son. I want an answer, now, and not a vague one either."

Josh kept his head down, not daring to look at Luke. "All of them, sir. I haven't gotten any done."

Luke swung a chair around and sat down resting his arms on the back of it. "You sure you don't want to talk bought it?"

Josh stiffened as he looked up at Luke. "About what?" What was he suppose to do now? He didn't want to tell Luke about his nightmares, but what was he suppose to do?

Luke shifted his gaze slightly. "Whatever it is that is bothering you, son. You aren't hiding it very well. I can tell you are trying to hide whatever it is and not worry your mom and me with it, but I think it will help you if you talk about it. Get it off your chest, so to speak."

Josh felt his stomach turn. He thought for a minute he was going to be sick. "What makes you think I am trying to hide anything?"

Luke smiled slightly. "Well, for one thing you have been calling me sir all day." Luke saw Josh flinch and wondered about it, but kept going. "For another, I don't remember a time that you were still doing school at six o'clock at night. Did you get any of your work done today yet, Joshua?"

Josh dropped his gaze. "Yes, sir. You are right, I haven't done any. I'm sorry."

Luke folded his arms over the back of the chair once more and waited. "So, son, are you going to tell me what is up? What has you so upset?"

Josh shifted uneasily. "Well, it's kind of hard to explain. You

17

see-"

At that moment the other kids burst into the kitchen. "Dad, it's all ready! Can we have our cook out now? Please!"

Luke smiled and his eyes softened. "Okay, we will be out there in a few minutes. Let's go."

The kids let out shrieks of laughter as they raced out side. Once the door slammed shut behind the last kid Luke turned back to Josh. "We are not done with this conversation. You will talk to me later. Come on, let's get outside and get this cookout underway."

Josh hesitated. "But I thought-"

Luke frowned. "You are just going to have to double up tomorrow. And this time no daydreaming."

"Yes, sir." Josh stood and started to put his books away.

"Joshua," Luke stopped him in his tracks. "Quit calling me sir. It makes me feel so old."

Josh bit his lip, and waited, "Yes, sir." Josh jerked suddenly, knowing he had just disobeyed, but he hadn't been able to stop himself. His stomach twisted, but he tried not to let Luke see how scared he was.

Luke shook his head and chuckled. "Get outside with your siblings and lets get started on this cook out."

Josh jumped up and ran out the door. He couldn't believe that Luke was going to let him participate, but he wasn't going to argue with it.

3

The next morning Josh again woke in a cold sweat. His dreams were even more real than they had been yesterday. What was he suppose to do? He couldn't go on like this. He didn't want to sleep, but he had to get some sleep. Every time he slept nightmares plagued him. He couldn't sleep. He shivered as he slowly rolled out of bed. He had to get over this some how. But how? He dropped to his knees and pleaded for help from the only one he knew who could give it to him.

"God, help me," he pleaded. "You gave me promises. Help me to stand on them. Really and truly, God, I need your help. I know I am not suppose to fear man, because you are with me. And nothing they can do can take you away from me, but I am very afraid. Please, please, help me. And please help no one else to find out."

He stood slowly and walked over to the mirror. He shook his head as he looked at himself. He let his hands trace over the scars that were on his chest. Tears burned his eyes. What kind of a monster did his dad have to be to put scares like that on a child or seven. He shook his head quickly. That life was over. He didn't need to fear it. Luke and Annie had taken good care of him and had never raised a hand to hurt him, and they sure hadn't hurt him just to feel the pleasure of hurting someone else.

He turned away from the mirror and gave his head another quick shake. Dwelling on his past wasn't going to help him at all. And it sure wasn't going to make him forget his nightmares. He pulled on his shirt and headed for the bathroom.

Luke was just coming out of his room as Josh headed down the hall. He stopped and waited on him.

Josh felt his stomach turn. He knew what Luke wanted, but he didn't want to talk about it, not now, more than likely not ever, though he knew he would have to some time; but after not much sleep and the horrible nightmares he had, he didn't want to talk to anyone. Slowly he walked up to Luke and stopped. He waited for him to speak.

"Josh," Luke's voice was quiet, but firm. "We need to talk about yesterday, and since we are the only two up, now looks like a good time."

Josh bit his lip as he dropped his head. "Yes, sir, I know we need to talk about it, but couldn't we do it another time."

Luke frowned. "I thought I said to quit calling me sir."

Josh looked up quickly and fear registered in his eyes. "I'm sorry," he barely stopped himself from saying sir again. He stepped back feeling himself panic. If he didn't call his father sir, his father whipped him till he remembered not to forget again. He knew that was why he had started in with Luke over the last few days. His nightmares were pulling him back to his old life even though he didn't live that life anymore.

Luke motioned Josh to proceed him downstairs.

Josh felt his skin crawl as Luke followed him. He tried to relax, but he couldn't stop worrying about what Luke would say or do to him. His nightmares and lack of sleep were affecting him in ways he wasn't realizing. And it was keeping his fear at high gear. He stopped as they entered the living room and waited for Luke to talk. He felt himself shaking.

Luke stepped around him and sat down on the couch. He motioned for Josh to sit next to him. "Joshua, we need to talk. I know you don't want to, but you need to. What was wrong yesterday?"

Josh looked away. His heart twisted in him. He didn't want to lie, but he didn't want to tell Luke about his nightmares. He didn't want to talk about it. It would only make it that much worse. It would only make them seem that much more real. He frantically searched his brain for something to say that wouldn't be a lie, but also, wouldn't reveal more of the truth than he wanted to talk about.

Luke waited silently, watching the emotions flit across Josh's face and the fear dance in and out of his eyes.

Finally Josh lifted his head and looked strait at Luke. "I-" there was a loud commotion on the stairs and the other kids burst into the room.

"Where's Mom? Are we ready for breakfast yet? What are you doing down here? When do we get to eat?"

Luke felt irritated with his kids for the first time in a long time. He had hoped to get Josh to talk, but he knew that wasn't going to happen now. "We aren't done." He looked directly into Josh's eyes. "Do you understand? We are going to finish this conversation."

Josh nodded slightly. For now he was just relieved that the other kids had shown up when they had. They had saved him from having to talk. If only he could have a good day and forget his nightmares, maybe Luke would forget about yesterday and life would get back to normal. He sighed as he shook his head. He may as well wish for pigs to fly. Luke wasn't going to forget, and he knew it.

Later that day, as the kids were finishing up school, Luke came home from visiting some people from the church who were in the hospital and let out a holler a he enter the kitchen. "Hey, everyone! I have some great news!"

The kids all jumped up and screamed. "What is it, Daddy! What!"

Luke laughed as Annie looked at him with a look of frustration, that he would excite the kid so.

"A new family is moving in down the road. We have new neighbors!"

Annie smiled broadly. "That is such good news." Her voice was soft, but Luke and Josh both heard the longing in her voice. They both knew she longed for neighbors closer by. Annie had grown up in the city. A move to a small acreage outside of a small town in Iowa was a hard move for her. She had tried hard not to complain, but it had been a hard change for her. Luke hadn't noticed how hard it was on her, but hearing the excitement and longing in her voice that a neighbor was moving in a mile and a half up the road made him realize how hard this life was on her. It also made him thank God

21

again for his wonderful wife and the blessing she was to this family and him.

"It has been such a long time since we have had neighbors so close. We must go and welcome them when they have settled in." She looked up at Luke. "Tomorrow is Saturday. Maybe we should go in the evening. That will give them plenty of time to get settled in. I don't want to bombard them, but I do want them to feel welcome. And maybe they will want to come to church on Sunday."

Luke smiled warmly at his wife. He couldn't believe how much he still loved her after twenty years together. "That is just what I was thinking." He glanced around the table at the kids. "I don't know how many or the ages, but they do have kids. I saw some of the stuff being unloaded."

Annie glanced around the table to see that all the kids had finished their school and were all looking at her with expectant eyes, except Joshua. Her stomach tightened. The boy was definitely battling something, but he wouldn't talk about it. It was keeping him very distracted,whatever it was, and that really bothered her. He seemed a little better today, but still very distracted and distant.

Josh saw Annie looking at him with concern in her eyes and he quickly straightened and tried to smile like nothing was bothering him.

Annie smiled at him, but the worry in her eyes didn't go away. She looked around at the other kids. "You kids can go on out and play till supper, but no running off. You are not to go down the road and try to see the new neighbors either. They will be moving in and they don't need to feel like they are being spied on. Just go play in the yard."

"Yes, Mom," came the chorus of voices, as the kids bounced out of their chairs and raced for the door.

Joy and Josh got up more quietly and headed out the door, following the rest of the kids.

Joy stopped on the steps. "So, are you going to tell me what is bothering you? I am guessing you aren't telling mom and dad, but are you going to tell me?"

Josh glanced at her out of the corner of his eye, "Your dad ask you to ask me?" his voice sounded angry, but he couldn't help it. He had started to talk to Luke twice and both times they had been interrupted. Not that that had bothered him, but why would he use Joy to try and find out what was going on? He felt anger rise in his heart.

Joy was taken by surprise. She knew Josh wasn't her real brother, but it had been so long since he had come to live with them that she had forgotten. She didn't really remember what it was like in her family before he was a part of it. She had been only five when he had come to live with them. He had always called her mom and dad, Mom and Dad, that she could remember. What had happened to make Josh refer to him as her dad, not just Dad?

"He isn't just my dad, Josh." Her voice was soft, but Josh heard the hurt running through it. "You know he loves you like a son, and I love you like a real brother. There isn't anything that can change that. So what if you weren't born in the family? God gave you to us later. I don't remember a time when you weren't my brother. And in answer to your question, no, Dad didn't ask me to ask you anything. You just looked so glum today and you were totally lost in space yesterday. I was just wondering. That is all. I thought maybe if you wanted to talk about it, it might help."

Josh eyed Joy with suspicion, then sighed. "Sorry, I didn't mean to be so mean. I didn't mean to hurt your feelings either. I know you all love me." He cleared his throat, "I just keep having these nightmares, and I don't know why."

Joy stood up straighter. "What kind of nightmares?"

Josh shrugged quickly. "Nothing I want to talk about. Just stuff that happened to me a long time go. It keeps coming back to me and I don't know why."

Joy looked thoughtful for a moment, and Josh knew she was thinking about what to say next. "Maybe you should ask Dad. He knows about that kind of stuff."

Josh looked down, then off across the yard. "I can't talk to him about it. I don't want to talk to him about it. I don't want him to know about it. I don't want to upset him. Besides that, I really don't want to talk about it, not just with Dad, but with any one. And if I try to talk to him about it, he will want me to explain and talk about it more and explain more, and I don't want to talk about any of it at all. I just want it to go away."

Joy turned to face Josh and waited till he looked at her, "You have been part of this family along time, Joshua. I don't ever remember you being afraid of anything. Surely you could talk to dad about this. Maybe it would help."

Josh studied he sister's face. Pain etched his heart. She had no idea what this type of pain did to a person. "You're right. I shouldn't be afraid to talk about this, but I am."

Joy smiled sweetly. "It wouldn't be any harder than talking to me. Dad cares about you. He wants you to talk to him. I see it in his eyes when he looks at you. He wants you to trust him. He wants to help you, if you would just let him. You know, kind of like God cares for us. But he won't barge in; we have to invite him. Dad might push you to talk a little, but that is only because he cares."

Josh smiled at his sister. He knew Joy was right. He knew Luke cared about it a great deal and wanted to help him, but that didn't take away the feeling that he still didn't want to talk about it. He took a deep breath, "Okay, Joy, I will talk to him. Not now, but maybe after supper, when all the kids are in bed."

"Awwww!" Joy protested.

Josh laughed, "That way no one can listen in on a conversation that they aren't meant to hear," he stressed.

Joy got the message. "Fine." her voice sounded irritated, but Josh knew she was faking it. She just wanted him to talk to Dad and get some help.

As soon as Josh and Joy went out the door, Luke turned to Annie. "How was he today?"

Annie shrugged. "I thought he was doing better, but then I started grading his school and-" she stopped and a look of concern fell on her face.

Luke was startled. "Annie, what is it?" He hadn't seen his wife look this distressed since she had her last miscarriage. He leaned over and put his arms around her. "What is it, Honey? Whatever it is we need to be able to talk about it."

Annie shook her head again as Luke let her go. She smiled up at him, then reached to a pile on the table and pulled out a few pieces of paper. "I told him I was going to be collecting his papers for the subject he was on every hour whether he was done or not." Her face paled slightly as she held the papers in her hands. Slowly she held them out to Luke. "I thought that we were getting somewhere and he

24

was busy doing school, but this is what I saw when I started to check his work."

Luke hesitantly reached out and took the papers. His mind whirled as he wondered what he was about to see. Slowly and fearfully he turned them over. His eyes widened as he looked at them, then widened even more as he started to realize what he was looking at. "Annie," he gasped.

Annie nodded. "I don't know for sure, but that is what it looks like to me. It's his dad that is bothering him. Something about his dad."

Luke stared in shock at the paper he was holding. Covering the paper where drawings of whips and angry eyes, sketches of a man and a boy. Tears came into Luke's eyes. "We will have to talk to him about it tonight. We better wait till after supper. Either we can send the other kids to bed early or send them upstairs to play."

Annie nodded, but tears were already streaming down her face. "Luke, what all happened to him when he was little. What would bring this on now?"

Luke looked at his wife and saw her tears. He reached out and pulled her into his arms. "Baby, it's going to be okay. We just need to talk to him about this and see what is bothering him. We don't know what happened to him when he was young, but obviously it wasn't a good thing." He glanced at the pictures again. "It is going to be fine. God has this all under control and he has a purpose for it."

Annie nodded as she got up. She turned from the table and started getting plates out for dinner. "We better get supper over with, so we can talk to him and see what is going on."

Luke nodded. "Are you okay?"

Annie nodded, but kept her back to him. "It'll be fine, Luke. Like you said, God has it all under control."

It seemed like just a few minutes after Josh and Joy had stepped out onto the porch, their mom was calling them in to supper. Josh and Joy hurried to get washed up before the whole gang came in.

The kids, all noisy from playing outside in the dirt, stormed into the house like an army. They pushed and shoved each other

25

joyfully as they waited for the bathroom, then raced for the table.

As they sat down to supper, Josh felt Luke's eyes on him. He glanced up at him, then looked away quickly. What was Luke going to say to him about the last two days? How much trouble was he going to get into? He knew he shouldn't have been doodling in school and he sure in the world shouldn't have doodled what was on his mind. But he had, and now he was going to have to talk.

He kept his head down, hoping Luke wouldn't say anything at the table with everyone else around.

Joy noticed the tension between her dad and Josh and silently prayed for them to be able to talk it out. She didn't want Josh to be in trouble, but she also knew her dad was worried about him and wanted to talk to him. She hoped Josh told her the truth. She prayed he would talk to Dad after everyone else was in bed, if not by his choice by her dad's.

Luke cleared his throat. "All of you bow your heads." He watched to be sure all heads bowed, even four year old Chelsey folded her little hands and bowed her head. He glanced at two year old Mary, who had just come to them a few weeks ago and smiled even more to see her little eyes close. He smiled in his heart. He rejoiced that God had blessed him with this wonderful family. How had he gotten so lucky? He bowed his head and tears came to his eyes and he started to pray. "Thank you, Heavenly Father, for the many many blessings you have given us. Thank you for this wonderful family. I love them all, Dear Lord. Please protect each one of us and help us all to desire to be more like you. Amen."

As he looked up, he caught his wife's eye, and she smiled at him. He smiled back as his heart swelled with love and thanks giving. God had truly and richly blessed them.

In his heart he let out a silent cry to God for help in talking with Josh tonight. He prayed God would help the boy tell them all that he needed to, and that they would know how to help him.

About halfway through dinner they were all surprised to hear a knock at the door. Luke looked up, "Who in the world could that be at this time of night?" his voice sounded as surprised as he felt.

Slowly he stood and headed for the door. Silently he asked God to give him the grace and patience he needed if it was child services again with another needy child. He and Annie had talked about this just a few days ago, and they had agreed that they didn't feel they could handle any more children right now. But what if God had different plans? He took a deep breath and opened the door.

"Good evening." He welcomed as he saw a man and woman and two kids on the porch. The woman was also holding a toddler three maybe four years of age. His heart twisted in him, was he right?

The man and woman smiled pleasantly. The kids just stood their looking on. "Hello!" The man's voice was deep, but friendly. "We just moved in down the street. We thought we would come and introduce ourselves since it looks like there aren't any other neighbors around for a little ways."

Luke laughed. Relief flooded him that is wasn't child services. *I know that is not the response I should have, Lord, but you know that Annie and I don't feel we can be good parents if we have more kids right now. If it is your will for us to get more you are going to have to prepare Annie and me.*

"Well, come on in. We were going to come over and visit you all once you had a chance to get settled in. I know how big of a job it is moving with a family." He stepped aside and motioned them in. "Please excuse us, we were just finishing up supper."

The woman flushed, embarrassed, "Oh, I am sorry. I told Jim this wasn't a good time to go visiting folks. Now here we have gone and disturbed your meal."

Luke shook his head. "No, no. I didn't mean that. It is wonderful that you came over. We are glad you did. The kids were wanting to run over to your place earlier this afternoon when I told them someone had moved in, but I wouldn't let them. So we are glad you all came over. They didn't want to wait till tomorrow."

The man laughed a deep laugh that seemed to shake the room. "Ours either. And since I have to start work in the morning, I didn't want Lilly to have to worry about them coming down here when we hadn't met you all yet. No offense, but you never know what kind of neighbors you are going to get."

Luke nodded seriously, "I know exactly what you mean. Well, come on in and meet the family."

The moment Josh had heard the man's voice he had frozen. He stared at the doorway and waited for Luke to bring the family in. He didn't know if he could handle it, but he knew for sure who the owner of that deep voice was. His stomach twisted in fear. He shook his head slightly. He had to be hearing things, he just had to be.

Then, he heard the voice again and knew he wasn't dreaming. But it just couldn't be, could it?

Silently he bowed his head. "Lord, help me not to be afraid. I know you are with me, but please help me not to be afraid." To his surprise and relief his fear lessened, then seemed to float away, that is until Luke walked into the room followed by a man and a woman and two teenage boys and a little girl of about three or four. The woman had dark brown hair, kind eyes, and was very obviously pregnant. The two teenage boys appeared to be about his age, and both had dark brown hair and eyes. The little girl had jet black hair and dark brown eyes. Josh saw them but hardly noticed any of them. His eyes were glued to the tall broad man who entered after Luke.

He sat as if froze when he saw the man and knew he wasn't imagining it. He felt himself shiver and he quickly looked away trying to hide his fear and his surprise.

"Everyone," Luke addressed them all, "these are our new neighbors." He motioned to them, then smiled sheepishly. "I'm sorry, I didn't even ask your names."

The man's broad grin seemed to light up his face. "I am Jim, and this is my wife, Lilly. These are our children." He motioned to each one as he said their names and they waved slightly. "Jared, Jordan," he motioned to the two boys about Josh's age. "And this is Julia. And baby Jay," he patted his wife's belly, "will be here in about four months."

Lilly laughed good naturedly, but she swatted at his hand a little. "Jim, really," she gasped. She flushed embarrassed.

Annie smiled as she stood. "It's good to meet you."

Luke turned to his family. "Well, I don't expect you to remember them all, but this is Josh, and Joy, then there is Travis, Tanner and Trevor, Tina, Gina, Chelsey, and Mary. He motioned to each one in turn. "I am Luke and this is my wife Annie." Luke chuckled. "I am sure your kids are wondering, because mine are also, so let me just tell you, Josh is fifteen, Joy is fourteen, Travis Tanner and Trevor are ten, Tina is seven, Gina is six, and Chelsey is four, and Mary is two."

Joy and the younger kids nodded politely, but Josh kept his gaze down and flinched when Luke said his name.

Luke frowned as he saw Josh's response. This wasn't like the boy at all. He was usually very friendly and outgoing, especially with kids his own age.

He tried to brush it off and not worry about it and hoped the company wouldn't think him rude, but a deep concern ran through him. Whatever was going on with his son, it was more serious then he had realized.

Luke smiled at the kids, "Why don't you all run along and play. I am sure you will find that much more fun."

The kids all shot out of their seats like rockets, and ran from the room taking Julia with them.

Joy rose and looked at her mom. "I can clean up in here, Mom, why don't you all go on and visit in the living room where it is more comfortable."

Josh looked at his sister with a smile. "I'll help you, Joy."

Joy shook her head. "You have company, Josh, go on and entertain them. I will be fine here. I am sure these two boys don't want to help out in the kitchen."

Jared and Jordan, both obviously taken by Joy's beauty and her smile, each flashed an award winning smile themselves. "Oh, we don't mind helping out at all. We help our mom at home all the time."

Josh saw the look of interest flash in both boy's eyes and his anger mounted. They had better not be making any moves on his sister. Yet something confused him. How was it possible that these two boys were his age? Lilly must have had them before she married his dad. Unless- Josh pushed the thought away before it had time to finish forming. He wouldn't think that; he couldn't think it.

Just thinking about it sent chills all through him. He looked again at the adults who stood watching to see if the young people were going to get along. Josh forced a nervous smile, but Joy's was real.

"Go on, Mom and Dad, we are going to be just fine in here."Joy saw her mom's smile and was glad she had volunteered.

Her mom needed a break. She needed to be able to talk to another woman. It meant a lot to her.

As the parents left Josh took the dishes to the sink while Joy filled it with water.

One of the boys, Josh was unsure which one, they both looked exactly alike, stepped up beside Joy. "I can wash and rinse, but I don't think I would do any good putting away."

Joy laughed, but she felt a little uneasy with him so close to her. Quickly she stepped away. "Well, I won't stop you if you are volunteering. But don't feel like you have to, really. You are company. I feel bad that you are helping us clean up. Really, I can do it on my own."

The boy laughed good naturedly. "I don't mind at all, but I tell you what, if you can guess correctly which one I am, I will let you tell me where everything goes and I will put it all away."

Joy laughed. "I don't have a clue which one you are, and I think it will be easier to put them away myself anyway." She tried not to be nervous, but something about the way he looked at her made her that way. She glanced over her shoulder to make sure Josh was still there.

The boy chuckled. "Fair. I am Jared, by the way. My brother Jordan and I are twins, but it is easy to tell us apart once you get to know us. I am the good-looking, charming one. He is the one who is always in trouble."

Jordan snorted. "I only get in trouble when you get me in trouble. She only has to know us a few minutes and she will be able to tell that. That is about all the longer you can keep out of trouble."

Joy giggled as she saw them scowl at one another. "I wonder, is it fun having a twin?"

The boys looked at each other and shrugged. "It's no different then anyone else, I guess, except that you always have someone to talk to and someone who understands how you feel."

Joy looked both boys over, then looked at Josh. "How old are you?" She knew Josh wasn't going to ask, but she thought if they were the same age, maybe that would help him start talking.

Jared laughed, and Jordan chuckled. "Fifteen, just. We won't be sixteen till December. How about you two?"

Josh finally relaxed a little when he knew the grownups were gone. It wasn't going to be easy to keep away from his dad. Was this why he had been having all the nightmares? Was God trying to warn him? Was his dad coming after him?

Joy flipped her hair back over her shoulders. "I just turned fourteen last week and Josh will be sixteen in October.

"What is school like here? We have to start next week. I don't know why we couldn't wait a few more months to move instead of us having to move a month before school is out. I guess Dad's job just couldn't wait that long. At least we will know two kids in school on Monday."

Josh shook his head and reached for the towel from his sister and started to dry the dishes. Joy scowled at him, but quickly went on talking as she headed to the table to get more dishes. "We are home-schooled, so you won't know anyone in school, sorry."

Jordan sighed. "It's okay. That is so cool that you are home-schooled. I wish my mom would do that with us. Do you like it?"

Joy shrugged. "It's okay. I like it the most that we have shorter days then kids in school and the fact that we are finishing up next week and the school kids still have to go to school for like four more weeks."

Jared frowned. "That is not fair. Why do you get out so much earlier?"

Josh smiled slightly, his sister's high spirits were helping him to relax a little more. "We can work ahead all we want, and we don't have play days like the kids in school do," he answered shortly.

Jordan shrugged. "Oh well, I guess we will have to just make the most of it."

As Josh leaned down to put away a pan he heard someone come into the kitchen.

"Boys, we won't be here very long. Just wanted to let you know in case you wanted to start a game or something. Don't make it a long one. It's late and your mother needs to get home and rest."

Josh jumped when he heard the voice and the pan he had been holding clattered to the floor. All the kids jumped.

Josh quickly looked away, hoping his father wouldn't recognize him.

Jim didn't seem to notice.

Jared grinned. "Sure, Dad, no problem. We'll just start a game of monopoly or something like that."

To Joshua's surprise, Jim laughed. "Get on, have fun." Jim

31

turned and walked out of the kitchen.

Josh stared at Jared as his father walked away. He never would have dared joke with his father like that. He wanted to tell himself he was wrong, that the man wasn't his dad, but he knew better. Did his dad recognize him? Would he say something if he did? Was that why they had come? Was his father going to make him leave Luke and Annie and move back in with him? Over his dead body would he ever live with his father again!

Joy snapped her figures in front of his face. "Earth to you! Josh!"

Josh jumped back and gritted his teeth as he rammed into the counter top. "Sorry."

Joy smiled. "It's okay, big brother. We got done without you."

Josh glanced at the dish drainer and lowered his gaze. "Sorry."

Joy didn't seem to mind, nor did she seem to notice that Josh was distracted. "Let's play a game!"

Josh shrugged as he glanced at Jordan and Jared. "You guys like to play games?"

"Sure," they said together.

"As long as it isn't too long. Dad said not to start a long one," Jordan added.

Jared laughed. "You know nothing longer than a few hours." His eyes glittered with mischief.

Joy ran out of the room to get a few games while Josh washed the table. He wanted to ask Jared and Jordan a ton of questions, but he bit his lip and kept them all inside. He didn't want them to figure anything out. He didn't want anyone to know that Mr. Jim Peterson was his dad.

As the kids were finishing up their third game of Uno, Jim and Luke walked in.

Josh jumped a little when they walked in, but tried to hide his uneasiness. He felt his whole being stiffened. He sat almost frozen and kept his head down. His shoulders hunched slightly forward as if his body was waiting for his dad to hit him. Luke noticed that Josh was acting uneasy, but he didn't think too much about it. Jim saw the boys reaction and felt his own uneasiness wash through him. Why was this man's son so nervous around him? He had noticed the boy jumped when they had come in the kitchen earlier. Did Luke hit his kids?

32

Jim felt his uneasiness grow. He knew more than anyone in this room how much you could hide with religion. Was that what this pastor was doing. He prayed not. He had lost his own son because of his selfish foolishness. He wouldn't want that to happen to this family. Not to mention, he wouldn't want the kids in this house to be suffering the way he had made his son suffer.

He tried to push away his uneasiness, but something about Joshua tugged at him. Somehow it reminded him of his son, but he wasn't sure how. Maybe it was just the name. He shrugged in his mind and tried again to push away his uneasiness.

"Boy's, it's time to head for home." Jim stated. He turned to Josh and Joy. "Thank you both for putting up with my boys." He chuckled, "I hope they didn't give you a hard time."

Joy smiled brightly, but Josh kept his head down and made no acknowledgment that he had even heard. "They were so hard to put up with," Joy answered with exaggeration in her voice. Her eyes sparkled with teasing and she giggled a little. "I mean, like, they were so hard to put up with, maybe you will bring them back tomorrow?"

Jim laughed, and Josh felt surprised that his laugh came from deep in his chest. He couldn't remember the last time he heard his dad laugh for real. He really didn't remember a time he heard his dad laugh a real laugh. The only laugh he remembered from his dad was that menacing chuckle he always gave just before he hit him.

"I don't think it will be tomorrow, but your dad did invite us to Sunday dinner after church, so we will see you then." Jim smiled warmly at Joy and Josh.

Joy glanced at Josh as she heard his quick intake of breath and was surprised to see how pail he looked. He looked as though he felt sick and he still hadn't looked up. He sat almost frozen the way he had been when Luke and Jim came in.

She turned back to Jim with a broad smile. "Okay, Mr. Johnson. Thanks. It will be fun having neighbors so close with kids our own age. We are sure glad you all came over."

Josh jolted a little when he heard the last name. His dad's name wasn't Johnson. When had Joy learned his last name, and what made her think it was Johnson?

Jim laughed again. "You may not think that if we make a nuisances of ourselves. Come on boys, let's go."

Luke looked at his kids then looked at the kitchen. "Thank you all for cleaning up in here. It looks great."

The kids all nodded and said your welcome, then the company headed for home.

That night in bed Joy wondered why Jim and Lilly had only the two boys then waited so long to have more. It seemed strange. Then she shook her head. Maybe they couldn't have any for a while. She shouldn't judge others without knowing all the circumstances.

Josh lay in his bed that night and let his tears fall. He didn't like to cry, but he felt he had to release his emotion somehow. How did his father find him? How had he gotten out of jail? Why didn't Jared and Jordan seem afraid of his dad? They had joked with him, and laughed with him. He hadn't ever been able to talk back to his dad in the slightest form. Did his father hit Jared and Jordan the way he use to hit him?

He shivered again. He doubted it. The boys hadn't acted afraid of getting in trouble for anything. They had laughed and joked and been silly, they had joked with his dad and never once flinched when he came into the room. There was no way that he was hitting them, at least not to the extreme that he had hit Josh.

His mind whirred. He felt confused and afraid. What was he going to do now? He couldn't just talk to his dad. He didn't want his dad to know who he was if he hadn't figured it out, and if he talked to him, his dad would know who he was. He couldn't talk to Luke and Annie about it. He didn't even want Luke and Annie to know it was his dad or even a relation. What would they do if they knew?

Finally, when he knew he was too scared and hurt to sleep, he sat up and flipped on the light. Grabbing his Bible he held it close. Silently he prayed for help and peace. Slowly he turned the pages of the Bible. Soon his eyes rested on the passage, "I know the plans I have for you, declares the Lord; plans to prosper you and not to harm you. Plans to give you a hope and a future."

Slowly he closed the Bible and lay it down. "God, I know you have my life in your hands, help me to leave it there. Help me to trust you with those plans," he whispered. "Cause right now, I don't know what you are doing, and I am afraid." Slowly he lay back down.

Tears once more surfaced. "God, what is so wrong with me, that he would beat me? Why did he hate me so much, but yet it doesn't seem like he is mean to them? Is it just me, God?

Finally his eyes closed in an exhausted sleep.

4

The family always got up early Sunday mornings. This morning, as Josh walked into the kitchen and looked at his family gathered around the table, tears sprang to his eyes. How much longer was this going to be his family? How long would it be till his dad made him move back in with him; or drug him out of here, and forced him to live with him. He shivered. He didn't ever want to see that man again, but he knew he would have to.

Luke looked up at Josh and smiled. He made a mental note to himself to talk with Josh today. He kept thinking about it, but it was never a good time to talk. Now, however, it seemed even more serious. Josh hadn't been himself since Friday night. Something was up, and he was going to find out what was going on. He had to. Something wasn't right and he had to talk to him and try to get him to talk before school on Monday. He couldn't put Annie through another stressful day, like the last few of days school had been. And the sadness in Josh's eyes was making him more uneasy. There seemed to be a shadow in his eyes.

"Been waiting on you, son." he tried to speak softly, but he noticed Josh still flinched.

Josh trembled. "I'm sorry, I didn't mean to keep you waiting." He slid into his chair, but he felt himself stiffen even more in fear. His eyes locked with Luke's and he couldn't look away. He knew he was over reacting, but he felt himself stiffen even more, just waiting for Luke to hit him.

Annie smiled at him, seeing the fear in his eyes. She cast a

36

glance to Luke which said as plain as day *leave him alone. He isn't trying to cause a problem, but something is bothering him.* "It's fine, son, but we don't want to be late, and we do have company coming after church."

Josh nodded, "Yes, ma'am."

Luke watched Josh as the boy slowly bowed his head. He sighed, then shook his head. God was going to have to help him and Josh be able to talk about this. Surely Josh would relax and get back to his normal self soon. Maybe all they needed was to have a good talk. Then he would see that he was loved and it was okay to talk to those he loved and who loved him about what was bothering him.

He bowed his head as the family all silently joined hands. Silently he thanked God for his wonderful family and praised him for his goodness. Then he prayed out loud thanking God for all his blessings, his wonderful goodness, and his mercy. When he said amen he looked up at his family. God was so good. He knew it was true. God would help him and Josh.

As the family drove to church about forty-five minutes later, Chelsey, all the sudden, started to cry.

Startled Annie looked over her shoulder, "Chelsey, honey, what is wrong?"

The little girl looked up at Annie and tears ran down her cheeks. "Mommy, I want to play dollies today when we get home, but if we are having company, what if Julia doesn't want to play with my dolls? What if she won't play with me?"

Annie laughed. "I am sure you and Julia will find something to do that you can both agree on, and you will have a great afternoon. Don't you worry. It's going to be fine, and you will have all kinds of fun."

Chelsey smiled, her tears of moments ago forgotten. "Okay!"

Travis and Tanner and Trevor frowned. "It's not fair. They don't have any kids our age. Why? We want kids to play with too."

Luke smiled. "Boys, it's going to be fine. You all could hang out with the older kids if you want. Otherwise you three do a fine job

37

of playing together all on your own."

Travis shook his head. "They won't let us."

Luke chuckled. "They might, if you play by the rules and behave."

Josh smiled and shook his head. He wished his problems were as small as Chelsey's. He then thought about how Annie had handled the situation. *Is that what God does for us?* He wondered. "*Are all of our problems that seem so huge to us, they are just small to God?* He hoped so, because right now his problems were BIG. He hoped God understood and had already taken care of the problem. Then he heard words, quiet and peaceful, whispered to his heart, "All things are possible with God. I will work all things together for good to them that love me."

He smiled. "Thank you, God," he whispered, "Thank you for taking care of it all. Thank you for Romans 8:28. Thank you that Mom made me learn it."

Luke stood in the pulpit and looked out at the congregation. "God always protect his children. There are no mistakes with God. He created everything and every one. Nothing takes him by surprise. Sin had to mar this beautiful world that God created. He didn't create us to have pain and heart ache, but because of sin that is what we have. God doesn't promise us if we become Christians we won't have bad times and we won't get hurt. His promise is that he will be with us when those bad times come. He will protect us when we fall. He will be with us and keep us, if we will let him."

Josh listened intently as Luke talked, but he was having a hard time keeping his mind on the sermon. The reason for this was his dad and the family he was with sat in the pew directly across from him. He kept seeing his dad out of the corner of his eye and then he would lose focus on the sermon.

He was surprised to see Lilly get out a small notebook and ink pen for their youngest child. He saw his dad look over at her and smile and his heart seemed to freeze. His father wouldn't have ever let him draw in church. In fact his father had whipped him if he so much as-

Without warning he sneezed. Quickly he put a hand over his mouth and nose to catch the next one before he made just as much noise with it. Luke kept right on preaching as Josh knew he would, but his stomach turned a complete somersault when he glanced over at his dad. His heart seemed to freeze then roar at the same moment. Jim was looking right at him.

Josh trembled. Was his father going to punish him for making a noise in church? Fear pricked his skin. Were his nightmares about to come true? Was this why he was having them? Was God warning him?

He glanced up at Luke then out of the corner of his eye he glanced at Annie. His stomach flipped again. He felt sweat form on his brow and he knew he was going to be sick. Quickly yet quietly he jumped up and went out.

Jim was watching Josh. And as the boy got up to go out, he felt something twist inside him. All of the pieces suddenly fell into place. He had been bothered the other night when they had first met their neighbors. He knew he had seen Josh before somewhere. The boy had looked so familiar, but he just hadn't been able to place him. Suddenly he could. At that moment it all became clear. Josh was his son!

Quietly he got up and followed the boy out, knowing he was heading for the bathrooms. He glanced back at the preacher. Luke hadn't seemed to even notice the boy was gone.

He slowly opened the door to the bathroom and stopped as Josh stepped out of the stall.

Josh saw his dad and froze mid step. The door swung back into him, but he didn't even flinch or take his his eyes off his dad.

The two stood staring at each other for a few moments, then Josh looked away. Fear lanced through him again. He didn't want to have to step back into the life he had lived for eight years. There was nothing wrong with his life now and he wanted it to stay that way. Why did his dad have to figure out who he was?

Jim kept staring at Josh finally he shook his head, "Son?"

Josh flinched and backed up a step. "Yes, sir?"

Tears stood in Jim's eyes. "Joshua, I can't believe it is you. I thought I would never see you again." He took a step closer to Josh. As he did, Josh took a step back. Jim shook his head again. "You knew it was me? How long have you known?"

Josh trembled, but looked his father in the eye. "Since I heard you at the front door. How long did it take you to figure out who I was?"

Jim again shook his head. He just couldn't believe it was his son standing before him. "I didn't till you headed back here during church. Why did you? I know I taught you better than to just walk out during church."

Josh stiffened. He took a small step away form his dad and felt his back brush against the wall. He was stuck in here with his dad, the last person on earth he wanted to be with. He felt himself start to tremble. As he looked up at his dad and his dad took another step toward him, he coward down. "I'm sorry." he whispered putting his arms up to shield himself from his dad. "Please, Dad, please don't I-"

As Jim looked down at his son cowering away from him in fear, and his heart wrenched. He felt conviction stab his heart stronger than it ever had before. "Joshua," He tried to keep his voice from shaking, but pain stabbed his heart again. "Son, I am not here to hurt you. I just didn't know why you left the service. I was worried about you." He looked down, then looked into Josh's eyes. "Does – does- does Luke, the pastor, beat you for making noises in church? Is that why you came back here? Oh, please, please, Son, tell me he doesn't treat you like I did. Please tell me you haven't had to live like that since you were taken away from me."

Josh shook all over. He felt his stomach turn. Suddenly he lunged up hoping he could make it to the toilet before he got sick on the floor, but he was too late.

Jim jumped back and barely escaped disaster.

Josh half fell, half stumbled into the stall where he emptied the contents of his stomach completely.

Jim quietly cleaned up the mess on the floor as Josh continued to empty his stomach. He felt his guilt. He had done this to his son. His showing up had hurt him again. Even without laying a hand on him, he was hurting him all over again. Pain ripped his heart. "Please, God," he prayed silently, "Please give us a chance. Please let him see that you have changed my heart and give us a chance."

He noticed then that Josh was quiet. And slowly he walked into the stall behind him.

Josh heard his dad and stiffened. He waited unmoving,

expecting to feel a belt across his back . He jumped when his dad lay his hand on his back. It was the first time he ever remembered his dad touching him without hurting him.

"I am sorry, Joshua."

He was surprised by the humility in his dad's voice. He sounded like he meant it.

"I am sorry for all that I have done to you, son. I didn't mean to hurt you like this. I would like the chance to talk to you about all that has happened to me, if you would let me."

Josh slowly stood and turned to face his dad. He desperately wanted to tell his father that he didn't ever want to see him again, and he had no interest in what happened to him. But through years of experience, he kept his mouth shut. In his heart he began to cry out to God, but outwardly he was quiet. *God, please help me. Please let this all just be another bad dream. Please don't make me have to live through this all again. Please!*

His father looked at him as though hearing his thoughts. "I know you probably don't want to hear it. I am sure you don't want to talk to me at all. And I don't blame you, son. Really I don't. You have every right to hate me."

He stepped out of the stall giving Josh room to get out and wash. "If you don't want to right now, that's okay; but someday, would you let me talk to you about it? I promise, son, I am not hear to mess up your life. I am not going to take you away from the family that you have come to know and love and that love you. I didn't come after you, and I won't tell anyone you are my son, if you don't want me to. We can just go on like it is now, and no one has to know anything. But please, will you forgive me for what I have done to you?"

Josh looked away from his father. He sounded serious. Was he or was he just putting it on?

Jim placed a hand on the boy's shoulder. "Will you at least give us a chance to talk? Will you give me a chance to tell you what all has happened in my life, son?"

Josh snapped his head up. "Don't call me that," he growled.

Jim looked into his son's angry eyes in surprise. "All right then, Joshua, what would you like me to call you?"

Josh bit his lip. Surprise ran through him, first of all that he had back talked his dad, and secondly that his dad hadn't back handed him for speaking; but he didn't let his surprise show. "Just call me Josh, like everyone else. No one needs to know that you know me beyond that. I won't tell anyone." He looked down as tears smarted his eyes. He didn't ever want to have to face his father, and now he was living next door.

Jim smiled weakly. He saw the hate in his son's eyes. He also saw the anger and pain. He wished he could go back and erase all those years, but he knew he couldn't. Time with Josh was going to take just that, time. "Will you give me a chance to talk to you sometime, Josh, about what has happened to me, about my life? At least give me a chance to get to know you a little."

Josh trembled. He didn't want his dad to know him and he didn't want to know his dad. "What do you want to know?"

Jim shrugged. "All about you and your life, about all that has happened in your life since- well, since – you know."

Josh looked his dad in the eye. "Why did they let you out?"

Jim's eyes widened in surprise that Josh would talk to him that way, but he bit his lip and looked away for a moment. "That is actually a long story, so- Josh, I was angry when the judged sentenced me. I was determined that I was going to escape. But days turned into weeks and months and then years. My cell mate started going to a Bible study. A pastor from the local church had started one for the men in the prison. He asked me to go with him. I went out of complete boredom. It was just something to take up time, but I ended up liking it. I listened to him, son. I was actually listening for the first time in my life. I went back the next week, then the next. Every week I liked it better. It was like all of those years I spent in church faking a religion, were so, well, I guess just that, fake. That preacher taught us right down the line, salvation and sanctification is the only way to Jesus. He told us that only by the blood of Jesus can we be saved and only by his blood can we ever be redeemed.

"He said we were all in prison because we had done wrong. Jesus loved us anyway, and he came to call us to repentance. It touched me in a way it never had before. I suddenly saw myself for who I was, and it wasn't pretty. I saw the hypocrite I had been, saw all the wickedness of my heart.

"He told us that it is only after we have a love for Jesus and have his love in our hearts can we ever have a love like we should for our fellow man.

"Son, it touched a place in me that I had kept hidden for years. It was almost like your mamma saying to me, 'Jim, you can't be the daddy you need to be to Joshua and the husband you need to be to me, till you let Jesus wash you clean. Loving Jesus is more than you seem to think it is. It may be a lot of things, but it's not a burden. It's a blessing. All he wants is your love.'

"Well, it so touched me, at that moment that I knelt down by my chair in the middle of that study and cried on the Lord Jesus to save me. I pleaded with him for forgiveness and promised him that if I ever had the chance that I would ask your forgiveness too. Then I discovered that it doesn't take a life time to be forgiven and cleansed. It only took God a moment to cleanse and make me whole. It took me to have faith. And he did the rest. All I had to do was ask.

"I realize that you don't have to forgive me, son, and if I were you I wouldn't want to forgive someone like me. But, son, please forgive me for all that I have done to you. It was so wrong. I never should have done it, ever. I know it probably still hurts you, some of the things that I did. I am so sorry. I wish there was a way that I could take back all the those things I did. I wish there was a way that I could go back in time and change everything, but I can't. I have to live with my choices, like you have to live with the scars of my choices. I am so sorry, son. Just think about it will you? I want you to know you really can forgive me. I don't want you to just say it, so please just think about it."

Josh stared at his dad in surprise. He had never heard or seen his dad like this. It took him a minute to nod slightly, "Okay, sir, I will." He looked down, fear still prickling his skin. Was his dad just trying to trick him into a comfort zone?

Jim smiled, encouraged by the small acceptance from his son. "Thank you, son. I won't try to pressure you, son."

Josh shivered, "Please, don't-" he stopped and his father read the fear in his eyes.

"What is it, son? I won't get mad. I promise."

Josh shook his head and turned away. "Nothing. Forget it." His mind whirled. He wanted nothing more than for his dad to never call him "son" again. He didn't want to be his son, and he didn't want anyone to know that he was his son.

Jim looked at him closely, searching his face. Suddenly it dawned on him what Josh wanted to say. To make sure he cleared his throat. "I am sorry, son- Josh. Is that it? You don't want me to call you son, but you are afraid to say it again. And I forgot and addressed you as son several times already. Haven't I?"

Josh flinched as Jim stepped closer to him. "I will try my best, Joshua. I will try. And know now that I am sorry for each and every time I mess up and bring back the pain of the past.

Josh looked up for a moment into his father's eyes. He was surprised to see the pain in them. He nodded slightly, "Yes, sir."

Jim grinned. "How about you stop calling me sir, and I will stop calling you son."

Josh felt the color drain from his face. How else was he going to address his dad? He wasn't going to call him dad.

Jim saw the panic in Josh's eyes and felt his heart squeeze again. "You can call me Jim for now, since you don't want to call me dad, or you could call me Mr. Johnson."

Josh's head snapped up, "Johnson? Your last name is Pe-" he trembled as he backed away from his dad and toward the door.

His dad nodded. "I know, son, but I – well, when I got out of prison I didn't want people to know me as I was. I changed my name. I wanted to be a better person. Guess I thought maybe if I could change my name, I wouldn't have to remember my past, or that I had lost my son, because of my own selfishness and temper. The authorities wouldn't give me any information on you. Nothing, not even where you had gone, or might be now. They told me to come back with a clean record in a couple of years and then they would consider it. I had no idea where to even begin looking for you."

Josh looked up at his dad as he backed even farther away. "How long has it been?"

Jim smiled slightly, but shook his head. "Four years ago, almost five. I asked about you as soon as I got out, but since they wouldn't let me find you I had to move on with life alone. I renewed my medical license and went back to that field. That is actually what lead me here."

Josh stiffened as his dad stepped closer to him.

Jim saw the discomfort in his son and knew he would have to bide his time. "I met up with Lilly about three and a half years ago. She came into my office for – just for reasons. It didn't take us long to fall in love. We married three months later."

Josh didn't know what to say. He had a million questions but he didn't know what he should ask or if he should. Finally, he looked his dad in the eye and risked a question he was afraid would get him whipped. "Does she know about you? Does she know what you use to do to me? Does she even know I exist?"

Jim shook his head slightly. "We have talked a little about my past. She knows I had a son whom was taken away from me. But she doesn't know why all I went to prison. She doesn't know the extent of what I did to you, Son. I kept some of that from her for my own reasons."

Josh shook his head. He wanted to tell his dad he still hadn't changed. He was still keeping secrets from his wife, hurting those around him. He was still the same. But he didn't dare. It hadn't been so long since he had felt his father's belt that he couldn't remember the pain connected with it, and he had no desire to feel it again.

Jim stepped closer to Josh. His heart yearned to hug his son, or just to touch him. "I realize I should have told her about you. I know that, and I know now that I have to; but I just don't know how I am going to do that. Please give me some time, son. It's going to take me while to work up the courage. She has things in her past that happened to her, and that is why I kept some things from her, but that is going to change."

Josh shook his head. "I don't want her to know that I am your son. I don't need another parent. I am just fine where I am. I don't want you or her for a parent, but don't you think she deserves to know what you did to your own child so that she knows what you may do to hers?" Josh sucked in his breath fast, as he realized what he had just said. "I'm sorry, Dad-" he looked away quickly, waiting and expecting to feel the sting of his father's hand across his face. He was surprised when his father touched his arm softly instead.

He jumped when he felt his father touch him, unsure of what was coming.

Jim saw the boy's pain and his heart ached again. "I am not that person anymore, Joshua. Please believe me. Please. I haven't touched her kids and I am not going to."

Josh looked away. He couldn't believe his dad. He wouldn't believe him. His dad knew how to put on a front and he knew it. He wasn't going to be fooled into moving back in with him, or even trusting him. Not now. Not ever. He turned quickly away. "I need to get back in there," he growled. He was worn out from this encounter.

His past seemed to press down on him harder.

Jim nodded. "Yeah, I guess we both do, before it's all over."

Josh opened the door and froze. People were coming out of the sanctuary. He glanced back at his dad. Jim saw the boy's fear and his heart went out to him, but it troubled him too. Was he afraid of Luke also? He smiled slightly at his son. "Go on out, son. I will wait a few minutes then I will go out."

Josh quickly left the rest room and almost collided with Mr. Magon.

"Joshua, just the boy I wanted to see!" The old man exclaimed.

Josh felt his pulse quicken. He was jumpy from the time with his dad and he didn't feel like talking to anyone right now. "Hi, Mr. Magon." He tried to smile and sound pleasant knowing his father was watching and listening.

The old man smiled a toothless smile. "Yes, sir. I need someone who would be willing to cut my grass and do yard work this summer. Are you interested in the job? I know you will do a good job and I thought I would rather ask you first."

Josh thought for a moment. "I will have to ask Luke and Ann-I mean Mom and Dad. I will let you know."

Mr. Magon smiled again. "Well, of course, you go on and ask them. You just let me know."

Josh nodded and walked on toward the door. He was stopped by three other members of the church and asked about working for them this summer before he made it to the door where Luke and Annie were standing shaking hands with people as they left.

Luke looked at Josh with concern in his eyes. He had seen Josh leave during the sermon and then Jim following him out. At first he didn't give it any thought, but neither one of them had returned, and he had become concerned. Now he looked at Josh and noted the sadness and pain in the boy's eyes. He shook hands with two more people then turned to Josh. "Son?"

Josh jumped and quickly turned to face Luke. "Yes, sir?"

Luke's concern grew, "What happened during service? Why did you go out then not come back in?"

Josh hung his head. "I'm sorry. I didn't mean to leave like that. I just-" he stopped unsure how to go on. He didn't want to tell Luke he had been so scared of his father that he got sick. What was he suppose to say?

Luke turned to shake hands with more people and Josh noted that his father and his new family were headed their way. His stomach turned sour. Luke smiled as he shook their hands. "Glad to see you all in church today. We are happy you made it. I hope you are also going to grace us with your presence for lunch."

Lilly smiled sweetly. "Yes, we are. And thank you again for the invitation. This was all so nice. I love the church. It really reminds me a lot of the one I grew up in."

Josh bit back a groan as he listened. He had forgotten about having to spend the whole day around his dad. He felt bile rise in his throat again. He turned quickly and swallowed hoping to rid the feeling.

"Joshua, just the boy I wanted to see!"

Josh bit is lip and willed his stomach to settle as he looked up at Mr. Less, one of the board members, with a smile. Arthur Less was a farmer who had a spread a couple of miles from Luke and Annie's place.

Mr. Less smiled showing perfect white teeth. Without waiting for Josh to respond to his greeting he went right on talking, "As you know summer is a very busy time for us. In fact, this year, it just seems to be more than my boy and me can handle. I was thinking on hiring some extra help around the place. We just can't get all the haying and things done by ourselves. It just seems that the list of things to do grows quicker than we can get them done.

"I was thinking if you are interested in the job, I will hire you on as soon as you are done with school. I know you are a good worker and I would as soon hire you as some of the other boys from town. I trust you and know you will give me a good days work.

"I will pay you eight dollars an hour plus lunch and supper if you are out there at that time. I realize we put in long days some of the time in the summer. But I will try to be fair to you. What do you say? There is a lot of manual labor, so if you aren't up for the job, just say so now."

Josh felt his pulse skip a beat. He wouldn't mind the labor at all. It would be a welcome distraction. He would enjoy it. And it would definitely keep him from having to see his dad most of the summer. Also, it should work him hard enough he would be to exhausted to dream. Maybe he could sleep at night. He turned to

Luke. Out of the corner of his eye he saw his dad looking at him. He shivered as his dad frowned at Mr. Less.

"Dad, can I?"Josh flinched when he called Luke dad in front of his dad, but he didn't want Luke to know how bothered he was about his dad.

Luke smiled, glad to hear Josh calling him dad again. It had been a long week with the boy seeming to be fighting with something. Whatever it was he seemed to be getting over it now. "Thank you, Arthur, for the offer. We will discuss it at home today and let you know tonight. I don't see any reason he can't, but we will need to talk to his mom before making any final decisions."

Jim felt his pulse start to race. He didn't trust Arthur Less. The man had a mean look in his eye. He knew he was a member of he church, and the board, and that he and his wife substituted for the Sunday school and youth group, but something in him twisted when he thought of Josh being out with the man. He wasn't sure what made him feel that way, but something about him made him nervous.

Josh sensed his father's disapproval and that made him want to take the job all the more. He didn't want his father to have any say in his life. He had lost that eight years ago, and he wasn't going to give it back to him. "Thank you, Mr. Less. I will discuss it more with my parents and let you know. I don't get done with school till the end of the week, so I wouldn't be able to start working for you till the week after that, if it works, and they say I can." Out of the corner of his eye he saw his father scowl.

Mr. Less smiled, "Good. We will see you tonight and talk more about it then."

Luke nodded as he shook hands with the man, "We will, and thanks."

5

Pain jolted Josh awake. Fear pricked his skin. He shivered. Finally he felt his breathing slow just enough to let him relax a little. *It was just a dream,* he told himself. *Stop being so chicken. This is stupid. Stop being so scared. It was all just a bad dream. Nothing is going to happen.*

It didn't help. Fear kept him shaking. Slowly he reached over and turned on the light. He sat up and rested his head in the palm of his hand. "Lord, I know you can stop these nightmares and take them away. I don't understand why I am still having them. Please take them away. And, Lord, please don't let anyone find out that he is my dad. Please don't ever let them find out what he use to do to me. Please."

Josh turned his head as he heard the door open.

"Josh?" Luke whispered.

Josh stiffened. *Please God, help me. Don't let him hurt me.* "Yes, sir?"

"Are you okay? I thought I heard you cry out."

Josh shivered. "No, I am fine. Sorry if I woke you. It was just a dream."

Luke walked in. He was startled to see how pale the boy looked. "Do you want to talk about it? Seems to me you have been having quite a few of these dreams lately. Maybe it would help if you told me what was bothering you."

Josh pulled back as Luke sat down on the edge of the bed.

"No, sir. I don't want to talk about it. That will just make it worse."

Luke smiled. "It seems that not talking about it really isn't helping you that much, Son. Are you sure you don't want to talk about it? It could help."

Josh nodded.

Luke shrugged and Josh saw the deep concern in his eyes. "Okay, let me know if you change your mind, son." He put his hand on Josh's shoulder. "I love you, son. I want to help you, but what ever is troubling you, God can help you so much more than I can. Just give it to him."

Josh nodded again, but kept his head down afraid that Luke would be able to see the fear in his eyes. There were times when he wondered if Luke already knew what was going on, but was just waiting for him to talk about it. More than once over the last eight years, God had talked to the man in one form or another, seeming to tell him things that, to Josh, didn't make sense; but Luke was always right. Did God really talk to Luke and tell him what he wanted to know?

Fear pricked his skin. *Please, God, don't tell him about this. Please keep it a secret for me, please. I don't want anyone to know.*

Luke sensed the trouble in Josh, but let it go, praying the boy would feel he could talk about it soon. He stood and walked to the door. Then he turned back. "Good night, son. I love you. Don't ever forget that. Your mother and I love you very much."

Josh nodded again. "Thanks. I love you both too." Tears sprang to his eyes. How much longer was he going to get to stay here? When was his dad going to make him leave?

Annie looked questioningly at Luke as he walked back into the room.

Luke shook his head. "He didn't want to talk about it."

Annie sighed. "How long are you going to let this go on, Luke? He didn't have this many nightmares when he first came to live with us. And they weren't this bad. What do you think happened to set it off? I know he was having a few last week, but since Friday it's been horrible. I don't even want to think about what he is going to be like in school tomorrow."

Luke shook his head. "I wish I knew. He has been so withdrawn the last week. Maybe getting done with school and starting to work for Less's will help him to get over whatever it is. Either that or wear him out enough, he stops having them."

Annie shook her head. "I hope so, but I doubt it. Something is wrong. I can feel it. I just wish you would make him talk to you about it."

Luke sighed as he turned to her. Seeing the worry in her eyes he smiled. He put his hands on her shoulders and rubbed them. "Honey, you know that isn't going to happen. I am not going to force him to talk to me, unless it seems to be threatening his life and I feel I should. We can worry all we want, but it isn't going to do any good. Maybe its time we stop trying to take care of it ourselves."

Annie smiled. "You are right. We need to pray about this. And while we are at it we need to pray that God gives me peace about him working for Arthur Less. I am just really uncomfortable about it all."

Luke felt a red flag raise in his mind. He hadn't been married to her for all these years and not learned that God often spoke through his wife and to his wife in a way he didn't talk to him. "What do you mean?"

Annie shrugged. "I really don't know. There is no reason to be nervous, but I am. It just makes me uneasy. I really don't know why."

Luke bit his lip. "Honey, why didn't you say something earlier, when we were talking about it to Josh?"

Annie sighed and pushed her brown hair back from her face. "Honey, he was so excited about this job offer, I didn't want to take that away from him. He needed something to encourage him and this seemed to do it. I just couldn't tell him earlier. I thought I would just take it to God and let him handle it."

Luke felt uneasy now. Was there something wrong? He looked into his wife's eyes. She was right. They needed to talk to God about it all, and let him handle it. "Let's pray about this," he whispered.

Annie smiled, silently thanking God for her wonderful husband who always reminded her to turn to God, he could handle all her troubles. *Thank you, God. Thank you.*

She slid out of bed and knelt on the floor next to Luke as they raised Josh to the Lord in prayer and handed the whole situation over to him. They asked God to help and heal Josh in a way that only he could. And to give them the wisdom to know what to do to help.

Luke rose to his feet and smiled. "Thank you, Lord, that we can always trust you no matter what the situation. Thank you for answering prayer. Amen!"

Annie smiled as she crawled back into bed. She still felt uneasy, but she tried to relax and trust the Lord. After all it was as Luke had said. The Lord was in control and He knew just what he was doing. She only hoped they weren't making a mistake. *Please help me to know, Lord, if these feelings are from you or not. Help me to know if I should be worried. Please keep my boy safe.*

Luke felt Annie's uneasiness and tried to push away his own worry. What was it about this situation that had them both uneasy? This sounded like a good thing. Josh was excited, or at least he seemed to be excited about it. So why were they both feeling so uneasy?

Help me, Lord. Please help me not to be making a mistake in letting the boy decide this on his own. Please help him to choose wisely. Please protect our boy, Lord. You are in control. Help me to remember that.

The following morning at breakfast Luke watched Josh closely. Again the boy seemed to be lost deep in thought. Was it over last night, or something else?

"Joshua, I need to talk to you before school this morning."

Josh jumped when he heard Luke talk to him. Looking up quickly he saw something strange in Luke's eyes. His stomach knotted. "Yes, sir."

The other kids quickly finished breakfast and ran off to play for a few minutes before school. Joy took the hint and left with them, though she was dying with curiosity about what was going on.

As the room cleared out, Luke cleared his throat and looked right into Josh's eyes. "Son, I know I told you this is your decision, and what you choose to do with your summer is up to you, and I know you told Arthur Less last night that you would work for him, but I have to tell you something about all this is making me very uneasy. I am not sure what it is exactly, but something is bothering me about it. Your mom is feeling that way too. We thought you should know how we feel."

Josh felt his stomach plunge. "Are you saying that I can't work for him?"

Luke shook his head, "No, that is not what I am saying, but I do want you to be aware that something about this is making me very uneasy."

Josh bit his lip. Maybe he should be concerned, but then he remembered the look in his father's eye yesterday when Mr. Less had offered him the job. His blood boiled. *He thinks that he can run my life. I bet he told mom and dad not to let me work for him.*

Luke stood slowly. "I just want you to think about it, son, please. I don't want you to get hurt. I will be honest with you, I was concerned when you acted interested in the job, but I didn't want that to bother you. Your mom and I are praying. I hope you are too. Just know that God has a good job out there for you this summer. I know you are starting to think about collage and other things and you need a job, but chose wisely. Please, Son."

Josh nodded. "Yes, sir. I will." He shifted uneasily. "Can I go now?"

Luke nodded. He saw the look of impatience, but something else flashed in his eye. He wasn't sure what, but it made him more nervous. What was really going on with Josh?

Josh walked out of the room and took a deep breath. There was no way he was going to let his father run his life. How dare his dad talk to Luke and Annie and try to keep him from taking the job at Less's just because he didn't want him to. "I will work there. I am not going to let him tell me what to do. Not now or ever again. He isn't my dad any more. I hate him." he growled under his breath.

A dark cloud seemed to cover him. He felt the sting of those words and knew that hate would block him from God. He pushed the thought away. *God understands about my dad. He isn't going to require me to love him. He isn't going to want me to obey him any more. He lost the right to be my dad.*

He pushed his uneasiness away, but he couldn't push away the emptiness he felt in his heart. He knew he had started a wall cutting him off from God, but he wasn't sure how to fix it. He would just have to keep pushing away his uneasiness. Surely this feeling wasn't from God.

Is it, God? You don't mean I have to love and obey him do you?

Children, He heard as clear as day in his heart, *obey your parents in the Lord, for this is right. Honor your father and mother.*

"But, God," he whispered. "My dad doesn't deserve my love. Nor does he deserve my respect. I don't want anything to do with him."

Again the words came back in his heart. *Children, obey your parents. Honor your parents.*

He sighed as he walked back down the stairs. He tried again to push his uneasiness away. He knew he had to obey God, but this time he just couldn't. He couldn't love his dad, and he didn't want to respect him. He forced the thoughts out of his mind.

If he worked hard, he could have all his school done today or tomorrow. Maybe he could start work early. That wouldn't give his dad another chance to try and ruin it for him. It would also help him to keep his mind off his dad and not have to have the chance of seeing him.

6

On Friday of that same week, Arthur Less called to see if Josh could come on Saturday instead of waiting till Monday to start work. Josh was excited to start, but Luke and Annie still felt uncomfortable with it.

At eight o'clock Saturday morning, Luke dropped him off at the Less farm, "I will be back to pick you up at seven. I am not letting you work any later than that tonight. Is that understood?"

Josh's eyes sparkled with excitement. "Sure thing, Luke."

Arthur Less walked out of the barn and waved. Luke waved back and waited till Arthur walked over to the pickup. He repeated what he had just said to Josh.

Arthur nodded. "That will be fine, Preacher. I'll bring him home for you. He'll be there a little after seven. That won't be a problem today."

Luke smiled. He turned his gaze back on Josh. "Behave and do a good job."

Josh nodded slightly. He was excited to be outside doing things this summer. He hoped it would be a good job. Something twinged in him as he thought about how uneasy Luke and Annie were, then a picture of his dad's disapproving glare on Sunday, when Mr. Less offered him the job, flashed into his mind. He pushed away all his uneasiness. He was not going to mess up this job, and have his dad say I told you so. He didn't want him to have any say in his life at all.

Luke waved and drove away, and Arthur Less turned to Josh. "Well, Boy, come on into the barn and we will get started for the day. We are working on the tractor and mower. When it's done Marcus or I will go start mowing hay. The other two of us will start working on the baler and racks. This is haying season."

Josh nodded. "Yes, sir." He followed Mr. Less into the barn. The big door was open and he could see that they had been working on equipment. He stopped. "Just tell me what you want me to do, Mr. Less."

Arthur smiled, but something in his eyes made Josh nervous. He quickly pushed the thought away. There wasn't anything to be nervous about, he kept telling himself, but the fear kept edging its way into his mind.

Mid afternoon Marcus left to go out to the field and start mowing. Josh and Arthur Less went back to the barn to start working on the baler and racks they would need in a few days.

For a while things were going great. Arthur had Josh running after things or helping him working on the baler, but then something changed.

Arthur Less shifted his position. "Joshua, go and get the screws that are on the bench and the impact that should be on the bench. Then I need three pieces of lumber for the floor. After we fix the floor I think I am going to have you change this tire. I don't think it will hold up under a load."

Josh nodded and turned to get the stuff that he had been told to get. When he came back he was surprised to see anger in Mr. Less's eyes. He set the stuff down and stepped back.

Arthur Less eyed him angrily. "You answer when you are spoken to, boy," he snapped. "Don't leave till you have answered me."

Josh was surprised. He looked up at Mr. Less. "I'm sorry. I didn't think to answer. I was just trying to get the stuff for you so you wouldn't be waiting."

Arthur Less stepped up to him and gripped his arm. Sparks seemed to shoot from his eyes. Suddenly he slapped the boy across the mouth.

Josh dropped his head. His cheek burned, but his anger mounted.

"I have had it already with your disrespect, boy. You want to

56

keep a job here you are going to show me respect," he growled.

Josh nodded slightly.

Arthur gripped his arm tighter and slapped him across the mouth again. "You want me to take you home right now, boy. You want to tell your parents you are too lazy and disrespectful to keep a job?" Arthur's eyes snapped.

Josh dropped his gaze. "No, sir." he muttered.

Arthur nodded and dropped his hold on the boy. "That's better. Now I think you need a bit more of a reminder."

Josh looked up at him with fear in his eyes.

Arthur Less saw the fear and reveled in it. He knew Josh's dad had beat him when he was little. He had been a close friend to his father till he had gotten thrown in prison, and he still blamed the boy for it. He chuckled to himself. He was going to make the boy pay for what he did even if his father was too much of a sissy to, now. He reached down and unbuckled his belt.

Josh saw and a shiver ran down his spine.

Arthur motioned to him. "Go on and get your shirt off, boy. You disobey around here and you are going to get punished for it. I will not put up with your disrespect."

Josh dropped his head. Slowly he turned away.

Arthur chuckled again out loud this time. "Get that shirt off, boy."

Josh shivered again, but slowly removed his shirt. As the belt slapped on his back, his only thought was that he had to keep Luke and Annie and his dad from finding out. Not only would they say they had told him, but he would probably get a worse whipping from his dad. He moaned as the belt snapped on his back again and brought his thoughts back to where he was and what was happening.

Arthur lowered the belt.

Josh slowly stood, pain shot thought his back.

Arthur smiled to see the pain in the boy's eyes. "You will be respectful to your boss, Joshua. I will give a full report of your behavior to your father."

Josh trembled but slowly nodded. "Yes, sir." Anger burned in him. His dad had set this whole thing up. He had walked right into a trap. What was he suppose to do now? He couldn't just quit. He didn't want to admit to Luke and Annie that they were right to feel uneasy about this. He bit his lip as he and Arthur went back to work. He would have to figure something out. He wasn't sure what, but something.

Later that same afternoon Josh felt someone grip his arm and jerk him around. Fear raced through him as he faced Arthur Less again. "You wasting time, boy?"

Josh trembled. "No, sir. I was just-"

Arthur gripped his arms tighter.

Josh cried out in pain.

Arthur smiled as he released the boy's arms. "Don't you waist time again on my clock, Joshua Peterson."

Josh moaned as he rubbed his arm slightly.

Arthur slammed his fist into the boys stomach. "Did you hear me?"

Josh gasped and doubled over in pain.

Arthur chuckled again as he grabbed his hair and jerked him up. "You hear me, boy?"

Josh felt his anger rise, but he forced it under control. "Yes, sir."

Arthur wanted to backhand the boy, but he made himself not. It wouldn't do him any good to leave a mark someone would see on the boy. If he did that, he wouldn't be coming back to work. He knew if Luke found out what had happened here and that he had struck him, he wouldn't be back.

He would have to make sure he kept himself in check and didn't leave a mark that could be seen. Then too he would have to come up with something to keep Josh from telling.

His eyes blazed as he looked at Josh. He wanted to beat him more, but he knew he couldn't today. He would have to bide his time. Slowly he released his hold on the boy.

Josh didn't move. He stood before Mr. Less with fear in his eyes. What was he suppose to do now?

Arthur looked him in the eye. "It's almost time to get you home, boy." He gripped Josh's face and pushed him back into the wall of the barn. "You tell your dad I had to beat you today, and he will do the same, boy. We already discussed this before I offered you the job. He assured me that if I needed to punish you while you were here I was suppose to and to let him know, and he would meet out the same at home.

Josh trembled. Had Luke really said that?

Arthur smiled. "So I will leave it up to you to tell him what happened so he can give you that same punishment at home. Understood?"

Josh felt the color drain from him face.

He glared at the boy.

Josh looked away. "Yes, sir. I understand." He determined then and there that he wasn't going to let anyone find out what was happening to him here. He would have to keep it a secret. If Luke and his dad were going to hit him the same at home as he got here, he couldn't take it. He would just have to keep Mr. Less from saying anything.

Arthur motioned toward the truck. "Let's get you headed home, boy. Your dad wouldn't like you to be late, would he?"

Josh shook his head. "No, sir."

Annie and Luke were sitting in the living room when he came in that evening. Luke looked up and smiled. "How did it go, Josh? Did you enjoy your first day?"

Josh shuttered, but forced on a fake smile. "It went great, Dad. I really enjoyed it."

Luke looked at him thoughtfully as though wondering if the boy was really telling the truth. "Did you eat out there?"

Josh bit his lip. He didn't think he could eat a thing with as bad as he hurt, but he wasn't going to tell Luke or Annie that. "I'm fine, Dad. I'm not hungry."

Annie smiled warmly as she stood. "Go on and take a shower, Josh. I am sure that after you have all the sweat washed off of you from the day you will feel differently. I'll go warm you up some supper."

Josh nodded, but felt his stomach knot. "Thanks, Mom. I will. A shower sounds great."

As he headed up the stairs he saw Luke watching him. He saw the look in Luke's eye and he felt his stomach turn. Was he going to be in more trouble?

7

Sunday morning, Josh sat in church next to Annie and the kids. He hurt worse today then he had yesterday. The belting he had gotten at work was now bruised on his back which made it uncomfortable to lean on anything, but sitting with his back held just enough away from the pew that it wasn't touching, but not so far away as anyone would notice wasn't comfortable either.

Arthur Less and his wife, their daughter, Emma, and he son Marcus sat directly behind them. Josh felt his emotions surge. Fear ate at him. What was Mr. Less going to do to him? Why did he have to sit right behind them? To make matters worse his dad and new family sat directly across from them again.

Josh felt the tension in his shoulders then in his back. He knew he shouldn't fidget, but he was having a hard time sitting still. He saw Lilly once again get out paper and pen for the little girl, then to his complete astonishment he saw Jared and Jordan passing a note back and forth.

Jim glanced at them a few times, but never said any thing.

Josh bit his lip. What was so wrong with him that his dad hated him so much? Why was his dad letting Arthur Less beat him for stuff that was so stupid, but he was letting Lilly's kids or his kids, whatever it was, play in church. He would have been whipped to a bloody mess by now. Why? What was so wrong with him? Why did his dad hate him so much?

Jim saw Josh watching him and he glanced over at him.

Josh saw his dad look at him, and he jerked his head back around. He trembled. Was he going to be in trouble now for not looking at the preacher? He wanted to look back at his dad and see if he was still looking at him, but he didn't dare.

Jim saw the look of fear that flashed on Josh's face, and a stab of guilt shot through him. He never should have come here. All he was doing was hurting his son. He wasn't sure what he was supposed to do at this point.

God, please help me to know what to do. I didn't want to hurt my son. Don't you think he has been through enough hurt for a boy his age already. Why did him seeing me have to be such a bad thing? What do I need to do, God? Won't you please show me?

Jim looked at Josh again, but the boy was still sitting ridged and looking straight at Luke.

Maybe they shouldn't have accepted the preachers invitation to dinner two weeks in a row. Maybe it was too much for Josh. But the truth was he wanted to spend as much time with his son as he could. He wanted to be as close to him as he could. He had already missed so much of his life he didn't want to miss more.

He shook his head. Maybe he should tell Lilly who Josh was. He knew Josh didn't want him to, but maybe he should anyway. Maybe Lilly would want to take Josh into their home. Maybe she wouldn't be apposed to the idea.

He shook his head again. He needed to talk to her, but he needed to wait a little longer. He didn't want to cause a problem. Not with the baby being on the way and all. He should have told her a long time ago. He should have explained why he had been put in jail. He just hadn't been able to when they first started dating. It would have been too much for her. She wouldn't have ever given him the chance to see that he was a changed person.

Now he was afraid of what she would say. Now he was afraid he had waited too long.

Again he pushed the thoughts aside. He needed to focus on the sermon for now. He could think about all of this other stuff later. He tried to hear what Luke was saying, but his mind continued to wander to the next isle over.

Josh trembled even more as he felt his dad watching him. What was he going to do to him? Did he know that Less had beat him

61

Saturday? Would he say something about it?

Fear edge into his thoughts. What if his dad was trying to get him back and he thought if he had Less beat him and he blamed it on Luke he could get him back. Why would he have Mr. Less beat him and not do it himself?

Josh shuttered as he tried to think about something else. Then he noticed that people were standing. Church was over. He felt a little guilty, because he hadn't heard most of it, but he couldn't do anything about it now.

As they were walking to the door he heard his mom and Lilly talking. He felt sick when he heard her say something about them coming over for lunch. He didn't want to be near his dad. It brought back too many memories, plus his dad might try to punish him for getting in trouble at work. What if he said something to Luke.

Mr. Less walked up to Luke and at the same time gripped Josh's arm.

Josh bit back a cry of pain as Mr. Less squeezed his arm.

"Luke if it wouldn't be too much trouble I would like to have the boy there at seven in the morning. We got hay down that needs to be raked and baled and all the chores to do before that. I could really use the boy's help if he is willing.

Luke glanced at Josh. He saw the look of pain in his son's eyes and he felt a wave of concern wash over him. What was Josh hiding? "We will talk about it today, Less, and let you know this evening."

Mr. Less smiled. "Oh, sure. No problem. We will see you tonight."

Jim had been standing back a little ways and saw the look of pain that flashed in his boy's eyes when Less had grabbed his arm and anger shot through him. If he found out that man had laid a hand on his son he was going to hurt him a whole lot more.

After lunch the younger kids all went upstairs to play. The adults sat around the table drinking coffee and chatting about things. Josh, Joy, Jared and Jordan went to the living room and started playing a game.

After a while, Jared, always the trouble maker, looked across the coffee table at his brother. Suddenly, Jordan felt something sting his cheek.

He looked up and glared at his brother. "Cut it out, Jared."

Joy giggled, but seeing that a fight was about to break out she quickly said she had to go upstairs for a minute and left the room.

Josh shook his head as his sister made a quick get away.

Jared laughed. He looked at Josh and shot a piece at him. Josh saw it coming and ducked. Jared laughed again.

Jordan glared at his brother harder. "Cut it out Jared."

Jared laughed harder and stood up to shoot another piece at Jordan. As he did so Josh grabbed his leg and jerked it out from under him. Jared slammed to the floor with a cry of surprise. Jordan laughed as Jared jumped up. He went at Josh with his fist flying.

Josh ducked and missed the first blow but that only served to infuriate Jared. Soon an all out wrestling match was being held in the living room. The boys slammed into the furniture laughing. Suddenly Jared landed a punch right on the large bruise on Josh's back.

He yelped and fell back. Jared jumped at him. But Jordan held him back. "Josh, are you okay?"

Josh rolled over and slowly stood. "I'm fine."

Jordan felt uneasy. He had seen Josh's bruised back while Jared and Josh wrestled. "Where are the bruises from, Josh?"

Josh jerked back. "What are you talking about?"

Jordan shook his head. His eyes looked sad as he looked at Josh in concern. "Josh, I saw your back when you were wrestling. You have a huge bruise on your back and it looks fresh. What happened?"

Josh trembled. What if the boy's told their dad? "It's nothing. It was just stupid," he muttered.

Jordan and Jared exchanged a glance. "Where did it come from, Josh? Did someone hit you?"

Josh shook his head. Fear filled him. "Please don't say anything, guys. It happened at work, but it was just stupid. It won't happen again, so don't worry about it. It's just one of those things. I was in the wrong place at the wrong time is all. It was stupid. Don't say anything to anyone about it, please."

The boys looked at each other again. They head the panic in Josh's voice and saw it in his eyes. They both glanced at each other knowing that it wasn't an accident that had caused the bruise. Jordan finally spoke. "So it was Mr. Less who did it, and not Pastor Luke?"

Josh nodded. "Yeah. I don't want him to know about it. Please, don't say anything."

Jordan sighed. "Whatever you say, Josh. You would know how he feels about someone hitting you more than we would, but you should tell someone. If Luke wouldn't care that someone was hitting you maybe you should tell our dad. He wouldn't let someone hit you just to hit you."

Josh shook his head. "Luke would care, but I can't, and besides it won't happen again so don't worry about it."

Slowly Jordan and Jared nodded. "Okay."

"What happened in here!" Jim's voice boomed from the doorway.

Josh jumped. He shot a glance at Jordan and Jared, but all they did was turn and look at him. Jared smiled. "Nothing much, Dad. We were just playing a little game."

Jim saw Josh stiffen and look down. Again he felt guilt wash over him. "You boy's get this room cleaned up. We need to get going in a little bit. It is almost time for church."

Jared frowned. "Already, Dad. Why can't we just stay here?"

Josh flinched when he heard Jared talk back to his dad. But when he heard his dad chuckle, anger ran though him. His dad was going to have Mr. Less beat him for being disrespectful and then let these two boys back talk him and argue with him, and he wasn't going to do anything to them. What was so wrong with him? Why did his dad hate him so much? Why was he the one getting beaten?

Jim saw Josh's jaw muscles tighten, but still the boy kept his head down and wouldn't look at him. "Boys, I already said it is almost time for church. Now you two help get this game put away and get the room cleaned up. It looks like you were wrestling in here, and that better not be what was going on. You know that is against the rules."

Jared flushed under his father's gaze, but didn't say anything. Jordan glared at his brother, but Josh trembled. Was his dad going to blame him for this? Slowly he looked up at him.

Jim saw the fear in his son's eyes and his heart broke. He shouldn't be scolding his boys, not right in front of Joshua. He didn't need to feel like he was the one in trouble. "Get this room cleaned up, boys. It's time to go," his voice was quiet, but had an edge running through it.

All three boys looked up at him. "Yes, sir," they answered in unison.

Jared and Jordan looked at Josh in surprise. "What are you answering for?" they asked. "It's us he is talking to."

Josh shrugged. "Come on let's just get this place cleaned up. We don't want your dad to get upset. He may decide you all can't come over anymore."

Jared and Jordan chuckled. "Dad wouldn't do that. Don't worry about it."

Josh trembled even more. Why did his dad let these boys disobey him? Why was he so lenient with them? It didn't make sense.

Josh decided to test the waters a little bit as they started to pick up the game. "How long have your mom and dad been married?" he asked, seeming to just be starting a conversation.

Jordan looked at him in surprise. "How did you know that they hadn't been always?"

Josh shrugged, but his muscles tightened.

Jared was the one who answered. "It's been almost four years now. Mom was dating a guy who was a real jerk. He got her pregnant with Julia. That was when Mom met up with Dad. He was her doctor. They started liking each other. Mom broke up with the jerk she was with a few weeks after she found out she was pregnant. It wasn't long before they were dating. They got married shortly after Julia was born, and she will be four next month."

Josh nodded pretending to be interested in the story. "I see. What happened to your real dad?"

Jordan was the one who answered this time. "He was killed in a hunting accident when we were less then a year old. We don't remember him at all. Mom lived with her parents for most of our lives. When we turned ten she decided it was time to live on her own. She moved to an apartment. That was when she started dating Greg Miller. He was horrible. He would hit her and then he got her pregnant, but mom wouldn't break up with him. We begged her to, but she wouldn't. That is until one day when she came home and found he had belted both me and Jared till we were bleeding. He had been doing it for a long time, she just hadn't known about it.

When she broke up with him he attacked her. We fought him off, but it was hard. He hurt mom pretty bad. When she and Dad started dating we were scared to death of him, but he was always so nice. He never yelled at mom. He was always nice to us. He started taking us to church. Mom got saved. Then things really were different at home, but it was a good different. When they got married it was great. Dad's been great. He hasn't in the whole time they have been together, ever raised a hand to me or Jared, or Mom, or Julia. It's been so nice. He loves us all as if we are his."

Josh felt his face pale at these words. *No, he doesn't. The reason he loves you is because you aren't his. You have no idea what he is capable of.* He looked up to say something to them and saw his dad in the door way. He froze.

Jim heard the boys talking and had stopped to listen. He heard the last few statements that Jordan had made and he felt a warm glow flow through him. Then he saw Josh's face and the glow died as though someone had thrown water on it. He understood the look.

Josh was more hurt then angry, but just the same, Jim figured he was wondering why he could beat him for so long and never touch these kids. He sighed. He would have to get a chance to talk to his son. Some time when they were alone, maybe he could explain why things were different now. He wanted his son to understand just how wrong he had been.

8

Josh stood and stretched. His back was killing him, but he didn't say anything. He knew it wouldn't do any good.

Marcus, Mr. Less's twenty year old son, stood and stretched also. Then he looked at Josh. "You ready for this?"

Josh shrugged. "I guess. If this machine would quit breaking down we could be half done by now."

Marcus nodded and gave a slight laugh. "Yeah, it's high time for Dad to buy a new one, but as long as this one keeps moving he will just insist that we keep patching it together and getting by."

Josh shrugged. "I guess if he is happy with it, it doesn't matter." A movement at the house caught his eye. He glanced that way and saw Emma, Mr. Less's fifteen year old daughter, on the porch watching them.

She saw Josh look at her, and she waved. "You boy's want a drink of lemonade before you head out?" she called. She pushed back her blond hair and took a step off the porch. "You can come in and get some. I just made it."

Marcus looked up at his sister then glanced sideways at Josh. "Sure." he called to her. "I will send Josh in to get it."

Josh felt an odd quiver run through him. Why was he suddenly so uneasy? He shouldn't be. In the two weeks he had been working here he had been in the house multiple times to get something before they headed to the fields. So why was he uneasy today? It really didn't make sense.

Marcus nodded his head toward Josh. "Go on in and get it. I'll hook up and be ready to go when you get out here with the drinks. Tell her thanks." He turned away before Josh could respond.

Josh felt that weird feeling ripple through him again, but he didn't want to make Marcus mad. He had already felt Marcus's wrath a few times since he had been working here and he really didn't want to feel it again. He could almost see his father's look of disapproval again, when he took the job. He stiffened. He wasn't going to live afraid. His father had nothing to do with him.

Marcus walked back around the baler. "Joshua! Go get us some drinks and get back out here. I am almost ready to go."

Josh jumped, "Okay," he snapped. He hadn't meant to snap, but his thoughts had drifted and put him in a bad mood again.

Whenever he thought of his dad, he felt that tightness in his heart again. He didn't want to hate him, but he wasn't going to make an effort to love him either. He took a deep breath and headed toward the house. He felt more and more uneasy the closer he got.

He stepped up on the porch and rapped lightly on the screen door. "Emma. Mrs. Less?"

Emma called out, "I am back here in the kitchen, Josh. Come on in. I have it ready for you."

Josh felt his nerves tighten and he looked back toward the barn to find Marcus watching him with a scowl. Slowly he opened the door and went in. "I can just wait out here, if you want to bring it."

Emma laughed good naturedly. "Don't be silly, Joshua. The house doesn't bite. Come on in and get a cold drink. Dad and Marcus have been working you hard enough today. You deserve a little break in a cool kitchen."

Josh slowly walked into the room. He had never felt this uneasy. He looked around quickly and suddenly realized why. "Where is your mom, Emma?"

Emma held out a cup of lemonade. "She went to my grandma's. My grandma isn't feeling well, and Mamma went to take care of her for a while. I don't really know for sure when she will be back. Grandma lives in California. I wish Mamma would have taken me with her. I miss my grandma."

Josh took a quick drink. "Do you have one for Marcus? I will just take it out to him. He is ready to go, so I shouldn't waste time."

Emma shook her head and her big blue eyes filled with tears. "I haven't ever seen you act like this, Joshua. In church you are always so nice and friendly to me. But since you have been working here you won't even hardly look at me. You haven't said more then twenty words to me since you have been here. Did I do something to make you mad at me?"

Josh looked away quickly. He felt guilty when he saw her tears, yet he had his reasons for staying away from her. He didn't want to upset Emma or her family, but he knew the kind of girl she was, and he didn't want someone to get the wrong impression with him and Emma. For, though her family hadn't said anything in the two weeks he had been working here, it was evident that she was pregnant. He didn't want someone to get the idea that he was responsible.

He shivered wondering what her dad would do to him, or Marcus even, if they thought he was responsible. He quickly took a step away from her as she stepped closer to him. "No, you didn't do anything. I was just thinking it is awfully hot out there and Marcus needs a drink also, and he is probably ready to go. I don't want to keep your dad waiting. He is paying me to work not cool off in the house."

Emma giggled as she stepped closer to him. "You are so cute, Josh." She put her hand on his arm and fluttered her long dark lashes at him.

Josh stepped away from her quickly and drank his lemonade hoping that would give him an excuse to get out of the house. *Help me, God,* he prayed.

Emma watched him drink it. "Can I get you some more?"

Josh handed her the cup. "No. Thank you, but no. It was good." He turned away from her. "I have to get back to work."

Emma placed her hand on his arm, again, stopping him in his flight to the door. "Josh, I really want to thank you."

Josh felt himself tense. "Thank me? For what?" He glanced back at her against his will.

Emma smiled softly and fluttered her eye lashes again. "Oh, you know. I have seen the way you look at me. You know."

Josh stepped away from her, but she kept her hand on his arm keeping him from fleeing. "Quit it, Emma," he said tightly. He didn't want to be rude, but he wanted her to leave him alone. Fear gripped him and he glanced around hoping to see a way of escape.

69

Emma sighed. "I know you know, Josh. Thanks for not saying anything about it." She dropped her hand losing all pretense of flirting.

Josh shrugged. "It's not my place to say anything. Does your dad know?"

Emma turned pale, "No, and I don't want him to," she shivered slightly.

Josh felt her shiver, and his heart went out to her, but he kept his distance. "I suggest you tell him soon." His voice sounded cold, but he couldn't help it. He didn't want her to get the wrong idea that he cared for her.

He took a step back, and this time she let him go without trying to stop him. "With as small as you are you aren't going to be able to hide it much longer," he added as he looked into her eyes.

Emma bit her lip. "You are right, I know, but I am scared to tell him. I am afraid of what he might do. I wish Mom was here. It wouldn't be so bad then. But she isn't, and she won't be in time. What am I going to do! Mamma would know what to do or say, but -"she burst into tears and hugged herself tightly, rubbing her hands up and down her arms as she did.

Josh nodded slightly. He understood how she felt. "I am sorry your mom isn't here Emma, but you can't just keep trying to hide it. I am sorry I have been ignoring you. I just didn't want someone to get the wrong idea about us."

Emma smiled up at him. "It's okay. Everyone else around here does it too."

Josh turned to go. Then he stopped and turned back. "Who was it, Emma?"

Emma looked away ashamed. Finally she looked back up at him. "Levi, my boyfriend. When I told him, he was so happy and excited. He wants us to get married. He wants me to come and live with him and start a family, but he hasn't got the courage to talk to Daddy yet. You see Daddy sort of doesn't know anything about him."

Josh shook his head slightly. "I am sorry for your troubles, Emma. I hope you and Levi can be very happy together."

Emma sighed. "If we ever get the chance. What is Daddy going to do when he finds out?"

Josh shrugged. "I have to get back to work, Emma. Thanks for the lemonade."

Emma nodded and Josh saw her tears as he turned to walk away. What a mess that girl had herself in.

Josh felt queer as he walked back out to the barn. He shouldn't have stayed in the house so long talking to Emma. He shouldn't have stood in the house and talked to her at all. As he walked in the barn, he looked around for Marcus. He thought he was hooking up the baler and rake, where was he? Suddenly he felt a hand on his arm like a vice. He froze.

"Have a nice little chat, boy?"

Josh felt his blood turn to ice.

Mr. Less spun him around to face him. "What were you doing in the house with my daughter, boy?"

Josh felt his stomach turn over. He felt again that sick feeling in his stomach. "Marcus sent me in to get us a drink."

Mr. Less scowled even more. "To get a drink, huh? Where is the drink then?"

Marcus walked into the barn then and pulled the door shut.

Josh felt weak to his knees. He had been set up, and he knew it. His dad was right. His stomach knotted with that realization.

Mr. Less gripped his arm tighter. "You went in for a drink, huh? When else in the last two weeks have you just gone in for a drink, boy? When else! What else have you helped yourself to!"

Josh tried to step back, tried to get away, but Mr. Less's grip was like iron. He winced as the man squeezed his arm tighter. "What do you mean?" His voice came out in more of a groan than he wanted it to.

Mr. Less's fist cut him off. "You been being a little too friendly with my daughter, ain't you, boy!"

Josh gasped. "I never-" again Mr. Less's fist stopped him, this time he saw stars before his eyes.

Marcus grabbed Josh's other arm and jerked him away from his dad. "You got my sister pregnant, brat, now you are going to pay for it. Is that why you took the job? You thought you could get close to my sister without anyone finding out? Thought no one would suspect it to be you since your dad is the pastor!"

Josh trembled as Marcus pushed him down. He looked at both men and his blood seemed to freeze. "I didn't do it." he whispered.

Marcus grabbed him and pulled him to his feet. "You hurt my sister, boy. Now you are going to pay for it. You have no idea what

71

pain is."

Josh trembled even more.

"I am going to make you feel pain like you have never felt." Marcus hissed.

Josh turned his head slightly and caught the punch with his cheek. He trembled. *Please, God, help me. Please don't let this happen!*

9

Pain was the first thing he felt as he tried to move. *It was just a dream,* he tried to tell himself. But then he tried to move again and knew this wasn't a dream. Where was he? What had happened? He tried to move again and pain exploded all over him. Darkness pressed in close around him. Finally he lay still and tried to think. What had happened to him?

Then he remembered going to the house to get a drink. He was right to be uneasy. It had been a set up. Marcus must have followed him to the house. He had heard at least part of what Emma had said to him. He had heard just enough to guess that Josh was the father of Emma's baby, and then he had gone for his dad.

Josh tried to move again. He had to get out of here before they came back. They wouldn't stop at one beating. They wouldn't stop till he was dead. His dad was right. He should have listened, but he had been too stubborn.

He trembled as he pushed himself to a sitting position. Then he stopped to think. He had to get out of here, but he couldn't just walk out. They would see him and stop him. Luke wouldn't be coming to give him a ride home. Mr. Less had given him a ride every day he had worked for him. That was how it had been arranged.

He shook his head. Had this been in Mr. Less's plans all along? Had he planned it since he asked Josh to work for him?

Josh shook his head. It didn't matter. He would just have to walk home. It was only two or three miles so it wasn't a big deal, but first he had to get out to the road and away from the house without them seeing him. He looked around the barn and noticed how much darker it had gotten. It was evening or later. How long had he been out? Did they think they had already killed him?

He let his gaze travel the walls wondering how to get away. Then he saw it, a back door on the barn. Fighting against the pain he pulled himself to it. Slowly he opened it and looked out. No one was there.

He was grateful for the tall grass around the barn. He lay down on his belly, and bit his lip. The pain that shot through him was almost unbearable, but he knew he had to do it. Slowly he pushed himself close to the ground and pulled himself toward the road. Slowly, inch by inch he made himself move forward.

"Please, God, I could use a miracle right now. I know you can help me. Please don't let them see me." He felt a sting in his heart and he bit his lip. He should have listened to his dad. He had been right.

Josh felt the sting in his conscience. He had been angry at his dad for talking to Luke and Annie. He had been angry with his dad for disapproving of this job, and even though he didn't like Mr. Less, he had taken the job to spite his dad. He felt ashamed. "I'm sorry, God. I am sorry I didn't listen. Please forgive me and help me. Please. Forgive me for not listening to Luke and my dad. Forgive me God, and help them to forgive me."

He pushed on, fearing at every moment someone was going to grab him. His body was stiff with pain and anxiety. Finally he made it to the road. Quickly and painfully he looked both ways then rolled across the gravel and into the ditch on the other side. As he landed in the grass, he bit his lip and forced down the cry of pain that rose in him. He had to do this and that was all there was to it.

He pulled himself along again till he was about half a mile down the road. Slowly he looked up and around. Did he dare walk now? Was he far enough away that they wouldn't see him? Slowly he stood. Pain shot through his chest and back. He didn't even look down to see how bad it was. He had to get home before he saw or he may not make it. With a quick glance around he began walking toward home. He was unsure of the time, and even as he started walking, though he didn't want to admit it, he was so confused he wasn't really sure he was walking in the right way. All he knew was it was dark and he had to get away.

He hadn't walked more then a quarter of a mile, when he heard a car coming up behind him. Fear gripped him and it took all his strength to not turn around or start to run, instead he walked closer to the grass as though he was just out for a stroll, but his body tensed ready to run if needed. "Help me, God. Please!"

The car slowed.

Josh tensed even more. Was he caught?

"Josh is that you?" It was Lilly, his dad's wife. She stopped beside him. "I thought that was you," she cried as he turned toward her. "What in the world are you doing walking out here at this time of night?"

He turned all the way toward her and flinched when he heard her gasp.

"Joshua! What happened? Were you in a fight? Was there an accident?"

Josh felt panic rise in him. He tried to sound calm. "Please, can you give me a ride home?"

Lilly nodded, "Yes, of course. Please get in, Josh, and tell me what happened. You look like you were attacked."

Josh opened the door. He flinched knowing he would make a mess out of her car. "Maybe I shouldn't-"

Lilly seemed to know what he was thinking. "Don't you worry about messing up my car, Joshua. I have two boys and there is nothing on you that hasn't been tracked in here before. Now you just get in and tell me what happened while I take you home."

Josh slowly slid in, but even with slow and careful movements his body rejected with pain. His stomach turned and he prayed he wouldn't get sick in her car as well. "I was just in the wrong place at the wrong time." He groaned as he shut the door. He felt surprised when he heard the worry in her voice and the passion. She sounded like she really cared that he was hurt.

Lilly felt sick as she saw the bruises on his face and the blood. By the way he was moving she guessed whoever it was that beat him up didn't stop at his face. Anger turned inside her. Why would someone have beat him up?

As they pulled into the drive at Luke and Annie's she looked at him again. "Josh, why don't I send Jim over. He can look you over and see if you need to get to a hospital."

"No!" Josh bit his lip, as he saw the surprise flash on Lilly's face. He guessed then that his dad hadn't told Lilly about him. He took a deep breath, as deep as he could with out it hurting, which wasn't very deep, "No," He managed a little calmer this time. His dad was the last person he wanted to know about this. He would join the Less's, not help him. He would probably tell him he deserved it for taking the job, when he knew his father didn't want him to. He dropped his head in shame. "It's fine. I'll be fine. Thanks for the ride." He bit his lip as he reached for the door handle.

Lilly saw the boy's pain, but was unsure if she should offer to help or let him do it on his own, though strong and built like a man, he was still a boy. Anger surged in her. Who would have beaten him up and for what reason? She was surprised he had been so objective about her getting her husband to help him, but that was probably the man in him not wanting help when he needed it. "Can you make it to the house alright, Josh? Or do you need some help?"

Josh stood slowly, his movement a testament to how badly he was hurting. "I can make it. Thanks for the ride."

Lilly's slow soft smile reached her eyes. "No problem. I glad I came along when I did."

She frowned slightly as Josh slowly walked toward the house. She had thought Mr. Less was suppose to bring Josh home every night. Why had he been walking? Again came the nagging question, who had beaten him up? She shook her head. She was going to talk to her husband about this, even though Josh had said no.

She understood he didn't want to take advantage of them being neighbors, but he needed a doctor's care. She backed the car out of the drive and headed for home. Her nerves were tight. She wasn't sure what to do, but she was sure her husband should at least look at Joshua and make sure nothing was broken. By the looks of the boy, she would say there was several things broken.

As she pulled into the drive at home, she felt tears slip down her cheeks. She had thought about it all the way home. She was sure it wasn't the pastor who had hurt Josh or he wouldn't have been trying to get home. But if it wasn't the Less's who was it? Had he been walking home and someone beat him up, or was it Arthur Less, even though he said he was such a good Christian. Did Christians act that way? Ever since Jim had introduced her to Jesus she had grown to love The Lord more and more every day.

She took a deep breath as she stopped the car. She bowed her head. This was what she should have done at the start. "Dear Lord, I am sorry I didn't give this to you at the very start. I guess I am still learning. Please help Joshua to be okay. Help who ever it was that beat him up to get caught. And please let Jim be able to help him if he needs to." She looked up with tears still streaming down her cheeks. "Amen."

She hurried to the house, not even bothering to get the groceries out of the car. She had to let Jim know what had happened, then she would have the boys help her unload the car.

Jim looked up when he heard the door open and was surprised to see that Lilly was crying. He rushed over to he. "Honey, what is wrong?" He gripped her shoulders gently and looked down into her eyes.

Lilly took a deep breath, but her tears still ran down her cheeks. She tried to talk, but whimpered instead.

Jim felt his heart turn over. What had happened to get her so upset. "Are you hurt?"

Lilly shook her head.

Jared and Jordan came running when they heard their dad's concern. They stopped short when they saw their mom crying. Fear ran through them both.

Jim looked up at them. "One of you get your mom some water."

They both stood there for a moment staring at him then Jordan turned to obey.

Jim turned back to Lilly and wrapped her in his arms. She sobbed even more. Her whole body shook with sobs. Jim felt his fear rise. "Lilly is something wrong with the baby? What is it? Please tell me."

Jordan appeared with a glass of water. Jim took it and thanked him then turned back to Lilly. "Honey, come on. I want you to drink this and tell me what happened."

Lilly took a deep shuttering breath. "Oh, Jim." she whispered as she took the glass. She slowly emptied it, handed it back to Jordan with a smile and whispered, "Thank you."

Jordan nodded, but glanced at his dad, unsure of what to do. He hadn't ever seen his mom cry like that. Not even after she had found out that her boyfriend had been beating him and Jared. Fear held him frozen to the spot.

Jim held Lilly out from him and gently rubbed his hands up and down her arms. He tried to calm the fear that was rising in him. He lead her into the living-room and gently sat her on the coach. He sat beside her and looked her in the eye. "Lilly, Honey, please tell me what is going on. What was that all about?"

Lilly took another deep breath. "Oh, Jim, it's awful. I was on the way home and saw someone on the road. As I got closer I could see it was Joshua. He was walking home from work. I stopped to give him a ride."

Jim's brow furrowed even as he felt his whole being tense. "I thought Arthur Less was giving him a ride."

Lilly nodded. "So did I, but when I got to him I saw why he wasn't. The boy had been beaten up badly. He was bleeding profusely. And he walked like he was in severe pain."

Jim felt his temper rise even more. He knew Less was a jerk, but had he really beaten up on Josh.

Jared and Jordan exchanged a look.

Jim saw it. "Boys, what do you know about this?"

Jared looked at Jordan again and Jordan shrugged. "Last Sunday when we were over there at Josh's, you know when we were wrestling, we saw a big bruise on his back. He didn't want to talk about it much, but he said that he had gotten it at work, and he begged us not to tell anyone. We wondered then if someone was hitting him, but since he begged us not to tell, we didn't figure we should."

Jim felt his blood boil. For a moment his vision became blurry. He stood up. "Boys, help you mom bring in the groceries and then get ready for bed. I'll be back later." He headed for the door.

Jared and Jordan looked after him in surprise. "Where are you going, Dad?"

Jim looked up at them. "I am going to check up on Joshua. I will be home when I am through."

Lilly nodded. "I was hoping you would do that." She took a deep shuttering breath. "I don't understand why anyone would beat him up."

Jim smiled at her, but his heart wrenched. He had kept it secret from his wife that Josh was his son, he hadn't told her about his past. Was God punishing him through Joshua? That didn't seem fair. Why make a child suffer for the sins of the parent? He pushed away his

78

uneasiness about it and hurried out the door. He had to get to Josh and see what was going on.

Annie was watching anxiously at the window. "Luke, he should have been home by now. I don't like it that it seems to get later every night. Mr. Less is going to have to be more careful about how long he keeps him out. The boy needs sleep as well."

Luke smiled as he wrapped his arms around her. "Honey, you know as well as I do that farming doesn't run on a scheduled start and stop time. He will get here when they are done for the day. It isn't that late yet. It's going to be fine. He likes working there, or he seems to."

Annie sighed. "I know but-" she stopped when she heard the front door. "I didn't hear Mr. Less's truck! Is that him?" She glanced out the window to see lights disappearing down the road. She hurried out into the hall and stopped short when she saw Josh lean back against the door. "Josh!" she shrieked. Panic washed over her as she saw the blood on her son's face and the way his exhausted body fell back into the door. "Luke, come quick!"

Luke stepped out and with one look at him ran to him. "Josh! What happened to you?" He grasped the boy's shoulders. "You've been hurt. Who hit you? What happened?" His angry and demanding voice brought fear into Josh.

He looked up at Luke and Annie, but his body trembled. He felt the dark vale of pain try to wash over him. He pushed it away. He opened his mouth to explain to Luke and Annie what happened, but found that he couldn't even begin to explain. It was too much. He leaned his head back again the door. A sob escaped his throat. Suddenly there was a loud knock on the door.

Josh felt the knock through his back. He jumped and looked up at Luke, his eyes wide with fear. Was Mr. Less after him already? Who would Luke believe, him or Mr. Less? Pain ripped through him. He knew who his father would believe. Would Luke be the same?

The knock sounded again and Luke waited for Josh to turn and answer it. When he didn't Luke frowned. What was going on? He released his hold on him. "Joshua, open the door." He could almost feel the fear in his son. What was going on?

Josh trembled and braced himself to be slugged as soon as he opened the door. Slowly he pulled the door open, but no fist greeted him, instead he saw someone he wanted to see even less then Mr. Less or Marcus. It was his dad.

Jim took one look at Josh and his eyes widened in surprise.

Josh saw the look and trembled. He retreated several steps into the house. Suddenly the pain and every thing that had happened registered and he started to shake. Jim stepped closer to him, and he shook even more.

He saw Jim reach out to touch him. Pain and fear gripped him tighter. He couldn't take more. He was already in so much pain. He saw Jim's hand coming toward him and he shrank down to the floor. "Please no, please! Please don't! I'm sorry! Please!" He pulled into himself and tried to cover his head with his arms. "Please don't! I didn't mean for it to happen! Please, Dad, I am sorry. Please don't hit me any more, please."

Luke and Jim both looked at him then at each other with a question in their eyes.

Luke squatted down beside his son. "Josh?" he tried to speak calmly, but his nerves were tight and fear edged his voice.

Josh looked up at him, but his fear was too great to register what was really happening. Suddenly it was as if his nightmares had come to life as he looked into his father's eyes. He jerked back smacking himself into the wall. "Please, don't! Please! I'm sorry. I didn't mean it! Please no! Please." He looked up at Luke with panic in his eyes. "Please don't let him touch me, please. I didn't do it!" He tried to edge away, but was up against the wall. Tears ran down his cheeks. He was ashamed to cry, but he couldn't help it. The pain in his body was too much.

Luke was confused. "Let who touch you, Josh?"

Jim squatted down beside them. "Josh, what happened?"

Josh screamed as his father reached out to him. "No! Please! No!" His body went ridged with fear as he tried to pull away from his dad.

Luke looked up at Annie and she quickly left to room to get some bandages and medicine.

Jim gripped his son's shoulder.

Josh felt his grip and his whole being trembled. "No! I didn't do it! I'm sorry!" He shrieked again as he tried to huddle even farther

80

into himself to shield himself from the pain that was coming. He was too scared to think, too scared to even know what he was doing.

Jim gripped Josh's arm firmly. He had to stop the boy's panic. He only knew of one thing to try. "Joshua Andrew Peterson, stop it right now." The command barked out, taking him by surprise. He hadn't sounded like that since he had gone to prison.

Josh froze in horror as he looked up into his father's eyes. The panic in him washed over him anew, but he bit back his cry of terror. In his panic, his heart told him his father was going to beat him even worse then Arthur Less and Marcus had, but he also knew it would be worse if he tried to fight it.

He stared at his dad with his eyes wide in fear, but made no more noise.

Luke stared at Jim as a horrible feeling settled into the pit of his stomach. "What did you say? How did you know his whole name." Fear and pain washed over him. This couldn't be Josh's dad, he thought. His last name was Johnson, Josh was a Peterson.

Jim looked down at Josh. He saw the pain and panic in his eyes and felt guilty. The boy hadn't wanted anyone to know about them so he hadn't even told Lilly. Yet when she had come home and told him about Josh, he was sure she knew something was up by the way he had run out of the house.

Josh bit his lip as his father looked at him, then looked away. He couldn't take any more of this. He groaned as the pain of the beating earlier washed over him again. He wrapped his arms around himself and tried to ease the terrible pain in his chest.

Jim hung his head for a moment then looked up at Luke. "I'm his father." he whispered. He reached out to remove Josh's shirt so he could see what all had been done to the boy, but Luke grabbed his wrist and stopped him from touching the boy.

Annie was just walking back up to them and froze when she heard this. An over whelming fear ran through her.

Luke sat stunned for a moment, pain and anger flooding him as he held Jim's wrist, keeping him from touching Josh. He looked at Josh and saw a fire in his eyes. "How long have you know, son?" his voice was soft, but edged with pain. "How long have you know he was your dad?"

Josh looked down unwilling to answer.

Jim frowned. "Answer him, son. Then we need to get you in to the couch and cleaned up. We need to see what the damage is."

Josh trembled, but he knew better then to disobey his father. He had learned that lesson long ago at the end of a belt. He looked Luke in the eye, and Luke saw his pain and fear. "Since I heard his voice at the door the first night they were here."

Luke sat speechless. How could that have been? No wonder the boy had been having such nightmares. Why had he felt he had to keep this a secret? Why hadn't he at least told them Jim was his dad? Was Jim the one who had hurt him?

"Is he the one who did this, son?" Luke's voice was hard and cold. He glanced at Jim then looked down at Josh.

Josh whimpered as he pulled into himself even more. He glanced at his dad, then looked at Luke. Slowly he shook his head, then gasped from the pain the small movement had caused. His dad hadn't hit him directly, but Josh was sure his dad was responsible for it in some way.

Luke slowly released Jim's wrists. "Sorry. I didn't mean to accuse you. It's just that-"

Jim nodded as he looked Luke in the eye. "I understand. If I was in your place I would probably have thought the same."

He turned back to Josh and reached down and lifted him from the floor. "Let's get you to the couch and see what all has been done." He tried not to sound harsh, but the emotions running through him at that moment made his voice sound raspy.

He felt Josh stiffen, and he felt a stab of guilt pierce his heart. He knew why Josh was afraid of him, and it was his own fault. In a way, he felt that the boy being hurt was his fault as well. He should have warned Luke and Annie about Arthur Less.

He looked up at Luke. "I will take a look at him and see if you need to take him in for any x-rays. We may need to do some in the morning if they don't need to be done in emergency tonight. Just to make sure everything is okay."

Josh started to tremble in pain as his father carried him into the living room. He wasn't sure if the pain he was feeling was greater or the fear. *Please God, help me to trust you. I don't know what to do. I don't know how to tell them what happened. Please, please help me.*

Jim felt Josh begin to shake. He looked down at the boy and saw why immediately. He knew most of it was from the pain he was feeling, but he was sure some of it was from his fear. The bruises on his face were one thing, but his shirt was torn and blood soaked. Lilly hadn't been exaggerating at all when she told him that Josh needed to be seen by a doctor. The boy was in bad shape. He wondered how he made it to where Lilly had found him.

Josh kept his eyes glued to his dad, too afraid to look away. What was he going to do to him? Beat him worse? Could he take more right now? Would Luke be able to protect him, or would Luke tell him it was his fault and he deserved it?

Jim slowly lowered him to the couch.

Josh cried out in pain as his back touched the furniture. He gasped as he realized what he had done, and fear flooded him as his eyes riveted on his father again. His body stiffened. He arched his back and tried to pull away. "I'm sorry, Dad. I didn't mean it."

Jim's jaw muscles tightened as he reached down and pressed gently on the boy's neck then moved down to his chest. Josh screamed again as Jim gently laid his hand on the boy's rib cage.

Jim felt concern flood him as he removed his hand and placed in on another rib. His heart clenched as again Josh cried out, though trying to hold it in this time. His body stiffened even more in pain. He saw the boy bite his lip trying to hold in the cry of pain.

"It's okay, Josh. I need you to let me know where it hurts. I need to see where all it is broken. You don't have to hold it back."

Luke squatted down by the couch close to Josh's head, as he was trying to stay out of Jim's way while he examined the boy. "What happened, son?"

Josh turned his head away slightly. He didn't want to answer. It hurt to talk, but it hurt even more thinking about what he had been accused of. "Nothing," he muttered. A sharp pain shot through his shoulder as his father gripped it firmly. He started to cry out, but managed to stifle it to a groan. His fear filled eyes looked up at his father.

Jim looked down at the boy with pain and anger in his eyes, a look that said clearly he knew Josh was lying. "Joshua, are you telling the truth? This is not nothing. If it is, what did the other guy look like? This is not just a fight among some teenage boys for fun. Now you answer the question you were asked, and you better answer it honestly."

Josh bit his lip as he dropped his head. He knew Luke would be ashamed of his lying. He took a deep breath and determined that he wasn't going to lie. He turned his head farther away to keep Luke from seeing the pain in his eyes. "It wasn't a fight. I didn't touch him," he muttered.

Jim nodded slightly. "Who was it, Joshua?" He waited for the boy to answer.

Luke waited quietly for Josh to answer also. He wasn't sure if he expected the boy to answer or not. So far he had said more to Jim in the last five minutes than Luke had been able to get him to talk about in the last month.

Josh looked up at his dad, and Luke saw the fear in the boy's eyes as he glanced past Luke and up at Jim. "Mr. Less," he muttered. "He said-" Josh stopped as Annie came back into the room with medicine and strips of cloth.

Jim took them from her silently and motioned for Josh to keep talking as he reached down and helped him sit up.

Josh caught his breath as pain shot through him, taking his breath away. He tried to talk, but that hurt even more.

Jim glanced at him out of the corner of his eye, but didn't press the issue of him talking. Instead he turned to Luke. "I am sorry I didn't talk to you about me being his dad. I should have told you as soon as I knew, but I didn't want to hurt you or him, nor did I wish to make you upset. You have all been so kind to us. And I can tell you have been kind to my son. I already told Joshua, and I am telling you now, I am not hear to take him away from you. That isn't my intent. I had no idea he was here. A job opened for me here, and I took it. That is what brought us here. I didn't figure out who he was till in church that first Sunday."

Jim stopped and looked down. "But I guess the boy isn't the only one to keep secrets. Lilly knows nothing about this. I kept meaning to tell her, but it just wasn't the right time. I just kept putting it off and putting it off and the longer I put it off the more afraid I became."

He shook his head, "We can work all that out later. For now, son, I want you to tell me what happened to you." Jim gripped the boys arm and wrist and pulled him to a seated position. His anger mounting even more when he saw the state of the boys shirt. He wanted to jerk the shirt off of him and demand to see his back, but he didn't. He didn't want to hurt the boy even more.

Josh glanced at Luke then at Annie. Tears smarted in his eyes, but he wasn't going to let them fall. He slowly turned his gaze back on his dad. "I didn't do it, Dad. I promise. It was a set up. Whatever he told you I did, I didn't do. I promise." He looked away. Fear ate at him. He felt it gnawing at his stomach. He glanced at Luke and saw pain in his eyes as well. He trembled. He wanted to beg Luke to keep him. He wanted to know that he would always be here with his family and not have to go back to living the life of pain and fear that he had to before. He bit his lip and would have turned away, were it not for the huge amount of pain he was in.

Jim leaned down and pushed his hand into the boy's back.

Josh felt the stab of pain and quickly caught his breath.

Jim looked down at him. "Hurt?"

Josh kept his head down as he shook his head slightly. It took every ounce of strength not to cry out in pain. He forced himself to not bit his lip from the pain.

Jim noted the boy's reaction, then pushed slightly on his back ribs.

Josh cried out in pain. He trembled, then dropped his head. "I'm sorry, Dad," he muttered. He felt the world around him start to fade. He hoped he wasn't going to pass out again, but he wasn't sure that he wasn't going to.

Jim shook his head slightly, but didn't say anything as he helped Josh lay back on the couch. He took a deep breath, and Josh wondered if he was trying to control his temper. "I think you may have a few broken ribs, but other than that it looks like just some major cuts and bruises." He reached behind Josh again and had him roll over. Then he pulled off the boy's shirt, motioning to Luke to look.

Josh gritted his teeth. He wasn't sure what all had happened today, but he knew there were bruises on his back from earlier this week, when Marcus had hit him, but he hadn't told Luke about it. He had been too afraid. He knew Luke and Annie had told him they were uncomfortable with the situation. He figured Luke would either get mad or say he deserved it.

Jim looked at the boy's back. He looked up at Luke and their concerned gazes met. "You going to talk about it, son?" Jim's voice was soft, and edged with pain and compassion.

Josh bit his lip. He didn't want his dad to ever call him son again. Anger shot through him as he looked his dad in the eye, "Why didn't you tell her about me?" He glared at him.

"You ashamed that I am your son? You don't even tell your wife what you use to do to me? You afraid she would dump you for fear of you doing that to her kids?

"Why do you hate me, Dad? Why can you feel fine with hitting me and acting like you have nothing to do with it? And it's all over stuff that is so stupid, but yet, things you wouldn't ever let me get by with, you never even speak to your other kids about?"

Jim felt the color drain from his face. That wasn't what he had meant to talk about. Still Josh was asking, and he would try his best to let him understand why he hadn't told his family about this part of his life.   Nervously he cleared his throat, "There are lots of different reasons, Joshua. I guess the main one was that I was afraid. I was afraid that she wouldn't want to marry me if she knew who I had been, if she knew what I had done to my own child." He stopped and looked down at Josh, then he knelt by the couch. "Son, could you ever forgive me for what I did to you? I promise it will not happen again. I am never going to hit you again, not like I use to for sure. I am truly sorry for everything I did to you. Please, can you ever find it in yourself to forgive me?"

Josh slowly turned his head. He was surprised to hear the sincerity in his father's voice, yet he still felt afraid that it was all a trap. He took a deep breath. Was Mr. Less lying about his dad? Had he only said that to keep Josh from telling that he was hitting him? *God, help me to trust you.* "It's okay, Dad," he whispered. "I forgive you, but-" he stopped too afraid to go on.

Jim turned his head to look his son in the eye. He saw Josh sink back into the couch with fear still shining in his eyes. "What is it, son? You can ask me. It's okay. I won't hurt you."

Josh looked from his father to Luke, pain ripped through his heart. "Do I have to go live with you?" He feared the answer, yet he had to know. He couldn't bare the thought of having to leave his family, but he knew that he could bare even less the fear that one day his dad would just come in and take him, better to have some warning.

Jim looked at Luke and a look seemed to pass between them that Josh didn't understand. Jim turned back to Josh, "Son, we will talk about that later. What we want to know right now is what happened to you other then the obvious. Why and who beat you up?"

Josh looked away from Jim and turned his fear filled eyes on Luke.

Luke saw the look and came up to the couch, having hung back not wanting to disturb father and son talking for the first time, he knew of any way, in almost eight years. Now he saw the fear in Josh's eyes and saw him start to tremble. He wondered how long they should make the boy talk. Wouldn't it be better for him to rest a little?

He rested his hand on Josh's shoulder lightly. "It's okay, Joshua. We aren't going to hurt you. We just need to know what is going on. You need-" someone pounding on the door interrupted what Luke was saying.

Luke turned toward the hall in surprise. Who would be pounding on the door at this hour? It had to be every bit of eleven o'clock at night. He glanced at his watch. Eleven forty-five! He shook his head. "I'll be back in a minute."

He knew, and Josh had lived with him long enough to know, that being a pastor meant putting your own needs behind that of others. There were many nights in the ministry that he had been called out of bed at midnight and one o'clock in the morning on an emergency.

Josh trembled as Luke walked out into the hall to answer the door. He quickly looked at his dad. Did he dare hope that his dad was honest and sincere? He had a feeling he was going to find out really quickly.

Luke opened the door still frowning slightly, that frown increased when he saw Arthur Less standing on the other side of the door.

Mr. Less stepped back a little surprised when Luke opened the door, but quickly regained his composer and pushed past him, storming into the house. "Where is he, Preacher! Bring that boy of yours out here. He is going to pay for what he has done. Where is he!"

Luke stood silently, his face void of emotion. Anger surged through him. So it was Less who had beat the boy up. Now the only question was why. "What are you talking about, Arthur?" Through years of practice from being in the ministry and having to stay clam, he kept his voice even.

"Get him out here! Quit your stalling, Preacher! He is going to pay for what he has done." Less screamed as he stormed past Luke.

Josh heard him and started to tremble. He glanced at his father and his stomach twisted in a knot. He wanted to tell Luke the truth, but now there wasn't going to be a chance. Who would his dad believe?

He waited in fear, for Luke and Mr. Less to come into the living room.

Jim heard Arthur Less screaming and anger surged through him. He saw the fear in his son's eyes and he knew it was Less who had beat him.

Luke stood calmly as Less raged on. Finally the man stood silent glaring at Luke. "What has he done to get you in such a state, Arthur? The boy just got home a few minutes ago. Why didn't you call me and tell me that you weren't going to bring him home? I would have picked him up. He didn't need to be walking home in the dark."

Arthur frowned hard. "Preacher, I think it would be best if the boy himself tells you what he's done, but I ain't leaving till he has paid for what he did."

Luke nodded slightly and motioned for Arthur to follow him into the living room.

Jim had walked to the doorway and stood glaring at Arthur Less. When Arthur saw him he smiled. "So you already here, huh. Did your boy tell you what he has been up to out at my place?"

Luke felt his anger rise. How many more people knew that Josh was Jim's son. Why had he not found out, or put two and two together. Now that he thought about it he could tell that Josh was bothered any time they were around Jim and the family. He had acted scared and nervous any time Jim was in the room. He should have thought. He should have asked the boy more direct questions. He knew he would have put two and two together if the name would have matched, but since they hadn't he hadn't thought about it at all.

As they walked into the room, Josh trembled and pulled himself up to face Arthur Less.

Jim frowned as he saw the boy start to stand, but he understood, in a way, and reached out to help him to his feet. Josh pulled back from his dad, and Jim noted the trembling in Josh and knew he was in a great deal of pain, but also saw that he was scared. Fear edged away in him. How long had Less been hitting Josh. Had it just started today? Had he done it since the boy had started working

88

out there? Why had Luke made him go back if Less was hitting him?

Mr. Less walked in and glared at him. He stormed across the room. "How dare you!" he screamed in the boy's face.

Josh bit his lip and dropped his head. His body jerked as he waited for Arthur to hit him.

Arthur grabbed the boy's arm and shook it slightly. His whole body tensed. He wanted to hit the boy, but he bid his time.

Jim tensed when he saw the man lay angry hands on Josh, but he waited to see what would happen. "I trusted you. I thought you were a good worker for me and a good helper. You were a helper alright weren't you, boy! Helped yourself to what you wanted didn't you, boy!" He gripped Josh's arms tighter and shook him harder.

Josh trembled even more. He knew he was almost sixteen and he shouldn't be afraid, but he was terrified. What was going to happen to him? His whole being began to shake in fear and in pain. He bit his lip to keep back the cry of pain that rose in him when Mr. Less squeezed his arms even tighter.

Luke cleared his throat. His anger surged. He could tell by the way Josh shied away from him, Less had hit him before. He tried to keep his voice even, but his anger still left an edge as he said, "Before we get all bent out of shape, Arthur, how about just telling us what he did."

Arthur Less glared down at Joshua. "I'll let your boy tell you. He needs to confess it." He gripped the boy's arms even tighter and fire shot from his eyes. Then he jerked the boy around to face Jim and Luke.

Luke turned his gaze on Josh and his heart went out to him. He saw how afraid the boy was.

Josh saw the look from Luke and fought to keep from running. If it hadn't been for the pain he was in he may have tried it, but instead he was stuck here with three men glaring at him and there was nothing he could do, but talk. Now Mr. Less stood behind him with a tight hold on his arms. His fear filled gaze went from his dad and then to Luke. "I didn't do it," he whispered. He bit his lip as Less twisted his arm behind him. "I didn't do anything! All I did was go in the house and-"

He fell back onto the couch as Arthur swung him around and back handed him.

He moaned in pain as he put his hand to his mouth. His breath came in a short gasp. It hurt to breath. It hurt to move. It hurt to lay. He felt a darkness try to close in on him, and he forced it away as he tried to move to get out of so much pain. He stopped when he felt a hand on his shoulder and another one on his arm.

He looked up and froze. He didn't know if he wanted to know who was gripping his arm, but he knew he didn't want to lay here and let them beat him to a pulp. His pulse quickened as he opened his eyes and saw his dad and Arthur Less standing over him. Arthur Less had a hold of his arm as if to jerk him to his feet. Jim had just placed his hand on the boy's shoulder.

Jim looked the man in the eye and tried to control his temper, but sparks were shooting out of his own eye as he growled, "What did the boy do, Arthur? Tell me. You know if it is worthy of punishment I will punish him." There was a sharp edge in Jim's voice as he finished.

Joshua trembled as he heard his dad's words. Was Luke going to let Jim beat him? Was his dad really going to whip him for what Less said he had done? The world started to spin around him and he closed his eyes and moaned.

Arthur glared at Josh, then glanced at Jim. He released Josh's arm and pulled a phone from his pocket. "Here. The boy left this at the farm." He held it out to Jim. "You may want to see it for yourself, let the pastor see as well."

Jim grabbed the phone and dropped it onto the coffee table. "I don't want a phone, Arthur. I want an answer."

Luke quietly walked over and picked up the phone.

Josh trembled even more, wondering what Mr. Less had put on his phone to make him look guilty.

Luke felt his heart clench as he looked through the boy's messages. He felt sick. In his heart he prayed for the right words to say. He hoped God gave him the wisdom to do the right thing. He thought he had raised Josh better then this, but it was clear the boy had fallen pray to a pretty girl. The question was how did Arthur find out about it. It looked to him as though the girl had willingly posed for the pictures.

Silently he held the phone out to Jim. He was worried that Jim wouldn't see the lie for what is was, because he was sure that it what this was. Josh wouldn't do this. Not when he was to be working. He wouldn't hurt a girl in that way. He didn't have it in him. He hoped

90

Jim would see it as a lie, but there was no way to know till it happened.

Jim scowled as he grabbed the phone, then he nearly dropped it. He turned his gaze on his son. Anger shot from his eyes. "Joshua! Is this true?"

Josh stared at his father in fear, but didn't move. He didn't even blink. He pulled back a little, trying to shrink into the couch.

Jim looked over at his son. "I asked you a question, son. I expect and answer," his voice was hard with anger, and sparks shot from his dark eyes. He prayed that Arthur Less was lying and that somehow the man had put this on the boy's phone.

Josh shivered as he heard his father's words. "I don't know, sir. I haven't read any of my messages for today," his voice came out a small whisper.

Jim set the phone down on the end table. "Joshua, you be honest with me, do you understand?" His voice had softened as he became more sure that this was a lie created by Arthur Less to make him mad at Joshua.

Josh kept his eyes glued to his dad. He didn't even dare to move so much as a nod. "I have only ever lied to you once in my life, Dad. You taught me a lesson that time. I haven't ever lied to you since. Not to you or anyone else." His voice was hard, but he couldn't help it. His dad had made sure he wouldn't forget that lesson and he hadn't.

Jim felt his neck muscles bulge and the muscles in his jaw tightened. "Joshua, did you get his daughter pregnant? Did you take these pictures of Emma?"

Josh knew the question was coming, but it still hurt to hear his dad ask. He looked over at Luke and tears stung his eye. Wouldn't Luke know he wouldn't do that. "No." His voice was little more then a whisper and he was afraid that his dad would take that to mean he was lying, but he was in so much pain he couldn't even speak any more. He felt the darkness trying to close around him again. Tears forced there way out of his eyes. He jerked his head to the side fearing his dad would hate him if he saw.

Jim saw Josh's tears and knew in his heart that the boy was telling the truth. He hoped that Luke believed him, but he couldn't make that happen. His voice softened as he gently laid his hands on the boy's shoulders. "What happened to you? Why do you have all these messages from her then? Why are there pictures of her on your phone. Are you dating her? Did you and she-"

"No!" Josh couldn't believe his dad was saying such things. Didn't he know that he wouldn't do that? "I didn't do anything, but be in the wrong place at the wrong time. That is all. And it was all a set up." Then he looked his dad in the eye. "What pictures?" he looked at Luke. "I don't have any pictures of any girl on my phone, and definitely not Emma."

His tears surfaced again as he looked pleadingly at Luke. "Please, Dad, please believe me. I didn't do anything to her. You raised me better then that. Please don't – all I did was – it was all just a set up."

He tried to pull away from his dad. Fear and pain raced through him as he saw his father's angry eyes watching him. "Please, believe me, Dad. I promise I am not lying to you. I didn't do it. Please. I promise. Please!"

Jim looked at him hard and gripped his shoulders more. It hurt to hear him call Luke dad, but he pushed the hurt away. He should expect it. The boy had lived with Luke for almost eight years. He knew he should be grateful that the boy felt loved enough to call Luke dad. "Who set you up, Joshua?" His voice was soft, yet stern.

Josh saw the look in his dad's eyes and his heart sank. He had seen that look in his father's eyes more than once in his life. A knot formed in the pit of his stomach and he felt it tighten more and more, till he wanted to throw up, but he knew that would just make the pain worse. He looked away. Why was he even trying? It wasn't going to matter if Luke believed him or not. His dad didn't, and that hurt. His dad was going to beat him and there was nothing Luke could do about it, because Jim was his dad.

Arthur Less looked from one man to the other, then turned his stormy eyes back on Josh. He grabbed the boy's arms and jerked him to his feet relishing the sound as Josh cried out in pain. "I ought to kill you, boy!"

Josh heard his father stand and he stiffened. Was his father going to let Mr. Less whip him. The world around him began to dim and he tried desperately to fight off the pain.

Jim stepped between Arthur and his son. "Joshua, turn around. I want Less and Luke and I to all get a good look at your back."

Josh felt the color drain from his face as he glanced at Luke.

He was his only hope. Would Luke believe him? His eyes pleaded with him to help.

Luke stepped forward. "Jim, we have no proof that the boy is lying. You are not going to touch him. Not in this house and not ever again. As far as the law is concerned he isn't your son, and as far as I am concerned you are not going to touch him. If you do, I'll see you back behind bars. Do you want that?"

Jim turned to Luke. "We will have proof, Preacher." He turned his stormy gaze back on Josh. "Joshua, do as you are told."

Josh bit his lip. He knew better then to try and disobey his dad. He had learned long ago that even if he was innocent the beating was not as bad if he just took it, than if he tried to convince his dad that he was innocent. With a fearful glance at Luke, wondering what was going to happen to him, he slowly and painfully pulled away from Arthur Less so he could turn for the men to see his beaten and bloody back.

Luke flipped on the over head light, and Josh groaned as he blinked in the bright light. He knew that in the dim light from the lamp his dad and Luke and Annie hadn't seen anywhere near as bad as it was going to be. Luke looked at Josh and gasped when he saw the welts on the boy's chest more clearly. He stepped closer, but Jim held out a hand to stop him.

His look was hard and his eyes blazed. "I said to turn around, boy." His voice was hard and threatening.

Josh glanced at Mr. Less, and seeing the satisfied smirk on his face, dropped his head and turned his back to his dad. He bit his lip as he felt his whole being tremble. What was going to happen to him? He heard someone unbuckling a belt. He stiffened, waiting for the leather to snap across his raw, bare back. He bit his lip harder hoping he wouldn't scream, and tasted blood. Was this really the only reason that Mr. Less had hired him. Was this his plan from the beginning?

Arthur pulled his belt from around his waist and raised it to smack the boy. Anger and a mean hungry glare burned in his eyes. Luke saw the look and his temper rose. He stepped forward to stop him, but as Arthur Less swung the belt down, Jim's hand gripped around his wrist stopping him. The pop of flesh on flesh was loud enough Josh jumped.

Luke saw the innocent look in Jim's eye, but also that it was hiding an anger, a deep hard anger. "Where did all the welts and marks come from on my boy's back, Arthur?" Jim's voice was quiet, but there was a hard sound running through it.

Josh heard it and trembled even more. That was his father's threatening voice, his do not cross me or you will be sorry voice.

Arthur looked Jim in the eyes and scowled. "How should I know? Probably the preacher, or didn't you know those in high authority in the church-"

"That's enough, Arthur!" Jim shouted.

Josh jumped and winced in pain. He started to turn around, but Arthur Less gripped his arm and kept him facing the other way. Josh felt his stomach turn as Mr. Less squeezed his arm harder again.

Arthur smiled. "Yeah, I didn't figure you would want the finger pointed at you. We wouldn't want to end up in jail or prison again now, would we? So now all you are doing is trying to hide behind me. Tell me to beat your boy, then hide behind your own lies."

Jim's voice was livid with anger. "I never told you to hit my boy, Less. You know that. You told the boy that though, didn't you. You knew if he was threatened with a worse whipping, he wouldn't squeal on you. How dare you-"

Annie stepped into the living room just then. When she started to speak Josh spun around and as he did he fell back onto the couch. His head spun in pain. He hoped she hadn't seen anything. He didn't want her to say anything to anyone else, like Joy or Lilly. He didn't want his dad even angrier at him. "There is a young lady here to see you, Joshua. I think you may just need to leave this alone for a while, and let the two of them talk." She frowned at the men.

Josh frowned as he sat back up. "What young lady?"

Annie smiled. "It's just Emma, Josh. I am sure it is fine. She won't bite. She said she had something she needed to talk to you about."

Josh felt his whole being start to tremble. *Can this night get any worse?* He felt his stomach turn. All this was going to do was make him look even more guilty. Had Arthur Less planned all this out? Had he made Emma flirt with him? Had Emma lied about being pregnant just to make her dad hit him more?

Annie smiled as she looked over her shoulder. "Come on into the living room, dear."

Josh bit back a groan. He was pretty sure her father had made her come to blame him as well. He saw his father looking at him out of the corner of his eye and he saw Luke's disappointed look. He shivered and wouldn't even glance at Mr. Less.

Emma stepped timidly through the door way. "Josh, I -" she stopped as she saw her dad standing there.

Anger blazed in his eyes. "What are you doing here, girl? Get back home where you belong. If I catch you with this boy again, I am going to kill him and you. How dare you let him touch you! Did you think I wouldn't figure it out!"

She dropped her gaze, then looked up at Josh. "I'm sorry," she whispered. "I didn't mean for this to happen."

Josh felt his heart go out to her. Was she here on her own, or for her dad? He wasn't sure, but he knew it didn't matter, it was going to make him look even more guilty, what ever the reason.

Jim looked at her closely. Tension was thick in the room. "What have you come for?" He tried to keep his voice kind, but he heard the tired edge in it.

Josh trembled not knowing what to expect.

Emma looked up at Luke with tears in her eyes. Then she looked at Jim, and he knew that her father had already informed her of who he really was. "Mr. Peterson, Pastor, Josh had nothing to do with me. It's my fault, not his. I'm sorry. I should have called or something, but I didn't figure out what my dad was up to till just a little while ago. I knew then that I had to tell everyone the truth. I didn't want Josh punished for something that he didn't do."

Luke turned his gaze on Josh as did Jim.

Josh wanted nothing more then to run away at that moment, but he knew he was in so much pain that he wouldn't get far, and if he did try to run the punishment would be way worse when he was caught.

Emma looked at all three men. She knew her condition was obvious. "Josh did come into the house earlier today. He came in to get a drink, because I asked him and Marcus if they wanted any. I was flirting with him, but that was because I was so scared. He saw that I was scared and asked me what was wrong. I didn't want to talk about it, but finally I told him I was pregnant.

"When I went outside a little while later to give him and my dad and brother a drink, they were standing out side the barn and Josh was nowhere to be seen. I asked where he was and they said it wasn't any of my business. I think it was my business. Where did you go,

Josh?"

Then she really looked at him and her tears ran down her cheeks. "Did they beat you up because of me?"

Josh looked away. He didn't want her to have anymore hurt than she already had.

Emma bit her lip. "I figured as much. But I didn't think that he had hurt you, till a few minutes later when I was heading back to the house. Daddy followed me and demanded that I give him my phone. It took me a while to figure out what he was doing, but I finally put two and two together." She looked at Josh again, "I am so sorry."

Arthur looked angrily at his daughter. "Get home, girl. This boy is going to pay for getting you pregnant. He is going to pay for all of it."

Josh sank onto the couch. Fear had been held at bay for a few minutes, but it was coming on faster. He felt his world shift slightly and wondered how much longer he could stand the pain he was in.

Arthur grabbed Josh and jerked him to his feet. "You going to deny to my face, boy, that you had anything to do with this?"

Josh looked down. He didn't want Mr. Less to see his pain or his anger. He turned his head away, and refused to look the man in the eye.

Jim and Luke both waited for Josh to answer, both praying in their hearts that this wasn't what it looked like.

Josh didn't look up. He could feel his father's eyes on him and knew Luke was watching him also. Would they believe him if he told them he didn't do it? Would Emma back him up or would she lie? Anger suddenly flooded him. He had already been beat up for this once. He had actually been beat and beat up, and he hadn't done it. He wasn't going to just stand here and take a beating again!

He looked up at Arthur Less with anger glaring out of his eyes. "I didn't do any thing to your daughter, and you know it. She was pregnant before I came to work for you. I haven't touched her. You know it, and so do I."

Arthur raised his hand to strike him, but Jim grasped his wrist again stopping him.

Emma looked at her dad with pleading eyes. "I told you that Josh had nothing to do with this. I told you it wasn't him." She looked at the others, "I promise, it wasn't Josh. He didn't do it."

Luke smiled at her tightly. "You telling the truth, or just trying to keep him out of trouble? If you didn't do anything, why does he have pictures of you on his phone."

Emma burst into tears. "Hold on a minute," she whispered. With one frightened look at her dad she ran from the room. She was back in less then two minutes with a young man at her side.

Josh looked at him in shock. Levi went to their church. He and Josh had been semi friends for years. As they had gotten older Levi had gotten wild and Luke and Annie hadn't allowed the boys to spend much time together.

Emma turned her gaze on her dad then glanced at Luke and Jim, but her eyes kept going back to her dad. "This is Levi, my boyfriend, and the father of our baby. It wasn't suppose to happen, but it did. We are taking responsibility for our actions. I talked to him a little while ago and told him I was pregnant. He tried to talk me into marrying him and moving in with him then, but I told him I was too afraid to tell my dad."

She looked her father in the eye, "But today, after I figured out what Dad was up to, I called him again, and we talked. I told him that Dad was blaming someone else for what we had done, and that I needed his help. That is why he is here."

Levi looked at Josh, "Sorry, Josh. If I would have known it was going to hurt someone else, I would have told her dad a week ago when I first found out. I knew her dad had a temper, and I guess I was afraid of facing him and owning up to what I did."

Josh looked away, but Luke saw him bite his lip and noticed his arm tighten around his waist. He saw the tightness around his mouth and knew his pain was getting worse. He saw the welts and bruises and he shivered. Her dad was meaner than he thought.

Luke looked over at Mr. Less. "There you have it, Arthur. Josh didn't do it, and there is your proof."

Arthur looked from his daughter to Levi to Luke to Jim then finally at Josh. Angrily he turned and stormed out.

Josh stood ridged looking from his father to Luke. What were they going to do to him?

Emma looked up at him with tears in her eyes, "Josh, I am so sorry. I never meant for this to happen. I didn't know that Daddy would blame you, and I had no idea he would beat you up if he did blame you. I am so sorry."

Josh shook his head slightly. He saw the pain and tears in

Emma's eyes, and his heart went out to her. "It's okay. Your dad did it. Not you. I forgive you." He looked over at Levi. "You better take care of her and get her out of that place, like now."

Levi nodded. He didn't want to even risk her going home to get her things, neither did he want to risk seeing her dad. If he beat Josh as bad as he did on the assumption that he had gotten her pregnant, what was he going to do to him now that he knew he was the one who had gotten her pregnant? He didn't want to end up like Josh or worse.

"My mom said she can come and live with us till we get a place of our own." He looked Josh in the eye. "I am sorry, Josh. I had no idea that someone else was going to take the blame for what I had done."

He looked down, then looked at Luke and Jim. His brown eyes filled with worry. "We need to go, but if there is anything else we need to do-"

Luke shook his head. "I think we have it all straightened out from here. Thanks." He turned to Emma and his heart broke. This girl had a hard road ahead of her and he hoped she had learned her lesson well this time, but he doubted she had. "Thank you for coming here. I know that had to have been very hard."

Emma nodded, then turned to Levi. "Let's go." They both smiled and waved as they headed toward the door.

Luke called after them, "Emma, how did Josh get pictures of you on his phone?"

Emma looked at him with a puzzled glance. "Josh has pictures of me on his phone?"

Jim nodded. "Very inappropriate pictures."

Emma flushed. "Dad must have got my phone. I know I shouldn't have taken those. Me and Levi were doing that one night. Check the day they were all sent, or he might have taken them with Josh's phone from my phone, but no, you know Josh wouldn't do that."

Luke nodded. "Thanks."

Emma smiled slightly. "Your welcome." They turned once more to go. Then Emma turned back. "I am really sorry that all this happened." She turned back to Levi. "Come on, let's go." Once they were gone both men turned back to Josh.

He faced them both trembling. He wanted to lay back down, but he didn't dare. His body throbbed with pain, and his head was

98

spinning in response to the pain.

It was Jim who cleared his throat. "I still want an answer, son. Who has been hitting you? Some of those marks are not from today." He stepped up to him and laid a hand on his shoulder, but Josh kept his head down, unwilling to let his father see his pain. His father's hands, however, did not miss the tremor that passed over Josh.

Jim saw the boy's fear and a fear of his own edged in. Had his son been living in the same life that he had been taken away from? Never in his life had he felt so guilty and ashamed. What had he done to his son?

Josh looked his father in the eye, but his mind raced frantically for an answer, because he didn't want to give his father the real one. He didn't want his father to know this wasn't the first time Marcus or Mr. Less had hit him in the last week, but he hadn't said anything because he didn't want to admit that Jim had been right to be concerned. And if Arthur Less hadn't been lying, he sure in the world didn't want to get hit at home, or from Jim.

Luke stepped up to him. "Jim, how can you tell they aren't from today?"

Jim gently put a hand on Josh's shoulder and turned him around.

Josh shivered when his father touched him. He hadn't ever felt a touch from his father, in his memory, that hadn't ended in pain, and right now he was in so much pain he didn't think he could handle more. Still his body stiffened as he waited to feel the sting of a belt across his back. He felt Jim touch his bare back. He jerked. Then winced in pain.

Jim pointed to a place on Josh's back "You see how these are fresher?" He pointed to another spot. "These here have scabbed over a bit, they are not so fresh. The bruises that are just starting to show color, are new." He pointed to another place, "And the ones that are no longer blue or greenish, but have paled to a yellowish, those are older."

Luke examined Josh's back, then looked up at him. He gripped the boy's arm and turned him back around to face him. "Well, son, what is your explanation for all of this? Who hit you?" The tears he felt stinging his eyes sounded in his voice. He couldn't believe this was going on and Josh hadn't said a thing.

Josh trembled even more as he looked from Luke to his father.

99

"I-" he looked down. He knew better than to try lying or even telling a half truth. His father would know. He sank back to the couch, squeezing his ribs with his arm, trying to get the pain out of his stomach and back, trying to make it less painful to breath and talk. He groaned before he realized he was going to, but when he heard himself, he bit his lip and tensed, sure his father or Luke would strike him.

Luke heard him and stepped closer to him as did Jim. "Son, are you okay?" Luke's concern grew as he saw that the boy's color was slightly gray from pain.

Josh looked up at the two men, but his stomach once again rejected the pain, and this time he couldn't control it. He felt everything start to work backwards and knew there wasn't anything he could do. He jerked up, but it was too late.

"Ow!" he cried as he got done, but it was more of a moan than a cry. Tears burned his eyes and his throat burned, but the pain he was in over powered everything else around him. The world around him spun in his pain.

Jim stepped over in front of him and gently but firmly laid him down. Silently and carefully he pushed on the boys ribs and then his stomach again.

Josh bit his lip and tried to keep from crying out when his father touched him, but a groan did escape his lips a few times when the pain was more than he could handle. And he felt his body jerk each time his father touched him. He was sure his dad was going to hit him more and cause him even more pain.

He cried out as Jim pushed down on his stomach. "Stop! Please, stop!"

Jim looked up at him with pain in his eyes. "You have a few broken ribs, son. From what I can tell that is all, besides being sore. You are a lucky, boy. I am going to wrap you up for tonight, but I would feel more comfortable if we took you to the hospital and got some ex-rays done just to be sure that is all that is wrong. I know you are in a great deal of pain, but with you throwing up, it makes me worry that there may be more than I can see wrong." He stopped.

Josh looked away. "Does she know, or are you hiding this from her?" he whispered.

Jim looked at him questioningly, "Why do you ask, son?"

Josh looked away even though movement of any kind was

getting even more painful. "You're going to make me come live with you, aren't you? She doesn't even know you have a kid, does she? Does she know you were in prison? Does she know it is for child abuse? You are going to make me go back and live with you, and your wife doesn't even know I exist."

Jim licked his lips, "Josh, it's not like that. I didn't come here to ruin your life. I wanted to find you, yes. When I first got out of prison I wanted to find you and bring you to live with me, and I would still love to have you with me, the way things should be; but I didn't come here for that reason, son. However, if some or most of these welts and bruises came from here, or I find out that Luke is the one who hit you around, than yes, you are leaving and coming to live with me."

"They didn't come from here," he groaned as his stomach once again began to turn. He didn't think the pain could get worse, but it was. He tried to move.

Jim looked at Luke. "That better be the truth, Preacher." He turned back to Josh, "Then where did they come from?"

Josh looked at Luke with tears in his eyes.

Luke looked back at him wondering what the boy was going to say.

Josh looked back at his father, a tremor started in him, but he couldn't keep this secret and hurt Luke. He had to tell his dad the truth no matter how scared he was. No matter if it really was his dad that had told Mr. Less to beat him.

"Less' place," he groaned at the effort.

The muscles tightened in Jim's neck. "When?" He tried to keep his voice light, but he couldn't. "Why? And why in the world did you let him and not say anything? I am assuming, anyway, that you didn't tell Luke. Because if you would have, I am pretty sure he wouldn't have let you go back, or made you go back."

Josh looked away then slowly looked back. "Why do you care?"

"Joshua." That was all Jim said, but that was all he needed to say. The boy knew not to cross his father again.

Trembling he looked his father in the eyes, "There hasn't been a day this week that he didn't hit me for something. Sometimes it wasn't him it was Marcus, but it was every day."

Josh saw the muscles working in his father's jaw. "Why did

Luke make you keep going out there?"

Josh looked up at Luke with tears in his eyes. "Luke didn't know. I never said anything, and he never saw."

Jim sat down beside him on the couch. "Why, Joshua?"

Josh closed his eyes wishing he could just disappear.

Luke squatted down by the couch so he was at eye level with Josh. "Son, why didn't you ever say anything? Why was he hitting you? Were you afraid to tell me? Why?"

"Yes, no." Josh took a shallow breath but the pain he was in was so bad he thought he would get sick again. "It was my fault. I did stuff wrong, or I did stuff he didn't like. He said I did stuff I wasn't suppose to do. He was just letting me know I was doing it wrong."

Jim placed a hand on Josh's shoulder. "That is not okay. He had no right to hit you. You could have told someone one. You should have told someone."

Josh turned his face away from his father in spite of the pain, "Are you going to take me away?" His voice was so quiet that Jim almost didn't hear him. He had to change the subject before his dad knew he hadn't told because he didn't want to get hit by him more.

Jim bit his lip. He wanted his son with him, but he was unsure what Josh wanted him to say. "I don't know, Josh. I don't want to hurt you by taking you away. But I do love you, and I would love to have you be a part of my family. I just don't know yet. And for now we don't need to worry about that. We need to worry about you."

Josh bit his lip then looked his father in the eye, "So, does Lilly know anything about me?"

Jim shook his head. "I guess that is the first place I need to start." He looked down at Josh. "You are right, I should have told her about it all a long time ago. I never should have hidden the truth from her."

Josh looked up at his father. He wanted to say so much, but at the same time he didn't want to talk to his dad at all.

Jim nodded slightly and stood. He looked over at Luke. "We need to get him to the hospital and get some of those ex-rays taken. We just need to make sure he is okay before I wrap him up."

Luke nodded as he reached down to lift the boy off the couch, but Jim was already picking him up.

Josh trembled as he felt his dad's arms on him. What was he going to do to him? He cried out in pain as his dad jostled him a bit to get him in the car. Fear trickled through him again, but this time neither Jim nor Luke said anything.

When they reached the hospital Josh had fallen asleep. Jim looked at Luke then back again at Josh.

Luke nodded. "The boy is in a lot of pain. I can't believe he can actually sleep through it."

Jim nodded. "Pastor, I want to tell you again, I am sorry for not telling you sooner who I am. The boy didn't want anyone to know, and for once in his life I didn't want to hurt him by making him tell you who I was. I thought we could just go on as it had been. But he is right, the more I am with him the more I want us to be a family.

I just wish I had been honest with Lilly from the beginning. I have my reasons why I wasn't, but that makes no difference. Josh is right. It is like I have been lying to her all this time." He hung his head. "I know she will forgive me, but I wish I hadn't done it. I wish I could just go back and erase the past, not just for me, but for him."

Luke nodded. "God doesn't let us do that. We always have to live with our choices. That is one of the reasons it is so important to make good ones the first time around. But God can use our mistakes to shape us into who we are, if we let him. He can use them to mold us into new creatures in Christ and to keep us humble. We just have to remember where we came from.

Jim nodded. "Well, we need to get the boy in there and get some pictures taken. I hope it isn't worse than it looks, but I am afraid that it may be."

As the men got out Josh groaned and opened his eyes. He tried to move, but pain shot through him at the slightest movement.

Jim opened the door and Josh looked up at him. He shivered and pulled back. "Josh, I am going to carry you in here and we are going to get some ex-rays. Don't worry. It's all going to be fine."

Jim reached for him, but Josh pulled away. "I'll walk," he muttered. He didn't want his dad to touch him. He didn't want him to have a reason to beat him. He was going to fight the pain and walk into the hospital if it killed him.

Slowly he got out. He saw Luke looking at him with concern. He stood slowly, but after a few steps he collapsed on the ground. He trembled as his dad knelt beside him. He looked up into his dad's eyes and the concerned eyes of Luke. "Please, don't hit me," he whimpered. "Dad, I'm sorry. Please don't hit me."

Jim shook his head to see his son in so much pain. He knew the boy was scared of him, but he couldn't help wondering if he was scared of Luke as well.

He put his arms under the boy and picked him up. It was then that he realized he hadn't even given Josh his shirt to put back on. He saw in the faint glow of the street lights that the boy's body was bleeding still.

He headed for the emergency entrance and Luke followed. Concern filled Luke. He wasn't sure what to do. He had no way of knowing if it was really all Arthur who had hit him, or if his dad was using Arthur Less to get to the boy. *God, show me what to do. Should I trust him with Josh? Is he only out to hurt him, or has he really changed and does he really care about the boy?*

One of the nurses at the station saw them coming and rose. "Dr. Johnston, we didn't expect you in tonight." She glanced down at Josh in his arms and gasped. "Doctor, what happened?"

Jim shook his head. "It's a long story, Milly. Can we get some ex-ray as soon as possible? I think the boy has a few broken ribs. We need to make sure nothing else if wrong, and see what all is busted up in there, before I wrap him up."

Milly nodded. "Sure thing, Doc. Right this way."

10

It was two o'clock Sunday morning when Jim carried Josh back into the living-room at Luke and Annie's, and gently laid him on the couch.

Josh bit his lip. Even though the pain killer had taken the edge off, his pain was still so great he felt sick. He managed to keep his cry of pain in. All that escaped was a slight groan.

Jim stood and looked down at his son. "I want you to stay down for a few days, son. Only get up to use the bathroom. Then back down on the couch or in bed. I don't want you up and around, and I don't want to have to repeat that. We don't need you busting yourself up more than you already have. Keep still, and we can hope that those ribs will heal."

He looked at Luke. "I know it's not easy to keep a boy down, but he needs to stay down at least a week to give them time to start healing. I'll check him over next Monday and see if he is good enough to be up and around. Until then he needs to stay put." His dark eyes seemed to challenge Luke.

Josh, though groggy from the pain killer, looked at Luke and Jim curiously. What was his dad mad at Luke for?

Luke nodded. "We will see to it that he stays down." Luke saw the look that Jim gave him. He shook his head. "Jim, I haven't ever hit your son. Yes, he has lived in this house for almost eight years. I - we have taken him in and loved him as a son, but I haven't beaten him. If

I ever have raised a hand to him and I am saying if, because there may have been one time, but I don't remember one at all, it would have been a swat on the bottom and that is all."

Jim nodded. "Thank you, Preacher, for all you have done for my boy." He looked down. "I'm sorry. I didn't mean to suspect you, but when I see him that beat up-" he glanced at Josh.

Luke looked down at Josh then back at Jim. "I'll see you out." Jim nodded.

As the men headed for the door, Josh pushed himself up a little trying to get some of the pain off his back. It didn't work. It just made his chest hurt worse. He looked toward the door where both men had gone and wondered what they were saying to each other that they hadn't wanted to say in front of him.

Luke followed Jim out the door and stopped on the front steps. He still wanted answers. He knew Jim had apologized before, but he didn't want an apology; he wanted an explanation. "Why didn't you say anything before about being his father?"

Jim looked away even though it was too dark outside to see Luke's face. He felt his shame. He took a deep breath and looked back to Luke. "I'm sorry, Preacher. I know this comes as a shock to you. I didn't intend to hurt you or your family. I had no idea he was here.

"When I figured out who he was, he was so scared of me I promised him I wouldn't tell. I didn't want to cause him more pain, Preacher. God knows I have done that to him way too much in his life. But then today when I saw him and wrongly assumed you where the one who – well, you know."

Luke shook his head. "I wish I would have known before tonight what was going on there. I should have been more careful. I should have kept a better eye on him. I had this uneasy feeling about him working there, but the boy never said a word about them hitting him or anything. I just assumed that everything was fine."

Jim shrugged. "I really don't blame you, Preacher. My boy is notorious for covering up his emotions and his feelings. I am not proud of this, but it is because of me. I trained him to do it, and I made him do it. I wish I could erase the past, Preacher. Why does God forgive, but not erase what we have done, especially to others? It just don't seem fair that my son has to live with the consequences of my actions."

Luke looked up at the night sky so full of beautiful twinkling stars. "That is a question I really don't know if I have the answer to, but I do know that every sin has a consequence. One who is a smoker all of his life isn't going to have a clean set of lungs if he gives his life to God. One who is an alcoholic isn't just going to have a healthy body if he gives his heart to God and quits drinking.

"God can often use our past, even if it is one we are not proud of, to shape us into who we are now. If nothing else it helps us remember his mercy. But He won't erase the past. I guess that is a reminder that we will pay for our mistakes, some of them for a long time, and hopefully that will keep us from making more in the future. Does that make any sense to you?"

Jim thought on what Luke had said. It did make sense, but he still wished his son didn't have to live with the scars of his past. "I do see it, Pastor, but I just wish that -"

Luke broke him off. "Jim, that is why God created forgiveness and why he grants mercy. Your son doesn't hate you. He may be afraid of you right now, but he doesn't hate you. Please believe me on this."

Jim sighed. He wished he could, but he just couldn't yet. Not when he had seen the pain and anger in Josh's eyes. He would have to pray more and more for God to help Josh forgive him, and now for Lilly to forgive him. He took a deep breath. It was time to go home and talk to her.

Josh was right about that. Lilly had a right to know everything. Whether she forgave him and still loved him or not was her choice, but she had a right to know the truth, the whole truth, about him.

Luke sensed the battle in Jim and silently prayed that God would help him tell his wife the whole truth, and that God would prepare her heart in the process and help her to accept him and love him more.

He clapped a hand on Jim's shoulder. "Well, Jim, we will just let it go for now, that you didn't tell me who you were. I don't know what I would have done in your place. I am just glad I am not in your place. You go on home and talk to Lilly and the two of you decide what you are going to do.

"We will pray that God will lead you in the way he wants you to go. We only want his will, and what is best for Josh. I know you have the right to him now that you are out of prison, but he is more than welcome to stay with us. He is one of the family here. So please don't feel like you have to take him. If Lilly doesn't want to or isn't ready for another teenager yet, please know that he is always welcome here."

Jim nodded slightly, "Thanks, Preacher. I need your prayers, and I do thank you for them."

Luke smiled, "Sometimes we find that the one thing we tried so hard to keep from people, the thing that is the hardest to tell them, they already know. Some how they already know."

Jim laughed dryly. "I wish that were true in this case, Preacher." He took a deep breath. "Well, I guess, I will know soon."

Luke shook his hand. "See you in church on Sunday, Jim. Or I guess in a few hours." he smiled. "Maybe you all can come over for lunch and we could all have a nice chat."

Jim thought for a moment. "We will see, Preacher. I really think it is our turn to have you. We have been over the last two Sundays, but with Joshua needing to stay put, we will see."

Luke laughed a deep jolly laugh. "Jim, how's about you just call me Luke. I am sure it is going to be fine. Lilly loves you and she still will. We will plan on you all coming over unless you call and say you aren't. Fair?"

Jim nodded. "We will do that, Luke. Thanks."

Luke nodded as well. "No problem, Jim. We will see you tomorrow or later today I guess it is."

Jim looked up, then turned to leave. "Thanks again, Luke. I wish there was some way I could repay you for all you have done for my son."

Luke bit his lip as a fear welled up inside of him. "Just don't take him away," he whispered low enough he knew Jim wouldn't hear as he was walking away.

Jim walked down to his truck and headed out the drive.

Luke watched till he was out of sight, then stepped back into the house. He jumped a little in surprise when he saw Josh standing in the door way. "What are you doing up, son? You heard what the doctor said. No getting up and walking around. Now you get back on that couch."

Josh trembled. He had tried to relax, but he couldn't without knowing what his dad and Luke were talking about. He risked a question before he turned back to the couch. "He's not my doctor. What did my dad say to you, Luke? He is taking me away, isn't he?"

Luke stepped up to Josh and helped him back to the couch. It wasn't till Josh was laying down that he answered."I don't know, son." He then looked Josh in the eyes. "Son, there is something I need to know from you." He stopped and Josh waited keeping his gaze down, too afraid to speak. Luke cleared his throat. "Joshua, has he hit you since you have seen him? Did he try to get you to keep who he was a secret?"

Josh bit his lip as he quickly turned his head so Luke wouldn't see his fear.

Luke waited silently, wondering what the boy was thinking.

Josh slowly turned his head back toward Luke, but still didn't look up to meet his gaze. "I was the one who wanted to keep it secret, Sir. It was me, not him. I begged him not to tell. I didn't want you to know who he really was. I was afraid if you did know, that you would make me go live with him. I figured you would be glad to be rid of me, especially with all that happened out at Less's."

Tears ran down Luke's cheeks. Josh had tried to be strong for so long alone, and he had no idea what the boy was going through now. "Son, I am sorry, I didn't realize what was going on at Less's place. I never should have let you go out there. Why didn't you tell me he and Marcus were hitting you?"

Josh shrugged. He knew good and well why, but he wasn't going to admit it, not unless he had to.

Luke waited a little while hoping that Josh would just start talking, but when it was clear that he didn't want to say more Luke sighed and stood. "Go ahead and sleep in here tonight, Son. I will see you in the morning."

Josh looked up at him and his stomach rolled. "Yes, sir." Slowly he let himself relax a little. He groaned as his back touched the cushions.

Luke sighed. "I am sorry, son."

Josh looked up at him. Luke was sure he saw pain and fear in the boy's eyes.

"I am sorry I lied," Josh whispered. "I should have trusted you, but he said that if I did, you had already said you would hit me as much as he did. He said my dad had made it clear also, that if I did anything he was to punish me and when I got home I would get the same or more."

Luke felt his heart break. No wonder Josh hadn't said anything, with that threat. It looked as though Arthur Less had beaten him several times, and then tortured the boy with threats till he was sure Josh wouldn't say a word.

Luke lifted one corner of his mouth in a brief half smile, hoping to relieve some of Josh's fears. "It's not really okay, son, but I forgive you. Just please don't do it again. If anyone hits you, tell me. You know I am not going to hit you for no reason. Have I ever given you a reason to think that? Josh, I love you, and I am not going to just hit you to hit you."

Josh nodded, then winced again.

Luke shook his head. He gently reached over and patted the boy's shoulder. "Probably best if you don't try to move for a while." he spoke kindly. He then stood and turned to go.

Josh bit his lip, "Yes, sir." Josh groaned again as Luke lay a blanket over him. He looked up at him in fear. "If I have nightmares tonight, Dad, I am just going to tell you right now, I am sorry for waking you up."

Luke smiled as he rested his hand on Josh's shoulder. "Son, don't worry about it. Just get some rest."

Josh nodded and closed his eyes.

Luke looked at the clock. Three o'clock in the morning. It wouldn't be long and it would be time for the boy's next pain killer. He knew he would have to set the alarm to wake himself and give it to him. Jim had already warned him that Josh wouldn't want to take it, but to make him whatever it took. He was going to need it. He sighed again and headed off to bed. This was going to be way too short of a night.

11

Jim sighed as he pulled up in front of his home. What was Lilly going to say to him? Would she be happy that he knew where his son was? Would she want Joshua to be a part of their family? Would she understand why he had kept this a secret?

He closed his eyes and bowed his head. "Dear Lord, you have been teaching me more about trusting you, and I guess this is one of those times that I need to have more faith in you. I am scared and I don't know what to do. I don't know how to tell Lilly what I need to tell her. I don't know if she will understand, or if she will care, or if she will be upset. I am afraid, God. Please help me to be completely honest with her. Help her to understand. Help her to trust me, even though I am not worthy of her trust. Thank you for bringing my son back to me. Thank you that he is okay. I know he doesn't want to be a part of my life right now. I know he doesn't want me to be a part of his. Help that to change. Please give me a chance to be the father I should have been to him. Give me a chance to be the father I want to be. In Jesus name, Amen."

He took a deep breath as he raised his head. He was glad that he had God to turn to. All of those years when he had just been faking a religion, what a waste of life. He had missed out on so much. The Bible was right; it just took a simple faith. Just trusting.

"Well, Lord, here it goes. Please go before me and prepare her for this. Please help me to say the right things in the right way. Just help me, God. I need it."

He smiled again as he felt an overwhelming peace flood his being. He knew that Lilly would care, but still he wondered what she would say. What feelings would there really be in her heart? Would she be willing to be a mom to Joshua? Were they ready for their family to add another teenager? After all, the baby wasn't that far from making it's entrance into the world.

He laid his head back on the steering wheel. What a mess sin had gotten him into. "God, I know that we have to live with the consequences from decisions that we have made, but also that you give grace and mercy to make it through. Help."

Again he felt that peace in his heart and he looked up with a smile. "Thank you, God. I know you are in control. Help me not to forget."

In his heart he heard the whispered words, *Ask in faith believing. And you shall receive.*

He took a deep steadying breath. In the time he had spent in prison and out he had learned to lean hard on the Lord in hard times, but his humanity kept getting in the way this time. "Lord, help her to be as forgiving as you are," he whispered as he walked into the house.

He smiled as he saw Lilly seated on the living-room floor a midst a pile of pictures she was attempting to put into albums. He stopped in the doorway and just watched her for a few moments, thanking God for her.   "Hey, beautiful lady," he whispered.

He glanced at the clock behind her on the wall. Three o'clock. He shook his head. "What are you doing up so late? You should have gone to bed. You need your rest."

She looked up and smiled. Relief flooded her. He had left so quickly when she had told him about Joshua, then he hadn't come back and he hadn't called. She was starting to worry that it was even worse than she had thought.

She stood and pushed back her brown curls from around her face. Her soft smile graced her lips. Her hand rested on her very round stomach, a reminder of the little life that was soon going to be coming into the world. "Well, if it isn't the most handsome doctor in town. What do I owe the honor of this visit?" She ignored his question. She knew he had to be exhausted and he hadn't even taken time for supper earlier.

He smiled as he entered the room and softly kissed her.

She stepped over the pictures with an awkward step. "Supper is ready. I kept a plate for you. The kids are all asleep. It is so late, or early I guess."

Jim shook his head. "Thank you, but I can't eat right now. I ah- I need to talk to you about something important."

Lilly looked up at him and worry clouded her eyes. It wasn't like him to appear upset or nervous when they needed to talk. She felt a flag of caution rise in her mind. "Did you find out what happened to Josh? Is it worse then you thought? What is wrong?"

Jim held her tightly in his arms. "Shh. I will explain it all. Just sit down and lets talk. Though it may be better to wait till a decent hour."

Lilly took a deep breath and tried to calm her jumpy nerves. "Okay, I am listening," she waited hoping he would go on.

Jim lead her over to the couch and cleared a spot for her to sit. "It's kind of a long story. Some of which I should have told you long, long ago. Please sit down."

Lilly felt her nerves suddenly tighten. What was going on. "What are you up to, Jim? What is going on?"

Jim shook his head as he waited for her to sit. Slowly he sat beside her and turned slightly so that he was facing her. He took her hands in his and held them tightly for a few minutes. "Honey, I have a few things to tell you that I should have told you a long time ago. I didn't mean to keep it from you so long, but I did. I am sorry. I didn't mean to lie to you, but that is what I have done in keeping them from you for so long." Jim felt tears sting his eyes. He let them run unchecked down his cheeks.

Lilly watched him closely with apprehension in her eyes. It startled her to see him cry, but she also saw that he was in deep anguish about something.

Jim saw the look and felt his throat constrict. He knew she had problems in the past, which was why he had kept this part of his past a secret. Again he prayed for God to soften his words and help Lilly to forgive him. Again he prayed for the right words to say.

He cleared his throat nervously, "You know that my past isn't perfect. I was in prison before we met, before I became a doctor again. Meaning I was a doctor, but then I got locked up. I had to renew my license when I got released. "

Lilly shook her head, some of the tension eased from her

shoulders. She actually felt a small bit of relief. This was a part of his life she had wanted to question him on many times, but never felt that she should. She had always felt that this was a part of his life that she wasn't welcome in. "Yes, Jim, you have told me. You told me when we first started to have feelings for each other. You said you wanted me to know, in case it changed how I felt about you."

Jim looked down. Shame filled him. He shouldn't have ever waited this long. Tears flooded his eyes. "Lilly, what I never told you was why I was there." He stopped and drew a ragged breath. "I always wondered why you never asked, but I was always too afraid to tell you. I was just grateful that you never asked." He looked up into her eyes and saw the love she had for him. He looked away, afraid that, all too soon, he would see that look turn into one of hate and scorn. He was so afraid that his life was going to fall apart. *Help me, God. I want to do what is right even when it is hard. Even when it may cost me, I want to live for you.*

"Honey, I am so sorry. I don't blame you if you want to leave me after I tell you what I am about to tell you. I know it is going to hurt you. And know now that I am sorry for what I did and for the pain it is going to cause you." Again he looked down at their clasp hands. His tears ran down his cheeks and dripped off of his chin.

Again Lilly waited. Fear etched her face. A nervousness started in her stomach, but she forced it away. She wanted him to tell her. She had so longed for this moment to come, she didn't what to fear it now. She wanted to reach out to him and comfort him. It frightened her to see him cry, but she was afraid if she made the wrong move he would stop talking, so she just stayed where she was and looked into his face waiting for him to tell her what he needed to.

Jim tried again to talk, but his mouth felt full of cotton. He cleared his throat again and finally looked up into her eyes. "I am not proud of who I was then. I wish I could turn back the pages of time and change decisions I made. I wish it could all be forgotten."

Lilly sat waiting, wondering what was coming. She wanted to ask questions, but feared that if she distracted him he wouldn't keep talking. She looked at him with passion in her eyes, hoping it would help him to know she loved him anyway.

Jim looked into her trusting eyes and felt another tear run down his cheek. "Lilly, the reason I was put in prison, was child abuse."

114

Lilly felt her throat constrict. She felt her eyes grow huge. She wasn't sure how she felt or what all she felt.

He saw the pain and pensiveness flash in her eyes and he prayed that God would help him to go on, and help her to hear and understand. "I was in for five years and they let me out. When I met you, and you had so much going on, then we fell in love – I didn't want to lose you. I knew some of the things that had just happened to you. I was afraid if you knew who I was and what I had done to my son, you wouldn't see that God had changed me. That he had forgiven me and made me a new creature in Christ. I was afraid if I told you the reason I was in prison you wouldn't love me. I had already fallen in love with you and the kids, I just couldn't handle the thought of you walking away. So I told myself, since you had told me that you knew God had changed me from the man I use to be in prison, and you said you still loved me when I told you I had spent five years in prison, that I didn't need to tell you the whole reason I was in there."

She sat up a little straighter and waited for him to go on sure there was more he needed to tell her. Why now? Had this episode with Josh made him think about what he had done? Did it make him feel guilty for what he had done to his son? Did it make him realize the pain he had put his child through? Why was he telling her all this now? What had happened to make him want to talk about all of this at three o'clock in the morning? Why was it so important to him now? It had waited for this long. Why now?

Jim saw the pain in her eyes, but forced himself to go on. "My son was taken from me when he was eight years old. He was placed in foster care. I was told that I was to be in prison for five years and then I had to reappear before the judge and he would decide my fate. They told me then, that it was unlikely that I would ever see my son again."

Pain washed over him again as he remembered the emotions that ran through him that day. He bowed his head.

Lilly caught her breath. She couldn't imagine what that had to of felt like. What kind of pain must have torn through his heart! No wonder he was so kind and attentive to her boys.

"When I got out of prison five years later, or I should say when the judge released me, though I am sure it was due to a lot of prayer, anyway, he told me then that I could have my son back. I wanted so bad to take him up on that, but I was just out of prison. I had no job, no money, no way to make a living. I didn't want to hurt him more than I already had. I was so afraid I would fail. I learned that he was in a good loving home, and he was doing great. So instead of even learning where he was, I told the judge that I needed some time to get on my feet before I took my son. I told him just not to disturb the boy and not even to let him know that I was out. I wanted him to be happy.

I asked the judge if I could leave him in foster care till I had at least gotten a job and knew I could provide him with a good home. The judge agreed and told me that when I was ready to be a father to my son, I was to come to him and he would help me get him back."

Jim felt his heart sting. "I never asked where he was. I didn't want to know. I was afraid if I did know, I would mess up. So instead of trying to find my son I renewed my medical license and started working in the hospital and clinic where I lived at the time. I was starting to get established and feeling like I could handle life, then I met you."

Here he stopped and looked up into her eyes. He was surprised to see that she was crying too.

She saw him look at her and she gave him a soft smile. She understood some of why he had kept this a secret, but it still hurt to know that he had lied to her.

Jim shook his head. "I could have killed that man the first day I saw you, sporting that black eye he had given you. I am just glad you got away from him." He shook his head, "But that gave me a small glimpse into who I use to be. And God showed me then how much he had changed me."

Lilly gave him a shaky smile as she remembered that day. "I am glad I got away too. That is one choice I wish I had never made. My kids had to suffer because of me," she stopped again overwhelmed at how much things had changed. "That is all in my past now, and yours. I belong to Jesus now, and so do you. I thank you for showing me that God still loved me."

Jim smiled back at her. "Yes, we both had much to be forgiven, but God did. He forgave us both and gave us both a new life and so much joy." He cleared his throat as emotions flooded over. He released one of her hands and placed his on her belly, that would soon be their baby.

"As we got to know each other better, I thought about telling you more about me, but it never seemed like it was the right time. When I asked you to marry me and you said yes, I knew I should tell you about my past and about my son, but I just couldn't. I couldn't ever work up the courage." He looked down.

"I was so afraid of losing you, but that wasn't all. I didn't want to fail at being a dad to your kids the way I had failed with mine. I never thought I would get to see my son again. I wanted to be the father to your kids I wished I could be to my son."

Lilly dabbed at her eyes. "So why are you telling me about all this now, Jim? Is it just what happened with Joshua? Has that gotten you so upset that you felt you had to talk to me now? What brought on all of this? Especially at three o'clock in the morning."

Jim wished that was all. He wished he could just tell her that was it, but he knew he had to come completely clean now or he never would.

He took a deep breath and looked down into her eyes, "Honey, I miss my son. I want him to be a part of our family. I have for a long time. I know this is a lot to throw on you at one time, and I promise you it will not change my love to your kids or to you or to our kids, I mean the baby. I promise you. I know this is a lot, and I understand if you don't want to with the baby and all.

"I will wait if that is what you want, but please, will you at least think about it? I promise it will just make my love grow. I have proven to myself with your children that I can be a good dad. I can love my son and your kids all at the same time. I can spend time with them. I can and have proven to myself that it is possible to discipline them and not abuse them. That was what I was so afraid of. But you have helped me. God has changed me, and you have helped. I am sorry, honey, I just -"

Lilly placed her hand on his lips. "Honey, I realize what you are saying. I can't imagine what it would be like to be separated from one of my children for so long." She stopped and looked at him with a question in her eyes. "How long has it been?"

Jim quickly counted in his head. Josh was taken from him the spring he was seven; he would turn sixteen in October. "It's been eight years," he whispered in surprise. "I didn't realize it had been so long. I mean, I did, but I didn't. I know some of that is because I got out of prison earlier than I thought I would. I can't believe it's been so long."

Lilly smiled softly as she counted in her head. "So he is the same age as Jordan and Jared?"

Jim shook his head. "He is a little older. He was born in October. The boys were born in December, correct?"

Lilly nodded slightly. She sat up a little straighter and smiled a real smile. "Thank you for finally telling me. You are right. You should have told me sooner, but I also realize why you didn't. You are right. I probably wouldn't have married you, but it would have been out of fear. In the years that we have been together you have been nothing but loving to me and the kids. Never once have you raised a hand to us, any of us. You have hardly even raised your voice at any of us, except the boys when they get way out of hand. You have shown in numerable ways that you love us. I love you too. And I am glad that I married you."

Jim looked unto her eyes and waited. He wanted to say more to her, but he also wanted her to have time to say what she was thinking and feeling.

Lilly placed her hand on his arm and gave him a soft loving smile. "I think it is a wonderful thing that you want your son with us. I am glad you want him. I can't believe you have waited this long to say anything. But where would we even begin to try to find him?" She looked at him with a bit of skepticism in her gaze. "And, just out of curiosity, what brought all this on anyway? Is it because of what happened to Josh tonight?"

Jim looked away slightly feeling his guilt once again. "I don't have to try to find him, Lilly. I know where he is." His voice was a hoarse whisper.

"But you said-"

"I know what I said. But that is what brought all this on, Lilly. You already know him, well, you have met anyway. I don't have to find him. I already did."

Lilly's eyes grew wide with surprise. "What! I have already met your son? And you didn't tell me?"

Jim placed his hands on her shoulders and looked deep into her eyes. "You helped him out earlier today, in fact."

Lilly looked confused. "Jim, I don't-"

"Joshua is my son, Lilly." His voice broke as he said it, and tears streamed down his cheeks. "It wasn't a reminder of what I use to do. It didn't remind me of my son. It was my son!"

Lilly gasped. "Joshua?" Then her eyes filled with apprehension. "Are you telling me you had something to do with what happened to him?"

"No!" Jim was surprised, then knew he shouldn't have been. With the way he was acting it was no wander she was wondering. "I didn't do any thing to him, Lilly, except help patch him up a while ago. I didn't even figure out he was my son, until two weeks ago in church. Remember when I followed him out of the sanctuary?"

She nodded.

"He didn't want me to tell anyone who he was. He didn't want anyone to know I was his dad. I promised him I wouldn't tell. But I shouldn't have promised that. I needed to tell you. And Luke and Annie should have been told before tonight, but it is what it is. I can't change it now. Just add it to my list of failures."

Again Lilly shook her head. "Jim, this will take a lot of time to get use to for him and us. Does he want to come and live with us?"

Jim looked down, then off into the distance. "I don't know, Lilly. I don't know what he thinks or feels about this. I didn't realize how much I missed him and wanted to be a part of his life before tonight. I don't want to disrupt his life, but-"

Lilly lay her hand on his shoulder. It wasn't going to do any good for him to beat himself up over the past. "You can't blame yourself over what happened to Josh today."

Jim shook his head. "Yes, I can blame myself. I should have been there for him. I shouldn't have ever hit him. I should have brought him home to live with me when I first got out of prison. I should have talked to Luke about how I felt about Arthur Less. I should have tried to take care of him better."

Lilly reached out to him and took his hands. "Let's think and pray about this, my love. We don't want to make a mess of things. Let's ask God what he wants, and if it is his will for you and Josh to be together. Let's ask God to help Josh to feel that way too."

Jim nodded numbly. He hadn't realized how draining it was going to be to tell her, but oddly in a way he felt refreshed and renewed. He hadn't realized what a burden he had been carrying.

Lilly bowed her head. "Dear Heavenly Father, give us guidance we pray and give us peace. Help Jim to stop feeling guilty about what he should have done and to know what he needs to do."

As Lilly prayed he felt God's love softly cover him and heard a soft whisper to his heart. "I will strengthen thee, yeah I will help thee."

"Thank you, God," he whispered. "Thank you for caring."

12

About five o'clock Luke was awakened by a noise from the living room. He sat up in bed and listened. There it was again. He heard Josh cry out and he leaped out of bed. He should have figured the boy would be having a nightmare. He hurried toward the living room, but stopped before he got there. The front door was standing open and he could hear a muffled voice from inside the room. Then came another cry from Josh. As quietly as he could he peeked around the doorway.

Josh groaned as he looked up at Mr. Less.

Less laughed as he towered over the boy. He grabbed his arm and jerked him to his feet.

Josh cried out in pain, then bit his lip. His whole body burned with pain and his vision was starting to blur.

Arthur Less chuckled wickedly. "You think it hurts now, boy, just you wait."

Arthur released his hold and Josh sank to the floor. His arm instinctively went around his ribs, trying to relieve the pain. He struggled to sit up. He had to get away somehow. He couldn't just sit here and let Mr. Less kill him. He struggled to get up, but was knocked back to the floor by a hard blow from Less.

He groaned as he rolled over trying to get away. Less pulled off his belt, but froze when he felt cold against his temple and heard the calk of a gun.

Luke growled out, "What are you trying to do, Arthur? You

get out of this house, and you stay out of this house. You ever attempt anything with my boy again, and this will be more than just a threat. Get out!"

Arthur turned to find himself face to face with a thirty-eight caliber. He shuttered and backed away. Then turned and fled out the door.

Luke followed and watched as the man disappeared into the woods. He holstered the gun with a sigh. What was going to happen next in this place? He hurried back to the living-room to find Josh writhing on the floor in pain.

Slowly he knelt beside him. "Son," he whispered.

Josh looked up at Luke, but the pain was shining in his eyes. "I'm okay, Dad. He only hit me a few times."

Luke saw the ugly welt on the boys cheek and knew it had to have been more then just a few, but didn't say anything. He just waited.

Josh groaned again as he tried to move.

Luke felt his concern grow. What were they to do now. Jim had told him to keep the boy still, and what happened? Less hurts him even more. Did they need to take him back to the hospital, or leave it be? He voiced his question to Josh.

"No, Dad, I'm okay. Just a little banged up. I'll be okay." He tried again to move, but the pain was too great. He looked up at Luke with fear in his eyes.

Luke saw the look. His heart hurt inside him. He carefully pick Josh up and laid him on the couch.

Josh groaned again in pain, but tried to keep Luke from seeing just how much pain he was in.

Luke sighed. "Josh, I am so sorry."

Josh shrugged. "It's not your fault, Dad. Thanks for helping me. If you hadn't come, he would have killed me," his voice broke.

Luke laid his hand on Josh shoulder gently. "It's all over now, son."

Josh nodded, but in his heart he knew it was far from over. Arthur Less had told him that he would kill him and he had no doubt that the man would try again. Fear raced through him. Had his dad really told Mr. Less to beat him? There was no way to know. He would just have to wait and see.

Luke rested his hand on Josh's shoulder. "Go ahead and try

122

and get some sleep, son. I will stay here and make sure you are okay."

Josh winced as he tried to nod. "Yes, sir." He lay still for a few minutes, but the pain inside him grew almost unbearable. He glanced at Luke and saw that the man was watching him with concern in his eyes. He was afraid to ask, but he knew he had to. "Dad, how long till I can have the next pain killer?"

Luke felt his concern grow even more. If Josh was asking for it he knew he had to be in a lot of pain. "I'll get it for you. It's about time for it anyway." Luke hurried to the kitchen to get a glass of water, then took it and the pain killer to Josh.

Josh winced again as he tried to sit up. Once he had taken it and sank back to the couch he glanced gratefully at Luke. "Thanks, Dad, for everything."

Luke smiled and nodded. "Get some rest, son. You are safe now."

Josh nodded slightly and slowly slipped back into sleep.

Sunday morning at seven o'clock, Josh awoke with a start. He looked over and saw Luke dozing in the chair. His head spun. What happened? He started to get up, but yelped in pain.

Luke heard the cry of pain and was instantly awake. He relaxed a little when he saw it was just Josh attempting to get up. "You aren't suppose to be moving much, son. Did you forget?

Josh let a soft moan escape as he sank back onto the couch.

Luke got up and stood over him. The welt on his cheek had now turned into a nasty looking bruise. The boy's eye was still swollen and now also bruised. He knew there was more than he could see and his heart seemed to ache in side of him. "How you doing this morning, son?"

Josh shrugged, then gasped in pain at the movement. He looked up at Luke. "It hurts," he whispered, but even talking sent a burning pain through his chest.

Luke nodded. "I'm sorry you are in so much pain, son. You can have the next pain killer in two hours."

Josh looked away, and Luke knew the boy was thinking that was an eternity away. "Your mom is going to stay with you this morning, son. I know you don't want to stay put, but you need to. You have to give your body time to heal."

Josh started to nod, but winced again in pain. "Okay," he moaned instead.

Luke sighed. "Josh, I am so sorry. I wish you would have said something before all this happened. Why didn't you?"

Josh shrugged. "I just couldn't." He turned his face away. "Please don't ask me, Luke. You wouldn't understand."

Luke frowned. "Try me."

Josh looked up into his eyes and trembled. Tears stung his eyes. "He told me you said he could hit me. He told me you agreed with him that if I needed a good whipping, he could give me one, and you would also, when I got home."

As Luke looked down at Josh, a pain filled his heart. "So to keep from getting in more trouble, you didn't say anything."

Josh bit his lip. A tear slipped down his cheek. "Yes, sir." he answered quietly.

Luke sighed. "I am so sorry, son."

Josh looked away.

"Josh," Luke's voice was quiet but firm, and Josh looked back up at him. "Son, don't ever try and hide the truth from me because you are afraid. I want to know what is going on. I realize you were afraid, but if you would have just told me, we could have stopped this."

Josh tried to nod, but gasped again in pain. "I'm sorry, Dad. I won't do it again. I should have trusted you."

Luke nodded. "Well, son, I need to go get ready for church. Your mom will be bringing your breakfast in here in a bit."

Josh started to nod, then stopped. "Thanks," he whispered.

Luke nodded as he left the room.

Shortly after church Josh heard the front door open and saw Annie look up anxiously. She had just given him another pain pill and was turning to leave.

Josh knew she was nervous about Arthur Less coming back, and he didn't blame her one bit. He heard one of the kids squeal and knew it was Luke and the kids back from church.

He looked toward the doorway and froze. His dad and Lilly stood there, with Jared and Jordan. Jim was holding Julia in his arms. He set her down as she started to squirm, and, laughing, she raced off chasing Chelsey.

He didn't dare move, but instead he stared at his dad. Jim walked in and smiled. "Luke tells me you had another run in last night."

Josh didn't move a muscle. His ridged body cried out in protest as he tried to jerk away from his father's touch.

Jim bit his lip in pain as he saw the boy's face. "Why, Josh? Why did he do this to you?"

Josh bit his lip and started to turn his face away. But then he stopped, and turned back. Anger suddenly flooded him. How dare his dad act like he had no idea what was going on. "I don't know, sir. I really don't know. Maybe you could tell me." Josh gasped as the words leaped out of his mouth. He couldn't believe he dared talk that way to his dad. Fear suddenly filled him where the anger had been.

Jim sighed. "Did he tell you it was me?"

Josh looked away, biting his lip.

Jim frowned. "I figured he would. Josh, I am not here to hurt you. I promise. I don't want to hurt you ever again."

Josh glanced back toward the doorway where Jared and Jordan and Lilly still stood. He looked back at his father with a question in his eyes.

Jim nodded slightly. "Lilly knows. I haven't told the boys, yet. I wasn't sure if you would want me to."

Josh shook his head slightly, then winced again in pain.

Jim smiled a sad smile. "Okay, Josh. I understand." He gently placed his hand on the boy's shoulder, but even at the soft touch he heard Josh's quick intake of breath in pain.

Silently he removed his hand.

Annie came in then and smiled at them. "Well, lunch is on the table. I am sure that after lunch the kids will want to hangout in here and play a game or something so Josh can join them.

Joy walked in at that moment and set her brother's plate down on the coffee table. She started to reach for some pillows to prop him up so he could eat, but Jim stepped over and gently lifted the boy and stuck the pillows behind him.

Joy smiled. "Thanks Mr. Jonson. I was going to do it myself. I am going to be a nurse someday. So Josh getting hurt is a perfect opportunity for me to practice my nursing."

Josh smiled at his little sister's dream. He could easily see her as a nurse and that surprised him. He hadn't thought of that from her before. He wondered what had brought on this sudden desire.

After lunch Jim, Lilly, Luke, Annie, Jared, Jordan and Joy all sat in the living room with Josh talking. They said nothing about Jim and Josh being father and son, but as they all got up to leave Jim turned to Luke. Why don't you let me stay with Josh tonight so Annie can go to church and be there with your kids."

Josh froze. He would rather die, then be left alone with his dad.

Luke saw the look of panic in Josh's eye. He knew the boy was afraid of Jim, but something inside him said that he could trust him. Jim was a changed man. God had worked a miracle in his life.

Josh started at Luke in fear. He couldn't' stay home with his dad. *Please, Luke, tell him no! Please don't make me stay with him!*

Jim saw the look in his son's eyes as did Luke and they both gave each other an understanding look. Lilly saw it also and her heart went out to Josh. She saw the fear he had toward Jim and she silently prayed that that fear would wash away. She prayed that he would see his father had changed. She knew Jim wanted his son with him, but she also could see with as scared at Josh was that wasn't going to happen. Not for a long time. They wouldn't do that to him.

Jim nodded as he turned to go. "Come on, kids. Let's get to church.

Jordan and Jared sighed as they said goodbye and walked toward the door. They thanked Luke and Annie for the meal and for letting them spend the afternoon there.

Luke nodded. "You're welcome. Thanks for the offer, Jim. But I think we better not this time."

Jim nodded again. "I hope this is the end of him trying to come after him."

Jared and Jordan exchanged a glance. Jim saw and turned to the boys. "What do you know about all of this?"

Again the boys looked at each other. Jared shrugged.

Jordan sighed, but it was him who turned to their dad. "Mr. Less hit him every day he was out there."

Jim stopped short. "What makes you say that? Joshua told me it was just a few times."

Jordan glanced at Jared again. "He told us," he whispered.

Jim felt his temper rise, but he kept it in check. His voice was even when he asked, "Why didn't you boys tell me?"

The boys shrugged. "He begged us not to. Said it would only cause more trouble. He didn't want to get in more trouble. We didn't want him to either. It didn't seem fair for him to get hit twice for stuff that was so stupid."

Jim frowned again, "Like what? What did Joshua tell you Less was hitting him for?"

"Like leaving the barn door open, or leaving a wrench out. Stupid stuff. Not stuff that he should have been belted till he bled for."

Jim felt his anger rise to the surface.

Luke saw the man's anger and, though he was experiencing some of his own, placed his hand on Jim's shoulder. "Let it go, Jim. The boy needs understanding right now and we can't take it out on Less, unless you want to end up behind bars."

Jim took a deep breath, then looked at Luke and nodded.

Jared and Jordan exchanged a glance. What was going on?

As the kids headed out to the car Jim turned back to Luke. "Lilly and I have talked about it, but we haven't reached a decision about Joshua yet. We want to be a family, but we don't want to ruin our friendship with you, or upset Joshua."

Luke nodded. "Thanks for caring." He took a deep breath. He knew that having to give up Josh was going to be the hardest thing he had done in his life, but he also knew God had given him and Annie, both a peace about it that was indescribable.

"We don't have to decide right away, Jim. God will guide you to the right thing in the right time."

Jim nodded. "Thanks for understanding."

Luke nodded also. "We will see you soon. Feel free to come over and spend time with him as much as you want."

Jim smiled. "Thanks, Pastor. I just might do that."

13

The following morning after the kids went out to play and Jim and Lilly were sitting at the kitchen table enjoying a nice fresh cup of coffee she looked up at him and asked, "Have you thought much more about Saturday night?"

Jim started, then smiled. "Only every minute. I am just worried. This doesn't just affect me and you, it wold affect him and it would affect the kids. And how are we going to go about telling the kids? Jordan and Jared and Joshua are already great friends so that should help, but being a friend and being a brother aren't really the same thing. I mean do we just tell them straight out? Or do we – oh, I don't know."

Lilly smiled. "I may have thought of something. After much thought and prayer I believe God has given me an option. Maybe we should take a breath. The kids need to bond before finding out that they are related. If they like each other it wouldn't be a problem."

Jim nodded. "I can see that, but the boys have already bonded. And Joshua already knows. But what did you have in mind?"

Lilly smiled. "It is really very simple, we just let the kids spend as much time together as they can. For example, we have Josh over for a sleep over, then they can get a feel for what it is going to be like. We can also. And it may help Josh to feel more comfortable. They don't have to know the real reason."

Jim nodded slightly. Maybe that would help Joshua feel better about him, but then again it might not. "There is just one problem with that. I have to tell Joshua what we are thinking. I don't want him thinking it is just for a night here and there. I want him to know I want him to come home."

Lilly bit her lip. "Will he say something to the others?"

Jim shrugged. He doubted that Joshua would say a word about it, but would he?

Lilly shook her head. "You are right; he needs to know. Just tell him we haven't told the other kids yet. Surely he will understand."

Jim sighed. "One of those times I wish I didn't have to deal with my past. When we dabble in sin it messes up our whole life. And not just ours, but the lives of those closest to us."

Lilly smiled and placed her hand over his on the table. "Jim, you know God has everything under control. You can't keep living like this. Families were meant to be together. We can do this. Let's just work through it one day at a time together. Okay?"

Jim nodded slightly, once again thanking God, in his heart, for this wonderful woman God had brought into his life. "When do you want to do the first sleep over?"

Lilly smiled. "I was thinking tonight since you aren't working today. You would have time to spend just with the boys. What do you think?"

Jim's eyes sparkled as he thought about being able to spend some time with his son, but then he shook his head. "We need to wait at least a week and give him time to heal. I want him down in bed for at least a week. And we need to talk to Luke and Annie about all this and see what they say. I should probably get in touch with the judge also and make sure that everything is legal."

Lilly smiled. "Let's go and talk to them today and see what they have to say." Her voice was full of excitement. "After we talk to them we can try and get in touch with the judge."

Jim shook his head. "I think I am going to try and get in touch with the judge first. I want to make sure we do this all legally."

Lilly saw the hesitancy in Jim's eyes and heard it in his voice. "What is the matter, Honey? Why are you worried?"

Jim looked up at her and she saw the tears that were in his eyes. "Lilly, what if my son doesn't want to live here?"

Lilly smiled. "Just give it a try, Jim. You never know what may happen."

Jim shook his head. "I don't think I can force him to live with us, even if the judge says he has to. I can't hurt him like that. Not now. Maybe it would be best to just leave it alone."

Lilly shook her head. "Jim, God created families to be together. Don't give up so fast. You haven't even asked him yet."

Jim nodded. "You are right. I will try to get in touch with the judge, then we can head over and see Joshua, and talk to Luke and Annie."

When Jim and Lilly showed up at the house later that day with no kids in tow, Luke and Annie knew they were there to talk about Josh. They had been praying about it ever since last night. They had seen the look in Jim's eyes as he had taken care of Josh Saturday and again as he had been with him yesterday, and they knew that even though he hadn't tried to get the boy to take to him, he missed his son and wanted to be with him.

Luke and Annie both had a calming peace about the whole situation. They knew that Josh didn't want to trust his dad, but they felt that God was taking care of the whole situation, and they were not afraid. So when Jim and Lilly showed up they were not surprised.

Josh stirred when he heard the knock on the door. The pain medicine he was on was also making him very tired. He heard Annie greet someone, then heard talking in the hall, but it was too quiet for him to figure out what they were saying, nor did he want to try. Pain was his constant companion and he tried to push himself up to get some relief, figuring the company was there to see him. But as he moved the pain increased. He groaned quietly, hoping Annie wouldn't hear him.

He heard footsteps approach the living-room and then stop. He glanced up to see his dad and Lilly walk in, followed by Luke and Annie.

Fear ran through him as he looked at his dad. He could see by the look on the man's face that he had something important to talk about. He stayed silent and frozen waiting for his dad to speak to him.

Jim knew the boy was waiting for him to speak; and something twisted in his stomach, knowing that he had placed that fear in his son's eyes. Again his heart ached as he saw the large bruise that was now prominent on Josh's cheek and around his eye."Joshua," he heard the hardness in his voice and he wished with all his might that he could erase it.

Josh turned his head slightly and flinched in pain and fear. "Dad?"

Luke felt the awkwardness between them and stepped forward to help. "Josh, your dad is here to talk to you about something very important. I want you to hear him out."

Josh looked Luke in the eye, but didn't respond. His eyes snapped. He wanted to refuse, but just like the last few days he knew he couldn't.

Jim cleared his throat and moved into Josh's line of vision. "We have talked and prayed about it and we think it would be good if you could come and live with us."

Josh felt his blood freeze as he glanced quickly at Luke, did he know this was why his dad was here?

Luke bit his lip. He knew Josh's dad was right and that the boy did belong with his dad, but tears burned his eyes. He saw the fear in Josh's eyes and knew that the reason the boy had suffered so with nightmares, was because of his father. Was it smart or safe to let him return to the man?

Jim went on. "It's not what you want, I know, son, and I don't blame you. But I think this is the best thing for all of us. We think it best to take it slow, son. Then if you still don't feel comfortable with living in our home, maybe we can talk about it and find out why. We think it best if we don't tell the other kids yet. Lets just see how it goes at first."

Lilly saw Josh open his mouth as if to speak, then shut it quickly and look away. She saw the tightness in his shoulders and the set of his jaw, and her stomach started to turn. How bad was the abuse that he had suffered from his father? From knowing Jim, she had thought last night, it was just the man had spanked him in front of the wrong person and gotten thrown in jail for it. Was it more than that?

Jim knelt down by the couch and flinched when he saw Josh shutter, then wince in pain. "Let me tell you what we are thinking, then you can tell us what you think of it. We are thinking, maybe we could start off with a couple of slumber parties. Then you and the boys can see more what it is like to be brothers. Well, you can. We won't tell the boys till later. Just let you all get to be better friends, then they will be excited to learn that you are their bother. What do you think? We are thinking a week or two from today. Give you enough time to be on your feet again."

Jim stopped. He was about to say that he wanted to have the move finalized before school started again, but he quickly stopped himself. He had to take it one step at a time. And though legally he could just make his son move in with him, he wasn't going to do it.

Jim held his breath as he watched Joshua. What would the boy say?

Luke looked down at Josh. The boy had his face turned away so the adults couldn't see what he was thinking or feeling. Pain ripped through his heart as he thought about the beaten boy who had come to their home almost eight years earlier. How could this be part of God's plan? How could they lose their son? Then he heard that soft still voice whispering to him, *My grace is sufficient for thee.*

He knew it was true. God was going to lead them and help them through this time as he had many many times before. God would lead and direct. He had everything under control. He would give them the strength to make it through this change.

Jim held his breath as he watched Josh. Pain etched on his face. He wanted so badly to reach out and hold his son. He wanted, so much, to prove to him that he could be a father, that he wanted to be his father, that he was sorry for the kind of father he had been. But he sat in silence waiting for Josh to say something.

Lilly slowly sat on the edge of the couch. "Josh, your dad told me about you and him. He told me everything Saturday night. I am sorry for how things use to be, but your dad is different now. God has changed him into a new man. I know you don't want to believe that is true and trust me on this, I know how you feel. I know you are scared to trust him. I know you are afraid that he is only trying to find a way to get to you, but he isn't.

"If we do a couple of sleepovers and you feel like you really can't fit or don't fit into our family, then we will talk about letting you stay with Luke and Annie, but please won't you give us a chance?"

Josh bit his lip. He didn't want to give his dad a chance. He didn't want to be anywhere near his dad, but he knew he couldn't say that to Lilly. He wondered if his dad had told her the complete truth. Slowly he turned his head so that he was looking at her and his dad.

"Okay," he muttered, "a couple."

Lilly smiled as she gently laid her hand on his shoulder. "Thank you, Joshua. I am glad. I know you aren't, but just give us a chance, please. We would love to be your family."

Josh felt anger fill his heart. *Why, God? Why are you making me live through this again. Please don't. Please don't make me live with him. Please!*

14

The following Saturday morning, Jared and Jordan hurriedly cleaned their room to make room for Joshua. They were talking excitedly about all the things they would do when he spent the night.

The boys had become fast friends and they were very excited that Josh was being allowed to spend the night. They had so many plans, they knew they wouldn't be able to do them all.

"He can sleep in my bed. I will take the blowup mattress on the floor." Jordan offered his brother with a sly smile.

"No way!" Jared contradicted. "I get the blowup. He can sleep in my bed. Its on the bottom bunk and that would work out better for him, since he still isn't completely better."

Jordan frowned. "That isn't fair!"

Jared looked at his twin brother and smiled. "I know what. Let's ask Dad if we can have two sleepovers. That way he can have your bed for one and he can have my bed for one."

Jordan smiled. "That's fair. Let's ask Dad, and if he says yes then he can have your bed this time, because you are right, his ribs aren't healed up yet. Even though he was up and around yesterday he wasn't moving very fast. And he still looked like he was hurting."

Both boys raced out the door to talk to their dad.

Josh grudgingly placed his pajamas in his back pack. "I don't want to go. Why are you making me?" Josh turned away from Luke and slammed his dresser drawer shut.

Luke sighed. "Joshua, we don't have a choice in this."

Josh looked up quickly. "Why can't you just tell him I changed my mind and don't want to come over for a sleep over? Dad, I don't want him in my life!" Anger burned in him. "I just want to stay with you. I don't want to be with him!"

Luke looked Josh in the eye. "First of all, son, you told them you would give them a try. And secondly, which I probably should have told you, when your dad was let out of prison he was also given full custody of you. We got a letter stating all that had happened. The judge indicated then that your father didn't seem interested in trying to find you, but if he came for you there was nothing we could do. You had to go with him. We went to a lawyer then, but he told us basically the same thing. If we were to try and fight or keep you away from your dad, he could put us in jail for kidnapping.

"I am sorry, Josh, there is nothing I can do this time. Just try to make the best of it, Son. You never know. Maybe you will like it. Your dad is a new creation. You have to admit the boys don't seem afraid of him, do they?"

Josh bit his lip as he turned away. At least now he understood why Luke and Annie hadn't said anything against this arrangement. "Okay, Dad, I will try, but-" Josh looked down afraid to ask, because he was afraid of what the answer may be. "Dad, do I have to go and live with him eventually. Is there really nothing you can do? Is that what you want?"

Luke blinked back his tears as he saw the pain and rejection on Josh's face. "Son, I don't want you to be anywhere, but here. But there is nothing I can do. He has all right to you. Unless he says otherwise, Josh, yes, you do have to go and live with him, if that is what he says. I am sorry. If there was something we could do to stop it we would. Son, I -" Luke choked up.

Josh nodded slightly understanding, "It's not your fault, Luke. I am the one who is sorry. I didn't mean to wreck your life." Josh felt his anger boiling. Why would God let this happen? It wasn't fair. Why did it seemed God didn't care?

135

Luke shook his head again and placed his hands on his son's shoulders. "You never wrecked our lives, Josh. We were very blessed to have you in this family. You will always be welcome here. Let's just get through this one day at a time, and be thankful that he is giving us this time. He could have just made you up and move in with him. Maybe he will change his mind and let you stay, not make you leave."

Josh looked at Luke with sadness in his eyes. "Yes, he will, and we both know it is coming."

Luke nodded slightly, "What God wills, Josh. Not us. God has this all under control."

Josh nodded again and glanced out the window in time to see his dad pull up. He knew he was stopping on his way home from work so he was probably in a hurry. With a sigh of contempt he reached down and grabbed his bag. "I'll see you in the morning," he muttered.

Luke nodded. "Have a good time, Josh. Please don't take it so negatively." He watched as Josh walked out the door. "God. Please don't let my son grow so bitter." he whispered.

Josh slowly walked down the stairs where the family was waiting to tell him goodbye. He smiled slightly. It looked as if he was leaving forever instead of just for the night. His stomach twisted and he knew that soon it would be forever. He knew that Luke and Annie had opted not to tell the other kids why all this was happening for some of the same reasons that Jim and Lilly weren't telling there kids, but he couldn't help but wonder if some of them thought it was suspicious.

Joy looked at him with sadness in her eyes. "It's not fair. I wish I had a girl I could go and spend the night with."

Josh gave her a weak smile. "Don't worry about it, sis. You will have your chance some day." *I just hope you really will enjoy your time, and that it won't be for the same reasons.*

Joy frowned. "It still isn't fair."

Josh felt his heart roar as he heard his dad knock on the door. "It's going to be fine, Joy. See you in the morning." He felt a sting in his heart. He knew in two weeks he wouldn't be able to say that anymore, and he feared what would happen to him when that time came. But if what Luke said was right there was nothing he could do about it, and he better not fight it. He didn't want to hurt Luke and

Annie.

Joy pouted a little. "See you in the morning, but I still wish I could go."

Luke smiled at his daughter as he walked up behind Josh. "Joy, that isn't even a good idea, for a girl and three boys to have a sleepover. You know that. No more about it. Period." He gave her a look and she snapped her mouth shut without another word.

Jim stepped into the house and smiled as he saw Josh ready to go. He hoped his son would at least give this a good try and not be glum about it. But he could tell by the look in Josh's eye that the boy wasn't happy about it at all, but he also saw a solid resolve and that made him feel a little better.

Josh looked up at him slowly, then he turned back to Luke. With fear in his eyes he mouthed, "Do I have to?"

Luke felt his heart break, but he nodded slightly "Have a good time, Josh. We will see you tomorrow."

Josh nodded firmly and turned to face his father.

Jim smiled broadly. "Ready to go, s-s- Joshua."

Josh stiffened. "Yes, Sir." he forced his mind into moving. He knew he had to do this. It was clear that Luke and Annie tried to do what they could, but there wasn't anything they could do to change the situation. He had to live with it, so he might as well start now.

Jim turned to Luke and Annie. "Thank you for letting him spent the night."

As if you gave them a choice, Josh thought as his father turned to go.

Annie smiled. "Be good, Josh."

He gave her a half hug and a smiled. "I will." Quickly he turned and followed Jim out the door.

Luke followed them out. He tried to smile as Jim turned to him. "This is going to be hard for all of us," he tried to speak softly so no one else would hear.

Jim nodded. "Thank you for being willing to try."

Luke nodded as he looked at Josh again. "Be good, son. I will see you tomorrow."

Josh looked back at Luke then at his dad. "Don't worry, Dad. I am sure if I get out of line, he will make sure I don't stay out of line."

Luke glanced quickly at Jim and saw the man flush in pain and embarrassment. "Joshua," hissed Luke, "That's enough."

Jim looked at Luke. "I wish I could erase the past. I am the one who made the memories he has to live with. Don't be upset with him."

Luke shook his head as he looked directly into Jim's pain filled eyes. "That is one of the funny things about memory. But God gives grace and mercy where it is needed. Let's just hope and pray he gives us all an abundant supply.

Jim nodded as he headed for the car.

Josh sat in the passenger seat and waved as they backed out of the drive.

Jim looked over at him and smiled. His voice was deep and full of emotion as he said, "I am glad you have agreed to give it a shot, Son. The other kids don't know anything about it right now, but that will change with time, I hope. Just give it a chance, Son. I am sure we are all going to be a very happy family together."

Josh didn't say anything. He just kept waiting for his dad to hit him. He wasn't sure when it was going to happen, but he was sure it was going to happen long before he wanted it to.

Jim felt the distance between him and Josh, and knew the boy had built an emotional wall that he was going to have to work hard to break down. As they pulled into the drive, then stopped, he turned to Josh. "Son, am I doing the wrong thing?"

Silently he prayed that God would give him the wisdom he needed to reach his son. That God would somehow show him how to break down that emotional wall. Was it possible, or was he just going to hurt his son even more?

Josh glanced at his dad out of the corner of is eye, but didn't dare say a word. Anger turned inside of him. Bitter, hateful, hurtful words rose to his mind, but he managed to bite them all back.

Jim reached over and turned the boy to face him. "Joshua, I made mistakes in the past, but I am not that person anymore. Son, please understand that I only want what is best for you."

Josh bit his lip as he saw the screen door opening on the house. "Don't you think you better stop calling me son, if you don't want them to know what is going on?" His voice was cold and hard, but he couldn't help it. He didn't want to be anywhere near his dad.

Jim nodded slightly. "Okay." It hurt more then ever to see the coolness in Josh's eyes. He sensed something in him that he hadn't sensed before. It seemed as though there was a deep bitterness, or a hatefulness that was just bursting in him, wanting to get to the surface.

He looked into Josh's eyes again. He hoped he was wrong, but something in him made him wonder how often since he had shown up, the boy had had his devotions. How many times had Josh talked with God, since he found out that he was out of prison? He feared the answer, but hoped that he would have time to talk to Josh about it in the night that he was here.

Lilly was at the door and Jared and Jordan came racing down the stairs as Joshua and his dad got out of the car.

"Josh! This is so cool. I am so glad your dad said you could come over, and that my dad suggested it." Jared cried.

"We are going to have so much fun, Josh!" Jordan joined in. "Just wait till you see all the stuff we have planned."

Josh smiled weakly at Jared and Jordan. He didn't like lying to them, in not telling them what was really going on, but it wasn't his place to tell them. Nor did he ever want to tell them why he had been taken away from his dad. So he quietly followed them inside and tried to act as though everything was fine.

15

The evening progressed without a problem and by bed time Josh was less frightened of his father, but still apprehensive. He saw how Jared and Jordan were with him and it started a longing in him.

Why didn't his dad care about him like that? Why had he always beaten him for the slightest thing, and now he was laughing and playing with them?

His heart jerked. Did his dad love Jared and Jordan and hate him? Was he the problem all the time? It was his fault his dad had hit him. He wasn't worthy of his dad's love. He had done something to make his dad hate him.

Again he felt that bitterness welling up inside of him. He felt a stirring of jealousy rising in him also. It frightened him. He knew he should pray and ask God to help him, but he just couldn't.

How could God love him and bring his dad back into his life? If God loved him, he wouldn't be so cruel as to let his dad back into his life. He would make his dad leave, and he would never have see him again. If God cared that is what he would do.

Josh felt the stab of guilt in his heart, but he quickly hardened it and pushed away the thoughts.

The night went well, and Josh was relieved that he didn't have nightmares that night. That was all he really didn't need right now. One more thing to explain. However, he knew the main reason he didn't have nightmares, was he was awake most of the night. His anger and bitterness were keeping him awake. He knew God was trying to talk to him, but he kept trying to push it away.

The following morning went extremely well, Jim spent time with the boys, and hoped that in Josh seeing him now, he would understand that he really had changed, not realizing the bitterness it was stirring up in his son.

When Josh headed home later that day he was surprised that his father had been with him that amount of time and hadn't once raised his hand to him. He hadn't even yelled at him, which use to be all he did. He felt a little more relaxed about the whole thing. Maybe his dad really did changed.

He quickly pushed the thought away. His dad was the best pretender he knew. There was no way he had changed. No way at all. He knew it would take time, but given time his dad would hit him. He had no doubt in his mind. He knew how well his dad could pretend.

The following week when it came time for the next sleep over Josh felt less afraid, but still very cautious, knowing that his dad could put on a good act for a long time.

This time Josh traded beds with Jordan. All three boys stayed up till way after four in the morning. They managed to keep things quiet for the most part, but by four thirty they were all extremely tired and none of them wanted to be the first one to admit defeat and sleep.

Jordan looked over at Jared and pulled a face at him.

Jared laughed loudly and did the same back to Jordan. Josh laughed at them both. He had never wondered what it would be like to have brothers before this, but he felt like he was going to get along okay with that part. All three were making such a racket that they all jumped when a sudden voice behind Josh startled them.

"Boys!" it was more of a deep rumble then a word.

Josh whirled around and Jared and Jordan looked up at their dad in surprise.

Jim eyed all three of them, but his gaze seemed to linger on Josh. "Have you slept at all?"

Josh swallowed hard, but shook his head. Jared and Jordan dropped their gaze. "No, sir."

141

Jim sighed. "Tomorrow is a big day, or I guess I should say today is a big day, boys. Try and get a little sleep or at least keep quiet so the rest of us can."

Jared and Jordan nodded. "Okay."

Jim turned his gaze on Josh.

Josh looked back at his dad with fear in his eyes. "Yes, sir." He swallowed again. Fear pricked his skin as he saw something flash behind his father's eyes.

Jim nodded slightly and headed back to bed.

Jared snickered as he looked at Jordan. "Guess we better get some sleep. I think Josh needs it."

Josh threw a pillow at him. "Go away."

Jared snickered again. "Yes, sir." he mimicked Josh's voice from moments ago.

Josh glared at him.

Jordan chuckled. "What is up with you, man. If anyone is going to get into trouble it's not going to be you. It will be us. It's our house. Dad's not going to get mad at you. He'll get mad at us."

Josh looked away. He wanted to tell them the truth, but knew it wasn't his place, besides his dad was going to tell them in the morning. He turned away from them completely and lay down.

Jared grinned as he picked up his pillow. Slowly he walked over to Josh. "Pillow fight!" he screamed as he slammed the pillow into Josh's face.

Josh gasped and grabbed the pillow from him.

Jared's eyes sparkled in fun as did Jordan's as he slammed his pillow into Josh from the back. Josh grabbed that pillow also. Quickly he slung them both at the boys then ducked as he grabbed his own pillow from the bed.

The boys laughed as they flung the pillows at one another. Suddenly Josh hollered as someone grabbed his shoulder. He felt his father's grip tighten down even more. Jared and Jordan froze in surprise; and then, seeing their dad, the bit their lips in fear knowing they had just willingly disobeyed him.

Jim scowled at them all. "I thought I told you all to be quiet," he growled.

Josh trembled, and his father feeling his fear slightly released his shoulder.

Jordan was surprised to see how white Josh was, but then he

figured he was the guest and probably figured he would be in trouble when he got home for being a problem at someone else's house. He tried to smooth it over. "You did, Dad, but it is just so much fun to have a pillow fight at a sleepover. Do you want to join us?" He held out an extra pillow to his dad. "It will do you good."

Jim laughed lightly as he looked at all of them again. "Get laid down and don't get up till at least seven in the morning."

Josh dropped onto the bed immediately and lay down, afraid of what his dad would do to him if he didn't. Jordan and Jared groaned as they slowly picked up their pillows and lay down.

Jim smiled as he saw them all laying down. "Now get some sleep, boys. I mean it. We have some very important things to talk about in the morning, and I mean at a descent hour in the morning. You all need to be well rested for this talk, am I understood."

"Yes, sir." they all three replied in unison.

Jim sighed as he left the room. He hoped that Josh didn't fear getting into trouble, but he knew by the way the boy had dropped everything and obeyed without a sound of protest that he still feared him, but he also had to admit that it was nice to have someone obey him immediately without complaint or protest. He knew that too, was because of how he raised him. He wished with all his might he could have that with Lilly's kids. He hadn't realized how much, though, till he had Josh here.

"Lord, help me, help him to see that I have changed." Slowly he made his way back to bed. It was nearly time to be rising for the day, but he hoped that the boys would at least get a little sleep.

Lilly smiled up at him as he walked in. "Get them to go to sleep yet?"

Jim shrugged. "Maybe. I am not sure who the instigator is in there, but one of them is up to mischief."

Lilly laughed. "Well, I would say it is Jared. He is the one who always likes to cause trouble."

Jim chuckled. But even as he did he couldn't help but feel a sting in his conscience when he thought about the look of fear in Josh's eyes. "They are just normal teenage boys." He looked over at her, "Honey, are you sure you are okay with another teenager in the house? I know it will be more of a strain on you then it will be on me."

Lilly looked at him questioningly. "Are you saying you don't want your son, Jim?"

He shook his head quickly. "That is not what I am saying at all, honey. I do want him. I want him now more than ever before and the more he is here the more I want him here. I want him to be a part of our family, to really be a part of our family, but I don't want to hurt you. If I had only told you at the beginning – or if you are afraid that I will show favoritism or not be the dad I should be to your kids, our kids-"

Lilly placed a hand over his mouth. "Jim, you stop that this minute. You know I love Joshua. You know that we have talked about this. I love him just as if he was my own. I love him just as much as my two sons. He is a very polite and well behaved young man. He isn't going to be a burden to me. You know that. What are you afraid of?"

Jim shook his head. "I don't want to mess up, Lilly. What if Josh is right to be afraid of me? Maybe I should just leave him with Luke and Annie? Maybe I shouldn't have stayed here. After I learned who he was, we should have just packed up and left. I don't want to hurt him. I don't want to be the man I was. But that is all I see when I look into his hate filled eyes. When he is afraid of me, that is all I can see, the man I was before. What if he is right and I really haven't changed?"

Lilly took his hands in hers. "We have been through all of this before, Jim. There has been a lot of prayer going into this change. We are not just letting go. We both thought this was God's will. We both prayed to make sure.

'Yes, you made some mistakes a few years ago, but God forgave you for those mistakes and made you into a new creature in him. You know that. You gave your heart and life to him and asked him to forgive you, and he has. Now we are looking at getting our whole family together for the first time. I couldn't be more happy. God brought us to this point and he isn't going to just abandon us. Please, honey, don't back up on God and his promises. You know and I know that he has guided our steps to this time and place."

Jim leaned over and kissed her. "I am so glad and thankful for you. I know you are right. I just don't want it to be a problem."

Lilly kissed him back, but her voice had a sharp edge when she replied, "Joshua is not a problem, Jim, and you know it. So don't act like it, and don't you dare make him feel like he is."

He nodded slightly. "I am sorry, Lilly."

Lilly looked at the clock. "Well, we may as well get up. It's six thirty. Shall we wait till seven to wake the boys. Will they have had enough sleep by then?"

He shook his head. "We can wake them at that time, but I doubt they are even sleeping.

He got up. On his way back from the bathroom he glanced in the boys room. He was surprised to find all three of them on the floor, soundly sleeping.

"Lord, please help them all to accept this," he whispered. "Please, help it to be the right thing."

By eight o'clock that morning Jim, Lilly and all four of the kids where seated around the breakfast table. Jim looked around happily at them all, but his gaze stayed the longest on Joshua.

Josh felt his stomach flip as he saw his dad looking at him. He felt his nerves tighten. He knew that look. His dad was about to say something, he was sure. Was he going to make him move in with them? Was he going to tell his kids who Josh really was? Fear trickled through him. He didn't want to live with his dad. He didn't want to be here. He thought of Luke and Annie and knew they were right, that there was nothing they could do about it. It didn't seem fair that his dad got to call all the shots in his favor. But he also knew that Luke had been right, he was just going to have to make the best of it and pray that his dad really had changed.

He bit his lip as he looked down, avoiding his father's eyes. He just had to make it through. There was nothing he could do about it. If his dad wanted to hit him again, he just had to live with it. He couldn't change the judges ruling, no matter how much he wanted to. "God help me." he prayed silently. "Jordan and Jared aren't afraid of him, but I am. Please help him to have really changed."

Josh suddenly felt guilty. He had no right to pray, and God had no reason to hear him. He had been angry at God since this whole thing started, and he had been doing his best to avoid God. His hate toward his dad had created a wall between him and God, and he knew the only way around that wall was to forgive his dad and ask God to forgive him.

Tears sprang to his eyes. He wanted to tell God he was sorry, and ask God to forgive him, but he didn't know how. Still he felt a tightness in his chest. How did he think he was going to make it through this without God?

16

After breakfast the kids were all getting up from the table, when Jim stopped them. He looked straight at Josh. "Stay here for a minute, I need to talk to you." He looked back at Jordan and Jared. "Don't go far I want to talk to you two in just a few minutes."

Jordan and Jared looked at each other. Why was their dad going to talk to Joshua about what happened last night first? It wasn't Josh's fault, and Josh was the guest. Why would he even talk to him about it?

They glanced at Josh, but he looked away.

"Dad, if it's about last night, we are sorry we got so loud, but it wasn't Josh's fault. We were the ones who kept keeping him awake. Please don't say we can't have a sleepover any more. We were just having fun, and we promise to do better next time." Jordan pleaded his eyes wide. "We didn't mean to make you upset."

Jim shook his head. "That is not what I want to talk to you about. Please go out. I will talk to you both in a few minutes. Joshua, sit down. I need to talk to you first."

The boys slowly walked out to the room. They were puzzled. Why was there dad talking to Josh? They looked up as their mom came down the hall way. They stopped her quickly before she walked into the kitchen. "Mom, what is going on? Why is Dad talking to Josh? He isn't his kid and it's not his fault we woke you up, it's ours. Is Dad mad?"

Lilly smiled. "It's going to be fine, boys. You will find out what is going on in a few minutes. Its good. Trust me. Everything is going to be great." She smiled softly. "Please keep an eye on Julia for me. I need to get in there with your dad."

"But, Mom," Jordan countered. "Dad was upset. He looked mad. Why is he talking to Josh about it and not us? Does he not trust us?"

Lilly smiled as she placed a hand on each of them. "Boys, just trust me this time. It is going to be fine. You will like this surprise. Really you will."

The boys turned back toward the kitchen. Was there mom right? Something just didn't feel right. Both of them felt nervous, but there was more to it. Was it jealousy they felt? What ever was going on, Dad was telling Josh about it first. Why? That just really didn't even make sense. They wanted to believe their mom, but whatever was going on, it didn't feel right.

As the boys left the room Jim turned to Josh. "Son, I want to know the truth, do you want to come and live with us?"

Josh swallowed around the lump the had formed in his throat. He wanted to tell his dad no, he didn't want to live there. He didn't want his dad to be part of his life, but he couldn't say that and he knew. He feared what the consequences would be if he should even start to say any of that. Yet, he knew better then to lie to his dad.

Jim waited, feeling the struggle inside of Joshua and praying that the boy would say yes.

Josh slowly looked up at his dad. He still felt his stomach turn in fear every time he looked his dad in the eye. "If you wish." he muttered. Everything in him wanted to refuse, but he remembered Luke's words and told himself it would be better for everyone if he just came willingly. He didn't want his dad mad at Luke and Annie.

Jim smiled, relieved that his son hadn't said no. "I do wish, son. I am very happy you will come here. I spoke with Luke and Annie about it yesterday. They agreed that we could move you in today, since I have the day off. Luke is busy with his sermon for tomorrow, but he thought if we could move you this morning, that it

148

would work best. That way he has the afternoon and evening to focus on his sermon."

Josh nodded. "Yes, sir. What ever you think is best."

Jim stood, glad that Josh was willing to at least give him a chance. "Good. I am going to call the others in here now and tell them the good news. Then we, you, Jared, Jordan and I, anyway, will head over to Luke and Annie's and pack up your stuff. I know Lilly wants to, but with Julia, and the baby being on the way, she needs to just stay here so she isn't trying to move things."

Josh looked up at his dad, slowly and hesitantly. "Dad," he gulped. "Could we-" he stopped too afraid to go on. He ducked his head a little, expecting in a way to feel the back of his dad's hand across his mouth, thinking his dad would consider his asking to be backtalk.

Jim looked at him closely, feeling the boy's fear. "What is it, Joshua? You can tell me."

Josh dropped his head, hoping to hide the tears that were in his eyes, but it didn't work. Jim saw the tears and his heart turned over.

Josh looked back up at him and took a deep steadying breath. "Could we wait till tomorrow or Monday to move me? Could I just have one more night with them to tell them goodbye?"

Jim smiled tightly. He didn't want to say yes, but he felt a prick in his heart. He should have known the boy would want time to say goodbye to the people who had been his family for the last eight years. He felt that he was being selfish. He hadn't even considered how hard this was going to be for Josh. He just wanted the boy to be happy that he was moving back in with his family.

He knew he should have thought, but, he reasoned, Joshua had known this was coming. He felt that same prick in his heart, and he knew he couldn't deny his son this request.

"Okay, son, if that is what you would like. I can take you there now, if you like, and you can pack. Since we were all invited there for lunch tomorrow, we will just move you home then. Okay?"

Josh nodded slowly, but tears stung his eyes. He realized this was going to be goodbye to the family he had grown to love, the family who had protected and cared for him for the last eight years. He bit his lip. Was everything going to change? He thought of his last year of school and his hopes to go to college in the spring.

One step at a time. I am always with you. I will direct your paths, He heard the soft words whispered to his heart and they gave him a small form of comfort. He also felt the sting of guilt. How cold God love him and be with him, when he had been trying to shut him out. *Help me, God.* He cried in his mind. He knew he had been wrong. *Help me.*

Jim looked at Josh seeming to sense his unease. "It was hard for you to ask me, wasn't it, son?"

Josh trembled, but nodded slightly. "Yes, sir, it was."

Jim smiled, glad to see that the boy was still going to tell him the truth even when it was frightening. "Thank you, Joshua. I hope that with time you can learn to trust me. I am sorry for what I have done to you, son, really I am. I hope in time you will see that I really have changed. God is real to me now. It isn't just an act.

Anger burned in him. He glanced up at his dad, but didn't say anything.

Jim saw the hate filled look. He bit his lip. "Joshua,"

Josh ducked his head. He knew he shouldn't let his anger show. "Yes, sir."

Josh heard someone come into the room and he turned his head slightly.

Lilly smiled at him as he looked her way.

Josh trembled as he looked back at his dad. Tears now stood in his eyes where the anger had been.

Jim took a deep breath. "Son, I have a question for you and I want you to be honest with me about it. Is that understood?"

Josh shivered. "Yes, sir."

Jim waited till Josh looked him in the eyes. "Joshua, how long has it been since you have spent time with God?"

Josh ducked his head.

Jim sighed. "Joshua, God loves you. He wants you to be talking to him about all your fears and cares. How long has it been, son? I want an answer."

Josh looked away, then slowly turned his tear filled eyes back to his dad. "I have devotions every day."

Jim sighed. "Joshua, that is not what I asked. I asked you how long it has been since you spent time with God?"

Josh bit his lip as he tried to keep his tears back, but slowly one fell down his cheek. "It's been a long time, Dad."

Jim reached out and placed his hand on the boy's shoulder.

"It's been since you saw me, hasn't it?"

Josh ducked his head even more. A trembling started inside of him and worked it's way out. Slowly he nodded, but he couldn't make himself look at his dad or at Lilly.

Jim sighed, "Son, I don't want you to be bitter. God doesn't want you to walk away from him. All bitterness and anger do is block you off from him."

Josh looked down at the floor. Something broke in side him, and his tears started to fall in earnest. "I know I was wrong to walk away from God, but I was so scared of you. I didn't know what to do. I don't know how to get back."

Jim reached out and pulled Josh to him in a hug.

Josh jumped and pulled quickly away. He looked into his dad's eye in surprise and fear.

Jim saw the look and again a pain stabbed his heart. He hadn't ever hugged his son, not just to hug him and let him know that he loved him. Guilt riddled his mind. He had hugged Lilly's kids in love every day at least once, but he had never given his son a hug in love.

"Let's take it to God together, son. I have a feeling we are both going to need his help." His voice was full of pain as he slowly bowed his head.

Tears stood in Lilly's eyes as father and son prayed together for the first time. When they were done Jim looked up at Josh and saw a tiny sparkle in his eye. He smiled. "Now, son, I hope you can learn to forgive me and trust me. I want us to be a family. Please give it a chance."

Josh looked into his dad's eyes and saw a sincerity there that hadn't been there when he was little. Something inside him at that moment told him that his dad was telling the truth this time. He nodded slowly, "With God's help, Dad, in time, I will. And thanks for caring about my heart."

Jim smiled broader, glad for this little bit of trust from his son. "Thank you."

He stood. "Well, how about I take you back to Luke and Annie's and let you get stuff ready for moving. Then I will talk to my family here." He looked at Josh and saw the boy flinch. "I am very happy that you are going to be a part of this family, Joshua. Thank you for giving me a chance."

Josh bit his lip. He wanted to snap that he didn't really have a choice, but he kept the words back. He may as well make the most of this, because it was happening whether he wanted it to or not. It was time for him to accept that, even though he had kept hoping that something would change.

Without a word he followed his dad out of the kitchen and toward the door. As soon as they walked by the living room Jared and Jordan bombarded them.

"What is going on? What's wrong, Dad? Why did you need to talk to Josh alone. What is happening?"

Jim smiled at the twins then at Lilly who had quietly followed them. "Every thing is fine." He placed a hand on each boy's shoulder. "I am taking Josh home. When I get back I want to have a very long talk with both of you."

Both boys glanced at Josh, but Josh kept his head down. He didn't want the boys to see his eyes, nor that there were tears on his cheeks. He was afraid, but he was also embarrassed.

Both boys looked back at their dad and nodded slightly. "Dad, it wasn't Josh's fault, last night." Jordan began. "Really. If any one is going to be in trouble it's me!"

Jared nodded. "That's right, Dad. He didn't even want to have a pillow fight. We started it."

Jim shook his head at the two of them. "Both of you calm down and go do the dishes. I will be back shortly. Then we will talk. He turned back to Josh. "Come on, son. Let's go."

Josh trembled to hear his dad call him son in front of the family. Would Jordan and Jared want him for a brother, or would they hate him. Would they understand why they hadn't been told who he was? He felt his stomach turn. This was going to be a hard change, but he pushed the thought aside. He had to just get over it, because it was going to happen. He may as well get use to the idea and quit wishing it was different.

Silently he followed his dad to the car.

Jim looked at him as they got in. "What is the matter, Joshua?"

Josh trembled. Would his dad hate him if he said what he was thinking? He looked up at him with tears still falling down his cheeks. Quickly he looked away and jerked his head, as though to get rid of all the tears. "It's nothing, sir. Nothing at all."

Jim shook his head. "Are you starting to lie to me, son?"

Josh bit his lip and ducked his head. He knew better then to lie. He hadn't considered it a lie. He had just hoped his dad would drop the subject, because he didn't want to talk about it.

He blinked hard and took a deep breath, still his voice trembled as he answered, "I was just wondering if your kids are going to want me in the family. What if they don't? How do they feel about all of this?"

Jim felt a sting as Josh said "your kids." He bit his lip to keep in a sharp retort and took a deep breath. "You are my son, Joshua. Yes, Jared and Jordan are also and Julia is my daughter, and when the new one comes in a few weeks or a month, it will be my child also, but just because they have a different mamma then you, doesn't make you fit in less. Jared and Jordan aren't my real sons, but I don't want to treat you differently because of that. I hope to treat you all the same and love you all the same. Do you understand?"

Josh didn't understand, but he nodded slightly anyway. He just wanted this conversation to be over. He wanted to be alone. He didn't want to be around his dad any more.

Jim smiled, unaware of the boy's feelings and hoping he understood. "Good, then let's get you to Luke and Annie's, and tomorrow you will be home to stay."

Josh shivered and sunk down a little in the seat as they drove the couple of miles to the house he had called home for the last eight years of his life, and would no longer. Tears once again burnt his eyes, but he forced them back. Crying wouldn't change anything. Luke and Annie already made it clear there was nothing any of them could do. His dad had the law with him and he was just going to have to deal with it.

He sighed, then turned to the one he had always been able to depend on. *Dear God, please help me to accept this. I am scared. Please help me not to be so scared. Please help it all to turn out all right. Thank you. Amen.*

He took a deep breath and felt the love of God sweep over him and knew no matter what happened to him or where he lived, God was always there.

17

Jim dropped Joshua off and headed back toward home. He felt cheerful. He was excited for this to take place. He didn't want Josh to stay another night with Luke and Annie, but he knew it was probably for the best. Joshua was right, he needed time to say goodbye.

Oh well, he must now set his mind to the task at hand and tell the rest of the family what was happening.

As he walked back into the house he smiled to hear Jordan and Jared arguing as they washed the dishes. He walked in behind them and put an arm around each of them. "Getting along good?" he asked.

They both jumped in surprise and shut their mouths.

Jim chuckled. These two were a handful. "When you are done, come to the living room. I need to talk to you both."

Jordan and Jared both nodded. "I think Momma is still in there with Julia," Jordan replied.

Jim smiled and headed to the living-room to talk to his wife before the two boys and their rambunctious spirits followed.

The boys finished the dishes and nervously walked into the living room. Their parents were sitting on the couch talking quietly, but they could tell by their faces that their conversation was also very serious. They stopped in the doorway and waited. Jared cleared his throat to make their presents known.

Jim stood up quickly, breaking off whatever he was saying. He smiled at the boys, but his eyes were serious as he motioned for them to come in. "Boys, come in and sit down. Your mother and I, well, actually I, need to talk to you about something very important."

Jordan and Jared once again looked at each other nervously, then they looked at their dad and mom. "Are we in trouble?" they said in unison.

Jim smiled. His eyes twinkled a little, "You should be after staying up all night, but no, that is not what this is about. Well, in a way it is. Just come and sit down, and I will tell you all about it."

The boys walked over to the couch and sat down nervously next to their mom. Ever since Jim had married their mom they had loved him like a dad, and he had loved them. They hadn't ever had more than a minor conflict of behavioral challenges, but they still felt nervous. They knew they had disobeyed, and they also knew they needed punished for it.

Lilly saw the looks on her boys faces and she almost laughed. They were sure they were in trouble for something. She looked up at Jim and he was looking even more nervous then the boys were.

He cleared his throat, but nothing would come out.

Lilly smiled at him in sympathy. "Just tell them, Jim."

Jim cleared his throat again. He looked at her with a smile. "Jared, Jordan, and Julia, your mom already knows, but we are going to be adding another member to our family."

The boys looked at him as if he had gone crazy. "Um, Dad, we already know that mom is going to have a baby. It's due in a couple of months, that isn't really a surprise to us," Jordan ventured.

Jim shook his head. "I am not meaning the baby, Jordan. It's not a baby we are adding to the family."

Jared looked at him hard, "But you said-"

Jim smiled. "I said we are adding another member to our family. You kids all know that I was married before I met your mom. What you don't know is that I had a child, a son. After my wife died I lost track of my son for – well, for reasons I am not proud of. You boys know that I was in jail for a while. After I got out of jail and met your mom I never thought I would see my son again, but I have found him." He smiled as he waited for the boys' response.

Jared and Jordan sat perfectly still for a minute and stared at him. "We have a brother? How old is he? Have we met him? When is he coming to live with us? Why didn't you find him before?" they questioned.

155

Jim held up his hand to stop the questions. "One at a time." he chuckled. "Yes, you have a brother. Yes, you all know him. He is coming to live here tomorrow after church. Which means we have a lot of work to do to get ready for him."

Jordan looked at his dad with a worried expression on his face. If his dad didn't want to tell them who it was, but they knew him, it must be someone they didn't like. Who could it be? He rapidly ran through his mind a list of boys that he knew and didn't like.

Jared peppered his dad with more questions, determined to find out who it was before he put forth any effort to get ready for someone else to move in to his family. "Who is it, Dad? Do we even get to meet him before he just moves in with us? How old is he? Doesn't he want to meet us before he moves in with us?"

Jim smiled a little broader. "He is almost sixteen, same as you boys. You have already met him, I already told you that. And he already knows you."

Jordan bit his lip trying to think. "Does he go to our church?"

Again Jim nodded, but this time his eyes twinkled in fun. He was enjoying the looks on the boys' faces. They were so sure it was someone they didn't like.

Lilly turned her face away from her sons as a smile played on her lips. This was going to be such a surprise to them.

Jared looked at him warily. "Oh, no, Dad, it's not Josiah is it. Please tell me we don't have to be related to him? I don't want him here. Please say he isn't our brother."

Jim shook his head. "No, Jordan, it's not Josiah."

Jordan frowned. "Is it Andy?" he murmured. "Oh, please, Dad, please say it's not him."

Again Jim shook his head. He laughed at the boys' worried expressions. "It is someone you boys will love to have as a brother, in fact, he has spent a few nights with you here, just recently."

Jared and Jordan both jumped to their feet in surprise and joy. "What! It's Joshua! How? When? Are you serious, Dad?"

Lilly laughed at the surprise on her boys' faces. "Yes, it's Joshua. He will be coming to live with us. And you boys had better not have another night like the last one was when he is living here."

Jordan looked from his mom to his dad. Something was bothering him, but he couldn't quiet put a finger on it. He looked at Jared and knew he felt the same way. "Dad, why didn't you tell us right away who Josh was? And why is he moving in now? Why did you wait so long?"

Jim looked at the two boys, then slowly turned and looked out the window. His heart wrenched. How much did he tell them?

Jordan bit his lip. What was his dad thinking? Was he going to answer him?

Lilly stood and took Julia in her arms. "I am going to put her down for her nap, honey, I will be right back."

Jim nodded, but both boys could tell that he really hadn't heard their mom. What was going on?

As Lilly left the room, Jim turned back to they boys. "Boys, we all make mistakes in life. I made a lot of bad choices and as so often happened those bad choices affected those around me. It hurt those around me. I wasn't a good father and the police had to take Joshua away from me because of that. During my time in jail someone cared enough about me to tell me about Jesus. I learned to love God. To really love him, not just to put on a show for others to see, but to have a real relationship with him.

"Learning to love God taught me how to love others as I should. When I got out of jail, the only thing I wanted to do was find my son. I wanted to tell him how sorry I was for being a bad father. I wanted to tell him I was sorry for hurting him so much. The only problem was I didn't know where to look, and I was afraid. I didn't trust myself. I was afraid that, if I did find him, I would hurt him more. I knew God had changed me, but I was afraid that I wasn't good enough to be a good father to my son.

"It happened by accident, or should I say God's grace, that I found him. I have known who he was for a little over a month who he is. You see a boy does a lot of changing in his teen years and at first I didn't recognize him.

"I didn't tell you kids who he was, because I wanted you to be good friends. I had hoped that if you were good friends you would be excited when you found out that he was actually your brother. We had him spend a few nights here, just to make sure it was all going to work, with you and with him. We didn't want to hurt him either. I wanted to make sure that he would want to live with us. And I didn't want to hurt you boys, or him. That is why we have kept it a secret from you. I'm sorry if you are upset that we didn't tell you, but I thought this would be the best way. Do you forgive me?"

Both of them stared at him in shock. Slowly they nodded. This was a lot of information to process.

Jim smiled a big smile, then reached over and hugged them both. "I want you both to know that this doesn't change how I feel about you. I love you. I love you all. And trust me my heart is big enough to spread it around."

Jared and Jordan both grinned. "Are you sure you want all of us boys together after last night?"

Jim laughed a great laugh. "I am sure. If you boys all want to have the same room we are going to move you into the guest room. It is bigger and there will be plenty of room for three beds if you two stay bunked and three dressers, with room to spare. If we left you in the room you are in now, there wouldn't be any room left, by the time we got another bed and dresser in there.

Jordan's smile lit up his whole face. "And the guest room is farther away from you and mom. So we won't be keeping you awake all night."

Jim shook his head. "You boys had better sleep at night, or I will be separating you. But for today lets see how much of this stuff we can get moved around so when Josh moves in tomorrow it won't be such a big job, and he won't feel like he is intruding on us.

The boys turned and raced up the steps. Their excitement was evident, but Jordan still felt uneasy, and now he knew what he was feeling. Did Josh know all this was going on, or did he not know until this morning? Why would their dad tell Josh first? It wasn't fair. Why hadn't Josh said any thing, if he knew?

Was dad going to give special treatment to Josh, just because he was his son? He looked over at Jared and saw that he was feeling similar fears.

Jared, the ever present trouble maker, leaned over to his brother and with a mischievous grin, whispered, "We will just have to see."

Jordan nodded. That was all they could do.

18

The following morning, before the family left for church, Joshua taped up the last box of things. He bowed his head. He didn't want this at all. He didn't want to be near his dad. Why did he have to go live with him? Had he changed?

Joy knocked on the open door. "Josh, can I come in?"

Josh sat back and looked up. "Sure you can, Joy."

She slowly opened the door and tears filled her big blue eyes. "I am going to miss you, big brother. You have always been there for me. I can't believe you are leaving. It's just not right."

Josh stood up and gave her a hug. "Hey, it's just down the street and you can come and see me. It's not like I will be moving a long ways away. Besides we will see each other at church three time a week."

Joy sniffed. "It's just not the same. I will miss you. I already do just thinking about it."

Josh smiled slightly and held her tighter. "Joy, I will still be there whenever you need me. But now I won't have the right to pick on you as much."

Joy finally smiled. "I give you permission to pick on me as much as you want. You will always be a big brother to me."

Josh smiled. "Okay, but that means that I get to terrorize your dates."

She laughed this time. "Make sure you do a good job of that."

Joy turned to go. "Mom sent me up here to tell you that breakfast is ready, and she doesn't want to be late to church."

Josh nodded as he looked around the room. His stomach felt empty, but he didn't think he could eat. "Tell her I will be right there."

Joy turned to go out the door then turned back, "I still get approval of your girl friends right?"

Josh threw his pillow at her and she ran down the stairs laughing. Josh felt tears sting his eyes. He was going to miss this family.

In church that morning Josh sat with Annie and the kids for the last time. Out of the corner of his eye he could see his dad and his new family. He still felt shocked when he saw Lilly give the little girl a coloring book and some crayons. He caught his father looking at him and he quickly looked away.

Jim saw Josh's quick movement and his heart hurt. He could see the hurt in Joshua, just in the way he was sitting. He wished he could undo his past. He wished he could go back and live his life again, and make better decisions with Joshua. Tears burned his eyes. He didn't know what to do.

He knew he had to talk to Josh and tell him how wrong he had been for the way he had treated him, but he was afraid the boy wouldn't believe him. He knew he had talk to him sometime. He needed to tell the boy again that God had changed his life, and because of God things were going to be very different this time.

He shook his head. He needed to get his mind back on the sermon. He would figure out what to do with Joshua later. *God, help me. Please help him to forgive me. Give us a chance at being a family. Thank you, God, for this step in the process.* He forced his mind back on the sermon. All he could do now was wait and trust that God knew what he was doing.

Sunday afternoon lunch was a long affair, the adults hanging around the table long after the meal was over talking and drinking coffee. Jim kept watching Joshua to see what the boy was thinking, but he never could tell. After a little while of them all at the table the kids had set up the card table and were now engrossed in a game.

Joy sat by her brother and tried to get him to smile. She had watched him all the way through lunch. He hadn't eaten anything, just pushed his food back and forth, and he looked like he was upset. She knew he didn't want to move away, and she couldn't understand why

160

he had to. Why couldn't he just keep living here like he had been? It was so hard to understand.

Josh felt tense, but he knew that it wasn't going to change. This was going to happen, and he may as well get over it. He kept glancing at Jared and Jordan, wondering what they were thinking about the change. Were they happy or mad? He couldn't tell. Would they want him for a brother, or would they rather him not live with them? They hadn't said anything about it.

Jared and Jordan, though subdued by Josh's solemn mood were excited to have Josh moving in with them. They were glad he was their brother, but they couldn't help but feel a little worried. Their dad had always spent his extra time with them, helping them with little things or teaching them how to build things, little things like that. Would that all change? Would he spend his time with Josh now, and forget about them?   They kept looking at Josh and wondering what he was feeling. He didn't seem very happy. Did he not want them for brothers? Maybe he was afraid his dad wouldn't be able to spend time with him now, because they were in the family.

Finally Jim stood. He looked over at the young people playing their game and smiled. "Well, I guess we better be getting home. We want to have Joshua all settled in before church tonight."

Josh looked up at his dad. A muscle jumped in his jaw, but he slowly stood.

Jim nodded to him. "Why don't you go ahead and get your things brought down, Joshua. The boys will help you."

Jordan and Jared bounced to their feet and happily followed their new brother upstairs. They were excited to show Josh their new room and let him know that they were all going to get to be in the same room together, but they had agreed not to say anything about it till they were home.

They practically ran ahead of Josh and grabbed the boxes out of his room, hurrying back downstairs to put them by the door, then back up for more. After a few trips they were done, and all Josh's things were piled by the front door.

Jim stepped into the front hall. "Tell you what," he said quickly, as though he had been thinking about it for a while. "Why don't I take everyone home, then come back and get you and all your things, Joshua." He wanted to give the boy a few privet minutes to say goodbye to this family, before he left their care.

Josh looked at him in surprise. He didn't figure his dad would care how he felt about leaving. "Okay, sir." he whispered. He felt afraid and unsure. What was he suppose to be feeling at a time like this, he wondered.

Jim smiled at Luke and Annie. "Thanks again for the great meal. We really do appreciate it. And thanks so much for all you have done for my boy."

Lilly smiled as well. "Thank you all so much for understanding. We want what is best for all of us."

Annie smiled through her tears. "I just have to trust that God has everything under control."

Lilly nodded. "Don't be shy about stopping by. We are only a little ways down the road, and we love company. You are welcome any time."

Annie nodded.

Jim motioned for Lilly and the boys to go out the door. Then he picked up Julia and turned to Joshua. "I will be back in a few minutes to get you, Son. Be ready." His voice sounded harsh even though he hadn't meant for it to.

Josh flinched, but nodded. "Yes, sir."

As they drove away Joy suddenly burst into tears and clung to him. "Oh, Josh, don't leave. Why do you have to go? Just stay here."

Josh bit his lip to keep his own tears back as he hugged her. "I can't, Joy. You know that. We have already talked about it." He turned away form her and one by one hugged all the other kids goodbye. He did good fighting off his tears till he came to Annie. Suddenly they ran down his cheeks. "Mom," he whispered. He put his arms around her in a quick hug. "Thanks for all you have done for me."

Annie hugged him tightly. "Son, you are always a part of this family no matter where you live. We love you. Don't be afraid to come back and visit us any time you want. Know that I love you as a son, no matter where you are."

Josh nodded slightly then turned to Luke.

Luke smiled and hugged him tight. "Son-" his voice broke.

Josh took a deep breath. "Thanks for being a dad to me. You know-" he broke off unable to say what he was feeling.

Luke nodded in understanding. "Son, you are always welcome here. I want you to know that. Don't be afraid to come to us if you need anything.

Josh nodded again and turned as he heard his dad pull back in. "Guess I have to go now." He turned back to Luke and Annie. "Thanks for everything."

Luke lifted a box and so did Josh as Jim swung open the door. Together they loaded up Josh's things and headed him toward his new home.

Jared and Jordan had moved most of their things the night before, so when their dad had dropped them off and went back to get Josh and his stuff, they stood on the front steps and waited for him to come back.

"Jordan are you worried about this at all?" Jared suddenly asked. The two hadn't really talked about how they felt about all this, but they knew the other was worried.

Jordan looked at his brother in surprise. "What do you mean?"

Jared shrugged. "Well, you know, Josh being Dad's real son and all. We are just his step sons. Do you think Dad will – you know, treat him better then he does us?"

Jordan laughed, though he was sure Jared heard the fear in his voice. "You are a goose, Jared. We have the best dad in the world. He treats us wonderfully. How could he treat Josh any better?"

Jared shrugged. He wasn't sure if his brother was trying to convince him or himself. "Oh, you know. I was just wondering that maybe, when things go wrong, or like we do something we shouldn't – all the blame will be put on you and me and Josh will get off the hook completely. You know stuff like that."

Jordan shrugged. "I guess with stuff like that, we are just going to have to wait and see. We have always gotten along fine before, just cause he will be with us all the time now, I don't see why that would change."

Jared nodded. "I guess, but maybe it wouldn't hurt to test the waters a little bit. You know, just to see."

Jordan shook his head. "Better give it a few days first."

Jared nodded again. "Okay. I will." Then he smiled. "But I know a good way to test them."

Jordan turned on his brother with a frown. He had that tone

that he had right before he got both of them into huge trouble. "What are you up to now, Jared? Last time you had that tone we spent two days in our room. Don't you remember that?"

Jared laughed. "Just a little fun. You know like a little pillow fight in the middle of the night or a wrestling match in the living room. You know just something simple.

Jordan's eyes sparkled. "Sounds like fun to me. I am sure Josh will join in."

Just then their dad and Josh pulled in. Both boys ran down the steps yelling, to help Josh take his stuff to their new room.

"Josh, just wait till you see. Dad moved us into the guest room so we can all three share a room. Isn't that so cool!" Jared cried. "Just wait till you see. It is so much bigger than our room was. Even with another bed and dresser in it we aren't crowded at all."

Jordan reached for a box.

Josh handed it to him and gave him a weak smile.

Jordan returned the smile with a big one of his own. "We are glad you are our brother, Josh. Don't worry about it. When Dad told us he had a son, and he was moving in with us, we were very worried about who it was. We were so excited when Dad said it was you! This is just so cool!" His eyes sparkled. "We get a new brother even if the baby turns out to be a girl."

Josh chuckled a little at this. He followed Jared and Jordan up the stairs to the room that was now to be his and his brothers. He tried to be happy, but he couldn't. He didn't want to go back to the life he had to live when he was little. Was it going to happen?

Jared and Jordan deposited boxes on the floor and stepped back.

"See!" Jared cried. "Isn't it so big. And one of the best things about it, is that it is farther away from Mom and Dad's room, so if we should have a pillow fight or something some night, we shouldn't wake them up."

Josh saw the mischief in Jared's eyes and knew he was already scheming. His stomach twisted. Did they ever get in trouble for all the stuff they did? Was his dad going to treat them all the same, or was he just going to beat him and leave them alone?

He tried to push the thought away. His dad hadn't tried to hit him yet, and he said he was sorry. He said he had changed. He needed to try and trust him, even though he didn't want to, and try to believe that he really had changed.

Jim motioned to Jared and Jordan, "I think you boys better leave Josh alone for a bit and let him get unpacked. We need to be leaving for church in about an hour."

Josh looked up at his dad.

Jim saw the fear in the boy's eyes and he knew it was going to be hard for him to make this adjustment, but he hoped that he would try cheerfully. "Yes, Josh, I would like you to sit with the family during service tonight. You can sit between your brothers if you like. Maybe you can get them to behave," he smiled slightly.

Josh looked away. He felt his stomach burn and a bitter taste filled his mouth. He swallowed and willed his stomach to settle. He couldn't let himself get sick, when he hadn't even been here an hour.

Jared looked up at his dad, "Can't we stay here. We won't bother him. We will help him. Promise. We just want to be together."

Jim looked Jared in the eye. "You had better not be planning any more mischief, young man." A smile twitched at the corner of his mouth.

Jared looked at his dad wide eyed, but with a teasing grin. "Dad, how could you even think that I would do something like that."

Jordan snorted. "The real question is how could he not think something like that."

Josh chuckled as Jared scowled at his brother. "I am not always bad."

Jordan thought for moment. "No, not always. There are some times when you sleep. Aw the peace." He pretended to be listening to quietness and smiled dreamily.

Jim laughed at them both. "Behave and don't keep Joshua from getting done with unpacking. I'll call you all when it is time to leave."

Josh didn't respond as he looked down. Jim turned to walk out of the room as Jared and Jordan chorused an okay.

As Jim left Jordan looked down at Josh who was sitting on the floor. "We figured we would let you have the single bed, and we would keep the bunks. Is that okay?"

Josh looked up at him. "Yeah, Jordan, that's fine." He looked at both of them. "Look, guys, I am sorry I had to move in like this and disrupt your family. And I am sorry I didn't tell you sooner who I was. It's just that – it's complicated."

Jordan shrugged. "I think it is cool. We were friends and now we get to be brothers that is even cooler. I mean, it's like a really long sleepover. It is totally awesome."

Jared smiled. "Yeah, we can always use another brother around here. I mean I'm glad you aren't a girl, that's for sure, unless it was one like Joy, but that wouldn't be good, because then I would want to date my sister and that would just be wrong. And anyway I can always use someone to pick on."

Josh looked up at him, "You want to date Joy?"

Jared flushed, "Well, I mean, she is pretty."

Josh grinned to see Jared squirm uneasily. "Forget it for a while, hot shot. Luke won't let her date till she is sixteen and that won't be till next year."

Jared groaned then seemed to recover quickly. "Well, Dad says we can't till we are sixteen either, so I guess that isn't so long to wait. It could be worse. It could be eighteen or something like that. When is her birthday?"

Josh suddenly decided he was keeping that information to himself. He didn't like the idea of Jordan or Jared dating Joy, but he kept that information to himself also. "Don't worry about it. It isn't your business."

Jared frowned, but didn't reply.

Jordan tried to smooth over the tension that was suddenly in the room. "Come on, Josh, let's get you unpacked, so you don't have to do it when we get home."

Josh turned to his stuff. "Thanks."

With the three of them working together they had Josh unpacked a few minuted before Jim hollered up the stairs to them that it was time to go.

Josh bit his lip. He didn't want to have to be in church with his dad. He took a deep breath. Now was a good time to see how much his dad had changed. He sighed. He didn't want to see. He just wanted to be away from his dad and not have to worry about it.

He followed Jared and Jordan down the stairs and out to the car still feeling his nerves jump in him. "God, help me. You alone know if Dad really has changed. Please help it to be true, God. Please don't let him hit me."

At church Lilly led the way to the pew they had been sitting in, right across form Annie and the kids. She sat down with Jim beside her on one side and Julia on the other.

Jim smiled as the boys walked in the other side of the pew. Josh trembled as he saw his dad looking at him. He sat between Jordan and Jared. His nerves were in an uproar. He felt like he was going to be sick, but he knew he had to fight it off. This was what his dad wanted, and he had to live with it. It wasn't going to do him any good to get sick in church.

God, please calm my nerves. I don't want to be sick. Please help me to be good. And help him not to hit me. Please don't let Jordan and Jared get me into trouble.

Luke looked over and saw Josh with Jared and Jordan and his heart ached. There was going to be a big open spot in their home without him. He knew he had to trust God to take care of him and them, but it was harder than he thought it was going to be, just knowing that Josh wouldn't be coming home with them again.

The service had barely started when Jared nudged him.

Josh tried to ignore him, but Jared continued to nudge him and then pinched his leg. Josh jerked, and barely stopped a yelp from escaping his mouth.

Jim looked over at them and frowned.

Josh wanted to sink down in the pew, but he knew that would just make his dad more upset.

A little while later Jordan snickered about something, and that cause Jared to snicker.

Both boys looked down and put their hands over their mouths.

Josh trembled. Was he going to get in trouble because they were being bad?

Jim snapped his finger. Josh again jerked, but he kept himself from glancing at his dad.

Jared and Jordan finally got themselves under control and faced the front once again.

When the sermon was over, Jim led all three of them outside. He didn't say much, but he pointed to the car. "Go sit in the car and do not get out of it till we are home, do I make myself clear."

Josh trembled. "Yes, sir." He turned and headed to the car, but stopped as he heard Jared protest.

"Oh, Dad. Come on. Why do we have to sit in the car. We were just trying to have a little fun."

Josh felt the color drain from his face. He wouldn't dare talk to his dad like that. His dad would whip him till there was blood. He waited to see what his dad would do to Jared.

Jim looked them both in the eye and pointed to the car. "Don't disobey me. Get in that car and do not move till I have granted you permission."

Jared and Jordan frowned, but turned to follow Josh to the car.

Josh bit his lip to keep back a moan as Jared and Jordan climbed in on either side of him. "What did we do?" grouched Jared. "I mean, just cause we got a little silly in church, why do we have to sit here?"

Jordan glanced over at his brother. "You and I did, but Josh didn't. Why is dad making all of us sit here?"

Jared scowled and started complaining again.

Jordan glanced at Josh and thought he saw a tear in his eye. He looked again, but couldn't be sure. Josh had slouched down in the seat and closed his eyes.

They sat and waited for about five minutes till Jim and Lilly and Julia came to the car and Jared didn't stop complaining the whole time. Jordan had started, but when he saw Josh something stopped him. What was wrong with Josh? Why didn't he complain? Of all of them he had the most right to.

When Josh heard the car door open he slowly sat up, knowing it was his dad.

Jim glanced back at the three of them. "No more complaining. You are all in trouble for the way you were behaving in church. We will talk about it at home."

Jared scowled even deeper, but finally closed his mouth.

Jordan glanced sideways at Josh. "Dad, I can understand why me and Jared are in trouble, but why is Josh? He didn't do anything."

Jim glanced back at his son.

Josh ducked his head, afraid that his dad would think he had put Jordan up to that. He shivered as his dad looked at him. "I said we will talk about it at home. All of you will be silent till we get there, am I understood."

Josh suddenly felt his stomach turn. He gasped, but knew he

shouldn't say anything. He felt it again, and knew he was going to get sick and he couldn't stop it this time.

Jim heard the gasp and turned to get after who had done it. When he saw the look on Josh's face gasped. "Jared get out!" Jim jumped out of the car and jerked the door open before Jared had time to even react.

Jared looked at his dad in fear, but jumped out of the car. Josh stumbled out behind him and barely made it in time. Jared stood frozen as Josh emptied his stomach on the parking lot and then on the grass. He looked at Jordan, and his brother shrugged.

Jim walked up behind Josh as the boy turned back.

Josh jumped. "I'm sorry, Dad," his voice was raspy. "I didn't mean to do that." He looked up and saw Luke coming their way. He bit his lip.

Jim turned to see what had bothered Josh.

"Josh, are you okay?" He asked as he walked up to them. "I saw you throwing up."

Josh took a step back from both men. "I'm fine, da – Luke." he stammered. "Just too much happening today I guess."

Luke smiled. "Okay. If you are sure."

Josh nodded slightly.

Jim turned to Luke. "Does he do this often?"

Luke shook his head. "Not often, but when he is really scared or upset, yeah, he gets sick. It usually takes a lot though." He put his arm on Josh's shoulder. "Are you sure you are okay?"

Josh pulled away. "I'm fine," he whispered.

Jim nodded. "Thanks for telling me, Pastor, that will help."

Luke nodded and turned to go, then turned back. "Josh, you be sure and come around once in a while."

Josh nodded slightly, but didn't say anything.

As Luke walked away Jim turned back to him. "If you are done, get in the car, son. We need to get home."

Josh shivered, but slid in the car, this time by the window with Jared in the middle. Julia sat upfront between Jim and Lilly. Josh wondered where they were going to put a car seat in a few weeks, but pushed the thought away.

When they got home Lilly took Julia in the house, saying she would be waiting in the living room when they came in.

Jim nodded and waited till she was in the house before he turned to the boys. "I am very disappointed in you. All of you know better than to behave that way in church."

Jordan opened his mouth to say again that Josh hadn't done anything, but his father's look silenced him.

Jim once again looked all three of them in the eye. Josh shivered. What was his dad going to do to them?

Jim cleared his throat. "All three of you go to your room and that is where you are to stay till morning. You are not having supper before you go, do I make myself clear? Go in the house, up to your room, and get ready for bed. Then go to bed. I don't want any arguing or complaining. In the house, up stairs and to bed, all three of you. Do you understand?"

"Yes, sir," Josh answered plainly.

Jared and Jordan both scowled, but muttered a, "Yes, sir," as they opened the door to the car and got out.

"But, Dad," Jordan started again. "Josh didn't do anything."

Jim's eyes shot fire at Josh then at Jordan. "I said get in the house, boys. Now, all of you obey me at once."

Once in their room Jared started complaining again. Josh didn't say anything, but he felt himself stiffen. If Dad was upset with them and told them not to talk, Jared was going to get them all in even more trouble.

Jordan apparently had the same thought. "Jared, be quiet. Do you want Dad up here?"

Jared glared at his brother, but snapped his mouth shut.

In a few minutes the boys were ready for bed. Jordan turned to Josh, "Sorry you are in trouble for us being loud in church. I know you didn't do anything. But I guess Dad doesn't."

Josh looked away as he climbed into bed and slid beneath the covers. He hoped that he wouldn't have any nightmares tonight, but he knew that was doubtful. "Forget it," he muttered.

Jared scowled at his brother. "He was so snickering. Just like we were."

Jordan frowned at his brother. "No, he wasn't and you know it."

Jared snapped his mouth closed and climbed up into his bed.

Just as Jordan was heading to open the door it opened and Jim stepped in. Lilly was with him. Josh sat up with a start, fearing what his dad was coming in for.

Jim smiled at the boys. "Thank you for all doing as you were told. He sat down on the edge of Josh's bed. Jared get your Bible. It is your night to read."

Josh barely turned his head to watch Jared get out of bed and get his Bible off the dresser. He climbed back up in bed and read a chapter out loud. When he had finished Lilly rose from where she was sitting on the side of Jordan's bed and took the Bible and put it back on the dresser. All of them closed their eyes and Jared started to pray. After he was done Jordan prayed. When he was done there was a pause of silence. Jim opened his eyes and looked at Josh.

Josh lay almost frozen in bed. His eyes were wide open as he stared in shock at his dad.

Jim smiled. "It's your turn to pray, Josh. We have family devotions every night. This is how we close out the day. You are now a part of this family and it is time for you to pray. We did this while you were here on sleepovers."

Josh nodded slightly. He had thought that was just an act put on by his dad. He was surprised to learn that it was a routine. He swallowed hard as he closed his eyes and prayed.

After Jim and Lilly had prayed they kissed the boys and headed out of the room. Again Josh lay there stunned. His father hadn't ever kissed him or told him he loved him, and tonight he had done both. Maybe he really had changed. He sighed as he let himself drift off to sleep. Only time would tell.

19

Josh slept good Sunday night and was grateful he didn't have any nightmares. Monday morning started out fairly well, and continued to go well throughout the afternoon.

When Jim got home from work, Josh was surprised to have him come in the house and offer to play some ball with the boys outside. After the game they all headed in for supper. He couldn't believe he had been with his dad a full twenty-four hours and his dad hadn't struck him.

But Monday night, though it started off quiet as their dad and mom told them good night and left the room, Jared's mischievous streak started to cause a problem.

Jared had been hyper all day. He was constantly picking on either Josh or Jordan. They had both gotten after him, but it hadn't stopped him. And now, as he lay in bed, a new idea came to him.

He was full of energy, even though he knew that Josh and Jordan were tired. He lay on his bed quietly hoping that his parents would go to their own room and go to sleep fast, so he could get up and goof off without them knowing about it.

He waited for what seemed like hours to him, but was really only about ten minutes. The house was still and quiet. He could hear his brothers' smooth even breathing, telling him they were asleep. Jared grinned to himself as he slipped out of bed. Ever so sneakily he crept up beside Joshua's bed. Quietly he got a hold of the sheet and gave a quick jerk.

Josh gave a quick gasp as he fell out of bed, startled awake. "What was that for?" he growled in an angry whisper, not wanting to wake anyone.

Jared laughed as he quietly snuck up to Jordan's bunk. He motioned for Josh to grab the sheet as well, and pull with him.

Josh shook his head and turned away. "No, way. We will be in trouble."

Jared shrugged and gripped the sheet tighter. Then with a quick jerk he pulled Jordan out of bed.

Jordan still half asleep, cried out as he hit the floor. Then, before he was even out of the tangle of sheets, he was after his brother. Both wrestled for a bit. Then, deciding that Josh had watched long enough, lunged at him and drug him into the tangle. The boys rolled into the beds and dressers, making a huge mess and a huge racket, which they were unaware of.

Josh who knew how to fight, made his way, quickly, to the top of the stack. The boys hollered and pulled him back down into the fight. Suddenly their door opened and a loud voice interrupted their game.

"Boys!"

Josh froze in fear as his dad entered the room. He quickly climbed off of Jared who was at this time sitting on Jordan who had somehow gotten a bloody nose in the scuffle.

Jim stood in the doorway with anger in his eyes. All three boys stood before him with fear in their eyes.

"What is going on here?" His voice seemed even louder in the silence of the room.

Jared shrank back. "It was just for fun, Dad. I didn't mean to make a mess. I am sorry."

Josh watched his dad's eyes. Fear ate at his stomach. He didn't want his dad to be mad at the other two. "It's all my fault, Dad. I started it." He forced his voice to remain calm.

Jared and Jordan both stared at him. Why was he doing that? Why was he taking the blame? Jared and Jordan both knew who had really started it. Josh hadn't even wanted to join in. They waited to see what their dad would say.

He looked hared at Josh.

Josh felt his pulse quicken. He didn't want to lie to his dad, but

173

if his dad was going to hit him anyway he might as well just hit him and not the other two. He looked back into his father's eyes without blinking.

Jim turned his gaze back to Jordan and Jared then to Josh again. "I want all of you in bed and the lights out and there to be silence in here. Do not make any more noise or bother each other tonight." He looked at Josh and took a step closer to him. "Understood?"

He felt his temper rise. Was Josh going to start testing the boundaries to see what he could get by with now? He hoped not, because if he was, Jim was going to make sure he knew where the boundaries were even if he didn't want to.

Josh trembled. "Yes, sir." He jumped back into be and saw that Jared and Jordan were quickly obeying as well.

Jim saw that they were all in their beds and went out, turning out the light on his way.

Jared looked toward Josh's bed, though it was too dark to see him. "Why did you do that, Josh? You know it was me who started it. Why did you take the blame and make Dad mad at you?"

Josh shrugged. There was no way in the world that he would tell the boys he didn't want his dad whipping them like he had done to him. "I just did. Don't worry about it."

Jared leaned over his bunk and looked down at Jordan. They both understood the other with that look. Was Josh also thinking that his dad would be more lenient with him? Was that why he took the wrap for it? They shrugged. It didn't really matter. Dad had let it go and none of them had gotten into trouble.

"Good night." Jordan mumbled as he rolled over and went back to sleep.

Jared muttered something as he drifted off to dream.

Josh trembled as he lay in his bed. He saw the anger in his father's eyes when he had looked at him. Was his father going to whip him for starting a fight? Was he just going to let him worry about it until morning, then whip him? He didn't want his dad to hit Jared or Jordan, and he knew that he wouldn't hit them if he admitted to being the one who started it. However, he also knew that if it wasn't him, his dad would probably whip all three of them.

Slowly he rolled over to try and go back to sleep, but it wasn't going to be easy.

"Get up!"

Josh groaned as he felt the pain in his body. He heard the sound of leather striking flesh. He looked up at his father and trembled. "Daddy, I am sorry. Please, No!"

Again he saw the anger in the man's eyes. Fear gripped him. He saw the man raise his belt to whip him. He shuttered and hovered down away from him. "Daddy, please. I am sorry. I didn't do it! Please!"

"Joshua!" the man screamed again.

Josh jumped and his eyes flew open. His head cracked on something as he flew out of bed.

"OW!" came the cry from by the bed.

Josh gasped as he saw Jordan there.

Jared moaned as he rolled over in his bed and muttered. "You two had better be quiet or dad will be back in here."

Josh was still breathing hard as he turned to look at Jordan.

Jordan looked at him as he rubbed his head. "I didn't mean to make you crack my head when you woke up." he grumbled.

Josh shuttered. "I'm sorry, Jordan. I-"

Jordan shrugged. "I guess you were having a nightmare. You were hollering in your sleep. I thought I would wake you up so you didn't wake up everyone else and have Dad mad at you again."

Josh nodded. "Thanks."

Jordan walked back to his bed still rubbing his head. "You have a hard head. That hurt worse then hitting my head on the top bunk when I sit up too fast." He turned his head to look at Josh, but couldn't see him well enough to see what he was thinking. "What was it about, Josh? The nightmare, I mean?"

Josh shuttered. There was no way he was going to tell them what his dad was really like. He wasn't ever going to let them see that side of his dad, not if he could help it. Not ever. "Never mind, Jordan. It was just a bad dream. Thanks for waking me."

Jordan rolled back over. "Good night, Josh."

Josh lay back down. "Good night, Jordan." It was only as he started to lay back down that he realized he was soaked with sweat.

Jordan rolled back over and looked at Josh. "Are you sure you are okay, Josh?"

Josh nodded even though he knew it was too dark for Jordan to see him. "It's okay, Jordan. Really. Don't worry about it. I'm fine."

Jordan shrugged as he rolled over and went back to sleep.

Josh lay in bed, forcing himself to stay awake. He couldn't dream if he didn't sleep, and he couldn't sleep. Not when sleep brought back all the nightmares.

The next morning as they all sat down at the table, Jim noted how tired Joshua looked. It puzzled him, but he let it go without comment. He would wait and see what happened later. If it didn't get better he would ask him about it, but maybe he was just having trouble getting use to a new place.

Shortly after breakfast he left for work with a warning to all three boys to get along and not cause trouble for their mom.

Later that morning Lilly asked the boys to clean out the car and wash it.

Jordan and Jared let out a glad whoop and ran to get the stuff they needed.

Josh followed them a bit hesitantly, unsure if Lilly had been addressing him as well or not. He stepped outside and saw both boys already by the car.

"Come on, Josh!" Jordan called. "This is our favorite job in the summer. We use to do it for all our neighbors too. It was a great way to make a little cash, but more so to have some great fun."

Josh walked toward them and saw that look in Jared's eye. Quickly he stepped back, but not far enough. Jared sprayed the hose in his direction soaking him.

Soon water was flying everywhere and the boys were having a grand time.

20

The days passed, and slowly Josh got use to the new family and the new home. He was still afraid of his dad, but so far the man hadn't raised a hand to him. Every time there was a conflict Josh became more afraid that his dad would whip him, but still, every time the boys got into trouble he took the blame on himself.

Jared continually got them into trouble, but Jordan was beginning to worry that there was something going on with Josh that they weren't seeing. He wasn't eating, so he was losing weight. There were dark circles under his eyes, and Jordan knew he was having nightmares almost every night. He saw a tension between his dad and Josh and wondered what it was. He started praying for them, but couldn't shake the fear that something was happening with Josh that he didn't know.

Jared still had a fear that his dad would show favoritism to Josh and this had sprung up a jealousy in him that he wasn't happy with. Still it never happened. Dad treated them all equally. No matter what had happened if there was trouble they were all in it together and they all got punished.

Josh slept little, always scared that his nightmares would give away something about his dad, or he would wake the others with them. He feared what would happen if his dad knew he was having nightmares. He forgot God's promise to be with him and instead let fear take hold of him. He feared that he would give away to Jordan and Jared and Lilly what his life had been like, but even more so, he feared that he would soon be forced to live through it all again. As a result of all his fear, he began to withdraw from the family.

Jordan and Jared knew that Josh wasn't sleeping well, and they figured it was because of the nightmares, for there were some nights when they would wake him because he was screaming in his sleep and other nights he would wake them as he gasped and bolted up in bed.

The boys began to wonder what was going on. They wanted to talk to their dad about it, but weren't sure if Josh would want them to. They were afraid that something was really wrong, but they were unsure of how to help. They tried to get him to talk, but he just told them it wasn't a big deal and not to worry about it.

July finally gave way to August and one morning at breakfast Jim decided it was time to talk with the boys about a few changes that were going to be happening very soon.

They were just finishing breakfast when he looked over to see Joshua asleep with his head on the table. He shook his head. What was going on with his son? The boy always said everything was fine, but he looked as though he was exhausted all the time. Was he not sleeping? He made a mental note to himself to talk with Jared and Jordan about it later.

"Joshua, get up," he ordered as Lilly stood to clear the table.

Josh jerked his head up. He couldn't believe he had fallen asleep at the table. "I'm sorry, sir." he muttered still half asleep.

Jim frowned. He wished that Joshua would call him Dad more, instead of Sir, but he also chided himself, because he was the one who had trained him that way. "Joshua, what is going on? What are you boys doing all night that is keeping you from sleeping?" His look took in all three of them, but his eyes stayed on Josh.

Josh looked away, afraid to tell his dad the truth, yet knowing better than to tell a lie.

His father shook his head and turned to Jared and Jordan. "Jared, Jordan, what is going on?"

Jared shrugged.

Jordan hesitated. Jared slept through most of the nights that Josh had nightmares, but Jordan woke with most of them. Should he tell his dad about them. He glanced at Josh and saw the pleading look in his eyes and knew that Josh wanted him to keep quiet.

"Nothing, Dad," he finally replied. It wasn't his place to say something. He didn't know all that was going on. And he didn't want to make the tension between them worse.

Jim turned his gaze back to Josh and frowned, "Your brothers don't seem to be as tired as you are. What is going on, son?"

Josh trembled. He wanted with everything in him to say nothing, or to tell his dad that everything was fine, but he had learned long ago, at the end of a belt, to never tell his father a half truth.

He looked up into his father's eyes and trembled even more. "I just haven't been able to sleep well, Sir."

Jim waited.

Josh saw the look in his father's eye and knew his father was going to consider that a half truth. He dropped his head. He was too ashamed to tell, but he knew he had to. "I have been having nightmares, sir," he whispered.

Jim nodded, suddenly understanding the boy's hesitance to talk. "We will talk about it later then, son."

Josh nodded slightly as his father looked at all three of them again. His stomach turned. What was his dad going to do to him when he talked with him alone? He trembled.

Jim was unaware of Josh's fear and continued on with what he was wanting to say. "It is time we talked about school."

Josh felt a new knot form in his stomach. He had been homeschooling since he had moved in with Luke and Annie. He hadn't given it a thought that he would have to go back to regular school. He bit his lip to keep back the groan that was rising in his throat as he realized this was going to change everything for him. He wouldn't be graduating in the middle of the year and going to college for the spring semester. Would he even be allowed to be senior this year, or would he have to do his senior classes over again that he had already completed?

Jim looked directly at Joshua. "I know that Annie home-schooled you, Josh, when you lived with them, but your mom and I talked, and we think it would be best for all concerned if we send you boys to school this year; what with your mom having the new baby and you all being in high school and in the same grade. I think it will be best.

Josh bit his lip to hold back his argument.

Jordan and Jared stared at their dad. "You actually talked about letting us stay home and do school here?"

Jim shook his head. "We talked about it, but not this year. Your mom is going to be too busy. You are entering your sophomore year of high school I think it will be good for you to be in a public school for this time in your life. You will have a few years left of school. We will see what happens at the end of this year. It will be good for you to be in school. Maybe you won't be fighting among yourselves so much."

Josh jerked his head up. There was no way he was going to do three years of high school again. He was a senior this year. Again he bit his lip. There was also no way for his dad to know that. He hadn't asked, so he hadn't been told.

Jim smiled at all of them as if it was a wonderful thing that he was doing. "We will go to the school in the next couple of days to get you registered. I think school starts like the twentieth or something like that of this month. We will get that all figured out when we get you all registered."

Josh bit his lip again and tasted blood.

"Joshua-" his dad intruded his thoughts.

Josh jumped when he heard his dad's voice. Quickly he looked up at him.

"Is there something you want to say? You are biting that lip so hard that you have it bleeding.

Josh trembled. He didn't want to talk to his dad about this, but he knew he had to. "I-ah-well- you see- Dad – I – I'm going to be a senior this year not a sophomore." He hung his head, waiting for his dad to hit him and call him a liar.

Jim looked at his son in surprise. "But you will only be fifteen when school starts! You won't turn sixteen till a couple of weeks after it starts."

Josh nodded slightly, "Yes, Sir. I did eighth and ninth in the same year and then I did tenth and eleventh last year. Annie has all my records and credits if you need them.

Jim sat stunned for a moment. Maybe Lilly was right. Maybe the boys being schooled at home would be a good thing. Slowly he shook his head. It wasn't a good time to let the boys do their school at home. Lilly didn't need the added stress of school, not with the baby on the way. The baby would be here by then.

He looked at Josh again and saw the fear in the boy's eyes. "All right, Son, I will go and talk to Annie about your records before

180

we register you boys for school."

Josh nodded slightly. He then glanced at Jared and Jordan. They were glaring at him, and he knew that somehow him being that far ahead of them in school was going to be a problem.

At that moment Lilly walked in with a hand on her stomach. "Jim, I think it's time," she gasped.

Jim jumped up and stared at her in surprise. "Already! It's not due for a few more weeks."

Lilly laughed. "Well, babies have been known to come early from time to time, my love." She groaned and sweat broke out on her forehead.

Jim turned to the boys. "The plan is for you kids to stay with Luke and Annie while mom is in the hospital. One of you go upstairs and get your little sister, now! We will drop you all off on our way to the hospital."

Josh bolted up the stairs and returned a few moments later with a still soundly sleeping Julia in his arms.

As they all bundled into the car Jared and Jordan started in. "Dad, can't we go to the hospital? Please, we can wait there. We will be good."

Jim shook his head. "You kids don't want to go wait around at a hospital all day. Luke and Annie will bring you after the baby is here."

But Jared and Jordan wouldn't let it lay. "Please, Dad. Mom, please, let us go. We will be good, I promise. Please let us go and stay at the hospital at least till it's born. Please."

Josh trembled. He wouldn't dare ever talk to his dad like that. When his dad said no, it meant no. If there was even a hint of disagreement, he learned that he was to keep it to himself, very quickly.

Jared and Jordan kept up their pleading till they were stopped at Luke and Annie's.

Jim glanced in the back seat and noted the look of fear in Josh's eyes. He wondered if the boy was thinking about his own mamma. He shook his head. How could that be? He hadn't been but two years old when his mamma had died. He surely couldn't remember her.

His head rang with Jordan and Jared's constant whine. Finally he gave in. "Okay, but only until the baby is born. Then you will go

181

home and no more arguments about it, am I understood?"

"Yes!" Jordan and Jared cried together.

Josh bit his lip wondering if there was going to be any consequences to staying at the hospital or for the boy's constant whine, but his dad said nothing more about it.

He simply picked up the sleeping Julia and ran into the house. After a few minute conversation at the front door he walked back to the car looking happy.

Lilly glanced over at him as he got in. "Jim, get moving we don't have much time."

Jim looked at her in surprise. Was she right? Then he saw how serious she was by the look in her eyes, and he hurried as fast as he could safely go to the hospital. He pulled up in front of the emergency door and started to get out, but Josh was already out and helping Lilly into a wheel chair. The other two boys were quickly emerging from the car.

Josh looked up at him, "Go on and park, Dad. I'll help her inside."

Jim looked at him in surprise, then nodded and climbed back in the car.

Josh pushed Lilly into the hospital and straight back to the delivery rooms. He rang the buzzer and turned to see Jordan and Jared running to keep up.

A nurse opened the door and smiled as she saw the boys. "Can I help you?" Then she saw Lilly. "Mrs. Johnson, is the baby coming?"

Lilly's face was white now as she nodded her head. Pain was evident on her face.

The nurse looked up at the three boys. "We will take it from here. You go on into the waiting room, just down the hall. We will come and get you when it is all over and you can come in and see your new sibling. Is your dad on the way? I hope so. He is the doctor."

Josh's face paled. "He was parking the car. I am sure he will be in soon." Josh felt his stomach tighten even more. His dad was still using the name Johnson. Why? Why didn't he use his real name?

The nurse nodded. "Alright, boys, go on. I am sure your dad will let you know when it gets here."

All three of then nodded in unison as they turned to go. They had no sooner stepped into the waiting room then their dad ran by.

182

Seeing them he stopped.

Josh looked up at him with tears in his eyes. "She's in there. You better go or you may miss it."

Fear laced through him. He had missed this fourteen years ago. He had missed being there for his wife. He had missed the birth of their daughter and in so doing he had missed her life which was so short and also the death of his wife. If only he had been there to help he could have done something.

Josh's words rang through his head again. *You better go or you'll miss it.* Those had been the exact words of his brother John when Mary, his first wife had gone into labor.

His face grew white with fear, and he turned and ran down the hall.

Josh watched his dad run off down the hall then looked at his brothers.

Jared and Jordan looked back at him, then looked at each other. "What was that all about?" Jordan whispered.

Jared shrugged, but Josh turned away. His mind was riddled with memories. He tried to push away the fear that ate at him, but he just couldn't do it. The memories coupled with the knowledge that his dad was still going under another name was making him sick to his stomach.

Was his dad not using Peterson because he didn't want anyone to know that Josh was his real son? He felt his stomach twist again at the thought. A burning started in the back of his throat and he jumped up and ran to the bathroom.

When he came back Jared and Jordan looked up at him with fear in their eyes then looked down. Josh sat down beside them and waited quietly not knowing what to do.

183

21

Josh sat in a chair with his head down. He remembered little of his mamma. He remembered little about what his dad was like before she was gone, but he remembered all too well what life had been like after she died. Would that happen again? What if something happened to Lilly?

Why was it some women could bring a baby into the world with no trouble and others died in doing so? It didn't seem fair. He shook his head. He didn't want to think about it. Slowly he stood and walked to the window. He saw Jordan and Jared watching him out of the corner of his eye.

Why didn't his dad get after them when they were silly or naughty? Why did he let them get away with back talking him? Josh knew if he had talked to his dad like they had on the way here, he would have felt the back of his dad hand on his mouth, even now, even though he was almost sixteen. He knew his dad said he wouldn't hit him, but if he did some of the things they did, he was sure he would.

He turned back to the door just as his dad walked in. He froze. Was it good news? His dad was smiling, so hopefully that meant it was good news.

Jim looked at all three of them with a broad smile. "It's here. Mom and baby are both doing great. Would you boys like to come back and see it?"

Josh hung back, suddenly feeling out of place and awkward.

But Jared and Jordan let out happy shouts and jumped up from their seats.

Their dad looked at them with a smile, "Quiet, boys, there are people here who are trying to sleep." Jim tried to sound stern, but he couldn't. He was too happy.

Both Jared and Jordan calmed down quickly, but not immediately. Josh was surprised that his dad didn't say anything more to them. Would he ever get use to seeing that in his dad? He knew he wouldn't ever try it to see if he could get by with it. He wouldn't get by with it. He didn't have to try to know that. It seemed so unfair that his dad didn't punish them for the naughty stuff they did, but yet he did him.

Slowly they all walked back to the room. The boys quietly opened the door and stepped in. All three of them hung back a little, unsure of what to do.

Jared remembered when Julia was born and wondered immediately if this baby was a boy or a girl. His dad hadn't said, and he hadn't asked. He wanted to be surprised when he saw it.

Their mom looked up at them with a smile. "Come on in, boys," she whispered. She looked exhausted and sounded just as tired.

Jared and Jordan stepped up to the bed and looked down at the small bundle in their mom's arms. Jordan gasp, "What a beautiful baby, Mom."

Josh again had that awkward, out of place feeling, and stayed back by the door. He felt like a stranger, an outsider. This wasn't his family. He didn't belong here. It was his dad's family, but not his. He took a step back, wanting to leave. Not wanting to be where he didn't belong.

Lilly looked up at him and smiled, but her heart tore. She saw the pained look in Josh's eyes and knew, somehow, what he was feeling. She wished that he would see that she wanted him to be a part of this family just as much as the rest of them were. She wanted him to know that she loved him as much as she loved the other kids, but she wasn't sure how. She just knew she had to keep trying, even though every attempt so far had just made him seem to pull away from her more. "Josh aren't you going to come and have a look?" she whispered.

He hesitated and cast a quick glance at his dad. Fear trickled through him. He wasn't sure how he should respond. He wasn't sure if his dad wanted him around or not. And he wasn't sure if trying to be a part of this family at the moment was going to get him into trouble or not.

Lilly saw the look and a frown creased her brow. Had Jim done something to his son? Had he said something to him to make him feel like he didn't belong?

Slowly and hesitantly Josh walked up to the bed and looked down at the small, sleeping baby in Lilly's arms. "He is beautiful, Lil - Mom." he whispered, so as not to wake the sleeping bundle.

Lilly smiled slightly that Josh had called her mom. She hoped that meant they were making a little progress.

Jared and Jordan looked at him in surprise. "How did you know it was a boy?" Jealousy ripped through them. They looked at their dad. Had he told Josh what the baby was and not told them. That wasn't fair! "You told him and not us! That's not fair! Why didn't you tell us?"

Jim held up his hands as though in defeat. "I haven't said a word to any of you." He looked at Josh with a smile. "What makes you think it is a boy?"

Josh shrugged, "He has good broad shoulders and looks like a boy. I just guessed."

Both other boys looked at their mom for assurance then glanced at their dad.

Lilly smiled and nodded, "Yes, boys, you have a new baby brother." She looked up at Jim and smiled even deeper. Love shone out of her eyes toward him.

Jim smiled. "That's right, boys. You have a new baby brother. I have a new son."

Josh heard the pride in his father's voice. His stomach turned. He wished his dad could sound that proud of him, but he knew no matter what he did, his dad was always going to be disappointed in him. Hadn't he said as much? Every time he had hit him, he had let him know just how worthless he was.

Josh shook his head. He couldn't think about that now. He couldn't live that way. He tried to push away his pain, but it kept coming up bigger and bigger.

He turned away, tears stinging his eyes.

Lilly had seen the pain in his eyes when his dad spoke, and something in her hurt worse. She saw the look he had when he glanced at his dad. She knew that Josh just wanted his dad to care about him. He wanted his dad to be proud of him and tell him that. She suddenly understood more than she had before. That look in Josh's eye, was a look that held such longing she wondered how she had missed it before. He just wanted his dad to love him.

She glanced at Jim. She was going to have to talk to him about this. She knew that Jim loved Joshua, but had he told him that in the time that Josh had been living with them? She tried to think back. Maybe at night when they told them goodnight, but that would have been just a generic to all the boys. Had Jim ever told his son that he loved him? She pushed the thought away. Surely he had when Josh was younger.

She smiled at the boys, pushing her worry aside till she could talk to Jim about it. "How would you like to hold him. Josh, why don't you go first."

Josh paled. He looked at his dad again. "I-"

Jim smiled and nodded. "Go ahead, Son."

Josh trembled as he stepped up to the bed. He didn't want to do something wrong. What if he did? He shivered. He had to do it all right. He just had to. Slowly he reached out and picked up the small bundle as Lilly held it up to him.

His fear increased as he looked down at the baby. Would his dad someday beat this baby too? He hoped not, but what if he did?

Josh felt a protectiveness rise up inside of him. He vowed to keep his little brother safe if he could. No matter the pain caused to him, he would look out for his little brother.

After Jordan and Jared had each had a turn Jim lay the sleeping baby in his bed and turned to Lilly. I am going to take the boys back to the house. I will be back to spend the night here with you. Luke and Annie said that Julia can stay with them. But," he turned to the boys, "you will go straight to bed at bed time and when you get up in the morning you will go over to Luke and Annie's, till we come home from the hospital. Is that understood? I realize that it is early afternoon, but there had better be no problems at home. If there is you can be sure this will not happen again. I am trusting all of you to behave."

"Yes, sir." the three of them said in unison.

Jim leaned down and kissed Lilly, then walked out the door.

The boys all said goodbye and walked out also, following

their dad timidly.

Jim was quiet as he drove the boys home. He wasn't sure if he should be leaving them alone for the night. He was sure that Josh would behave, but he wasn't sure about the other two. He looked at them all as he parked in the driveway. "I am trusting all of you to behave. When bed time comes I want you all to go straight to bed, no goofing off. No playing around. Go to bed, go to sleep. When you get up in the morning, call the pastor. Him or Annie will come and get you. Got it."

"Yes, sir." the answer came in unison.

Jim nodded. "Alright then. There are leftovers in the fridge for supper. I don't want any fighting over any thing. It's only two o'clock so you have a while to get a long." He gave them all a pointed look. "Good night. I'll see you tomorrow." He looked Josh in the eye. "Behave."

The boys got out and watched as their dad drove away. Then in unison they all three turned and headed to the house. It was early yet, and the small amount of lunch they had eaten in the hospital had worn off long ago.

"First stop is the kitchen." Jared announced as they entered the house. "I am starving."

Josh and Jordan agreed. It didn't take them long to warm up leftovers and make sandwiches. After they ate they sat down in the living room and played a couple games. After the games were finished they decided to find more to eat. By the time they were done with that it had grown dark and they decided to go up stairs. It seemed so different at home without their mom and dad.

22

As they got ready for bed Jared got an ornery streak again. "It's nice not having mom and dad at home. Not that I would like for it to be that way all the time, but it is nice just for one night, just us boys being here." Jared grinned and Josh and Jordan instantly knew he was up to something. "You know it's kind of like a camp out, only more comfortable, and we have a bathroom."

Josh shook his head as he got into bed and laid down. "Don't sound too much like a camp out to me."

Jared laughed, "Josh, do you know the best part about parents not being home?" Jared gripped his pillow tightly and stepped toward Josh's bed, hoping Josh wouldn't look at him.

Josh heard the mischievousness in Jared's voice and turned his head just in time to see the pillow head his direction.

"No one here to tell us to go to seep!" Jared cried. "It is way past time for us to have a pillow fight!"

Josh rolled to get away, but Jared smacked him with the pillow anyway. Jordan let out an excited, wild yell and leaped out of bed, pillow in hand.

Josh held back. "But Dad said-"

Jordan laughed. "They won't ever know, Josh. Come on, just one good old fashioned pillow fight. It will be lots of fun." Jordan and Jared both stood ready to pounce whether he said yes or no.

189

Josh looked at them, knowing what they were thinking. He trembled. What would Dad do to him, if he found out? Then he thought of all the things that Jared and Jordan did that his dad use to whip him for. He hadn't ever even swatted them that Josh had seen. He shrugged. Maybe it would be fun. He reached up and gripped his pillow. In one quick movement he was out of bed. He jerk and swung at the same time slugging Jared with the pillow.

Jared stumbled backward from the force of the hit and ran into Jordan who slammed his pillow into him, making him stumble the other way.

Jared, half blinded by laughter, swung his pillow hard, but there was no one in front of him. All he hit was the lamp, which fell to the floor with a crash and shattered.

Jordan and Josh froze. All three stared in horror at the broken lamp.

Josh looked at Jared and Jordan, who looked back at him, their eyes wide. Josh knew someone had to take charge and he figure from the looks of them, it was going to have to be him. "We had better get this cleaned up. Jared get the dust pan. Jordan get the vacuum." He ran and got the broom.

With the three of them working together, they had the mess cleaned up in no time, but the trouble still remained of who was going to tell their dad that the lamp had been broken, because they disobeyed.

Josh shivered as he thought about it. He glanced at Jordan and Jared. They were looking at him, with fear in their eyes. Jared said in a small voice, "Who is going to tell Dad what happened?"

Josh bit his lip. Fear trickled through him, but he didn't let it show. He didn't want to tell his dad, but he didn't want the others to be on the receiving end of his fathers wrath either. He took a deep breath. "I'll do it," he whispered.

Jordan let out a sigh. "Good. Maybe we won't get in so much trouble then."

Josh looked at him questioningly. "What do you mean?"

Jordan shrugged as he glanced sideways at Jared. "Oh, you know, with you being his son and all, and us just being his step sons, if you tell him, it will probably go over better. You know, like, he won't be so mad. If Jared or I told him, we would probably get sent to our rooms for the evening with no supper, but if you tell him, maybe he will just shake his head at us, and tell us we should have been better behaved or something like that."

Jared shrugged. "Yeah. You know he wouldn't punish you as bad as he would us. So like Jordan said it's best if you tell."

Josh stared at them in disbelief. Did they really think that Dad was going to give him special treatment! He shook his head. He would get special treatment alright.

He trembled. He was sure from watching over the last couple of weeks that, Jordan and Jared were right about one thing, his dad would punish him different from them. He shook his head as he trembled. His back tingled in remembrance. How bad was his dad going to hit him?

It wasn't just for the lamp, but for everything. Josh had quietly taken the blame over the last couple of weeks, for anything that had been done that shouldn't. The water fight in the bathroom, which moved out into the hall and got the carpet wet, the wrestling match in the living room, Jared getting a bloody nose because someone had punched him, the other two misbehaving in church, the broken board on the bed when they had been jumping on it. Josh shivered again.

Each time he had taken the blame. His dad hadn't hit him, but he felt his father's anger rising. What would he do to him this time? So far all three boys had been sent to their room with no supper about five times, but this was bigger than that. Their dad had trusted them to be alone, and they had disobeyed him on purpose. They had known what the rules were and they deliberately broken them.

Josh moaned as he thought about what his punishment would probably be. Then he looked at Jordan and Jared. Had they done this on purpose to get him in trouble? Were they doing all these things to get him in trouble and see what would happen?

He shivered, lay down in bed and rolled over to face the wall, "Your right. He won't punish you the same," he muttered under his breath. Why did his dad hit him and not them? It didn't really make sense, and it wasn't fair.

Jared looked at Josh laying in bed and shook his head, "What did you just say?"

Josh bit his lip. He wouldn't let the boys know what his dad had done to him in the past. It wasn't right to tell and make them afraid of him too. "Nothing. Don't worry about it."

Jordan glanced at Jared and they both shrugged, fell silent and climbed into bed.

Josh awoke a little while later with a scream. He was dripping with sweat. Fear gripped him as the realness of his dream surrounded him. "God," he whispered, "You told me you would be with me and help me. I need you. Please help. I don't want Dad to hit them, but I don't want him to hit me either. Please help. Please."

He shivered.

Jordan rolled over and saw Josh sitting up in bed, "Josh, what is wrong?" he whispered. He had heard him cry out.

Josh shivered even harder. "Nothing, Jordan. Don't worry about it. Just a dumb dream."

Jordan shrugged and rolled back over to go back to sleep.

Josh trembled again. "God, I know you have everything under control, but if he is going to hit me, would you just have him do it and get it over with. Please don't make me live like this. Please."

The following afternoon, Jim and Lilly stopped by Luke and Annie's to pick them and Julia up on their way home from the hospital in the new mini van Jim had purchased that morning. On the way home, Jim noticed that all three boys were unusually quiet. He was use to Josh being quieter, but there was something about him this time, something that said he was troubled about something.

Lilly smiled, "I haven't seen you three this quiet before. What is going on? Is something wrong?"

Jordan glanced sideways at his brothers, both of whom shook their heads at him. "Just don't want to wake the baby, Mom." he answered softly.

Jim glanced in the mirror and saw Josh's face grow paler. He instantly knew that Jordan wasn't telling the truth. Not the whole truth anyway. He was keeping something from them. Jim felt his stomach turn. What had the boys done now?

They walked to the house in silence. Once they were inside, Jim turned back to the boys. They all looked at him guiltily. Jim frowned. "All three of you go to the living room. I am going to help mama to bed and then I will be back down to talk to you. Understood?"

"Yes, sir," Jared and Jordan answered together.

Josh hung back a little.

Jim frowned and stepped toward him.

Josh jumped back and looked his dad in the eye. "Yes, sir," his voice shook slightly. Jared and Jordan noticed it and glanced at each other again.

As Jim turned toward the stairs with Lilly, Jordan watched Josh. In the moment that his dad had stepped toward Josh, Jordan saw something different. Inside he felt hurt. Josh wasn't just faking it. He saw it in his eyes. He was scared of Dad. Why? What had Dad done to him? A cold knot started in his stomach. What was really going on?

Jim helped Lilly into bed, leaned down and kissed her, then lay the sleeping infant beside her. "Now, you won't have to get up to get him when he is hungry. I don't know how long I will be with the boys."

Lilly smiled. "Going to see what is making them so quiet?"

Jim nodded, but his eyes looked thoughtful. "Will you be okay here?"

Lilly nodded. "We will be fine. I think we all just need some rest." She looked down at the baby, "Look at him. Do you think he already knows we are home? He seems to."

Jim shrugged, distracted by the trouble with the boys.

Lilly smiled as she placed her hand on her husband's arm. "I am sure it is nothing. They probably just had a little spat and they don't want to tell you about it, because they don't want to disappoint you when you left them here by themselves."

Jim wished he could believe that, but he was pretty sure it was more.

Lilly smiled at him slightly. "Just think about what I said before, honey, with Josh."

Jim nodded again. "I will, sweet heart, but I am just not sure it's true."

Lilly smiled weakly. "Jim, he just needs to know you care."

Jim nodded and turned to go. "Get some rest, honey. I will be back soon."

As he walked back down the hall toward the stairs, he passed the boy's room and noticed it looked different. He looked again to be sure. Yes, it was. The lamp was missing. What had they done with it? He shrugged and headed back downstairs. He would have to ask them about that, after he found out what was wrong with them. Why were they being so quiet? What had they been up to?

All three boys were seated on the sofa when he reached the room. He stopped just outside the door and peeked in. Josh sat with his head down, looking guilty of some wrong doing. The other two sat there looking pensive, but not acting as if something was amiss.

"You boys have something you want to say?" he asked as he stepped in the room.

Josh jumped, but the other two just looked up at him.

Slowly Josh raised his eyes to look at his dad. Fear ran through him. Jared and Jordan said Dad had never hit them, but what was going to happen this time? He just hoped his dad didn't hit them too. "It's my fault, Dad." he whispered unsure of how to start.

Jim raised his eyebrows. "What do you mean your fault?"

Josh kept his eyes glued to his dad as he stood, not allowing himself even a sideways glance at Jared and Jordan. "I disobeyed you and-and started a pillow fight last night. We knocked a lamp over and broke it." He trembled as he looked straight into his dad's eyes. He wished he could back away from his dad as fear raced through him, but there was no where to go except to sit back down on the couch, and there was no way he was doing that.

Jim nodded slightly wondering if it really was Josh's fault, or if the boy was just taking the blame for it. He looked over at Jared and Jordan. "And what do you two have to say about this?"

They both hung their heads. "We are sorry, Dad. We didn't mean to break the lamp. It just accidentally got knocked over, and it broke. We are sorry."

Jim looked at all three of them with pain in his eyes. "It's not just the lamp that concerns me. I trusted you. You all three heard me last night when I told you to go straight to bed and not to be goofing off. But you deliberately disobeyed me and had a pillow fight. I want to know whose idea it really was, and who really started it."

194

Jared hung his head. He knew he was to blame, but he felt something rise in him. Why was their dad acting liked he didn't believe Josh had started it? Favoritism. That's what it was. He like Josh better because he was his actual son. Jared felt his temper rise. Dad didn't want to admit to it being Josh that started it. He wanted them all to get punished equally. It wasn't fair that if he admitted to it, he was sure, Josh would get off scott free and him and Jordan would be the ones in trouble. *Josh was the one who broke the lamp,* he told himself. *It's not fair. Dad is just playing favorites and won't believe Josh did it. He thinks Josh is too perfect.*

Josh knew his dad would demand and answer and he knew the other two were not going to tell who really did it. If they did his dad would punish him for lying. Slowly he lifted his eyes. "I did, Dad. I already told you."

Jim frowned at him as he reached down and unbuckled his belt. Pain stabbed his heart. He didn't want to hit any of them, but he had to let Josh know where the boundaries were. He couldn't just let this keep going. It just seemed like the boy was trying to see what all he could do without getting punished.

It was time he showed the boy with a little more clarity where those boundaries were. He had to show him there were going to be consequences when those boundaries were crossed. Sending him to his room didn't work. Going without supper and being sent to his room hadn't worked. He didn't want this to happen, but he couldn't just let it go any more. Even though the boy was fifteen, he had to learn.

What more would he do if he didn't punish him now? He didn't want to know. It was time to put a stop to this little act of rebellion Josh was displaying. He knew Josh knew to obey. "Seems to me you were the one behind the water fight last week and the wrestling match a few days ago."

Josh flinched. He knew what was coming, but he didn't say anything. He only hoped that his dad wouldn't whip him in front of the other two.

Jim felt his heart begin to hammer. "It also seems to me that if there has been a fight in the house over the past month and a half that you have been here, it has been you who started it. What do I need to do to you, Joshua? Sending you to your room hasn't worked, making you go without supper hasn't worked. Is there only one kind of punishment that you understand, Joshua?"

Josh trembled as his father pulled off his belt. He looked up at him with fear filled eye, then dropped his gaze. "Yes, sir." His voice broke. He wanted to fight it. He wanted to tell his dad the truth, but he knew if he did Jared and Jordan would be in trouble too, and he would just get a beating for lying.

Jared and Jordan trembled also. They hadn't ever been hit, except for the time their mom had dated the man who had hated them and he had belted them every day, until their mom found out about what was going on and dumped him. But Dad had only spanked them once or twice and it had only ever been with his hand.

Jordan suddenly felt guilty. Josh wasn't to blame for this. He hadn't wanted to fight. He wasn't the one who had started all the fights. Jordan and Jared had done that to try and get Josh in trouble, Jordan knew. But Josh had willingly taken the blame so they wouldn't get into trouble. He had done it even though he knew his dad wouldn't like it. Jordan suddenly saw something in Josh.

Josh had known his dad would hit him. He knew his dad wouldn't favor him over them, but he had taken the blame anyway. That was what he had said yesterday when he was in bed. He had just tried to keep them from knowing what he was scared of. Jordan hung his head in shame. Yet he wasn't ashamed enough to admit the truth.

Jim gripped Josh's arm tightly with one hand and the belt with the other. "It's time for you to understand something, son. You are not going to get away with breaking the rules. You know to behave and I don't know why you are having a time of rebellion, but it is going to stop now. Is that clear?"

Josh dropped his head. "Yes, sir."

Jim turned to Jared and Jordan. "Both of you go to your room. I will be up to talk to you both in a few minutes."

Josh trembled as his brothers left the room, leaving him alone with his dad.

Jim turned back to him after the other two had left. "Are you just testing the boundaries, son. Do you not know where they lie anymore?"

Josh dropped his head even lower.

Jim sighed. "Son, I don't want to have to do this, but you are leaving me no choice. Why are you doing all these things? You have continually picked fights with your brothers, you have deliberately disobeyed me, now this. Why, son? Why?"

Josh shook his head. He knew what was coming. He looked at his dad and slowly pulled off his shirt and turned away from his dad so his back was toward him. He trembled even more as he waited.

Jim felt himself pale. Why did this have to be? Slowly he raised his belt. With one hand he gripped Josh's arm with the other he swung the belt, but he didn't hit him across his bare back as he use to do. Instead he brought the belt down across his bottom. Pain ripped through him with each snap of the belt and he wasn't sure who was being hurt worse Josh or him. His heart hurt more when he felt the boy stiffen in fear.

After several swats he lowered the belt and released Josh's arm.

Slowly Josh turned to face him. He knew his dad wasn't done, so why was he stopping? He trembled as he faced his dad.

Jim felt tears sting his eyes as he looked at Josh. "Don't you ever make me do that again, son."

Josh dropped his head. "Yes, sir."

Jim sighed, trying to get a hold of his emotions. "Go to your room, son. I will be up to talk to you and your brothers later, but you will also join them in the no supper punishment and you will remain in your room the rest of the night."

Josh slowly walked out into the hall. He frowned as he saw feet disappear ahead of him. Anger surged through him. His brothers had seen and heard everything. They knew they were to blame and then they had to watch him get punished. He pushed the thought away. At least his dad hadn't beat him this time.

Jared and Jordan were both crying when he entered the room. They ran over to him. "Josh we are so sorry. We didn't mean to make him hit you. We didn't think Dad would hit you. You hasn't ever hit us. He hasn't ever even acted like he would. We thought you were just being silly, being scared of him. We are so sorry."

Josh shrugged and looked away from them as he sank down on the bed. "It's fine. At least he didn't hit you guys too. At least it

197

was just me."

Jared and Jordan looked at each other. They didn't feel that way and they knew if they had been the one in trouble they wouldn't have felt that way either. If they would have been the one spanked they wouldn't have thought it fair that the other had gotten away with it.

"Josh we are sorry. We were jealous of you. We thought Dad would give you special treatment, we didn't think – we will tell him we were to blame not you." Jordan started.

"Don't." Josh snapped. "It's not worth talking about. And it's not worth you both getting in trouble for. Just forget it."

Jared bit his lip. He wasn't sure that he wanted to just forget it, but he wanted even less to be spanked.

Jordan stood in front of Josh. "You knew he was going to hit you, didn't you? You knew it last night when you said you would tell him, that you would take the fall for what happened. You knew then that he would hit you. How? Why did you think he was going to hit you? He hasn't in all the time you have been here. He hasn't ever stuck any of us. How did you know he was going to start now?"

Josh shrugged. "It doesn't matter Jordan, just forget it. It's over. No point in talking about it."

Jordan frowned again, but slowly walked back to his bed. "I am sorry, Josh."

Josh shrugged. His heart hurt more than his rear, but he was afraid of what had started here.

A few minutes later there was a knock at the door. "Boys," their dad called from the other side. "Can I come in?"

Josh slowly stood and opened the door.

His dad looked at him, surprised that he was the one opening the door. "Can I come in?"

Josh stepped back. Fear trickled through him. Was his dad going to hit them all?

Jim walked into the room.

Josh saw his dad's shoulders slump a little and saw the tears in his eyes.

Jim looked at his son and saw the fear in his eye. He felt so guilty for putting that fear back in his eyes. "Josh, I want to start with you."

Josh trembled, but slowly stepped up in front of his dad and waited without speaking.

Jim sighed. "Son, I am so sorry I had to hit you. I didn't ever want to do that again. And I don't ever want to have to do that again, but, even though you are fifteen, you needed it. You have to learn to obey and respect authority. Do you understand?"

Josh bit his lip to keep from telling his dad to teach it to Jared and Jordan, not him.

Jim sighed again. "I am sorry, Joshua."

Josh nodded waiting to feel the sting of the belt again.

Jim turned to Jordan and Jared. "As for you two, is there something you want to say to me?"

Jordan looked guilty, but Jared quickly shook his head.

Jim sighed. "I don't think Josh is totally responsible for everything that happened, is he?"

Jordan and Jared both shook their heads.

Josh felt himself stiffen. Was his dad trying to call his lie so he could hit him more?

Jim nodded. "I didn't think so." He paused. "You boys will do extra chores around here till you have worked off the cost of the lamp. You will all work together and I will hear no argument about it. Is that understood?"

"Yeah, Dad," Jared and Jordan replied.

Jim looked at Josh. "Son?"

Josh jumped and jerked his head up so he was looking at his dad. "Yes, sir. I understand."

Jim nodded. "Good. I will have a list of things for you to do tomorrow along with the normal."

"Yes, sir." They all three answered in unison.

"You will all stay in this room for the rest of the night. No sneaking out. No supper. I will call you for breakfast in the morning. And I better not see you out of here before that, except to take a shower."

All three nodded again. "Yes, sir."

Jim nodded. "Good. Joshua, I want you to get in the shower now. I have something to talk about with your brothers."

Josh looked at them quickly, then looked at his dad. He wanted to beg his dad not to hit them, but he knew he couldn't and even if he did it wouldn't change what his dad did. Slowly he walked out of the room. He longed to eaves drop as Jordan and Jared had

199

done, but he knew his dad would punish him more for it so he walked away.

Jim turned back to Jordan and Jared as Josh walked out of the room. "Boys, I don't think you are being very honest with me, are you?"

They both looked at him, then at each other, then back to him, but remained silent.

Jim sighed. "I don't know what is going on, but you both need to stop picking on him. I don't know why you think I am going to love him more than I do you. I am not. You are all three important to me. Don't you understand that?"

Jordan nodded. "Yes, Dad. We are sorry. We didn't mean to get him into trouble. We didn't mean to break the lamp."

Jim sighed. "Get along from now on. Understood?"

They nodded. "Yes, sir."

Jared felt something well up inside him as his dad spoke. He wasn't going to stop. His dad did like Josh better. He was sure of it. He felt jealousy run through him harder than before.

"Okay. When he gets back here, Jordan you go next and Jared last. And don't stand in there and waste all the hot water." Jim looked at both boys with a hard look.

They both laughed. "Yes, sir."

Later that night when everyone was asleep, Josh thought he heard something. Slowly he sat up in bed and listened. Then he shook his head. He had to of imagined it. No, there it was again. Was someone coming up the stairs? He shivered without knowing why.

Slowly he lay back down and waited, wondering if he would hear the sound again. Then he saw the door open. He bit back a scream, then relaxed when he saw his dad.

Jim motioned to him and he slid out of bed. Fear trickled through him. Slowly and quietly he followed his dad down the stairs and out the door. In the night air he shivered even more. His dad lead him across the yard to the garage.

He frowned but followed. Once he was inside the garage he heard his dad close and lock the door. Only then did he really start to tremble. He felt his dad grip his arm.

"Get that shirt off now, boy. You think you are getting away with what you have done?"

Josh bit his lip, but slowly obeyed. He should have known this was coming, but his dad had seemed so sincere tonight, he had wanted to believe him.

He bit his lip to keep back the cry of pain as the leather belt snapped on his back. The pain was worse than he remembered. Again the belt snapped, then again. He trembled in pain as the strikes got harder and harder. He quit counting at twenty and wondered how many more he could take without crying out. Then the belt snapped the back of his neck.

He yelped and jerked away. He knew he had only been seven when his dad had beaten him before, but he still remembered the pain. He also remembered the whipping got worse if he made a peep.

His father chuckled and he trembled. He knew it was his dad, but the chuckle didn't sound right.

It was too dark to see much, but he felt his arm gripped in a vice like squeeze.

Then he felt his own belt being unfastened. He started to shake in fear. What was his dad doing to him?

"Get them off, boy," came the growled order.

Josh shook too hard to move, but as the belt snapped on his chest he obeyed. He shook harder as his dad gripped his arm as he had earlier that day, but he knew this was going to hurt a whole lot worse.

He yelped with the first swat, and felt a hand smack his mouth. "Shut up, boy, or I will gag you."

He bit his lip to keep it back, but with the next swat which was across his legs he let out another yelp. Pain laced through him. How long would his dad keep this up. Was he really that mad at him?

He saw something dark headed for his mouth and he tried to turn away, "Please, don't," he gasped. Suddenly he found himself pinned up again the wall and a bandanna was forced between his lips. He tried to cry out, but couldn't. Fear trickled through him. Just because he was older now, he was sure his dad was going to beat him a whole lot worse than he did when he was seven.

"Leave it in there, boy, or it will get worse." The man tied it tight behind the boy's head. Then raised the belt again.

Josh tried to turn away, but there was no where to go. He wanted to scream, but he couldn't. *God, Where are you? Help me, please!*

As the morning light lit up the sky the belting finally stopped.

Josh moaned in pain as he felt himself pulled to his feet. If he didn't know better he would think this was his Uncle John not his dad. His dad hadn't ever hit him in the legs. He had always smacked his back or his bottom, but his uncle hadn't ever cared where he hit him, just so it hurt.

He trembled as he looked at the man.

John looked down at his nephew. He had waited for this moment ever since he had learned that this was his nephew. He would keep the boy believing it was his father hitting him for as long as he could, but he had to keep Josh from talking to anyone, even his dad. He felt anger surge through him when he thought about his brother being put in jail because of the boy. Then he felt more anger gush through him when he thought about all the pain his brother had been in because of Joshua.

He pulled out his gun as he pushed the boy back into the pickup.

Josh whimpered as he saw the gun. Was his dad going to get rid of him? Was he that much trouble? Was his dad just going to finish him off and be done with him? Why had he made him come here then? Why hadn't he just left him with Luke and Annie, if he really didn't want him?

Maybe it had been Lilly that thought his dad had wanted him and his dad hadn't wanted to admit how much he hated him. He trembled as he felt the gun in his stomach.

"You will not let on to anyone that I have been hitting you. Is that clear? If I can tell that I have been hitting you or you let on in the slightest bit to someone else, I will whip you harder tomorrow. Do you understand? You tell anyone what is happening and you know what will happen."

Josh got the threat loud and clear, but even the threat made him uneasy. It wasn't like his dad to threaten to kill him. To whip him yes, but kill him?

John saw the boy's reluctance. He gripped his face between his hands and forced Josh to look at him. "This is how it is going to be, boy. Do you understand?"

Josh bit his lip. "Yes, sir."

John smacked the belt on his already raw and bloody back. "Get dressed and get back into bed then. Don't you dare let on to anyone."

Josh slowly nodded as he pulled on his shirt and pants. He bit his lip in pain as the clothing touched his skin.

He watched as his dad slipped out of the garage and headed to the house.

He waited a few minutes and then slipped out into the morning dawn. Quickly, but painfully he ran to the house, slipped in and walked quietly toward the stairs. As he reached the top of the stairs he breathed a sigh of relief. So far so good. His brothers hadn't caught him yet any way. If they did, would they tell Dad, just to see if he would be in trouble when he was told to stay in his room? He bit his lip. Would his dad hit him more where the boys could see if they knew he had been out?

He reached for the door knob, but gasped as someone suddenly grasped his arm and spun him around and pinned him to the wall. He bit his lip to keep in the scream of fear and the cry of pain as he looked into his dad's eyes.

His mind raced as he thought of his father's threat just moments ago. Was he testing him?

"Joshua," Jim whispered angrily. "What are you doing out of your room? What where you doing downstairs? I told you not to come out till I called you for breakfast. Why did you disobey me?"

Josh shook. What was his dad going to do to him? He again remembered the threat. What was the right answer? Maybe his dad was testing him to see if he really could keep it secret. He trembled. "I'm sorry, Dad," he whispered. Tears sounded in his voice and he tried to turn away fearing his father was going to strike him again.

Jim frowned. "Were you eating, son?"

Josh hung his head. He had thought about sneaking into the kitchen. He was starving, but he hadn't. He had made himself come straight up stairs.

Jim took the boys silence as an answer. "Get back in your room, Joshua. Because you disobeyed me, you will come down and sit at the breakfast table and watch us eat, but you will not." Jim felt his heart wrench in pain as he saw the fear in Josh's eyes. "Do not disobey me, son. I thought I taught you better than that."

Josh dropped his head. His stomach cramped in hunger. Was his dad going to beat him and starve him to death? Did he want him out of his life that bad? Again the question filled his mind, why had he brought him here then? Why hadn't he just let him stay with Luke and Annie?

Jim frowned, deeper. "Joshua, are you listening to me?"

Josh looked up at him and Jim was surprised to see the pain in Josh's eyes. Slowly he released his hold on him.

Josh bit his lip again, to hold back a sigh. "Yes, sir."

Jim nodded and motioned for him to get in his room. Then he continued down the hall.

Josh trembled as he walked into his room. How was he suppose to keep it all a secret? He lay down on his bed with a moan. Slowly he rolled onto his stomach, hoping that would hurt less. It did some, but not much. Exhausted he closed his eyes in sleep.

Jordan heard Josh come in. He looked over at him in surprise. What had he been doing out of there room so early? Didn't he know Dad was serious about not leaving the room till breakfast. He heard Josh moan, and he bit his lip. What was going on? What would cause Josh to moan as if he were in pain? He thought about saying something, but quickly decided against it. If Josh wanted to talk to him that would be fine, but he wasn't going to ask. Not yet anyway.

23

About an hour later Jim knocked on the boy's door quietly. "Come down for breakfast boys, but be quiet as you do. The baby didn't sleep well last night, and Mama is resting now that baby is sleeping. Come on. We better get breakfast over with and get you all over to the school to get you registered. Then I have to get to work."

Jim waited.

Jared slowly opened his eyes and rolled out of bed. "Okay, Dad." he mumbled.

Jordan rolled out of bed next. He glanced at Josh's bed, and felt his stomach knot slightly. Josh was soundly sleeping, but he was laying on his stomach and his one arm was wrapped around his ribs as if he was in pain.

Jim looked at Josh also, and frowned. He reached down and shook him slightly. "Joshua, get up, son." He knew Josh had been up an hour ago and it surprised him that the boy had gone back to sleep.

Josh cried out in pain as his father's hand touched him. Quickly his eyes came open and he rolled over, falling out of bed. Trembling he scooted back. Fear filled him as he looked up into his dad's eyes. "I'm sorry, Dad, I didn't mean it." he whispered.

Jim nodded slightly. "We will talk later, son. Get up and get dressed. Time to get going on the day." As he turned to go back downstairs he felt an uneasiness in his heart. Why was Josh so scared of him? Why would he cry out from a light touch?

205

Josh nodded. "Yes, sir."

Jim turned back to him, nodded then turned and walked out.

Josh slowly stood and looked over at his brothers. Did they know what happened? Did they know that he was out of his room last night?

He grabbed clothes out of his dresser and hurried to the bathroom. Jim saw Josh head into the bathroom with his clothes and he frowned. He walked over and knocked softly on the door. "Josh, what are you doing?"

Josh trembled even more. What was his dad doing?

"Joshua, answer me now. What are you doing? Open this door now. You are not going to take a shower; you just took one last night. Open up."

Josh looked at himself in the mirror and shook his head. What now? Was he going to forbid him to change in privacy so Jordan and Jared would see what he had done to him last night. How could his dad not be tired this morning? It didn't make any sense.

Jim waited a moment, but when Josh made no attempt to open the door he opened it.

Josh jumped as the door swung open and he spun around to face his dad. He trembled as he backed up into the counter. "Dad, I-"

Jim scowled at him. "You don't need to be getting changed in the bathroom, son. You have a room. It's not going to kill you to change in front of your brothers, unless you are trying to hide something. Are you?"

Josh shook his head vigorously, but stepped away from his dad as he did. "No, Sir."

Jim stepped up closer to him.

Josh trembled. What was his dad going to do to him? Just then His stomach rumbled loudly. He flushed. Did his dad still think he was lying this morning? Well, he was, but that was because his dad told him he had to.

His heart pricked him. He knew he shouldn't ever lie, but what was he suppose to do? *Help me, God. I don't know what I am suppose to do, but I need you now more than ever. If he is going to hit me like this, God, I need strength. And if he isn't going to let me eat, I definitely need your strength. Please don't let the others find out what is happening.*

Jim waited for Josh to respond, but the boy just stood with his head down waiting, as though waiting for Jim to hit him. His conscience smote him. He shouldn't be being so hard on Josh. The poor kid had enough changes happening in his life, and Jim had just been expecting him to be happy about it. He hadn't thought about how hard it would be for Josh to adjust. He should have expected some of the behavior he was seeing.

The boy was mad and acting out. He thought he understood, but it still wasn't okay that he was acting that way.

He cleared his throat. "I'm sorry, son. I should have been easier on you. I know you aren't use to having a brother around you every minute of every day. Get dressed and get downstairs. After breakfast we have to head to the school."

Josh bit his lip. He wanted to go back to Luke and Annie's. He wanted to just finish school at home. He wanted to beg his dad to let him do it, but his fear kept him from asking. He didn't want his dad to hit him any more, but he knew it was going to happen. He just had to let it all settle. He had to learn to live with it. He was right. His dad hadn't changed. He just got better at hiding it.

Jim snapped his fingers.

Josh jumped and realized he had no idea what his dad had just said.

Jim sighed. "Get downstairs. Hurry it up."

Josh nodded slightly. "Yes, sir." He hurriedly shut the door. "God, help, please," he whispered as he rested his head on the wall. "Please help me."

Jared and Jordan sat at the table waiting. Was Josh ever going to get down here?

Jim walked over to the stairs, and forgetting the baby, he hollered, "Joshua, get down to this table now!"

Josh stumbled as he ran down the stairs. He stepped into the kitchen timidly, half expecting his dad to strike him. When he didn't, he was surprised. His stomach cramped again. He was starving. It wasn't fair. Why was Dad making him watch them all eat? That was torture. He figured that was why his dad was making him do it. Just another way to hurt him.

Jim looked up at him. "Come on, Son, let's get done with breakfast. We have got to get you all three registered for school, and I have got to get to work. Let's not waste time. Get started eating.

"When I bring you boys back home, I want you to behave for your mom. I want you to help her all you can today. She doesn't need to be up and around. And she doesn't need to be doing anything extra. Understood? There will be absolutely no problems or even fun fights between the three of you, is that understood? Your mom has enough to do with Julia and the baby. You all need to help, not stress."

He looked at all of them and his dark eyes seemed to darken even more. "There is a list of things for you all to do on the fridge. You will have it done when I get home tonight. Is that understood?"

All three nodded and Jared and Jordan quickly poured their cereal. Josh sat silently. Jim looked at him questioningly, but said nothing till they had finished praying and the other two were eating, and still Josh hadn't made a move to get breakfast. "Joshua!"

Josh jumped and looked up at his dad. He blinked hard hoping his dad wouldn't see the pain in his eyes. He wanted to get away from here. He just wanted to be alone.

Jim frowned. "Son, I just told you we are in a hurry, now get your food and get to eating."

Josh shivered. There was no way he was falling for that kind of a trick. His dad had done this before. He looked away.

Jim frowned. "Joshua?"

Josh bit his lip. He dared not look at his dad again.

Jim sighed. "Suit yourself, if you aren't going to eat then get ready to go."

Josh stood. Again his stomach cramped in hunger. For a moment he considered eating. Maybe it would be worth it. He shook his head. There was no way he was eating, not when Dad had told him no. There was no way it would be worth it later, when his dad hit him for it.

About an hour later the boys found themselves standing in the office of the high school while their dad talked to the secretary about getting them registered. She smiled a lot and seemed friendly, but

Josh still wished he could be home. Why did everything have to change? He had his life figured out. Then his dad had to come and ruin it all.

He sighed and shook his head. *I thought you had told me this was what you wanted, God. Why is everything messed up now? I don't understand. How am I suppose to follow your will for my life, when its not a possibility right now? I don't want to doubt you, God, but I am having a hard time trusting you. Please help my faith. I need you to keep me.*

Josh lifted his head as a door off the side of the office opened and the principle walked through. Josh froze. It wasn't possible, was it?

Jim turned at the same time and his eyes grew wide.

The principle stopped in the doorway and his eyes grew round also.

Jared and Jordan stared in shock. If they hadn't known it wasn't their dad coming out of the principle office, they would have been fooled. The two men, the principle and their dad, looked exactly alike. Everything about them was the same. Their smile, their eyes, their forehead, their body shape and form, the way they walked and held themselves. It was just unreal. They both looked at their dad again as if to make sure he was still standing with them.

Josh sucked in his breath. A shiver suddenly ran through him.

Jim took a step toward the man. "John is it really you? I can't believe it."

John looked at him with the same look. "Jim?"

Both of them stopped for a moment. Then they stepped toward each other and embraced. "I can't believe it. The last I knew you were in prison. What happen? Look at you. And this must be Josh." he turned his steely gaze on Josh. His eyes seemed to shoot fire.

Josh froze. Those eyes, that voice. Was it possible? He shook his head. It couldn't be, could it. How would John have known where he was?

Jim laughed. "John, I just can't believe it is you. What are you doing out here? I thought you were working back in Maine. Why the move?"

John shrugged. "Just needed the change. Needed to get the boy out of the big city. We have all adjusted well to being here. Still not like where we grew up, but oh, well. Its the best we have for now."

Jim smiled again. "I need to get these kids registered for school John. You know Josh, of course, and these other two are Jared and Jordan. I am remarried now. We just had a little boy, the wife had two and another one on the way when I met her. We make a family. How is your family, Lucy and Jonathan? Are there any more?"

Josh saw a mask slide over his Uncle John's face. It was as if a cloud had descended on him.

He shook his head. "No, there is no more. It's just me and Johnathan. Lucy died seven years ago. Car accident. Dumb drunk driver swerved in front of her." He shook his head again, "That was another reason for the move a few years back. We both needed a change."

Jim shook his head. "John, I am so sorry. I wish I would have known. If I would have – I should have tried to get in touch with you when I got out, but-"

John shook his head. "Don't." He looked at the boys, then turned back to his office, "Now, let's get these boys registered for school. It's a good thing you came in today, by the way. School starts on Thursday."

Jim looked at him in surprise. "As in tomorrow, Thursday?"

John nodded. "Started doing that here of late, because they think the kids adjust better to a short first week. So Thursday and Friday are half days, then school starts full swing on Monday."

Jim shook his head. "Sorry I took so long to get them in and registered then. I thought we had a few more weeks of summer."

John nodded. "We should have. This starting before September is ridiculous. If they want kids to adjust well to school they should just wait to start till it is time to start, but they didn't ask my opinion. Probably wouldn't have listened if I would have given it any way.

Jim nodded. "You are probably right."

John pulled the paper work out of a file cabinet. "Just fill these out. I assume they are all three going into tenth grade."

Jim nodded absently.

Josh stiffened. There was no way he was going to go through two more years of school then he had to. He bit his lip for a moment, debating on what he should say. He had already told his dad he was going to be senior this year, had he not heard him. "Dad," his voice

210

was timid and almost too soft to be heard.

Jim looked up at him. "What, son?" He felt his temper rise. He knew Josh wasn't excited about going to school and he figured they were going to have a discussion about it right now. He knew this wasn't the place, but he knew it was coming so it might as well happen here.

Josh trembled. "I'm a senior."

Jim looked at him in alarm. "What!" He slammed his fist down on the desk and stood up to face his son. His eyes snapped. Josh had to be lying!

Josh ducked his head. He saw the anger in his dad's eyes and he didn't dare say anything else.

Jared and Jordan both looked at him, with a jealous glare in their eyes. They remembered Josh telling their dad that a few nights ago when Dad had been talking about putting them in school, but apparently with all that had been happening lately, their dad forgot.

John looked up at him quickly. "We will need your transcripts from your other school. How in the world are you a senior, boy? You aren't any more then fifteen."

Josh bit his lip and looked down.

Jim understood his son's hesitancy and felt bad that he had been sharp with him. "He was home-schooled the last seven years, John. I can ask his foster mom if she has his records. Will that work? I am sorry, I should have thought of that."

John nodded, but his eyes shot sparks at Josh.

Josh trembled even more. Now more then ever he wanted to do school at home. He was scared of his uncle and he didn't mind admitting it. The man had a mean streak worse than his dad.

Jim sighed. "I won't have it to you before tomorrow unless she can get it in a few minutes. If she can I will drop it off on my way to work.

John nodded. That's fine, Jim. Just bring it by." He looked at all three boys, "You three come to my office first thing in the morning. I will have your schedules for you then. Okay?"

"Yes, sir." they all said in unison.

Josh felt his uncle watching him, and he shivered. What was going to happen at school with his uncle as principal? Was his dad going to say something to Jared and Jordan to let them know who he was. Evidently not, because they left the office a few minutes later and nothing was said.

That night Josh was again awakened by someone standing quietly by his bed. This time he put a hand over his mouth to keep him quiet and motioned for him to follow.

Josh slowly did. His temper flared. Was it his dad or his uncle? He wasn't sure. The two of them were identical. When he had been very little he remembered them trying to trick him with who was who. He hadn't ever been able to tell them apart. As he got older he learned the only difference in their appearance was his uncle had a small mole on the side of his neck that his dad didn't have. But since it was dark he couldn't see whether he had a mole or not. He knew he didn't dare risk it.

The man led him to the garage again. And again beat him mercilessly.

In pain a few hours later he quietly climbed the steps and crept into his room. As he lay down, he groaned. He bit his lip to keep back another moan as he rolled over. He didn't know how much more of this he could take and keep someone from finding out.

Jordan awoke when Josh came in. He lay silently in bed and watched him. He heard him groan as he lay down. Curiosity about got the better of him, but he forced himself to stay laying down and not let Josh know he was awake. What was going on, though? He wanted to find out more then ever. Maybe he would just have to keep himself awake, and when Josh snuck out he would have to follow him.

Josh lay in bed in too much pain to sleep. How was he suppose to live like this? Why did he have to? "I guess you were right to warn me in those dreams, God, but it hurts a whole lot more then I remembered. Please help me know what to do. Please. I'm scared, God. Really scared. Please help."

Jordan strained to hear what Josh was saying. It sounded like he was praying, but he couldn't be sure. Finally he drifted back to sleep, but his wonderment didn't go away.

24

Fists flew as the boys dove at each other.

Kids all screamed as they watched the fight. This was one of the most exciting things that had happened on the school yard for several months.

Josh felt his anger rise as he slammed his fist into Johnathan's stomach. Suddenly he felt stronger hands grip both his arms and pull him off the bigger boy.

He jerked, trying to get back at Jonathan.

Johnathan looked at Josh. Then shook his head. "Stupid kid," he snapped. "You gave me a bloody nose."

"That's enough of this." The voice was cold and hard and Josh knew the instant he heard it who it belong to. He froze.

John looked at the crowd. "All of you get back to class. If there is any more of this and you all are caught watching you will be punished as well." He gripped Josh's arms tighter. "You two get to my office."

Josh tried to jerk free, but his uncle tightened his grip. Josh wanted to cry out in pain, but he forced his mouth closed.

John pushed Josh ahead of him into the office, Johnathan followed.

"Well, what do you two have to say for yourselves?" he asked coolly.

Josh hung his head.

Johnathan glared at him. "He started it, Dad. He said something bad about Mom, then about you."

Josh's head jerked up. "I didn't either," he yelled.

John back handed him, making his head snap to the side with the force. "You be quiet, boy," he growled. "You will not yell at my son, and you will not misbehave in this school. You want to pick a fight, fine. You are going to find out just what happens to boys who start fights at this school."

Josh dropped his head. Tears burned the backs of his eyes, but there was no way he was going to let them fall.

John turned back to Johnathan. "What did he say?"

Jonathan shook his head. "I can't remember. It made me so mad, I told him that if he wanted to pick a fight he just did. And he said something about not being afraid to fight, because you are a softy for a principal."

Josh started to tremble. He knew exactly where this was going to take him.

John looked at him with a frown. "Johnathan go back to class. Josh and I need our own private meeting."

Josh bit his lip to keep from whimpering.

Johnathan turned to go. He smiled menacingly at Josh. He knew that Josh was his cousin, but he enjoyed watching him get a good thrashing. It was funny to see him in so much pain. He knew his dad wanted a reason to whip him as much as he could, he had said as much last night.

Josh glared at him as he left. When he was gone, Josh slowly turned his eyes on his uncle.

John glared at him. "You just have to test it out the first few days, Josh? Just curious how much you can get by with, on the first day?"

Josh felt his anger rise even more. He wanted to beat Johnathan to a pulp. He may take the blame for stuff at home, but he wasn't going to here. "No, sir." He locked his knees to keep from shaking in fear.

John unbuckled his belt. "You will be sorry for what you did, boy. Trust me. You will not pick a fight, and you will not insult others, and you will not ever best my boy in a fight. You understand all that?"

Josh nodded. He bit his lip to keep back the cry of pain as his uncle jerked him around and jerked off his shirt.

214

John chuckled as he saw the welts already on Josh's back from the night before. He raised the belt and brought it down with a loud smacked. The sound of the leather on Josh's flesh served to calm his temper only slightly.

John smacked him again. He was determined to make the boy yell.

Josh felt himself sinking to the floor as lash after lash fell across his now bare back. He forced himself to stay quiet. Fear that his whipping would get worse if he made a noise made him more determined than ever not to make a sound. When Uncle John finally stopped hitting him, he tried to stand, but didn't have the strength. He hadn't eaten anything since the night that Jimmy had been born and the boys were home alone. That was a few days ago.

John frowned as Josh stayed where he was. "You want more of the same, boy?" He wanted to beat him more, but he knew if he wasn't careful someone would find out what he was doing to him, and that would be the end of it.

Josh groaned as he tried to move again. Everything in him rejected.

John grabbed him and jerked him to his feet. "No more, boy. You best learn you can't escape me now. You try to tell, I will say it was your dad and he will be back in prison for life. Then think of your poor mom. She will have all of you kids to care for and no man to help."

Josh didn't dare look up.

John gripped his arms and slammed him into the wall.

This time, he couldn't hold the cry in.

John looked pleased that he had made the boy scream. "You want to behave, or do you want more?'

Josh shuttered. He knew it didn't matter what he wanted, he wasn't going to get what he wanted. He was going to get hit anyway.

John pushed him down. "Get your shirt on and get to class, boy. Now. And you better not snitch."

Josh nodded. "Yes, sir, I won't."

John frowned and motioned for him to leave.

Lilly picked the boys up from school that afternoon. She noticed a small bruise on Josh's cheek, but she said nothing. Probably just a boy squabble, she thought to herself. She was sure whatever it was, it would come out eventually.

Josh saw the look Lilly gave him and looked away. He didn't want to invite a question.

When they got home, the boys stayed busy in the yard, cleaning up brush and leaves. Jared and Jordan gave a glad cry when they saw their dad pull in, but Jordan noticed Josh held back a little, looking afraid. He frowned. What was happening with him? Why did he seem scared of his dad all of the sudden. He had seemed scared of him before, but since Jimmy had been born it was different. He seemed, Jordan didn't know, all he knew was he didn't like the feel he got. It was like ever since Dad had spanked him he acted like everything he did, Dad was going to hit him for, even if it wasn't anything wrong.

Jim smiled at the boys as he walked up. "Thank you, boys." He gave Jared and Jordan both a half a hug as he walked up to them in the yard. "How was your first day of school?"

Jared and Jordan glanced at Josh and saw him stiffen as they stopped in front of him. Jim reached out to give him a hug, but Josh stepped away. They decided for once to have pity on him and not mention what had happened with Johnathan.

"It was great!" Jared answered with enthusiasm. "I like all my teachers. I think I will do good in all my classes. Jordan and I are in all the same classes. Isn't that cool, and we get to sit together in a couple of them."

Jordan smiled at his dad, but he gave a sideways glance at Josh, wondering what he was going to say. "It was good. Everything was fine."

Jim looked to Josh.

Josh bit his lip and looked away, but Jim had already seen the bruise on his son's face.

"Joshua, how did your first day go?" He felt his anger rise. What had happened to Josh at school to give him a bruise on his face?

Josh bit his lip and tasted blood, finally he looked up at his dad. "Fine," his voice was cold and unconvincing.

Jim nodded slightly obviously not convinced. "Who was the fight with?"

216

Josh felt his knees start to buckle. He looked his dad in the eye. "It doesn't matter," he muttered. He forced himself not to fall only by locking his knees.

Jim stepped closer to him.

Josh shuttered and backed quickly away. "Just another senior, trying to strut his stuff to the new kid. It was nothing, Dad, really."

Jim shook his head. "I don't agree with you, Josh. And I think you are trying to hide something from me."

Josh looked down.

Jared and Jordan did the same.

Jim nodded. "I am right aren't I."

He looked at Jordan and Jared, both boys looked down. "You both know something about this too, don't you? One of you had better start talking. What happened at school?"

Josh trembled, but knew he had to tell his dad something or all three of them would be in trouble. "Don't, Dad. It's not their fault. It's mine. I didn't want to tell." He looked into his father's eyes. "Can I talk to you alone?"

Jim eyed Joshua with suspicion, "All right, Joshua. Come on into the house. You two," he turned back to Jordan and Jared, "Finish up this pile and then come in. I am sure supper is almost ready."

The boys nodded, but glanced at Josh, wondering what he was thinking. Was he going to fess up to everything or was he just trying to get out of finishing in the yard? What all would he really tell?

Josh paled as he walked in front of his dad to the house. He didn't want to tell anything, and he for sure didn't want to tell about the whipping he had gotten. Afraid that his dad would give him one to match it,he thought it would be best if he just didn't say anything at all. But he wasn't sure what all to say. How much would be enough for his dad to let it go, and not enough to give away what all had happened?

He shivered again as he thought about what was coming tomorrow at school, and fear of what his dad would do to him tonight, if it was his dad whipping him at night. He was beginning to have his doubts that it was him.

Jim stopped the boy in the living room. "Alright, son, we are alone here. Tell me what happened."

Josh looked down. Slowly he raised his eyes and looked strait at his dad. "I got into a fight."

Jim nodded. "I can see. Who with, son."

Josh shivered again at hearing his dad call him son. Tears burned his eyes, and he looked quickly away so that his dad wouldn't see. "It doesn't really matter does it?"

Jim shook his head. "Are you testing me to see if you can get away with fighting in school?" His voice held the warning that Josh had heard many times before, but it was also as if his dad was hurting.

He looked up at his dad. He saw sadness in his dad's eyes, which surprised him. Why was his dad sad. He figured he would readily welcome the chance to whip him during the day, with a reason, instead of always waiting till night when no one could see.

Jim sighed again. "Josh, I know I haven't been a good dad to you. I know that I messed up when you were little, but I want to be a good dad. I want to do the right thing. I want to raise you to be a good man, not a man like me, or like who I was. I want you to be honest with me, and with everyone else. I also want you to get along with others. I want you to be able to control your temper, and accept the consequences when you don't graciously. Now, tell me who the fight was with, and what it was about."

Josh recognized the command not request. He looked away again. Fear trickled through him. "Just another senior trying to strut his stuff to the new kid. I just happened to be in the wrong place at the wrong time, Dad. I didn't try to get tangled up in a fight. I'm sorry."

Jim eyed him with more suspicion. "Are you telling me the truth, Son?"

Josh bit his lip as he looked down. He had told the truth, just not all of it.

Jim sighed. "Son, this better not happen again. Am I understood?"

Josh nodded slowly. He looked up at his dad and waited. What was his dad going to do? Was he going to let him go, or was he going to whip him, then let him go. He saw a struggle going on in his dad's eyes and his stomach turned. Was his dad going to make him go without eating again?

He groaned at the thought. He was starving. If his dad made him go without, how much more did he have to tell to get supper? He debated with himself whether or not to say more. He stood waiting, hoping, bed without supper wasn't going to be an option tonight.

Jim sighed as though he hated what he had to say next. He

watched the fear in Josh's eyes, but wasn't sure what the boy was thinking. He was afraid the boy wasn't telling him the whole truth. *Help me, God, I don't know what to do.* "Josh, are you telling me the truth? Do you not know the name of the boy, or are you just lying to me?" He gripped his arm. "Tell me now, no more stalling, what is the name of the boy you were fighting with?"

Josh looked down again. His shoulders sagged. Did he dare tell his dad? He looked up and knew the answer. If he didn't tell he would be going to bed with no supper, or worse have to sit and watch them eat and not be aloud to eat, or he would get whipped, maybe both. He took a chance on the truth and prayed that his dad wouldn't hit him, not now anyway. "Johnathan." He muttered.

Jim stopped. A glare entered his eyes. Fire seemed to shoot from them. Why couldn't Josh and Johnathan get along. They never had been able to. "Why?" He heard the pain in his own voice.

Josh turned away waiting for the first strike.

Jim gripped Josh's arm. "I asked you a question, son, I expect an answer immediately. Why were you fighting him?"

He looked up at his dad. He couldn't say, "I don't know," his dad would skin him alive. He racked his brain for an answer, finally he settled on the truth and hoped his dad would take it for what it was. "I acted in self defense. He was tormenting me about being too young to be a senior. I tried to ignore him, but he wouldn't stop. When I tried to walk away. He pushed me down. It wasn't much of a fight. I came up and gave him a slug and about that time Uncle John walked up, and took both of us into the office for fighting."

Josh stopped and prayed his dad wouldn't make him go on. He didn't want to admit to what Uncle John had done to him. His chest fell as he sighed.

Jim waited, wondering if his son would continue, but he saw the pain flash in Josh's eyes and was sure he knew what had happened, or he at least had a pretty good guess. He wished Josh would just admit it, instead of being prodded. "Go on, son."

Josh shrugged. "Nothing much left to tell."

Jim nodded thoughtfully, "So, if I told you to take off your shirt, what would I see, son?" Jim was surprised to see the fear and pain flash across Josh's face.

Josh locked his legs to keep from falling as he heard his father's request. Was he going to make him take off his shirt? He trembled as he looked into his father's eyes. "Dad -"

At that moment the front door opened and in walked Jordan and Jared. Both boys were in good spirits and bounced into the living room. "We are done, Dad. Can we have a barbecue?"

Jim looked at them in surprise. He hadn't thought of doing a barbecue in a long time. "I don't think we have the stuff for it, and Mom already has supper ready, but I'll tell you what, I will get the stuff and we can do that tomorrow. That will be a good way to give your mom a night off and be a lot of fun. We can celebrate the first week of school being over with a big barbecue."

Both boys leaped up and down with excitement.

Lilly stepped into the room with a smile. She had heard the boys request and her husbands suggestion. "Thank you all, but for tonight, lets go eat supper before it gets cold."

Jim turned to look at Josh. "We are not through with this, son," he whispered.

Josh trembled as he heard his dad, but he nodded. He knew better than to think that his dad would just drop it. He sighed as he followed the family to the kitchen, where Julia was coloring and waiting on them for supper.

Later that night Jordan awoke to Josh slipping out of his bed. He watched quietly wondering what he was going to do.

Josh heard the tap outside the window and knew what was happening. With an under breath moan, he rolled out of bed and quietly slipped out the door and down the stairs unaware that Jordan was following him.

Slowly he stepped off the front porch and waited. It didn't take long for the strong arms to grip his and half lead half drag him toward the garage.

Jordan smiled to himself. It was about time Josh got in trouble for something he had been doing. He wondered why Dad was taking him out of the house in the middle of the night though. It really didn't make any sense. He watched and waited for several minutes wondering what his dad and Josh were doing. Was Josh getting a spanking? Was Dad just talking to him? What was going on in the garage? He didn't dare open the door, but maybe he could get close enough to hear.

He crept forward silently, and as he did his conscience pricked him. He knew Josh hadn't done anything at school, yet he had been in trouble there. He knew Josh hadn't been the one who had done all the stuff at home, but he had taken the blame.

He sighed. He didn't want to admit it, but he hoped that his dad wouldn't spank Josh. It wasn't fair if he did. Josh hadn't done anything wrong. Jordan knew he and Jared had been picking on Josh a lot here lately, but he didn't think his dad would really hit Josh or them.

Besides Josh wasn't the one who started the fight today, and he shouldn't have been the one to get in trouble for it, but it looked like Dad was going to punish him too. Oh well, it was Dad. He was sure it wouldn't be anything serious. Dad wouldn't punish *him* with a spanking, anyway. Then a sound met his ears and he stopped still in his tracks. After hearing it a few more times, he turned and fled to the house and up to his bed.

Tears burned his eyes. It was his and Jared's fault. Dad was spanking Josh, and it was because of him and Jared. Why was Dad hitting Josh? Why not hit him and Jared? Why? Josh had only been standing up for them. They had been the ones to really pick the fight, Josh had just been the one to step in and fight it, keeping Johnathan from making mush out of them.

Jordan closed his eyes. "I am sorry, God," he whispered. "I didn't mean to make Dad hit him. Please make him to stop. And help Josh to forgive me. Please don't let Daddy hit him any more."

He wasn't sure what Dad would do if he caught him watching, but if he was hitting Josh for the fight at school, when Josh hadn't been the one at fault, would he hit Jared and him because they had caused it? And would he hit him if he was watching what was happening in the garage? He buried his face in his pillow. "Please make Daddy stop, God. Please don't make Josh be in trouble because of me. I am sorry."

25

Josh bit his lip trying to keep back his cries of pain, but once and a while a moan did escape. He tried hard not to let his dad see how much pain he was in, but he knew he couldn't hide it for much longer.

There was a wicked laugh and John grabbed Josh by the hair and pulled him to his feet. "There will be no more fighting in school, boy. You got that. No more!" He smacked the boy again.

Josh cried out in pain, then bit his lip again. He didn't want to be gagged again. Again the belt struck his raw back. He trembled as he fell to the floor again with the belt cracking on his back.

Again the man caught him up and pushed him into the wall.

Josh felt the cold of steal on his stomach and his breath caught in his throat, even though he knew it was a pistol.

"You going to say a word about what is happening out here? You going to let on to anyone?"

Josh tried to turn away. But he was too afraid to fight much. "No, sir. I won't say a word."

"You going to act like you're in pain? Or let anyone else see what has happened to you, boy?"

Josh hung his head. "No, sir." When was this going to end?

John smiled, satisfied for now, he still had Josh convinced that he was being beaten by his dad, not his uncle. "Then get back in that house and get to bed where you belong. It won't be long now till it is time to get up. And don't wake anyone when you go in, or else."

Again Josh felt the belt across his back. Again a cry of pain ran through him. He bit his tongue and stopped it just in time.

When his dad, he thought, finally stopped and motioned for him to go out, he quietly pulled on his shirt and pants and walked to the house. His body ached from the whipping, not just tonight, but yesterday and the night before, but also from no sleep, or hardly any.

He moaned as he lay down in bed. Tears burned his eyes. Why was Dad doing this? Was he so wicked that his dad was willing to risk the whole family, just to whip him? Again he felt tears in his eye. It just didn't seem like the dad who had talked to him earlier in the day. If he had wanted to whip him, why had he waited? Why didn't he just whip him and get it over with? It didn't make sense. Besides he didn't hit like Dad. He hit with more anger or something.

Josh shook his head. His life was just becoming one bad dream. Always repeating, day after day. He had to stop thinking about it. It wasn't going to make it stop.

Jordan woke when heard Josh's groan as he lay down in bed. Sleepily he looked up at the clock. He couldn't believe it was already five thirty in the morning.

He bit his lip as he looked over toward Josh's bed. Was he getting a spanking every night? Was that why he was acting like he was in pain? Jordan felt guilt rip through him. He was glad Dad hadn't hit him and Jared also, but why in the world had he hit Josh so much? It didn't make any sense at all.

Why would he hit Josh at all? Josh had been innocent. He hadn't done anything.

The boys woke the next morning to their dad hollering up the stairs. "Get up, boys. I am going to be up there in less then five minutes and you all three better be out of bed and dressed when I get up there."

Jared and Jordan instantly rolled out of bed, but Josh, though he heard his dad, couldn't quiet register it in his sleep deprived mind.

He moaned as he rolled over.

Jared glared at him. "Come on, Josh, get up. You heard him. Get up, but I guess it doesn't matter for you anyways does it. It's not like you would get in trouble." He glared at Josh wanting to jerk him out of bed, but he didn't. Instead he ran out the door to be the first one in the bathroom.

Jordan glanced at Josh, and bit his lip. "Josh, I am sorry for everything yesterday."

Josh looked up at him. "What do you mean?" He tried to hold back the groan as he tried to move to get more comfy.

Jordan flushed. "I sort of heard you go out last night, so I followed you." He was surprised to see Josh stiffen and grow pale. "What?"

"I heard what Dad was doing to you. I am sorry, Josh. I will tell him it was my fault and not yours."

Josh shook his head. "Don't, Jordan. It will just make it worse. Don't make him mad at you too."

"But I feel like-"

"Don't." Josh cut him off. "Just don't follow me again. And don't say anything about what you heard. Okay? Please."

Jordan stared at him in surprise as Josh slowly sat up. "But, Josh-"

Josh shook his head again. "Please don't say anything, Jordan. Don't let on that you know. If he thinks I told you-" Josh stopped unwilling to go on. Too afraid of what would happen to say it out loud. Suddenly there was a loud knock on the door. Both boys jumped as their father stuck his head in the room.

"Boys, I said it was time to get up. Now get up and be ready to have breakfast in less then five minutes, or you may not be getting any."

Josh bit his lip as his father turned and walked away.

Jordan looked at him with sympathy. "I won't say anything for now, just because you asked, but if it gets worse, what then?"

Josh looked away, but slowly rolled out of bed. His body cried out in protest as he tried to move. He gritted his teeth. "We will see if that happens."

Jordan's eyes flashed. It better not happen again, because if it did, he didn't know what he was going to do, but he wasn't going to just sit around and let it happen. No way!

Jared rushed into the room. "Come on, guys. Dad said to get ready."

Josh flushed, grabbed his clothes and hurried, as much as his battered body would let him, to the bathroom.

Jared snorted. "To good to change in front of us, huh? We'll see about that!" he yelled after him.

Jordan shook his head. He had a feeling Josh was going out so they wouldn't see how bad his beating was. "Leave him alone, Jared. Can't you see that Dad isn't favoring him. We have picked on him and let him take the blame for everything the last few weeks, okay, since he moved in. Dad hasn't ever once favored him. Can't you see he isn't going to. Let's just leave him alone."

Jared glared at his brother. "So you like him better now, is that it?"

Jordan shook his head. "I don't like him better than you, but we are friends. You are too. You know that. We were all great friends till he moved in and we started acting jealous. Let's just start being friends and brothers again. Okay?"

Jared thought for a moment. He knew his brother was right. "Okay. We will. Let's both stop all the picking. He got in enough trouble at school yesterday for a while, anyway."

Jordan nodded, but didn't say anything to Jared about what happened to Josh last night. He felt unsure of how to say it.

Jim hollered up the stairs again. "Boys, get down here and get breakfast. We need to leave in fifteen minutes.

Josh opened the door and paled as he saw the two boys still there waiting.

Jordan walked quickly. "We better hurry. Dad isn't sounding very patient today."

As the boys walked into the kitchen, Jim looked up and smiled. "It's about time. Hurry up. I am dropping you off at school, and Mom is going to pick you up again today." He looked directly at Joshua. "What took you so long?"

Josh bit his lip, but Jordan spoke up quickly. "You know how it is when we all have to use the bathroom, Dad. It just takes a while to get everyone through it."

Jim nodded, but the look of pain in his son's eyes didn't go unnoticed. "Get to eating. We can't be late."

As the boys sat down he continued. "I am not sure how all it's going to work the rest of the week, or I guess next week. This week of school is over. We will just have to see. It sure will be nice, Joshua, when you get your license."

Josh stiffened. What was his dad planning to do to him now?

The boys hurried through breakfast, then ran upstairs to get their books and were out the door in less than fifteen minutes.

As Jim dropped them off, he again admonished them to have a good day, and gave Josh another warning not to be fighting. "I will see you all tonight when I get home."

The boys nodded and waved, then headed to the school to face another day.

Josh cried out in pain as the belt cracked on his back. He tried to turn so the next lash didn't hit directly in the same spot, and the belt snapped across his belly.

Tears stung his eyes as he sank to the floor and covered is head with his arms. Again the belt snapped. Tears fell this time, but he tried to blink them back.

His chest burned, but the fear of what was coming was even worse then the burning. He felt John grip his arm and jerk him to his feet.

John glared at him. Anger and hate shot from his eyes. "You think you are going to pick a fight on the school property, boy, you are going to pay for it."

Josh bit his lip, to keep back the sharp retort. Johnathan had picked the fight, not him. Johnathan had thrown the first punch, not him, but Johnathan wasn't going to get the blame for any of it, and he knew it. Nor was Johnathan going to take part in any kind of punishment for being in a fight.

Josh groaned as John pushed him into the wall and slammed his fists into the boys ribs. He felt the breath leave his lungs and sank to the floor in pain.

John kicked him in the ribs.

Josh tried to keep from crying out, but the pain that ripped through him was even worse then the time he had been beaten by Arthur Less and Marcus.

John jerked him to his feet and flung him against the wall again.

Josh felt the wall at his back and sank down slowly to the floor. He grimmest as his uncle walked toward him.

"You going to keep this up all year, son?"

Josh looked away, but his uncle was going to demand an answer. He cried out again as the belt snapped.

"Answer me now!"

Josh whimpered, then hung his head.

John heard the boy whimper and a satisfied smile crossed his face. He snapped the belt on his back again. "Answer me!"

Josh sank to the floor, then slowly looked up at John knowing the beating was only going to get worse, no matter what he did. "No, sir."

John smiled. "You better quit then, hadn't you, brat."

Josh dropped his head.

John kicked him and he cried out again. "Get going. Your brothers are going to be wondering what is taking you so long. It's time to head home."

Josh forced himself to his feet and pulled on his shirt. He tried to walk as though he didn't hurt, but couldn't. Slowly he walked out to the yard where Jared and Jordan were waiting for him.

Both boys looked up as he approached.

"Have you been in the office all afternoon?" Jordan cried.

Josh looked away.

Jared bit his lip as he looked at his brother. He wondered what all had happened in there. He could tell just by the way Josh stood and walked, he was in pain.

Josh bit his lip. He tried to keep the pain out of his voice as he answered. "Yes. Please don't say anything."

The boys' eyes widened. "I am telling Dad! He shouldn't have hit you. That's not right. You didn't do anything." Jordan snapped. "There is no way he should have hit you in the first place, and he hit you for a few hours?" Jordan's eyes snapped as he looked at Josh. "Don't try and talk me out of it. Dad isn't going to hit you too, if anything else he will -"

Josh paled. "Please, don't tell, please. If you do, I'll just be in worse trouble."

Jared snorted. "Dad will come and clean the principal's clock. You wait and see."

Josh bit his lip. "Please, don't say anything. Please. He won't do anything to the principal. I'll just be in worse trouble. Please keep it a secret, please."

Jordan bit his lip. He agreed with Jared, but after hearing what was happening between Josh and their dad last night, he was afraid that maybe Josh was right. "Come on let's go. Mom is probably waiting out front. It's a good thing we don't take the bus, cause he would have made us miss it today."

Josh put his arm around his ribs as he followed trying to ease the horrible pain.

Lilly smiled as she saw the boys walking up. "How was your day?" She stopped at the look of pain in Josh's eyes. "Josh, is everything okay?"

Josh dropped his gaze. "It's all fine." He shot a sideways glance at Jared and Jordan, willing them to keep quiet.

They both bit their lips. He saw the flash in Jared's eye, and he was sure that he was going to say something. He looked again in Jordan's direction. Jordan shrugged slightly, unsure of what to say.

As they drove home, Jared and Jordan spoke about their day, and asked their mom how hers was, but didn't say anything about what had happened in school. They weren't sure what to say. They didn't know if they should squeal to their mom or not. Would she be able to help?

Jordan was afraid Josh was right, and saying something would make it worse. Jared was mad that Josh didn't want to say anything, and he wanted to talk to his dad anyway. He didn't see how that could make a problem.

When they got home the boys quickly changed into their work cloths. Then headed out to the yard to finish the work from the day before. Josh forced himself to join them, but Jordan told him to go back in.

Josh shook his head. "I'm okay. I don't want to leave you two alone."

Jared scowled at his brother. When Josh walked to the opposite side of the yard to rake up the leaves there, he spit at him. "How dare you tell him he doesn't have to help. He didn't get in that much trouble. Just cause he had to go to the principal's office, doesn't mean that you need to tell him that he doesn't have to help us. That was stupid. Do you realize how much more we have to do if he doesn't help? It was his own fault he got in that fight, and I am going

228

to tell Dad."

Jordan cast a sideways glance at his brother. "What is the matter with you, Jared? Why are you mad at him?"

Jared shrugged. He really didn't know why he felt so mad at Josh. He just knew he had a huge fear that their dad wasn't going to like him and Jordan anymore, and he was going to favor Josh. He didn't know how to put it into words, and he really didn't even know why he felt that way, he just did. He wanted to get Josh in trouble. He wanted his dad to see that Josh was nothing but trouble and him and Jordan were good. He wanted to be his dad's favorite.

Jared looked at his brother with a scowl. "I'll prove to you that he is being favored by Dad."

Jordan felt his stomach knot. Why was he worried? What was Jared up to? "What do you mean, Jared? Don't go planning on getting me into trouble with you."

Jared shook his head. "No it won't be anything like that. I will just prove to you that if there is a problem and Dad sees it, not just letting Josh take the blame for it, but if Dad sees it, we will end up the ones in trouble, or at least one of us not him."

Jordan shook his head. "Don't, Jared. Josh never tried to hurt you. He has taken the blame for every crazy stunt you have pulled, and you know it. Dad should have whipped you several times, but he didn't because Josh took the fall for you."

Jared eyed his brother. "And what did Dad do to him? Nothing, that's what. He didn't get a spanking or even so much as a good scolding, which Dad has given us. If it was our faults we probably would have been spanked or we would have had to spend a day in our room with no meals. I am going to prove it."

Jordan felt uneasy. Should he tell his brother about what happened last night in the garage with Josh and Dad?

He shook his head and looked down. Not yet. Not unless he had to. Jared couldn't keep a secret to save his life, so not unless it looked like he needed to squeal was he going to. He was pretty sure what happened last night could get his dad in a lot of trouble.

Jared looked toward where Josh was working, and a smile formed on his lips. He was going to make Josh sorry for trying to be Dad's favorite. He would make sure by the end of the day or at least the week Dad knew about everything that happened at school and every fight that Josh had been in.

229

26

At six o'clock the boys went into the house and washed up for supper. Lilly smiled at them as they came up to the table. "Got the work all done, boys?"

Josh shook his head. "Not yet. Maybe by tomorrow night."

Jared glared at Josh. Was Josh trying to be their mom's favorite now? He felt his anger toward Josh grow. He was going to prove to his brother that Josh was just trying to be the favorite, and he was going to make Josh sorry for it.

Josh looked over at him at the same time Jordan did, and Jared realized that his mom must have spoken to him. "I'm sorry, Mom. I wasn't listening, I was just thinking about something that happened at school today."

Josh stiffened and so did Jordan. Was Jared going to squeal?

At that moment the front door opened and Jim called out, "Hello, every one. Sorry I am late. I was kept up at the office." He walked into the room with a smile. "Lilly, honey, you didn't need to keep supper waiting for me."

She laughed. "I didn't really. The boys just came in."

Jim nodded as he looked at each of them. "The yard looks good, boys. By tomorrow night it should look great. Thank you all for doing such a great job. I am sorry we didn't have the barbecue tonight. I had a woman come in around four, who was in labor. I couldn't leave till she delivered. Sorry. How about tomorrow night?

After the yard is finished."

Jared and Jordan both beamed with pleasure, but Lilly frowned as she glance at Josh and saw him shrink back a little in his chair.

Jared suddenly spoke up, "We would have had more time to work on it if someone," he drawled out the someone, "didn't get in trouble at school and go to the principal's office. He made us late getting home."

Josh froze as he felt his dad turn and look at him. Why had Jared said anything? They had agreed that Josh would tell his dad if his dad needed told.

Jim turned his gaze to Josh with a frown. "Son, what is this all about?"

Josh glanced at Jordan.

Jordan shrugged and glance at Jared. He was mad at his brother, but he knew what Jared us up to.

Josh bit his lip as he looked down at his plate.

Jim frowned at him. "Joshua, I asked you a question, son."

Josh stiffened his shoulders. Slowly he raised his gaze to meet his dad's. He felt his jaw muscles tighten as he saw the anger in his dad's eyes. "What is all this about?"

Josh dropped his gaze. He felt too afraid and ashamed to say anything, and he didn't want to say anything in front of Lilly anyway.

Jim tightened his jaw. "Go to your room, Joshua. I will be up to talk to you in a few minutes, and you had better have some good reasons, or you will be finding yourself without supper."

Josh pushed back his chair and stood. Anger raged inside of him. This was the first night since Jimmy had been born that he hadn't gotten in trouble before supper. He felt his stomach cramp. He had gotten to eat last night, but his dad had made him throw it up when he whipped him last night. Was he ever going to get to eat again?

He kept his eyes on his dad, and Jim saw the fight in his eyes. He raised his eyebrow. Slowly Josh dropped his gaze and walked out of the room. He was defeated and he knew it.

Jordan bit his lip at the defeated slump he saw in Josh's walk. What all had really happened to him at school? And what all had happened last night? What was he afraid would happen if his dad knew about today?

Jim watched his son walked out of the room and turned back

231

to the table in time to see a satisfied smirk on Jared's face. It puzzled him. He thought the boys had been getting along good. Was Jared just trying to get Josh in trouble or had the boy really gotten in trouble?

He leaned down and kissed Lilly softly. "I guess supper will have to wait a little bit longer. You all go ahead. I will talk to him and then we will eat. There is no sense in all of us having to eat it when it's cold."

Lilly looked up at him with a smile. "Just don't take too long up there."

Jim nodded with a smile. "We will be down in a few minutes."

Jared felt disappointed that Dad had made Josh go to the bedroom. He wanted to see what all was said, and what Dad would do. He had to prove his point to Jordan, that Dad was favoring Josh.

Jordan looked at his mom and saw the worried frown that she wore. Was she worried about what was happening to Josh and their dad too? Did she know that Dad was hitting him at night? Jordan shook his head. Mom would not stand for that. She hadn't ever let Jim even give them a spanking unless it was really necessary, and even then he had only ever used his hand and swatted them just a few times. He had always had to, or tried to, punish them without violence. But would Mom do that with Josh, or would she feel it wasn't her place?

Jordan dropped his head. Jared was right. Dad was showing favor, but it wasn't to Josh, it was to them. He wished he knew what was going on upstairs, but Mom looked at him and nodded. "Pray, Jordan. Dad is right, no sense in all of us eating a cold supper.

Jared scowled, but bowed his head and waited for the prayer to end. He felt a prick in his conscience. He knew he shouldn't be jealous of Josh, but he was. And he didn't know what to do about it. He didn't want to say sorry, not yet. He wanted to prove to Jordan that he was right.

Jim walked up the steps and opened the bedroom door.

Josh heard the door open and slowly turned to face his dad. "Yes, sir?"

Jim stepped into the room and shut the door. "Son, why were

232

you in the principal's office?"

Josh looked down. "I just got into some – trouble today, that's all."

Jim shook his head. "Josh, you haven't even been in school a week. What is going on?"

Josh dropped his gaze. "I'm sorry, Dad, I was just in the wrong place at the wrong time again." Josh wondered if his dad would consider that a lie. He had been, but it was because Johnathan had searched him out.

Jim crossed his arms over his broad chest. "Boy, are you telling me the truth? Because that sounds an awful lot like what you said yesterday."

Josh shuttered but looked up into his dad's eyes. "Dad, – I -"

Jim stepped up to him.

Josh bit his lip, scared to death at what his dad would do to him. He knew what his dad was capable of doing to him, but what would he do to him?

Jim gripped his arm. "How long is your detention to last, son? How long did he give you?"

Josh turned his head slightly hoping to keep his dad from seeing anything suspicious, but didn't answer.

Jim shook him a little. "I asked you a question, son. You had better give me the answer."

Josh trembled. He still couldn't bring himself to look up into his father's stormy eyes. "A week," he muttered.

Jim frowned as he released his hold on Josh. "And just when were you going to tell me this? Why did I have to hear about it from Jared?"

Josh felt his whole body flinch. "I was going to tell you, Dad, really I was. I just thought I would wait till-" he stopped. He was about to say till after supper, but he was afraid if he mentioned that, his dad would make him go without it. He bit his lip. He knew he had already said too much.

Jim eyed him warily. "Joshua, what are you trying to do? Do you want me to beat you? Is that it? Are you just trying to see how far you can push me before I hit you? Son, I don't want to hit you, ever. But you have got to stop pushing all the limits. And if you do something that is whipping worthy, son, I am going to whip you. Is that understood?"

Josh trembled even more. "Dad, I-"

Jim interrupted him. "Was this problem at school your fault?"

Josh shuttered. It was no use to try and tell the truth. His dad was going to beat him anyway. He may as well accept the blame and maybe the whipping would be less severe "Yes, sir."

Jim nodded. "Then, for the week you have detention, you will also go without supper. No snack and no supper. Is that understood?"

Josh felt his knees grow weak, but he forced himself to answer. "Yes, sir." He dropped his head even lower and pulled away from his dad a little more. Fear gripped him. How was he going to make it a week with no food. His uncle beat him through the lunch hour so he didn't ever get lunch and now no supper.

Jim sighed. As he started to speak Josh raised his eyes to look at him, out of pure habit and learning from when he was little. "Son, I don't like having to punish you, especially when I don't know the whole story. But for some reason you are not learning well. When you get hungry enough, you will be willing to listen and obey."

Josh dropped his head again, as he stood before his dad. He hadn't felt this hungry since, he really couldn't remember when, but then he had been in too much pain to eat breakfast and his uncle was beating him through lunch, so he hadn't had anything to eat since yesterday, and that had only been a little bit. Still he knew his dad meant what he said.

"Yes, sir," he murmured again. "I understand."

Jim nodded. "You may stay in your room for half an hour. After that you better join the rest of us downstairs."

Josh nodded, but still kept his head down. "Yes, sir." Tears sprang to his eyes and he tried to blink them away, ashamed.

Jim shook his head and turned and walked out. He felt sick. What was happening with Josh? He didn't remember his son ever being a trouble maker. Why now? Luke had said that Josh was always wonderfully behaved. What was happening? Slowly he walked back down to he kitchen.

Lilly looked up as he walked in, but said nothing. Fear nudged in her mind. What was happening between Josh and Jim?

She felt uneasy. Was she suppose to get involved or leave it alone? She supposed she should leave it alone, but if he started to hit Joshua, she was stepping in. There was no way she was going to stand for him abusing his child again.

Jim looked up at her with pain in his eyes. "Josh won't be joining us for supper," he said dryly. He looked at Jordan and Jared, "And don't either one of you boys try to sneak him something either. Got it."

Jared bit his lip. This was working out so well. Now he had a way to get Josh in even more trouble. He slipped a biscuit off the table as they were finishing up.

Jim saw out of the corner of his eye, but made no move to appear that he knew. He just watched and waited. Was Jared the cause of all the trouble? Jim felt puzzled. Would Josh hide the truth to keep his brother out of trouble?

Jordan asked his mom if he could hold little Jimmy for a while, and when granted permission, he took the baby and headed for the living room. Jared said nothing, but slipped out the door.

Jim waited till Jared was far enough away he wouldn't hear him following and slipped out the door after him. He followed him up the steps, making no noise.

Jared slipped up the steps and into the room.

Josh lay on the bed sound asleep.

Jared was disappointed. His plan wasn't going to work after all. He walked over to the bed and smacked Josh on the back to wake him up.

Josh was startled by the smack, but the pain that ripped through him was even worse. He let out a startled yelp and rolled over, sitting up at the same time. His mind raced as he tried to place where he was and what was happening.

Jared took a step back, startled himself by Josh cry.

Josh looked up at him with pain in his eyes. "What?"

Jared hesitated. Maybe he shouldn't try and get Josh in trouble. Quickly he pushed the thought away. He held out the biscuit. "I brought you something to eat."

Josh shook his head even as his stomach cramped with hunger. "Dad said I can't, Jared, but thanks."

Jared was disappointed. He was sure Josh would eat it. After all he hadn't eaten any lunch. "Come on, Josh. Dad won't know. And besides, this is Mom's homemade biscuit. They are the best."

Josh shook his head again. His stomach cramped so hard he thought he was going to be sick. He quickly looked away. "Thanks, Jared, but Dad said I can't. So I can't."

Jared sighed. "Fine. Whatever," he snapped. He was angry that he hadn't been able to get Josh to eat, but kind of impressed by Josh's obedience.

Josh weakly lay back on the bed and rolled so his back wasn't touching the mattress. "I'm sorry, Jared, but Dad told me no, and I don't want to disobey him."

Jared glared at him. "Whatever. You are just playing favorites. If Jordan had brought it to you, you would have eaten it to get it out of sight quickly so he wouldn't get into trouble, but not with me. You think that I have to take it back down, and then I will be in trouble, because I will get caught. All I was trying to do was be nice to my brother and you are going to make me get in trouble."

Josh bit his lip. "Jared, I am not playing favorites." He sat up again and could see the hurt in Jared's eyes. "You know that. I haven't played favorites since I have been here and I didn't play favorites before that."

Jared held out the bread to him. "Then eat it, Josh. Come on, it's been weeks since you had a meal, or really much of anything to eat.

Josh hung his head. He didn't know the boys had noticed. He felt his conscience prick him, but he slowly reached out and took the biscuit. He knew he would be in big trouble if his dad knew, but could it hurt just to eat a little. He was starving and he hadn't had anything to eat in a few days that he hadn't been forced to throw back up..

Slowly he bit into the biscuit. His eyes widened. It was delicious! He glanced at Jared and the boy smiled at him then turned and walked out.

Jim stood just outside the door as Jared walked out. He gave no indication that he had seen the whole thing, but waited to see what Jared was going to say. "What are you doing, son?"

Jared jumped a little. "Nothing, Dad. I was just coming up to let Josh know we were done. I also needed to get my math, I have some homework." He stopped as he turned back around. "I guess I forgot to grab it."

Jim nodded. "Sneaking food to your brother, are you?"

Jared shook his head. "No, sir. I wasn't doing that."

Jim felt shocked. He couldn't believe that Jared would look him in the eye and lie to him. He gripped the boy's arm and turned him back to the bedroom. "We will see about that."

Jared bit his lip as Jim opened the door.

Josh looked up expecting to see Jared or Jordan. He jumped when he saw his dad. The partly eaten biscuit fell to the floor.

Jim shook his head as he walked into the room. "Joshua, where did you get the food?"

Josh trembled. Was Jared just trying to get him in trouble? "I-"

Jim didn't wait for an answer, instead he drug Jared over to stand beside Josh . He looked at Jared. "So you didn't bring your brother food?"

Jared shook his head. "No, Dad, I didn't."

Jim frowned again. He couldn't believe that Jared could stand there and lie to him. He saw Josh tremble. "Jared, are you lying to me?" He looked the boy squarely in the eye.

Jared suddenly saw his dad angry. He hadn't ever been angry in the time that he had been married to Lilly. At least not where the boys could see. He had gotten upset with them, but this time he was angry.

Josh trembled. As his dad stood before both of them.

"Josh, where did you get the food?" he questioned.

Josh bit his lip. He didn't want to lie to his dad, but if he told the truth Jared would be in trouble.

Jim turned to face his son. "Joshua, I asked you a question, now you will answer me. Where did you get the food?"

Josh looked down, but didn't answer.

Jim frowned. Was Josh going to lie to him also?

Jared glared at Josh. Was he going to tell on him?

Jim waited.

Josh slowly looked up at him. His whole being was trembling.

Jared saw how scared Josh was, and he almost laughed. Dad wasn't going to do anything serious to them. What was Josh so afraid of? At the worst it would be sent to bed now, instead of in a few hours.

Jim watched them both. "If you are not going to tell me, then you may both stay in your room for a while." Jim turned and walked out. Anger raged inside of him. He made his way down the hall. He knew why Josh wasn't talking. The boy had reason to fear him, but he was surprised that he wasn't going to just tell on his brother to get himself out of trouble.   What surprised him the most was Jared lying to his face and not even flinching about it. This meant that it had

237

happened before. How many times, he wondered? He shook his head and took a deep breath. He had to cool off a little before he dealt with this.

He walked back to the kitchen where Lilly was washing the dishes with Julia's help. He smiled as he walked up to the four year old and lifted her off her feet. "How about you running along and playing, Little Princess. Daddy needs to have a talk with Mommy."

Julia giggled as she ran out the door.

Lilly smiled as she handed him the next plate. She stopped at the worry she saw in his eyes. "What's wrong, Jim?"

Jim shook his head, then tuned to look her in the eye. "Lilly, I know I haven't spanked your boys on your request, but just a few times and I have always gotten your approval before doing it, but I am afraid that is going to have to change."

Lilly waited, wondering why he was saying this. If the boys needed a spanking then he needed to give them one.

Jim hesitated. "Jared openly lied to me tonight." He told her what had happened.

Lilly shook her head. "Jim, I never meant to make it so you couldn't punish the boys. I want you to be their dad. You know if they need punished. If they do, then I want you to punish them. I want us to raise them together. Please don't feel you have to come to me for permission to spank them." She looked at him with concern in her eyes. "But I also don't want that to go overboard. With my boys *or yours*. They are all ours and we need to work together to raise them. Please don't feel like you can't be their dad."

Jim nodded as he put his arm around her. "Thank you, Love. And just so you know, I second that. I want you to be Joshua's mom."

She smiled. "Don't worry, honey. I am sure it is all fine. He probably just wanted to help his brother. It will be okay. And just so you know, I think you are being kind of hard on your son. He needs to feel like you care about him, but all he feels for you is fear. I see it in his eyes, and in the way he is when you are around. He is scared you are going to hit him."

Jim nodded. As soon as the dishes were done he made his way back up the steps for the next confrontation with his boys. He sighed. Lilly was right. He was expecting too much out of Josh. He was being too hard on him. He expected him to obey promptly and with out argument, but how many times had he allowed, in front of Joshua,

Jared and Jordan to argue with him? And he hadn't even gotten after them? No.

He sighed. He had some confessing he had to do. Then he had to take care of some business.

Jared glared at Josh as their dad left. "Why didn't you eat it fast. Then Dad wouldn't have known. You were just trying to get me in trouble, weren't you!"

Josh looked away. He didn't understand what was happening with Jared. Why weren't they friends anymore?

Jared stormed to his side of the room then back. "I tried to be nice, and what do I get? I get in trouble, because of you. You are such a – a – a, I don't even know what you are. Favorite child, just because he is your dad. Well he loved us before you came here."

Josh was stunned. He had realized that his dad treated the boys differently, but he would have thought Jared would be grateful for that. He shivered. Was Jared jealous of him?

Jared glared. "All you want to do is get me and Jordan in trouble."

Josh stiffened. "Jared, that is not true and you know it. All the countless times I have taken the blame for the crazy stuff you did, how can you even think that?"

Jared stood nose to nose with him and glared. "I can say it as much as I want. This is my house and my family. Not yours. You have been there every time something has happened and yeah you have taken the blame. That just proves my point. Dad hasn't done anything to you for all the stuff you have taken the blame for. You are such a little kiss up. I hate you. Dad use to love us, now you get all his attention."

Josh backed off a little. What was Jared's problem? His words stung. Josh tried not to let it show, but it hurt deeply. He already didn't feel like he belonged in the family, and Jared had just confirmed it. Did Jordan feel the same way?

Jared glared again. This time he was going to make sure he proved his point to Jordan and to Josh. He swung.

Josh saw the fight coming and ducked. But Jared came from

the other side and swung at him again.

Josh tried to block his brother, but then Jared slammed a fist into his jaw and the fight was on. Josh jumped to the side, and swung back. His fist met with Jared's jaw and Jared stumbled back, his lip bleeding.

He swung angrily.

Josh ducked and swung again. Then swung around and slammed into Jared knocking him to the floor.

Jordan came in at that moment and froze. Josh was sitting on top of Jared holding him down. Jared was swinging as best as he could and kicking for all he was worth.

Jim walked up behind Jordan. His eyes widened. He wasn't sure what was going on, but he knew that this was enough. It was time to punish them all and get things back to order around here.

Jared swung again and pushed.

Josh looked up at that moment and saw his dad. He breath froze. He couldn't move.

Jared swung again, this time, with Josh distracted, he managed to get lose. He jumped to his feet and slugged Josh in the ribs.

Josh grunted from the impact, but managed not to cry out even though the pain at that spot was almost unbearable. He didn't make a move to fight back.

Jared lunged at him again.

Jim cleared his throat.

Jared looked up and saw him and his expression changed, but to Jordan it didn't look like Jared was surprised. It looked as if he had expected his dad, almost hoped he would be there.

"Both of you get up and get over here," he ordered.

Josh slowly stood and moved in front of his dad.

Jared stepped up in front of him too. The boys stood shoulder to shoulder facing him.

Jim looked at Jared then at Josh. "What is going on?"

Both boys looked down.

Jim felt his anger rise. "I asked a question and I expect an answer. One of you had better tell me or both of you will feel a belt on your backside."

Josh paled slightly, but made no move to speak.

Jared looked at him angrily. "He started it," he snapped.

Jim looked at Josh. "What happened?"

Jared felt his temper rise. He wanted to be the one to tell. He needed to be the one to make up the story just to prove to Jordan that Dad was going to favor Josh. To his surprise Josh didn't defend himself. He didn't deny having started the fight. He just stood there silently.

Jared grew even angrier. "He made me bring him something to eat. Then when you made us stay in here, he was mad that he was in trouble and told me that it was all my fault. He said that he wished we weren't even brothers."

Jordan saw Josh flinch, and he wondered why Jared was making up all of this.

Josh was sure that the lie Jared just told was going to cost him more than the fight if he didn't argue it.

Jim turned to Josh. "I want to hear your side, son."

Jared scowled. He looked at Jordan with an I told you so look in his eyes.

Josh remained silent.

Jim felt his anger rise. What would make his son say such a thing? Why would he wish that Jared wasn't his brother? "Joshua, you had better start talking."

Josh trembled. He didn't know what to do. Should he tell the truth. He bit his lip. His dad wouldn't believe him. He looked up and saw the anger in his dad's eyes and he shuttered again.

Jared glared at him harder.

Jim cleared his throat. "Is what he says true, Joshua? Did you start the fight? Did you ask him to bring you something, if you got in trouble? Were you expecting to get in trouble?"

Josh dropped his head again. He didn't want to lie to his dad, but he knew his dad wasn't going to believe him. What was he suppose to do? He glanced at Jared and knew it was hopeless. Why was Jared so mad at him? The sting of Jared's words still rung in his mind, and he turned slightly away. Jared was right. He didn't belong here. He wasn't wanted here.

Jim reached down and unbuckled his belt. "Joshua, you know I told you when you moved here it would be different, and I wouldn't hit you. But you have brought this on yourself." He looked at Jared. "You too."

Jared paled. "Why am I in trouble? I didn't do it!"

Jim felt his muscles bunch. "Jared, you-"

241

Jared stared at him. "You don't believe me because I am not your son, is that it. If Josh said I had started the fight and it was all my fault you wouldn't be punishing him. It's not fair. Why do you love him more? Just cause he is yours and I'm not?" Jared stormed.

Jim felt tension build in his neck and shoulders. "Jared-" He gripped his arm. He wanted to smack his mouth and then belt him for the way he was talking.

Josh looked up. "Don't, Dad. It's my fault. I started it. I was the one responsible for it all. He didn't do anything. I'm sorry."

Jim looked at him in stunned silence. Was he telling the truth? "Did you ask him to bring you food, son?"

Josh shuttered, knowing he was going to pay dearly for this if he lied and said yes, but he couldn't stand the thought of his dad whipping the others. "Yes, sir."

Jared felt as if Josh had kicked him in the stomach. Why was he taking the blame?

Jim slowly pulled off his belt the rest of the way. "Jared and Jordan go out."

Josh bit his lip.

Jordan wanted to beg his dad not to hit Josh, but he didn't know what to do. He didn't want Jared in trouble either.

Jared scowled. "Why? You don't want us to see that you are just going to act like you punish him, but you aren't going to are you?"

Jim felt his temper rise even more. "Jared, go out into the hall. I will deal with you in a few minutes," his voice was low, but more of a deep growl than words.

Jared frowned again, but slowly followed Jordan out into the hall and shut the door behind him. Then he turned back with his ear to the door to listen still sure that his dad was just going to act like he was going to spank Josh. He wasn't going to do anything.

Jordan frowned at Jared. "You are unbelievable. Do you not realize that Dad whipped him last night for nothing? He came into our room and drug him out to the garage and hit him. Why are you making it worse for him? Didn't you see the principal hit him today at school? You know it was all your fault and he took the blame for you. You are unbelievable."

Jordan sat down in the hall with a disgusted grunt.

Jared still wasn't listening to his brother. He was too busy wishing he could see what was going on on the other side of the door to even hear what his brother had said.

Jim turned to Josh as the boys went out and closed the door. "Son, are you lying to me?"

Josh trembled. "Why do you ask?"

Jim frowned. "You are, aren't you?"

Josh looked away. "Please just let it go, Dad. Punish me and leave him alone. It is my fault."

Jim gripped his arm. "That is not what I am asking you, Joshua. I asked are you lying to me?"

Josh bit his lip. His dad shook him slightly, and he felt the burn on his arm.

Jim let his arm go and sighed. "Joshua, I don't want to hit you, but this time, I have to. I can't just keep letting you get by with stuff. I thought I taught you never to lie to me a long time ago. Does that lesson need relearned?"

Josh nodded slightly.

Jim gripped his arm tightly. His face drained of color as he raised his belt. He brought it down on his sons legs with a loud smack.

Josh jerked. His dad usually hit him on the back. He bit his lip to keep back a cry as the belt smacked him again. He was grateful he didn't hit his back this time, because he was sure if he had, he would have found out that he had been being hit at school.

After about twenty swats Jim lowered the belt. His heart felt broken. "Don't ever make me do that again, son. Is that clear?" He choked on his own tears.

Josh didn't respond. He knew he would be whipped tonight, so why was his dad acting like it hurt him so much to spank him now?

Jim raised his voice slightly, "Jared, come in here."

Josh felt his face pale. "Dad, don't punish him because of me, please."

Jim looked his son in the eye. He couldn't believe Josh was still holding up that it was his fault. The fact that he didn't want his brother punished was a pretty good sign it wasn't his fault. "Joshua, go out to the hall with Jordan. I have let all three of you get away with way too much. It is going to stop here and now. Do not back talk me. Go to the hall."

Josh trembled as he opened the door.

Jared stood there crestfallen.

Jim called him in again.

Slowly he walked in the room with a glance toward Joshua that said how mad he was.

Josh sank to the floor as the door shut. He rested his head on his knees. He thought about his dad hitting Jared and bile rose in his mouth.

Jordan saw the pain in his brother's eyes. "I'm sorry, Josh. I don't know what has come over Jared. I don't get why he is so mad."

Josh shrugged. It really didn't matter. His dad was hitting him anyway. Nothing was ever going to change that.

A few minutes later Jared opened the door. He glared at Josh even more, but said nothing with his dad there. He knew if he did, he would be in even more trouble.

Jim called all three into the room. "Sit down, boys." He motioned to Josh's bed. He waited till all three were sitting facing him with Jordan in between Jared and Josh. "I don't know why you are all having a hard time getting along, but I do know that, that is going to change. I don't want any more arguments out of any of you. I don't want any more fighting, and since you can't seem to even have a friendly fight, I mean no fighting period. No wrestling matches, no pillow fights, nothing. Am I understood?"

Jared and Jordan looked up at him, "Yes, Sir."

Josh bit his lip as he dropped his gaze. If he said yes, and Jared picked more fights he would just get in worse trouble.

Jim cleared his throat, waiting on Josh's answer. "Joshua, am I clear?"

Josh slowly lifted his gaze. He saw the anger in his father's eyes, and fear gripped him hard. "Yes, sir," his voice came out barely above a whisper.

Jim frowned at all of them. "Now, to give you all time to think about it, you are going to stay in this room the rest of the evening together and getting along. When you get back from school- never mind I forgot tomorrow is Saturday, so when you get up in the morning you will find that there are lots of chores for each of you to do. And you are all on kitchen duty till farther notice, together. Understood?"

The boys understood that he was making them work together to get along.

"Yes, Sir," they answered in unison.

"Good. Then you all can start right now with cleaning up this room before bed time. I will be up in a while to see how you are doing." With that he turned and walked out, closing the door most of the way behind him. He walked down the hall, then tiptoed back to the partly open door and listened. Wondering what all he would hear.

Jared scowled at Josh and Jordan. "See I told you, Jordan. Dad likes him better. It's only because he admitted part of the blame, that he got spanked. Otherwise, Dad would have only spanked me."

Jordan glanced at Josh and opened his mouth to say something, but Josh quickly put his hand on his arm, stopping him. Jordan sighed. "Jared, why are you so mad at Josh? He tried to get Dad not to spank you. He took the blame even though you are the one to blame-"

Jared glared at his brother. "Get away from me!" he screamed. Suddenly he leaped on his brother and sent him to the floor.

Jordan was startled by his brother's attack, but quickly recovered and both boys rolled across the floor slugging one another and yelling.

Josh reached down to stop them and was jerked into the fight. "Guys, Dad said no fighting. Are you trying to get into more trouble."

Jared pushed him backwards. "Go away if you aren't going to join. We can fight if we want to. You are not the boss."

Josh bit his lip as he stepped back.

Jim couldn't hear much of what the boys were saying, but he heard the thud and then heard Jared screaming at one of the others. He sighed as he opened the door. He waited as they fought for a few minutes. He sighed. Josh stood to the side unsure of what to do. He walked up behind him and put his hand on his son's shoulder.

Josh felt Jim's hand on his arm and froze.

"I thought I said no fighting." Jim's voice was quiet, but it got the point across loud and clear.

Jared and Jordan jumped to their feet.

Jim looked them both in the eye, then slowly shook his head. "You both deliberately disobeyed me, and you didn't even wait ten minutes. Get over here."

Jared paled. Dad wasn't going to take it easy on him this time he was sure. He had only swatted him a few times with his hand just a few minutes ago, but this time Jared was sure the belt wasn't just a threat.

Jim pulled off his belt and turned to Jared. "Get over here."

Jared paled even more, but walked over to his dad. "But Josh started it, then he got out as soon as he heard you coming."

Jim raised the belt as he glanced at his son.

Josh made no move to deny it, but Jim saw him flinch.

"Be quiet, Jared." Jordan hissed. He didn't understand his brother at all.

Jim gripped Jared's arm. Then bent him over under his arm and swatted him with the belt five times.

Jared cried before his dad started and let out a yowl every time he was swatted.

Jim let him go and turned to Jordan.

Jordan trembled as his dad bent him under his arm. He knew he deserved it but he didn't want it. He whimpered with each stinging swat, but managed to stay a whole lot quieter then his brother.

When Jim released Jordan he turned to Josh.

Josh trembled, but came close enough his dad could touch him.

"Where you involved in this, Son?"

Josh bit his lip and looked away.

Jim felt his temper rise. "I thought I raised you to obey me without hesitation, son. I guess you have forgotten some of those lessons, so they need to be relearned."

Josh stiffened. What was his dad going to do to him?

Jim gripped Josh's arm and bent him as he had the other two. Slowly he raised the belt.

Josh bit his lip as the first swat came, then the next. He wasn't sure which was more painful, the belt or his ribs from the beating he had received at school, now agitated by his dad squeezing them.

Jim swatted him several more times then he had the other two.

Jordan bit his lip. Why was Josh getting more then him or Jared? Josh wasn't even in the fight. He had just tried to get them to stop.

After about twenty swats, Josh groaned. He was sure he was

246

going to have a hard time sitting for a while.

Jim heard the groan and stopped. "Now, when I say no fights I mean it. All of you work together to get this room cleaned and then get to bed. No more arguments. Josh you go get in the shower, when you are done, Jordan, then Jared. Then to bed. I don't want to hear a peep out of any of you the rest of the night. Is that clear?"

Jordan and Jared hung their heads. "Yes, sir."

Josh trembled, but slowly nodded. He did not even dare to say "yes, sir" aloud.

Jim turned and walked out the door closing it behind him.

Jared glared at Josh. "You are such a spoiled brat. I hate you."

Josh bit his lip as he turned away. Jared's words hurt more then the belt had.

Jared frowned. He wanted Josh to take a swing at him. He wanted to get him into even more trouble.

Jordan scowled at his brother. "Shut up, Jared. Leave him alone. He didn't do anything to you. Why are you trying to get him in trouble?"

Jared glared back at Jordan. "Well, we never got whipped till he moved in. It's his fault!"

Josh turned away. Jared had no idea what being whipped even was, he thought. Anger turned inside of him, but he knew he had to keep it in check. His dad had made it clear who would get the brunt of the punishment around here.

Jordan stepped up to Jared and looked him in the eye. "He didn't do anything just a minute ago and dad gave him more swats then he gave both of us put together. Do you think that is what being a favorite is, is that what you want?"

Jared scowled at his brother but shut his mouth and grabbed his clothes and ran for the shower.

Josh and Jordan looked at each other. Now what were they to do? Dad had said for Josh to got first.

A few minutes later Jim came back up the stairs. He looked into the boys' room and frowned. "Joshua, did you take a shower yet?"

Josh trembled as he looked at his dad, and cast a sideways glance at Jordan. "No, sir."

Jim stepped into the room. "I told you to go first, son. Why didn't you obey me?"

Josh bit his lip and looked down.

Jordan tightened his lips. He didn't understand why Josh was covering for Jared. All Jared was trying to do was get him in trouble.

Jim gripped Josh's arm. He forced himself to stop before he shook him. "Why did your brother go first?"

Josh kept his gaze on the floor. He didn't dare tell. Jared already hated him.

Jim again reached down to unbuckle his belt again. His heart broke. He didn't want to start and he didn't want to keep on hitting him, but he wasn't going to stop with out Josh learning his lesson. All that would do was more harm than good. "Son, what are you doing? Do you not understand how much this hurts me? But you are going to obey me. What I say is what goes, and it goes immediately. Understood? When I ask a question it you are to answer immediately."

Josh bit his lip as he father raised the belt again.

Jordan felt anger rise in him. Josh shouldn't be in trouble for this. It wasn't his fault. "Dad, stop, please!"

The snap of the belt interrupted him. Jim turned to him. "What?" He turned back toward Josh slightly.

Jordan trembled. "Dad, Josh didn't do anything. Jared grabbed his cloths and ran off to the bathroom before Josh could."

Jim looked at his son then gripped his arm and forced him to look up at him. "Son, is that true?"

Josh nodded slightly. "Yes, sir."

Jim released his hold on Josh. "Then why didn't you say something?"

Josh looked away. "It doesn't matter," he muttered.

Jim heard and this time his heart smote him. "Tell me the truth next time, son. Do not lie to me. Please, son, no more lies. I do not want to ever have to hit you again. Please don't make me."

Josh nodded slightly "Yes, sir." He didn't understand why his dad was saying that, when in a few hours he was going to beat him unmercifully and not even care. Maybe it wasn't his dad; maybe it was Uncle John? He pushed the thought away. It had started before school. How would Uncle John have known were to find him.

Jim turned and walked out of the room and to the bathroom. Both boys heard the door open and shut, then they heard Jared yelling.

Josh ducked his head.

Jordan looked over at him. "It's not your fault, Josh. He did it. He deserved to get a spanking."

Jim walked back into the room a few minutes later. "Joshua, get to the bathroom."

Josh jumped up, grabbed his clothes and ran.

Jim frowned as he looked at Jordan, "Do you have any idea what is going on with your brother?"

Jordan flushed. "Jared?"

"Yes, Jared." Jim answered impatiently. He knew instantly what the answer was, but he wondered if Jordan was going to tell him the truth or not. He suddenly wondered how long he had let these two lie to him and not even realized they were lying. He suddenly realized what all he had let them get away with. A bitter taste filled his mouth.

Jordan looked at his dad and saw the anger in his eyes. He decided to risk it and tell the truth, hoping not to get Jared in more trouble than he already had himself in. "Jared is jealous of Josh. He thinks that since Josh is your son, and we aren't by blood, that you love Josh more."

Jim nodded. "Do you feel that way?"

Jordan hesitated. "I did when he first moved in, but I have been watching and you haven't been showing favoritism. You haven't even with Jimmy. You have still loved us the same, or more."

Jim smiled. "Thank you for telling me."

Jared walked into the bedroom his face resembling a thunder cloud. "Why did you send him to the bathroom before I was done? He is so impatient. Knocking on the door, just to be a problem. Telling me to hurry up, just to get me in trouble. It's not fair."

Jim frowned at Jared. "I think we have had enough for tonight, son. Get to bed and no more of this foolishness, am I understood?"

Jared looked his dad in the eye as though trying to decide if he should push it and say one more thing. He snapped his mouth closed and climbed into bed.

Jim smiled slightly. That was the first time since his marriage to Lilly, that he had told the boys to go to bed and Jared hadn't whined about it in some way. He felt his heart constrict again. He wouldn't have let Josh get by with that for a second, not even once. He felt his heart break as he realized he had been playing favorites, but not what Jared was afraid of him playing. He had been harder on Josh, because

249

he was his son, than he had been on Jared and Jordan.

"Good night, boys. Both of you read your devotions while you are waiting on Josh. Then, Jordan, shower, and I want silence in this room. All of you go to bed."

Jordan and Jared both got up and got their Bibles.

Jim turned and walked out of the room.

Jared listened to see if his dad would go spank Josh like he had him, but he didn't. He scowled. It just wasn't fair. Josh got away with everything.

Jordan listened wondering the same thing, but was relieved when he didn't hear the bathroom door. "Why can't you get over this jealousy, Jared. You know, if anything, Dad is harder on Josh then he is on us."

Jared snorted, "Whatever. Leave me alone." He knew his brother was right and he shouldn't be jealous, but he wanted to be, for some reason. He wanted to pick fights and get Josh in trouble. He just wanted to prove to himself and his brother that it would change, and Dad would, at some point in time, like Josh better and treat him better.

Jordan sighed. Did he dare tell his brother what he had overheard last night. He shook his head. Not yet. Jared wouldn't believe him anyway.

Josh walked in and picked up his Bible. Jordan heard a quiet moan as he lay down and he wondered what all had happened in the principal's office earlier that day, but he didn't ask. He didn't want Josh to get upset. Instead he got his clothes and headed to the bathroom.

Jared glared down at Josh as he read his Bible. His anger burned inside him and he didn't even see what he was reading, he just glared at his brother till Josh got up and put his Bible away, then lay down.

Josh felt Jared glare at him, but he tried to let it go. If being his dad's favorite meant what it seemed to mean, he would gladly give this place to Jared, but he knew that wasn't what it was. Why did his dad hate him? He wished he could have said no about moving here. He sighed, rolled over to get the pressure of his back, and within minutes was sound asleep.

Jordan came in a few minutes later and was surprised to see Josh already asleep and Jared laying in bed staring at the ceiling.

Jared was usually the one who went to sleep fast. He shrugged and turned out the light. "Good night, Jared."

Jared snorted. "Good night, Jordan. See you in the morning."

A few hours later Josh was startled awake. He looked up and saw his dad standing over him. "Get downstairs now," he snapped.

Josh trembled but slowly got out of bed and followed him out the door.

Jordan heard Josh moving around and slowly opened an eye. He saw his brother slip out of the room. He got up quietly and slugged Jared. "Josh, is sneaking out. Let's see what is going on," he whispered.

Jared, who usually took quite a while to wake up, woke up instantly and rolled quietly out of his bed. Then followed Jordan out the door, down the steps and outside.

There was no one in sight. They stood there confused for a moment, then Jordan headed to the garage.

Jared followed wondering what was going on. Was Josh running away? He didn't blame him if he did. Jared knew he had been a horrible brother to him. He didn't blame him if he hated him, when he had tried so hard to get him in trouble this evening. He didn't know what was wrong with him.

Jordan motioned to him, and Jared followed his brother to the garage. A murmur of voices sounded from inside. Something snapped, and they heard a groan. Again came the snap, then again a weak moan.

Jared felt his stomach knot. Was Dad hitting Josh, because of him? He leaned forward to hear better, and he thought he was going to be sick. Again came the crack and then he heard Josh cry out in pain.

The boys looked at each other with wide eyes. Fear raced through them both, as they wondered what was happening in the garage.

Josh stumbled and fell to the floor. As the whip snapped on his back again, he cried out. He felt himself being grabbed and he tried to roll away, but didn't make it that far. He whimpered, as again the whip snapped on his back.

"You make another sound, boy, and I will gag you so you can't."

Josh trembled even more. He knew his dad had a temper, but this seemed to be extreme even for him.

Another crack of the whip, and he cried out again.

"That did it!"

Josh felt something being forced in his mouth. He tried to pull away, but found that he couldn't. He gagged on the bandanna. It pulled back on the sides of his mouth and kept him from opening or closing his mouth all the way. When the next whipping sounded, he tried to cry out only to have his spit soak the bandanna making his mouth dry.

He moaned and dropped his head. He didn't remember his dad ever doing this to him in this extreme. He wished this was his uncle instead, but he knew it couldn't be. How would his uncle get into the house? How would he know which bed was Josh's?

He tried to blink back tears as the whip snapped him again. *God, please, help me. This is worse then a nightmare. Please help!* He groaned again. Would this never end?

Jared and Jordan stood outside the garage for a long time. They didn't hear another sound from Josh, but they did hear the strange snapping sound. Both of them felt bewildered. What was going on? Finally Jared whispered, "We better get back to bed, before we get caught.

Jordan nodded and the boys quietly snuck back into the house.

At five thirty in the morning, the man finally lowered the whip.

Josh lay on the floor in too much pain to even move. His hands had been tied behind his back a few hours before, when he had attempted to fight back. Tears burned his eyes as he felt the ropes released. He wanted to cry out as he was jerked to his feet and his

252

body slammed into the wall, but the gag was still pushed in his mouth.

"You going to tell anyone, boy? Or do you want a worse whipping to remind you to keep your mouth shut?"

Josh dropped his head. Then he felt cold steel on his stomach. He froze as he saw the barrel of a gun. His head spun.

"Let me tell you one thing, boy. If I can tell at all today that I gave you this whipping, or if anyone else can tell it, I am going to whip you even worse tomorrow night. Do you understand?"

Josh nodded slightly, afraid to move, yet afraid not to. He felt himself relax a little as the gag was removed from his mouth.

"Get in the house and don't let me see any sign of you getting this whipping or any other whipping you get. Is that understood?"

Josh dropped his head. "Yes, sir." He walked out of the garage and shivered. How much more was he going to take? He wished he could just run, but he knew that wouldn't work. Where would he go to? Any where he thought of his dad would find him all too soon. Then he knew he would regret running, cause the whipping would get even worse.

He quietly slipped in the house and up to bed, his back and legs throbbed. He wondered why his dad was beating him so much like his Uncle John. It didn't seem like him.

He lay down in bed and whimpered. He bit his lip. He couldn't take a chance on his brothers hearing. He would just have to do the best he could to keep it from showing. He felt his mouth and groaned again. The gag had hurt, but his mouth still hurt and he knew he had burns on the sides of his mouth from it.

Jordan heard Josh come in. He wanted to say something to him, but he didn't dare. He was afraid it would just get Josh in more trouble. He wondered how long Dad had hit him. He was afraid to think about it.

27

Sunday morning Joy raced up to Josh as they came out of Sunday school. "Josh, Josh! Look! It came!" She held out a white envelope. "It came in yesterday's mail."

Josh looked at the mail in Joy's hand, and his heart sank. It was from the college he had felt the Lord leading him too this coming spring when he had graduated, but that wasn't going to happen now.

He felt his heart sink deeper. "Just throw it away, Joy. It doesn't matter any more." He felt as hopeless as he sounded. If he got another whipping like the one his dad gave him last night he wouldn't be alive in the spring anyway.

Joy was stunned. "But, Josh, it's what you wanted. You said that you felt this was where God wanted you and this was where he was leading."

Josh shook his head. He didn't want to have to explain everything. Slowly he reached out and took the letter. At that moment the church piano started to play. He folded the letter quickly and put it in his pocket. "Thanks, Joy. I need to get in there and sit. Dad doesn't like me out here when it's time to start.

Joy nodded. "I know. See you after church. I can't wait to see if you are really excepted. Are you coming over for lunch?"

Josh shrugged. "I don't know. Come on lets get in there, before we are late."

The two quickly went in to the sanctuary. Josh slipped into the pew beside Jared. His heart sank as his dad looked over at him. Was he going to be in trouble, just because he hadn't gotten in here before the music started?

His body seemed to cry out in pain. He didn't know how much more of this he could take. He looked up at Luke, then looked quickly away. He longed to tell him what was happening, but he knew if he did there would be consequences to pay.

Luke was startled when he saw Josh at church that morning. The dark circles under his eyes said plainly that he wasn't getting enough sleep, but there was something else about him that bothered Luke. He tried to place it as he watched him. Was it just the way the boy looked at him or was it more. He frowned. The defeated slump of his shoulders, the beaten down way he stood, the fear that seemed to cloak him, Luke felt something inside him twist.

As they were leaving he stopped him knowing that the boy talking to him was a slim chance, but he had to try. "Josh, is every thing okay? I haven't had a chance to talk to you since the baby was born. How are you handling things at your dads? Come here and talk to me."

Josh jerked as Luke lead him aside, and Luke saw the panic in his eyes. "Everything is fine." He tried to pull away. "Please, Da-Luke, I can't talk about it. Please don't ask."

Luke frowned. "Josh, everything isn't fine. What is wrong? You seemed to be getting along fine for a while. Why are you-"

"Dad, please-" Josh interrupted then stopped and his face paled as he glanced behind him to make sure his dad hadn't heard. "I mean Luke, everything is fine."

Luke nodded. "If there is something wrong, Josh, please don't hesitate to ask for help. Please tell me, if you need me."

Josh nodded, but turned away. "Thanks."

Luke felt the boys pain, but didn't know what to do. Luke sighed as Josh turned away and he stepped back up by the door. He smiled at Jim as he walked up. "Hi, Jim. The wife would like it if you all could come for lunch today."

Jim looked at Luke and smiled lightly. "Thanks for the invite, Luke, but I think we need to go home today. The boys started school this week and," He glanced at Josh then back to Luke, "I think Joshua needs to get some sleep. He doesn't seem to be handling school well."

Luke nodded. "I noticed he seemed tired."

Jim nodded as well. He glanced around and saw no one else

waiting to leave, so he turned back to Luke. "I wish I could say it was just tired, Luke. I don't know what it is. The boy is shutting down. He won't talk to me, he won't talk to Lilly. He is picking fights at school and at home. I thought if he was going to have an act out from moving in with us, it would have been before now. I don't know what to do. I don't want to hit the boy, Luke, but what do I do to let him know when he has crossed a definite boundary and he knows it? I can't just let it go unchecked or undisciplined. What do I do?"

Luke frowned in thought. "I had that trouble with him some last spring, but that was all. Are you sure he is doing it on purpose? Are you sure the others aren't just letting him take the fall for it?"

Jim sighed. He had thought about that, and he was worried about that. "I just don't know, Luke." He shook his head. "Tell Annie, thanks for the invite, but I think we better just go home today." He turned to Lilly. "Lets go. I am sure the kids are outside already."

Lilly smiled and waved as they walked out the door.

As Jim, Lilly and the kids left, he bowed his head. "Dear Lord, you know what is going on with Joshua. Please protect him. Please don't let his dad hit him."

Monday morning came all too soon for Josh. He knew what was going to happen at school and he was afraid of what would happen at home if he said anything.

Jared felt guilty for all that he had done to Josh. After hearing what had to have been happening the other night, he knew he had been wrong. He never should have tried to get Josh in trouble. Why had Josh just willingly taken the blame for everything, when he knew what the cost would be? But Jared knew why. Josh had taken the blame, because he hadn't wanted him and Jordan to get into that big of a punishment.

Jared felt his conscience prick him. Josh had known what his father was capable of. He knew what would happen to him if he had pushed to far, that would be why he had acted afraid of his dad.

Jared tried to push his uneasiness away, telling himself it wouldn't happen again, but in his mind he still wondered if his dad was going to love Josh more than him and Jordan. He knew he wouldn't but he was still having a hard time believing it for some reason.

Monday afternoon when Luke picked the boys up from school he grew even more worried about Josh. As the boys walked to the car he could tell Josh seemed to be in pain. He stumbled once and saw Jordan grab him before he fell. He saw the boys say something, but they were still to far away to tell what was being said. His concern grew.

What was happening to Josh? He had noticed in church yesterday that he had seemed to be losing weight, but now he really saw him, and he felt sick. Josh looked sick. He smiled at them all as they climbed in his car. "Hi, boys. How was school today?"

He glanced in the back. Josh kept his head down and made no reply. Jared and Jordan both looked up with a smile, but he saw worry in Jordan's eyes. "It was fine. Thanks for picking us up."

Luke smiled. "No problem. Glad to do it. I was just on my way home anyway."

He dropped them off and decided that he was going to have a very serious talk with Jim. Either Jim was beating and starving him, or something was up at school. He didn't know which, but he was going to find out.

He watched as the boys disappeared into the house and his determination grew. He was going to find out what was going on. And this time if it was Jim hurting him – He shook his head. He couldn't believe it was him. He saw the sincerity in Jim when they talked. God had changed him, but what was going on with Josh? He needed to find out.

28

Slowly, for Josh, the month of August gave way to September, then October. Things didn't get better at school, they got worse, and John continued to beat and terrorize Josh at night as well. Josh was still unaware that it was his uncle and because he thought it was his dad, a wall had grown up between him and his dad.

Jim saw Josh withdrawing from him more and more each day, and though he tried to talk to him and do things with him, Josh refused to let his guard down. Jim wished he could take back the spanking he had to give Josh. To him that was when his son withdrew from him the most. He knew Josh was afraid that he hadn't changed, and every time Jim looked at Josh he felt his guilt even more.

Jordan began feeling more and more guilty as he watched the strain growing between Josh and his dad, but he didn't know what to do. He knew stuff was going on, but he wasn't sure what all it was or why.

Jared continued to be jealous of Josh and tried to get him into trouble every chance he got.

On the first Monday in October Josh had again been sent to the principal's office and whipped thoroughly. Johnathan had made sure that he was the one who caught all the blame for the fight and Jared had even helped him.

Jordan had told Jared off when school was over and they were waiting for Josh in the parking lot, and waiting for their dad to get

258

there, but it ended up that their mom picked them up, because at the last minute their dad had a woman come in in labor.

Jordan had decided enough was enough and he was going to tell their dad what was happening. When his mom pulled in he wasn't sure what he should do.

Lilly told them what happened with their dad as they climbed in the car. "Where is Joshua?" She asked as she looked back at her two boys. "Why isn't he out here with you two?"

Jordan bit his lip. He knew Josh feared them telling Mom and Dad, because he was afraid that Dad would spank him at home, but he couldn't escape the feeling that he should say something. Out of the corner of his eye he saw Jared open his mouth to answer and he quickly cut him off. "He had some stuff to get out of his locker. He should be here any minute."

Lilly looked at Jordan in the mirror. Then she looked at Julia and Jimmy asleep in their seats and decided that now was not the time to have a discussion with the boys. That could wait till later, but she did need to talk to them.

At that moment Josh came out of the school and headed their way.

Lilly smiled as he climbed in, but Jared scowled. He was hoping Josh would take longer and have to tell his mom that he was in trouble. He thought to himself, trying to come up with a plan to tell his dad. He needed to do it at just the right moment. He wanted Josh to get in big trouble. Suddenly a sly smile came to his face. He had the perfect idea!

When they got home Josh started to head up to their room, but Lilly stopped him. "Dad wants you boys to get all the leaves raked up and taken care of today. So go ahead and get changed and then take care of that. I am going to start supper. When you boys are done in the yard, I want some help in the house. The floors could use a good scrubbing."

Josh bit his lip, but didn't say anything. The pain he was in was making him sick. He wanted to sleep and he had a mountain of homework because he had been in the principal's office through his last two classes. He knew he couldn't say anything, but okay, so he turned without a word and headed out the door. As he did he heard Jared start to protest.

Jared moaned. "Aw, Mom, do we have to scrub the floors?

They will just get dirty anyway. Why do we have to scrub them today, it's not even Saturday?"

Lilly frowned at Jared. "Watch it young man, or you will be doing all the scrubbing by yourself."

Jared snapped his mouth closed and followed his brothers out the door.

As they raked he got madder and madder. He looked over and saw Jordan holding open a bag while Josh put the leaves in it. Anger surged through him. Why was Jordan so nice to Josh, didn't he see what Josh was doing?

Josh leaned down to pick up another pile of leaves. "Thanks for not saying anything to Mom."

Jordan shrugged. "I didn't figure it was my place, but I am pretty sure Jared is planning to tell Dad. I don't think I can stop him."

Josh paled slightly, but didn't say anything more. He groaned slightly in pain as he picked up the rest of the leaves and shoved them in the bag.

Jordan longed to ask Josh about him sneaking out at night, but for some reason he couldn't bring himself to. He wasn't sure why, he just couldn't.

Josh stood and tried to stretch a little, but felt his muscles reject as he did. He bit his lip to keep back a cry of pain and it escaped as a groan.

Jordan looked away, not wanting to make Josh feel even worse. "I think you should tell Dad," he muttered. "He has a right to know what the principal is doing to you. It's not fair and it is not illegal. Why don't you tell on him?"

Josh turned away. "Let's get this job done, Jordan. I don't want Dad to be upset when we don't get done on time."

Jordan scowled. "You are changing the subject, but it doesn't change the fact."

Josh looked up at Jordan. "Dad isn't going to care what they are doing to me. He would care if it was you or Jared, but he isn't going to care that it is me. Just trust me on this one, please, Jordan."

Jordan's eyes seemed to snap. "But, Josh-"

Josh's look silenced Jordan's protest. "Trust me, Jordan. Dad will punish me more if you tell him. He will whip me worse than the principal if he finds out that I have been in trouble at school."

Jordan frowned again then turned back to the leaves. Josh was wrong. Dad wouldn't punish him for nothing, and that is all it was. Josh hadn't done anything. He hadn't picked the fights at school. He hadn't done any of the things that that brat Johnathan accused him of. Why was Josh so sure his dad wouldn't believe him? Jordan knew his dad would care. "Come on, let's get done," he muttered as he turned away. He was determined if Josh was sent to the principal's office one more time, he was going to tell his dad. Josh could argue all he wanted, but he was going to tell.

As the boys were filling the last bag, they heard their dad's car drive up. Josh slowly stood, biting his lip, fighting against the pain. Fear filled his dark blue eyes as he waited for his dad to get out of the car.

Jordan saw Josh's pain and felt the guilt strike his heart again. Maybe he should talk to his dad, without Josh knowing. Maybe he should see what his dad really thought about the principal hitting Josh, but in his heart he was also afraid. What if Josh was right and his dad hit him, because he had been in trouble at school? He didn't want Josh in even more trouble.

Jim smiled at them as he got out of the car. "Thanks, boys. It sure is looking wonderful. How are my boys doing today?" He ruffled Jordan's hair and gave Jared a one armed hug. He reached out to Josh, but Josh saw his father's hand heading toward him and quickly stepped away.

Why did his dad always act so nice to him when he was home? Why did he act like he loved him, then at night beat him so badly? Tears stung his eyes and he looked quickly away so his dad didn't see.

Jim felt a pain stab his heart as he saw fear in his son's eyes. How he wished more and more every day that he could erase the past. He knew that was impossible and his son hating him so much was his own fault because of who he had been, but he longed to love his son.

261

He wished the boy would let him get close to him, but every time he tried it just seemed to drive him farther away.

God, where is your mercy and grace in this?

"Why don't you all join me in going to see if supper is ready? It looks like you are all done with the yard." He smiled warmly at all of them, but saw Josh look away before he even started to speak.

The three boys nodded and Jared and Jordan walked beside their dad on the way in the house. Josh trailed behind. He felt tears form in his eyes, but quickly blinked them away. Would he ever feel like he belonged here? No. But maybe some day his dad would stop hitting him. Maybe he would just get over it. Maybe some day he would love him. Some day.

Jim looked back at Josh. He knew something was wrong with him, but he was unsure how to find out what it was. "Come on, Josh. Step it up a little. Mom is probably waiting."

Josh nodded as he stepped closer to his dad. "Sorry," he muttered. "I didn't mean to make you slow down."

Jim reached out and put his arm around the boy. He was more surprised to feel Josh shiver then he was when Josh actually let him touch him. But he was even more surprised to see pain flash in the boy's eyes. Just what was going on?

During supper, Jared tried to think of something he could do to Josh to get him into trouble, but his mind was drawing a blank. He glanced at his dad and saw him watching Josh. He looked at his brother and frowned. Josh hadn't eaten any of Mom's good supper. All he was doing was pushing it around on his plate.

"Joshua," Jim's voice was stern.

Josh jumped and looked up at his dad, then looked down again. He knew by the tone of his dad's voice he was in trouble.

Jim frowned. "Are you not hungry, son?"

Josh looked away slightly. He was starving, but he was in so much pain he knew if he tried to eat it was coming back up.

Jim saw the fear in his son and it puzzled him. He hadn't had to spank the boys in quiet a while, why was Josh acting so afraid of him? "What's bothering you, son?"

Josh looked up and met his father's gaze without blinking as he had been taught to do. "I'm just not hungry, Dad." That was a lie, he was starving, but he was in too much pain to eat.

Jordan bit his lip. He wished there was something he could do

262

to help his brother.

Jim sighed. "If you aren't going to eat then you may as well get started on your homework, son."

Josh paled. What was his dad going to do to him when he saw how much homework he had? He had been being able to work on it, most of the time, before his dad got home. But tonight he had a lot and he hadn't been able to work on any of it.

He gave Jordan a quick glance.

Jordan saw his brother's fear and felt his guilt. He shouldn't be keeping a secret from his dad. He needed to tell him. But he knew Josh didn't want him to, and from the way his brother was trembling in fear he knew he was afraid that he was going to be in trouble at home.

Lilly rose and started to clear the table. "Come on, boys. Let's get this table cleared so you can get started on your homework."

Josh stood and help Lilly clear the table.

Jared and Jordan slowly followed. Then they headed up to their room to get their books.

Jim was startled when he saw the boys coming back down with their book. It looked as if Josh hadn't done any school work that day. He waited till they were all three seated at the table then he walked up behind his son. "Joshua, why do you have so much homework?"

Josh jumped. Fear shot through him like lightning.

Jim frowned deeper. "How much did you do in study hall, son?"

Josh bit his lip and dropped his head.

Jim waited.

Jared and Jordan exchanged a glance. Was their dad mad at Josh because he had homework? That didn't make a lot of sense.

Josh struggled against telling his dad he hadn't had a study hall all year. He had spent his study time in the principal's office. Fortunately that was one of his afternoon classes. Otherwise he would be in real trouble. Most of the time the beatings stopped in time for him to make it to his other two. He just usually ended up back in the principal's office before the last one was over.

Jared suddenly saw his chance to get Josh in trouble. "It's kind of hard to study in study hall when you spend all of your study hall in the principal's office.

Jim looked at Jared, then back at Josh. Fire seemed to shoot from his eyes. "Joshua?"

Josh sunk lower in his chair. He couldn't bring himself to look at his dad. "Yes, sir." his voice was barely a whisper.

"Why were you in the principal's office, son?"

Josh bit his lip. His dad wouldn't believe the truth. What was he suppose to say?

Jim waited.

Josh trembled. "Just stupid stuff."

Jim knew the vague answer his son was giving was a cover up, but for tonight he decided to let it go. "It better not happen again. I better never see you coming home with this much homework again. Is that understood?

Josh nodded, but kept his head down.

Jim sighed. "Go ahead and work on your books, boys. But by ten o'clock you are heading to bed." He gave Joshua a firm look. "All of you."

Josh nodded. "Yes, sir."

By nine forty-five all the boys were done with their homework, but Josh had a test tomorrow and Jared and Jordan had a couple of quizzes that they needed to study for.

Jim smiled as he came into the kitchen and saw the boys picking up the books. "Good job, boys. I hope anyway."

Josh shuttered.

Jim noticed, but let it go. He couldn't blame his son for being afraid of him. It was his own fault. "Well, you all might as well head up and get ready for bed. Mom and I will be up in a few minutes to pray with you."

Josh slowly stood and headed for the stairs. Was his dad going to beat him? Did he already suspect stuff going on at school?

As the boys headed up to their room Jared got an idea. It had been a long time since they had had a good pillow fight. He knew Dad had told them to go to bed, but something in him couldn't resist.

As they were entering their room he gave Josh a hard push. Unknowingly he pushed on Josh's back which was very painful from the whipping the principal had given him.

Josh bit his lip and somehow managed to keep back the cry of pain the surfaced, but barely.

Jared raced to his bed and grabbed his pillow. A minute later he swung with a mighty force knocking Josh to the floor.

Josh felt his anger rise. What was Jared doing? Trying to get them all in trouble!

Jordan let out a whoop and dived for his pillow. Soon all three where having a great time. But as the pillow fight got longer the fun turned into a battle.

Josh felt his anger mounting as he fought with his brothers. He knew if his dad caught them they would all be in trouble, but he couldn't stop himself. He had so much anger burning in him he had to let some of it out.

Suddenly Jared walloped him in the back.

Josh let out a yelp and swung around. Anger shot out of his eyes. He lunged at his brother and slammed his entire body into him knocking him to the floor.

Jared was suddenly afraid of Josh. He saw the anger in him and knew that this was no longer a fun fight for him.

Josh slugged him in the face.

Jared screamed and struggled to get away.

Jordan saw what was happening and ran to help his brother. He slammed into Josh and knocked him off of Jared, but Josh jumped up and swung again.

His anger mounted. He had enough of this. He hated his life. He was tired of getting whipped. He wasn't going to just sit by and let it happened. He lunged at Jared again and knocked him to the floor.

Jared let out a yell of fear.

Jordan grabbed Josh's arms and tried to pull him off his brother, but Josh arched his back and twisted throwing Jordan off.

Jordan was suddenly afraid. He hadn't realized how strong Josh really was. He knew he had muscle, but he hadn't realized just how much. If he didn't stop him, in his anger he was going to really hurt Jared or him or maybe both.

Jared was screaming as Josh slammed his fist into his brother's face. "I am not going to take any more!" he screamed. He slugged Jared again.

All Jordan saw was blood. He rammed into Josh and knocked

him to the floor. Josh rolled to the side and rammed into Jordan's legs knocking him to the floor. He rolled on top of him and would have slugged him, but his fist was stopped mid-swing by a hand gripping his wrist.

He jerked his arm and yelled, but slowly felt himself being dragged off his brother. He jerked and fought. "Let go of me! I hate you! Let me go! Leave me alone!"

Jim had never seen his son this mad before. He didn't know what had started it, but he did know this was not going to go unpunished. He struggled to keep his son from getting loose.

Josh jerked and fought. "Get away from me! Let me go."

Jim finally managed to get both of his son's arms pulled behind him.

Josh felt the restriction, but he knew it was fight or pay and he wasn't going to pay without a fight this time. He jerked again. "Let me go!"

"Joshua." Jim tried to keep his voice calm.

Josh jerked again.

Jim turned the boy to face him.

Josh saw his dad and jerked harder. "Let me go! I hate you! Leave me alone! I hate you! I hate you!" He swung his leg out trying to kick his dad.

Jim's hand snapped out before he quite realized what he was doing.

Josh's head snapped to the side with the force of the blow. Instantly the fight in him died. He knew he shouldn't have tried to fight, but he needed to let his anger out. He hunched up slightly as though waiting for his father to strike him again, but jerked himself to the side and looked at his brothers.

Fear trickled through him as he saw Jared's mouth was bleeding and he had a bruise on the side of his head. He looked at Jordan and saw that he was bleeding too, but looked less beat up then his brother.

He knew he was the one who did it and panic washed over him. What was his dad going to do to him?

"Just what is going on here?" Jim's voice was soft, but Josh heard the threat that was in it.

Josh breathed hard as he glanced again at his brothers.

Jim saw that Josh was calmer and slowly released his hold on him. He turned to Jared and Jordan. "Are you two okay?"

Jared couldn't believe how quickly Josh had changed from fun fighting to dangerous. His anger and jealousy toward his brother grew. He looked at his dad. His vision was still a bit blurry. "Do I look fine? No, I am not fine!"

Josh looked at him and snapped. "You are fine. Shut up!"

Jim gripped his son's arm and backhanded him.

Josh's head again snapped with the force of the blow. He felt moisture on his chin and knew his mouth was bleeding. Slowly he looked back at his dad, and again felt the back of his hand across his mouth. He moaned, but slowly turned back toward his dad again. Again his dad struck him. This time he stayed with his head down.

Jim looked over at Jared and Jordan. "Both of you come here. Stand beside your brother."

All three boys stood before their father and waited.

Jim sighed. "What happened? I sent you all up to bed."

Jared looked at his father with innocents. "It was just suppose to be a little pillow fight, but he just blew up." He looked at Josh with a scowl.

Jim turned to Jordan.

Jordan saw the look and wished with all his might that he didn't have to tell. Slowly he raised his eyes. "We were just having a fun pillow fight. I am not sure what happened, but Josh got mad and started beating on Jared. I tried to get him off and he turned on me."

Jim looked at his son.

Josh looked away. He knew by the look in his dad's eyes that he was going to pay dearly for this.

Jim stood there for a moment as though thinking. "Who had the idea of a pillow fight? I told all of you to get ready to bed and go to bed. Did you think you had time to do that and have a pillow fight before we came up to pray with you. I want to know the truth. Who started this fight?" His voice was hard a livid with anger.

Jared looked away. He had hoped that Josh would again take the blame, but he could see by the look on his face that he wasn't going to this time. "I did, Dad. It has just been so long since we had one, and it sounded like such fun."

Jim looked at Josh again. "What is your side to this story?"

Josh looked away.

Jim saw the pain in the boy's eyes, but also fear. Well this time

267

he had better be afraid, because this wasn't going to go with just a few swats and a hope that it wouldn't happen again.

Jim sighed. "Joshua, what made you beat on your brothers?"

Josh looked up slowly. "I was mad."

Jim nodded. "I could see that. Why were you mad?"

Josh looked away again. He couldn't tell his dad the truth. He just couldn't. "I just was."

Jared stared. Was all Josh was going to get just a talking to?

Jordan waited wondering what was going to happen.

Jim looked at Josh then at the other two. His jaw muscles were working and all three knew that he was trying to decide what he was going to do to them.

Finally Jim looked at Jared. "You the one who started the fight?"

Jared couldn't believe it. Josh had beat him up and all Dad cared about was who had started the fight. Slowly he nodded, but he felt his anger mounting. He just knew it. Josh was going to get away scotch free.

Jim slowly unbuckled his belt. "Take off your shirt, Jared, and come here."

Jared stared in fear at his dad, but slowly pulled off his shirt and walked up to him.

Jim sighed. "This had better never happen again, son. Turn around."

Jared felt his anger rise. Why was he the only one who was getting punished? It wasn't fair. "It was Josh's fault, Dad. I only wanted to have a friendly pillow fight, but when I told him that I was going to tell you what he was hiding under his bed, he attacked with vengeance."

Jim snapped the belt across his back five times. Jared yelled with each smack. Slowly he lowered the belt. "Look at me," his voice was hard. "What was he hiding."

Jared looked at Josh.

Josh bit his lip. He didn't have anything under his bed that he shouldn't. What was Jordan talking about?

Jared walked over to Josh's bed and pulled what looked like a magazine from under the mattress.

Josh felt the color drain from his face as he saw his dad's eyes flash. He knew instantly what it was and he knew he was going to be whipped severely if he even tried to deny it was his.

Jim took the magazine from Jared and turned to Josh with fire in his eyes. "I will deal with this in a minute," he growled.

Josh bit his lip to keep back the whimper.

Jim took a deep breath and turned to Jordan.

Jordan saw the look in his dad's eyes. Fear trickled through him, but he slowly pulled off his shirt and turned around.

Jim struck him five times and turned to Josh. His eyes snapped. "Come here, son."

Josh trembled, but slowly stepped in front of his dad. Which was he going to be punished for first, the fight or the magazine?

Jim eyed him with anger in his eyes. "Get your shirt off." His voice seemed deadly to Josh. He felt his temper rise high. There was no way he was going to let his son get away with this. No son of his was going to be looking at this dirty stuff.

Josh trembled and took a step back. "No." He knew that he was going to get it way worse then the other two anyway, but there was no way he was going to let Jared, Jordan, or his dad see what had been happening to him at school and here.

Jim gripped his son's arm. "You will take it off on your own, son, or I will take it off of you. You are not going to let your anger take possession of you like that again. Do you understand?"

Josh trembled. He wanted to back away, but he knew it was useless to try.

Jim gripped the boy's arm tighter. He raised the belt and brought it down with a loud snap on Josh's back.

Josh bit his lip to keep back the cry of pain. Again and again the belt snapped his back. Josh felt moisture through his shirt and knew that he was bleeding.

Jared and Jordan looked on with wide eyes. They hadn't ever seen their dad this mad before.

Jim smacked Josh again. He could see wetness on the boy's shirt, but he didn't stop. This behavior had to stop. He had to show Josh where his boundaries were. He had to know he had crossed one to many. Again he brought the belt down with a loud snap. "Get your shirt off, son," he was breathing hard from the exertion.

Josh trembled and tried to pull away. "No, Sir."

Jim gripped the boy's arm tighter and raised the belt again. "You are going to obey me son, be it in pain or not."

269

Josh trembled, but bit back the cry of pain as the belting got worse.

Jared stared in fear as it went on and on. How long was his dad going to hit Josh? He saw Josh drop his head, and knew that he was in pain. Why didn't he just take off his shirt?

Jordan shivered. Just how long was his dad going to hit Josh?

After about twenty minutes Jim lowered the belt. "Look at me, Joshua," his voice was as hard as steel.

Josh slowly turned.

Jim's eyes snapped. "Get your shirt off."

Josh bit his lip as he back away slightly. He knew he would have to when his dad dragged him out to the garage later, but he really didn't want his brothers to see the state of his back. "No." his voice was weak, but Jim heard the defiance in it.

He gripped Josh's arm again and again brought the belt down on his back. Josh fell to the floor after a few more blows. Whimpering he pulled into himself and prayed that the beating would stop.

Jim felt his pain and anger grow with each strike to his son. Pain in hitting him; anger in what he had done to get this whipping. "You are never to look at that trash again, son! Not ever. Do you understand?"

Jared couldn't believe his dad was hitting Josh like this. His dad hadn't hardly ever given them a spanking, but the beating he was giving Josh was worse than Jared had ever seen or thought.

Jim grabbed his son's arm and jerked him to his feet. "Go to the bathroom, son." Jared and Jordan didn't need to see all of this.

Josh walked slowly in front of his dad to the bathroom.

Once inside Jim shut the door

Josh felt his dad grab his shirt and he knew he was in for it. He tried to pull away, but couldn't. He whimpered as his dad jerked his shirt off of him and again snapped the belt across his back. Again and again it struck. He tried to keep back the cry of pain, but at last as the belt snapped he cried out.

Jim heard the boy cry out and knew Josh had had enough. This was one lesson he wasn't going to forget soon. He stopped and jerked his son to his feet.

Josh trembled even more as he stood before his dad.

"Don't you ever let your anger get the better of you again, son. I didn't want to have to do that, but you have done nothing but push the boundaries since you moved in. But this boundary you should know isn't just mine. Do you know where they lie now?"

Josh looked away.

Jim sighed. He knew that defiant look in his son. "Turn around again, Joshua."

Josh looked up at his dad with tears in his eyes. Slowly he turned away from his dad. There was no way he was going to answer. All that would do is make him get a worse whipping.

Jim bit his lip, but slowly lifted the belt again.

After several more smacks he stopped. "Do you know now, Joshua?" he whispered. Pain was wracking his heart as he watched his son bleed. Silently he pleaded not to have to hit him again, but Josh wouldn't answer him.

In pain of heart, he raised the belt again.

This time Josh cried out with the first smack. The cry broke his heart, but he smacked him again.

Josh saw the determination in his dad, and knew that he was going to get beat him till he obeyed his dad, but he feared if he did, his dad would beat him tonight for being a sissy.

Jim stopped once more. "Do you know where your boundaries are now, Joshua."

Josh looked up at his dad with pain in his eyes. "Yes, sir."

Jim nodded. "Good. Now you better tell me honestly, do you have any more pornography in your room?"

Josh jerked away from his dad. Anger ripped through him. "No."

Jim gripped Josh's arm tightly. "You had better not be lying to me, son. If I find any in there, you are getting twenty lashes with the belt for each thing I find. Is that understood."

Josh trembled. He knew his dad was serious. "Yes, sir," he answered weakly.

Jim turned so he was looking directly into Josh's eyes. "So knowing what the punishment is I am going to give you one more chance to change your answer if you want to. If you tell me the truth now there won't be any more punishment. Do you have any more pornography in your room?"

Josh pulled away slightly. "I told you no, Dad. I don't have any."

Jim nodded solemnly. "Head in there, son, you are going to

prove it to me."

Josh trembled. What if Jared had planted more then just under his bed.

Jim followed his son into the bed room. "Move your mattress, son."

Jared and Jordan stood silently as Josh moved his mattress. Jordan was surprised to see how many welts and how much blood was on his brother's back.

Jared tried to hide a smirk knowing what his dad was looking for and knowing what he was going to find. He hoped Josh got in a lot of trouble for it.

After the mattress was moved and nothing had been found Jim turned to Josh's dresser. "Open the bottom drawer, son."

Josh trembled even more as he opened each drawer and his dad searched through them. He found nothing. Then Josh came to the top drawer. Slowly he opened it and he paled slightly seeing there was indeed at least one magazine in it.

Jim saw his son stiffen and knew that he had found where the boy was hiding stuff. He pushed him aside and reached in the drawer. His heart hammered harder as he pulled out five magazines. Slowly he turned to look at his son with magazines in hand and pain in his heart.

Josh whimpered and backed away. He wanted to beg his dad not to hit him. He wanted to scream out that they weren't his, but he knew in his heart that his dad wouldn't believe him if he said they weren't his. He also knew that he would get a worse beating if he tried to deny them being his.

Jim gripped Josh's arm. "I told you what would happen, son. Did you think I was lying or that I wouldn't find them?"

Josh hung his head.

Jim sighed as he raised the belt.

Jared and Jordan both stared at their dad with wide eyes. Josh was already bleeding. They couldn't believe that their dad was going to hit him more.

Josh whimpered as the belt smacked his back. Lash after lash sounded and he felt the wetness of blood.

Jim smacked him harder. "You will not look at this stuff again! Am I clear, son! You will not be like your mother!"

Josh jerked as the belt struck him again. "What?" he

whispered.

Suddenly the door opened and Lilly stepped in. She gasped when she saw Josh bleeding and his dad hitting him. "Jim, stop. What are you doing?"

Jim slowly lowered the belt. "Turn and face me, son." his heart was sick. He realized what he had said and a pain jolted him. He realized he was taking his anger out on Josh, for something that wasn't his fault.

Josh slowly turned, but kept his head down.

"Do you understand?"

Josh nodded slowly. It hurt to move and he knew it was going to hurt to speak, "Yes, sir." He bit his lip against the pain. He didn't understand and he didn't know what his dad was talking about when he said he was not going to turn out like his mom, but if his dad was going to stop hitting him, he was fine with that.

Jim nodded.

Lilly stood speechless. Both her boy's backs were bare, but she didn't see any sign that Jim had touched them. "Jim, boys, what is going on in here?"

Jim sighed. "I long over due lesson in obedience, Lilly. That is all. And purity."

Lilly stared at him in shock. "Do you think that by beating your son till he bleeds that you will get him to obey?"

Jim looked at her but it was Josh who spoke.

"It's okay, Mom. I deserved it."

Lilly looked at Jim again with contempt in her eyes. "Are you still needing to punish Jared and Jordan?"

Jim shook his head no.

Lilly's eyebrows raised even more. "So you won't touch them and you whip Josh till blood flows?"

Josh looked away. "Mom, it was my fault. I kept fighting him and refusing to obey. And he warned me what the punishment was and how many lashes I would get if I lied."

Lilly looked at Josh sharply then looked at Jim.

Jim saw the look and nodded, it was time for the night to be over. "Boys, let's all pray and ask God to help us control our tempers and our tongue. All of us, me included."

Slowly the boys all knelt down. It was then that Lilly saw a slight welt on Jordan's back, but nothing like what Josh looked like.

Josh hung back. His body was wracked with pain. He didn't think he could kneel, but his dad had made it clear what would happen if he didn't obey. He was too afraid not to try.

After praying together Jim stood and looked at the boys sharply. "Shower and bed, boys. No fighting, no arguing."

All three nodded. "Yes, Sir."

Jim nodded and him and Lilly walked out.

As soon as they were out of the room Lilly looked at Jim and he burst into a fountain of tears. He took her hand and lead her into their room where they could talk without the boys hearing.

Lilly stared at him in shock. "Jim, I can not believe after all the things we have talked about and all that you promised that Joshua, you would beat him like that. What has come over you?"

Jim placed his hands gently on Lilly shoulders. "Honey, please don't hate me, but I am not done punishing him."

Lilly's eyes widened. "Jim, you have whipped him till he can barely move. Don't you dare touch him like that again."

Jim shook his head, "To stop now would do more harm than good," he whispered. "If I am going to stop now, I shouldn't have ever started I should have just let it all go."

Lilly looked into his eyes. "What are you talking about, Jim."

He sat her down on the edge of the bed and knelt in front of her. "I came up to talk to the boys and they were fighting. When I started getting after them Jared told me that Josh was mad cause he told him he was going to tell on him, because he had found something under Josh's bed.

"Josh flew into a rage and started beating him up.

"I asked Josh what he was hiding, but he refused to answer me. I went over and looked and found a porn magazine."

Lilly's face paled slightly. She couldn't believe that Josh would do such a thing. Surely he knew that was wrong? She looked at Jim with pain in her eyes.

Jim nodded slightly. "Yes, I got angry. I took him into the bathroom and belted him. I asked him if he had any more in the house. He told me he didn't. I told him if he was lying to me I was going to give him twenty lashes for each thing that I found. I then asked him again if he had anything else hidden in his room. I wanted to give him another chance to tell the truth and escape a whipping. But he refused to tell me anything.

274

"We went back into his room and I searched his dresser drawers." Jim hung his head. Tears ran down his cheeks. "I had no idea he had that much in the house. I didn't have a clue he had any, but five more magazines," his voice rang with pain.

He looked up at Lilly. "I can't go back on my word now, Lilly. The boy needs thirty more lashes. I have to do this. If I am going to stop short I am going to do more harm then good. Then he will think I will stop short next time and it will be more serious."

Lilly nodded. "I understand, Jim." she whispered. Her tears were now flowing just as freely as his. "Just don't hit him any more than you have to."

Jim nodded. His face paled as he headed back to the boys room. He paused outside the door. "God," he whispered. "I need you to help me. I don't want to hit my son any more show me what to do to get him to listen."

Almost that quickly a thought came to him. He gasped, then nodded. That was the answer. Slowly he opened the door.

Josh jerked around as he saw the door open. Jared and Jordan sat on their bed with their eyes wide. Fear was evident on every face, but his gaze stayed fixed on Josh.

"Son."

Josh trembled. Was his dad going to hit him more? "Yes, sir?"

Jim stepped up to his son. "You know your whipping is not over."

Josh bit his lip. Slowly he stood. He trembled as he faced his dad, but without blinking or hesitating he removed his shirt and slowly turned around.

Jim bit his lip hard as he saw the boys bare back. Had he really whipped the boy that badly? He knew he lost his temper for a while, but had he done that?

He cleared his throat knowing this was going to be one of the hardest things he had done in his life. "Joshua, take off your belt."

Josh jerked around to face his dad. His face lost all it's color. He trembled. Fear ran through him. He tried to fight off the whimper that rose in his throat, but he couldn't. He took a step back.

Jim saw the fear in his son's eyes and gripped his arm tightly. "Do as you are told son."

Jared and Jordan stared at the scene before them with horror in their eyes. Was Dad really going to hit Josh more? Hadn't he done enough.

Jared felt his guilt even deeper, but fear of his dad beating him worse than he had Josh, kept him from telling the truth.

Jim looked Josh in the eye. Josh looked his dad in the eye for a brief moment, then slowly lowered his gaze. He knew he had to obey. To fight his dad was just going to make the whipping worse. Slowly and fighting tears he reached down and unbuckled his belt.

Jim watched the pain in his eyes growing. "Take it off, son."

Josh looked at his dad with pain in his eyes, but slowly obeyed.

Jim nodded as the boy pulled his belt off, then to Josh's complete surprise Jim pulled off his own shirt and turned his back to his son. "I am taking the rest of your beating, son, and you are going to give it to me. Thirty lashes. Get started."

Josh's eyes grew wide and he dropped the belt and backed away. "No, Dad. Please, no."

Jim turned and gripped Josh's arm. "You will, son. Be it with more of a beating to yourself or not, you are going to hit me with that belt thirty times. Now get started."

Josh felt all the color drain out of his face. He reached out and picked up his belt. What was his dad doing?

Jared and Jordan looked at their dad in surprise then in horror at Josh.

Josh bit his lip and painfully brought the belt down on his dad's back.

"Harder." Jim ordered.

Josh smacked him again.

"Harder." Jim ordered again.

Josh trembled, but brought the belt across his dad's back again.

Jim felt the sting, but knew his son was holding back. Josh could hit a lot harder than he was. After about five blows he turned and gripped Josh's arm. "Son, I said to hit harder, now you are going to hit till you hit hard enough, then you will hit me thirty times, so you better start hitting me harder. Do you understand?"

Josh's face paled even more. "Please, Dad, I-"

Jim slapped him hard across the mouth. "Do not argue and do not plead for it to stop. This time you are the one making it longer, and it will last till you have belted me thirty times, hard. Now get to it."

Josh whimpered as he raised the belt and his dad turned again. Pain ripped through him as he brought the belt down with a loud crack and a stinging blow on his dad's back. He instantly saw the red welt from the belt. Again he brought the belt down as hard as he could. Again the welt almost instantly rose on his dad's back.

Jared and Jordan watched in horror as Josh belted their dad. Jordan saw the tears running down Josh's cheeks, and he wondered how many were from what he was being forced to do and how many were from the pain he was in.

Josh felt the pain in his back and shoulder with each blow he brought down on his dad. He didn't dare stop until his count reached thirty, nor did he dare go one over, sure his dad was counting, but he wasn't sure how many he had done, because he wasn't sure what all his dad would count.

When his mental count reached thirty he dropped the belt and as his dad stood and faced him he backed away trembling.

Jim saw the pain and fear in his son's eyes and he hated himself for putting it there. Pain shot though his back as he stood straight. "Are we ever going to have to repeat this, son?"

Josh wanted to tell his dad again, that he hadn't touched the porn nor brought it into the house, but he knew his dad wouldn't believe him and that would just lead to another whipping.

"No, sir." he whispered, still wishing he could shout out the truth and his dad would believe him.

Jared bit his lip hard. He hadn't meant to do this. It had all gone way too far. He never should have been jealous of Josh. Josh wasn't trying to play favorites, and Jared knew it.

Jim looked Josh in the eye. "You ever look at that stuff again and you will get way worse. Do I make myself clear?"

Jim waited till Josh had nodded, then turned to the other two. "All of you get to bed. Josh, you get started on the first shower."

Josh nodded slightly as he turned away from his dad.

Jim waited till Josh was out of the room then turned to Jared and Jordan. "Did either one of you look at the magazines Josh had?"

Jared and Jordan both shook their heads. "No, sir."

Jim nodded. "Good. I better never catch either one of you looking at it. If you do, you remember this. Because you will be getting a whipping to match the one your brother got or worse. Do you understand?"

Jared and Jordan both stared at him in fear for a few minutes then nodded slightly. "Yes, sir."

Jared bit his lip. He knew he should tell his dad the truth, but fear that his dad would hit him like he had Josh kept him from saying anything.

Jim nodded. "Good. Goodnight, boys."

The boys nodded. "Good night, Dad."

Jim nodded and walked out of the room.

That night as Josh was in the shower and Jared and Jordan were having their devotions Jared felt his heart constrict. He had been reading the beatitudes and his sin was heavy on his conscience.

Jordan heard his brother sniff and looked up in surprise. "Jared, what is wrong?"

Jared shook his head. "I have been so awful, Jordan. I have disobeyed Dad. I have let Josh take the blame for things he didn't do. I have lied. I am a sinner." He felt his guilt even stronger now. Why had dad beat Josh so badly when he found the porn. He didn't even ask Josh if it was his, he just started hitting him for it. And what had he meant about Josh turning out like his mom? He had never felt so guilty. Why had he let his dad hit Josh so long?

Jordan sighed. Finally, Jared was admitting his wrong.

Jared burst into tears. He rolled out of his bed and knelt down beside his brother's bed. "God, forgive me. I have been so wicked. I didn't want Josh to be a part of our family. I was mean and hateful. Please forgive me. Wash me clean. Please help me to be more like you. Please forgive me and help Josh to forgive me too."

He stood with a smile. From now on he knew things were going to be different. God had made him a new person. He had forgiven him. "Thank you, God." he whispered. "You are a wonderful God." In his heart he knew he was going to have to admit to his dad, that he was the one who had set Josh up. His heart jerked in fear. He would wait till morning when Dad had cooled off a little. But he knew what he had to do.

Later that night after the boys were all in bed, a dark figure slipped into the boys' room. He stood angrily beside Josh's bed. He glared down at the boy for a moment then gripped his arm and jerked him out of bed.

Josh felt himself jerked out of bed. He let out a startled cry as his back hit the floor. Though still wrapped up in his blanket he looked up at his dad with fear filled eyes and whimpered as he tried to scoot back from his dad. What was his dad going to do to him?

The man glared down at him. "Get up and get outside, boy," he snarled.

Josh trembled even more.

The man reached down and grabbed Josh by the hair at the back of his neck. He jerked him to his feet and drug him out the door.

Josh cried out in pain, but that only caused his dad to jerk his head back and push him sharply. He grunted as he fell down the steps. Before he could make a sound as he hit the bottom, he felt his dad's angry grip on his arm and felt himself being drug to his feet and out the door.

He cried out in pain again as his dad pushed him to the floor of the garage. He looked up in pain and tried to back away, but his dad grabbed him and pushed a gag in his mouth, then pushed him to the ground one more time.

Josh moaned as his head struck the floor. He wanted to beg his dad to stop, but he knew when his dad had him hit him earlier that night, that this was coming. He whimpered as his dad gripped his arms and drug him across the concrete floor.

He tried to scream as he felt the rough concrete rip his back, but the gag kept him from uttering more than a muffled groan. When they reached the far side of the garage where there was no light his dad stopped and jerked him to his feet.

Josh glared at his dad with hate and anger in his eyes, but quickly looked away as his dad jerked his shirt off of him and tied his hands in front of him with duck tape. He closed his eyes and prayed for help as his father pulled off his belt.

Jared and Jordan were both awakened by Josh's cry. They both watched quietly from their bed in horror as their dad jerked their brother to his feet and drug him out of the room.

They followed as silently as they could, wondering what their dad was going to do to Josh.

They watched in wide eyed horror as they saw their dad drag Josh across the floor of the garage, then, though they couldn't see, listened as they heard a belt snapping; and though they didn't hear a sound from Josh they knew that their dad was hitting him.

Jared looked at Jordan with tears on his eyes. "I never meant for Dad to take it this far," he whispered. "I didn't mean for him to hit Josh like this."

Jordan sighed and both boys made their way back to the house. They were at a loss as to what to do. Should they tell mom what dad was doing? Should they let it go? What were they suppose to do?

They discussed it quietly until they fell asleep. There was still no sight of Josh.

Tuesday morning when Lilly called the boys to breakfast, Jordan rolled out of bed and shook Josh who was still soundly sleeping. He didn't give it a thought to being careful with his brother and gripped his arm tightly as he shook him.

Josh groaned as Jordan touched him.

Jordan bit his lip. "Josh, it's time to get up. Mamma is calling us for breakfast."

Josh slowly opened his eyes. He knew he hadn't been asleep very long, but he was afraid if he let on, his dad would find out. He drug himself out of bed and slowly and painfully made his way to the bathroom. He looked in the mirror and bit his lip. Sixteen today! His birthday!

He groaned as he remembered the last birthday he spent with his dad. Quickly he pushed the thought aside. If it happened again, it happened again. Could he beat him any worse then he had last night? He doubted it.

His body still wracked with pain. His back was still oozing with blood. His lip was bleeding, and he had a large welt on the side of his face from his dad hitting him in the garage in the night.

He shook his head again. He understood his dad beating him. What he didn't understand was why he thought he had to drag him across the concrete and rip his back up. One other thing he hadn't understood was what his dad had said about his mom last night.

He looked down at himself again. Why did his dad hate him so much? He slowly walked down the stairs to breakfast, half expecting his dad to beat him again.

Jared and Jordan where already seated at the table. Lilly sat there holding Jimmy in her arms. "I am sorry, boys. Dad had to leave early this morning. He said he hopes to be back early afternoon and take you to the court house, Josh."

Josh looked up quickly. "Why?"

Lilly laughed. "To get your license."

Josh felt himself pale. What was his dad up to? "Really?"

"Yes, really. Get done with breakfast and get ready to go. I am going to be driving you to school today." Lilly watched Josh with pain in her eyes. She saw the welt on the boys cheek and figured it was from Jim. She knew Jim had felt horrible about hitting his son last night, but she also understood that he had said something and he was going to sick with it.

She knew he was feeling guilty still about it this morning and that had been part of the reason he had left early. He hadn't wanted to face his son after whipping him before bed. She felt her heart go out to both of them and prayed silently for God to heal the rift between them and help them to forgive each other.

All three boys hurriedly ate their breakfast. Jordan and Jared were again fighting a little jealousy. It just wasn't fair that Josh was two months older than them. Just because of that he got his license first. But they both swallowed it, knowing it wasn't Josh's fault, and he wouldn't brag about it either. Both Jared and Jordan were wondering if also, if dad had left early this morning because he didn't have the nerve to face Josh in the daylight.

There was no way to know, but Jordan knew if things got any worse between Josh and Dad he was going to have to tell Mom, or someone who could help. Josh couldn't survive more of what his dad did to him last night. If it meant he had to tell on Jared, he would. That thought, though, gave him a sick feeling in his stomach. What if Dad hit Jared like he had Josh? Fear trickled through him.

Help, God! I don't know what to do. Please help. He silently prayed.

As Lilly dropped them off she cautioned them. "If Dad isn't here to get you, you may need to at least start walking home."

"Okay," they all three said in unison then headed off to their classes.

Lilly watched them and bit her lip. She could see that Josh was in pain, and she hoped that no one question him today. But she knew she wouldn't blame him if he told someone. Jim shouldn't have hit him as he did. She didn't want to have Jim in jail again, but she wasn't going to let him hit his son like he had either.

She sighed and drove away with a silent prayer in her heart that God help her know what to do. And for protection for Josh.

29

"Get him!"

Josh jumped to the side as Johnathan threw a punch. He ducked as the next punch came his way and threw one of his own.

Johnathan suddenly slugged again and knocked Josh to the ground.

Josh cried out in pain, but didn't even have time to move before his cousin jumped on him and slammed his fist into his stomach. Josh cried out again.

Johnathan slugged him over and over.

Josh tried to get away, but there wasn't much he could do with Johnathan sitting on him. Pain ripped through him.

"Stop it at once!"

Both boys looked up to see the principal headed that way. "What is the meaning of this!"

Johnathan looked his dad in the eye. "He stole my knife!"

Josh pushed himself to his feet. "I did not." He bit his lip. He felt like he was going to throw up.

Johnathan pointed to the ground, "See it's right there where he fell." He reached down and picked up the knife.

Josh trembled as the principal gripped his arm. "Get into the office, boy. We have punishments for the likes of you, and I would think that by now you would be tired of learning them."

Josh bit his lip and glanced at his brothers.

Jared and Jordan stood silently. What could they do?

When the principal led Josh away Jared nudged his brother. The other boys all started to drift away. "Let's go see what he does to Josh. You and I both know he didn't steal the knife."

Jordan nodded. "We know it, but I don't think that the principal is going to care about the truth. But it is nice to see you caring about what happens to him."

Jared shrugged. "Come on lets just sneak in and see what is going on." Jared didn't tell his brother, he didn't care about what happened to Josh. He wanted to see him get a whipping. It would just serve him right for always trying to play favorites with Dad. Then he felt his conscience prick him. He knew dad had been way harder on Josh then he had been on Jordan or him last night. And he also knew that last night wasn't Josh's fault, but still Josh had said nothing.

Jordan bit his lip. "Okay," he said at last. "But we have to be quiet. We don't want to get him in even more trouble. And we sure don't want to get caught and get into trouble."

Jared nodded and the two silently snuck to the office.

Josh groaned as he fell to the floor. The belt smacked his back again and again. He felt sick from the pain, not only the pain from his uncle's hitting him, but his fight with Johnathan earlier, and from the repeated beatings of the nights since he had moved in with his dad.

He trembled as his Uncle John pulled him to his feet. Fear trickled through him as he looked the man in the eye.

"How old are you now, boy?" he snarled.

Josh heard the anger in the man's voice and he wished he didn't have to answer. "Sixteen," he whispered.

Uncle John smiled a wicked smile. "Take off your shirt, boy." His command cracked like a whip.

Josh wanted to refuse with all that was in him, but he was afraid that if he did the whipping would get even worse then it already was. He hesitated.

John gripped his arms and slammed him into the wall. He slugged him in the stomach, then, as he was going down in pain, slammed his knee into the boy's chest.

Josh cried out in pain as he fell to the floor.

John scowled at him as he kicked him repeatedly. "Get up, now! Or suffer the consequences!" he stormed.

Josh tried to stand, but fell as his uncle kicked him again.

John grabbed him and pulled him to his feet again. He jerked the boys shirt off of him. Then picked up a whip from in his desk draw.

Josh bit his lip and dropped his head. The first smack ripped skin. He bit his lip harder to keep back the cry of pain, but on the fifth smack it came.

John jerked the boy around and just stopped himself from hitting the boy in the face. It wouldn't do any good to leave a mark for the boy's father to see. Instead he brought it down on his stomach.

Josh jerked. Pain throbbed in him. And he felt himself fainting. Then all of the sudden he was pulled back with a snap of pain. Again he wished he could faint, but again his uncle pulled him back as the whip snaked across his back leaving a line of blood.

Jared and Jordan peeked into the office and were horrified by what they saw. They quickly ducked back, so the principal wouldn't see them and that make things even worse.

Jared's eyes were wide. I didn't realize it was that bad," he whispered. The boys quickly slipped out of the school. Just as they reached the outside the bell began to ring.

Jordan looked at his brother. "I think we need to tell Dad when we get home. I know that Josh doesn't want us to, but I think we should anyway. We can't just let this go on. He is going to kill him."

Jared nodded. "I agree. We need to tell him tonight. This has to stop." Jared felt tears sting his eyes. Is this how it had been every time he went to the principal's office? Was that why Josh had always seemed in so much pain?

Both boys went on to their classes, but both of them worried about their brother the rest of the day. What was going to happen to him? What was happening to him? Was he still in the office, or had the principal let him go on to class? They knew they would just have to wait to find out.

The last bell rang and Jared and Jordan hurried out of school. They looked around eagerly for Joshua, and finally spotted him walking their way.

Jordan noticed that he was walking slowly, his arm squeezed his ribs and he looked like he felt sick. Pain for his brother rushed through him. He had to talk to Dad, before it was too late.

Jared felt guilty as he watched Josh walk toward them. Just yesterday he was jealous of his brother and wanted to get him in trouble, but this was worse punishment then he had ever dreamed. What was worse was, he knew Josh hadn't done anything to deserve it. Johnathan had caused all the trouble. He felt his temper rise. He wished he could clean that kid's clock.

Pray for your enemies. He felt it more then heard it, but he knew it just the same. He gasped. God surely didn't mean that he was to pray for Johnathan when he was intentionally hurting Josh! *Pray for your enemies.* He heard again. Slowly he took a deep breath and let it out. "Okay, God," he said without realizing it.

Josh and Jordan looked at him. "What?"

Jared flushed. "Oh, just a reminder that we are suppose to pray for our enemies."

Josh shuttered visibly as the three of them headed toward the road. "I think I need that reminder, too. Thanks, Jared."

Jared shrugged. "Well, that may be me, if you consider how I have been treating you the last few weeks or months. I'm sorry, Josh. I know you aren't trying to be a favorite, and I know that I was just jealous." He looked over at him. "Forgive me?"

Josh smiled. "Sure," he looked over at Jared then at Jordan. "I guess now we can finally be brothers?"

Both boys nodded.

Josh looked up and stopped. "Is that Luke? I mean Pastor Luke out there?"

Luke honked the horn and motioned to the boys.

They ran over to him.

"Hi, boys! Your mom asked if I could give you all a lift home. She didn't want you to have to walk and since I was already in town she asked if I would mind. Climb in."

Josh sighed in relief. At least that would be that much less pain. They all three slid into the back seat.

Luke looked at them with a smile. "Let's go."

As he dropped them off he stopped Josh. "Is everything going good, Josh? You look like you're upset or something. He hasn't been hitting you, has he?"

Josh shook his head. He wanted to tell Luke everything that was going on, but he knew he shouldn't. "I'm fine."

Luke nodded. "Okay. Happy birthday, by the way."

Josh smiled weakly. "Thanks," he wished it would be a happy day, but he was pretty sure he was going to be in even more trouble again tonight. "Thanks for the ride home." It felt good to know that Luke still cared about him. It also felt good to know that he hadn't forgotten him. "I can't believe you remembered."

Luke looked at Josh strangely. "You did live with us for the better part of eight years, Josh. Of course I remember."

Josh flushed. "Thanks." Again he wished he could tell Luke everything, but then he felt the knot in his stomach where the gun had been slammed into it last night and he knew there was no way he could ever say anything.

Luke nodded. "Any time, s-Josh. See you later."

Josh nodded.

Lilly smiled as the boys walked in. "Josh, don't bother changing into your work clothes."

Josh stopped on the stairs. "Why?"

Lilly's eyes twinkled. "Your dad plans on being home in a couple of minutes, and he is going to take you to the court house. He had a few things to finish up at the clinic before he came home, so he called and said he wouldn't be able to pick you up from school, but he should be home in a few minutes."

Josh froze. "What for?" Surely his dad wasn't going to turn himself in for hitting him, so why was he going to take him to the court house?

Lilly was astonished to hear the fear in Josh's voice. "Josh, what do you think for? Your sixteen. Time for you to get your license. Did you forget so soon? We just talked about this at the breakfast table this morning."

Josh relaxed visibly.

Suddenly the front door slammed. "Joshua!"

Josh's breath caught in his throat as he heard his dad scream. Slowly he turned and saw Jim, he thought, walk into the room.

He gripped Josh's arm and backhanded him.

Josh fell back a little from the force as much as the shock. He felt moister on his lip and knew it was bleeding. He didn't dare ask what he had done. Instead he stared at him in fear.

Jordan and Jared also froze as they watched their dad. They had never seen him this angry before. Not even with the porn magazines last night.

Josh trembled as his dad pulled off his belt.

Lilly sucked in her breath. She had never seen her husband so angry. In all the time that they had been together he hadn't ever raised so much as his voice to the kids, and definitely not a hand or belt to them in anger, though he had spanked them a few times. The angriest he had been was last night, but that hadn't been anger as much as it had been pain.   When he had walked out of the boy's room last night after hitting Josh, he had broke down and cried. It had hurt him so much to have to hit his son, but he had to get Josh to obey. He couldn't just let him get away with his disobedience. He had done it too long. It had hurt him so badly to hit him last night, that Jim hadn't slept at all. He had been so heart sick he couldn't even face the boy that morning. That had been why he left for work before the boys were even up.

If it had made him that heart sick, how could he be so mad now, Lilly wondered? She saw the fear in Josh's face as he looked up at his dad.

Josh looked the man in the eye, and suddenly his eyes widened. It wasn't his dad. It was his Uncle John. Though they were identical twins, and it was almost impossible to tell them apart, his uncle had one small mole on the right side of his neck that his dad didn't have.

Josh stumbled backward. If his uncle was pretending to be his dad now, was he the one who was whipping him at night? That would explain why his dad didn't seem to know why Josh was afraid of him, and why he had repeatedly said he didn't want to strike him. Why he had repeatedly tried to love him and Josh hadn't let him. It would also explain why his dad never seemed tired in the mornings, after he had been hitting him all night.

As the pieces started falling into place, John saw in boy's eyes that he knew who he was, and his blood ran cold. "Go to your room, boy. Now!"

Josh bit his lip, but slowly turned to obey. He knew if he refused someone else would more than likely get hurt. He hoped his dad didn't come home and get hurt. John probably thought he was gone till six which was when he normally got home. Slowly he turned and walked out the door, but he didn't go to his room. He stood out in the hall listening to make sure his uncle left everyone else alone.

Lilly frowned at him. "Jim, don't you dare beat that boy."

John glared at her. "He needs to learn a lesson. He was stealing at school. He isn't going to be stealing. Never." He looked at Jared and Jordan. "You two stay down here, do you understand?" he growled.

Jared and Jordan nodded wide eyed. They hadn't ever seen their dad like this.

Lilly's eyes widened as she looked at him. "Jim, don't you dare hit him in anger. You know how much it bothered you last night."

He turned to her with a deep scowl. "Don't you dare tell me how to discipline my son again."

John saw the hurt register in Lilly's eyes. "I will punish him as he needs and you will be quiet about it," he snarled. "The boy needs a good beating and I have let it go, and let it go. He has become more and more disobedient. Today was it. He won't be stealing and getting away with it. I am drawing the line. You will stay out of it."

Lilly felt tears start to run down her cheeks. Jim had never spoken to her that way.

John chuckled to himself as he walked out of the room and headed to the boy's room. This time the boy was going to get a whipping to remember and this time everyone was going to think it was from his dad.

Lilly started to follow, but stopped as Jordan laid a hand on her arm. "Mom, don't. You know Josh wouldn't want you to get hurt. It would hurt him more if you got hurt then if he did."

Lilly burst into tears as she sank onto the couch. Just as she sat down her phone rang through with a message. She opened it and looked at it with a puzzled frown.

Jordan and Jared both looked at her questioningly.

Lilly looked up at them, and her confusion registered in her eyes. "It's from your dad. He says to tell Josh he is sorry that he isn't going to make it home in time to take him to get his license." She look up at the boys. "What is going on?"

Josh trembled as he shut the door a few moments before his uncle reached the top of the stairs. What was he going to do? He was already hurting. Hadn't Uncle John hit him enough today? Why did he have to do this?

He jumped as the door burst open.

John didn't give him a chance to say anything. He grabbed him and backhanded him. Then slammed him into the wall.

Josh cried out in pain. Then sank to the floor with a moan. How long was this beating going to last?

John finally lowered the whip. "You going to tell anyone, brat?"

Josh whimpered. He felt ashamed of the sound, but his body burned with pain. Blood soaked his back.

John reached down and jerked him to his feet.

Josh bit back the scream that rose in his throat and muffled it into a moan.

"I asked you a question, boy. You going to keep quiet?"

"Yes, sir," his voice was full of pain.

"You better keep the rest of them quiet also, do you understand. I hear that you snitched about who I am and what I have been doing and you won't live to regret it. Got that?"

Josh shuttered at the hate in the man's voice. His knees buckled and, as his uncle released his arm, he fell to the floor.

John scowled at him and kicked his stomach.

Josh moaned again as he tried to roll away.

John glared at him. "Get one thing straight, boy. You pick a

290

fight with my son, and you will regret it."

"Yes, sir," he moaned again.

John knew he had to hurry and get out of here before his brother came home. He figured he would be home early today with it being Josh's birthday. He laughed as he thought about giving the boy so many whippings on his birthday. But as he glared down at Josh anger rose in him. He kicked him in the ribs again.

Josh cried out in pain.

John wrapped his hands around the boy's neck and jerked him to his feet. He squeezed the boy's neck tighter, making sure his threat was loud and clear. "Get cleaned up and keep your mouth shut about what is going on. You got that?"

Josh whimpered again as he gasped for breath. "Yes, sir," he groaned. He gasped again and sank to the floor as his uncle released his hands. He struggled to get air back in his lungs. He heard John laughing, then he heard the door shut.

He gasped in pain and curled into himself. This had to stop, but how? He couldn't tell Dad, so what was he suppose to do?

Lilly heard Jim coming down the stairs and she pulled Jared and Jordan into her. How could he hit his son this long? She and the boys had heard the strikes. She was glad the baby was sleeping and that Julia had gone over to the pastor's house for a while to play.

She looked up at the doorway expecting him to come in, but instead he stormed past the doorway and went out the front door. This was almost as confusing as his message.

Jordan ran up the stairs to check on Josh. Jared and Lilly hurried to the front door and, not seeing any sign of him turned and went upstairs.

Jordan ran into the bed room and stopped in horror as he saw Josh laying on the floor. Blood soaked his body and his breathing was weak.

Josh looked up at him. "Don't, please. It's not -" he stopped as he tried to move. The pain took his breath away. "Help me," he gasped. He felt ashamed to ask, but he had to move and he couldn't on his own. He also knew he was going to have to hurry to get cleaned up before his dad came home and saw.

Jordan hurried over to him and slowly helped him sit up. "Was this because of the fight at school?"

Before Josh could answer Lilly walked in tears were streaming down her cheeks. "Josh, I am so sorry. I don't understand why he is doing this. Was this what he was like before?"

Josh looked at his mom with pain in his eyes, "It's okay, Mom. Really, it's okay. This isn't your fault."

Lilly shook her head. "He is not going to be hitting you." Her fear was evident. If Jim would hit Joshua this bad, what would he do to her boys, or even Julia and what about little Jimmy? Tears ran down her cheeks as her anger mounted. She knelt down on the floor by him. "Josh, I am so sorry. I never would have – if I only would have known, I wouldn't have-" Her eyes flashed. "He isn't going to do this again, Josh. I promise."

Josh looked at her and shook his head. "Mom, it's not what you think. Please just let it go. It wasn't -"

Jared and Jordan both looked at each other as Lilly interrupted him. "Josh, it was not necessary. I don't care what you did. This is not going to happen again. I don't care if you robbed a bank, your dad isn't going to beat you like this."

Josh laid his hand on her arm. "Lilly, he isn't going to hurt anyone else. I promise. It's just me. Let it go this time, and when he gets home don't say anything, please."

He bit his lip. Should he tell? He looked up at Lilly again, and knew if he didn't she would leave his dad. He realized that is probably what his uncle wanted to happen. "It wasn't Dad, Mom. He didn't do it. Just don't say anything to him. Please. I don't want him to get hurt."

"What do you mean, Josh?" Lilly felt even more confused. She had heard her boys come up with some wild stories before, but this one started out sounding like it was going to top all of theirs.

Josh bit his lip. "It was his twin. Uncle John is the principle at the school. He got mad about something today. I guess he wanted to pretend to be Dad so he could hit me. Please don't say anything to Dad about it."

Lilly frowned, but said nothing as she helped him up and to the bathroom where he could wash up. Just then Jimmy started crying and she hurried to look after him. Still her mind whirled with all that Josh had said. Could this day get any more weird or confusing?

Josh slipped back to the bedroom and found Jared and Jordan still their.

Jared was crying. "I'm sorry, Josh."

Josh shook his head. "Jordan, help me out with this will you?"

he held up a long strip of cloth.

Jordan looked at him questioningly.

Josh groaned as the pain in his body seemed to increase. "I am pretty sure I have some cracked ribs. Help me wrap them up."

"Josh, I don't have a clue what I am doing."

Josh leaned over to try and get his breath. "Jordan, I have seen Dad do it and I know that I can. Please just help me. All you have to do is wind it up tight.

Jordan sighed. "Okay. But don't you think Dad-" he stopped.

Josh frowned. "I would rather Dad not know. Maybe I am being a coward. I just don't want to risk him getting angry at me too."

Jordan sighed. He understood, but would Dad really do this to Josh, maybe it was the principal last night, and maybe it was him here just a little bit ago too. Strangely that thought made him feel better. But at the same time he couldn't help but wonder if Josh was lying. He took the bandages from Josh and slowly started to wrap his brother's ribs.

Josh bit his lip to keep back a cry.

The sound of the door downstairs brought all three of the boys to attention.

"I am home!" Jim called. "Where is everyone? Lilly, boys, where are you all? I stopped off at Luke and Annie's and picked up Julia. Hello."

When Lilly heard Jim her stomach cramped. Was Josh telling a lie or was it the truth? Did her husband have a twin? Would he really impersonate her husband and hit their son? She didn't know what to believe. After the whipping he gave Josh last night for looking at the pornography she really didn't know whether to believe Josh that it wasn't him today. Had I not been for last night she would believe him with little hesitation.

"Upstairs feeding the baby," Lilly called. She sounded almost normal and Josh hoped she wouldn't say anything.

Josh paled. "Hurry up, Jordan. Don't let Dad see what happened to me. Please."

Jordan pulled the bandage around him again. "Jared, go stall him," he hissed.

Jared jumped up and raced out the door.

Josh bit his lip. "You have to pull it tighter," he moaned.

Jordan flushed, but pulled the bandage a little tighter. He

shook as he saw Josh flinch even more in pain. "Is that too tight?"

Josh shook his head slightly, knowing if he opened his mouth at that moment he was going to be sick.

Jared flew down the stairs. "Hi, Dad. Back from work, huh?"

Jim looked at him questioningly. "Yeah, imagine that." He looked at Jared strangely. "What is going on, son?"

Jared bit his lip. He hoped that Josh wasn't lying to cover for his dad. What if he was? What if his dad was the one hitting him? He did have to admit that John, the principal at school, did look identical to his dad, and that would explain why they had acted like they knew each other so well when they had first met. But if it really was his dad's brother, why hadn't his dad said something about it? It didn't really add up.

Lilly walked down the stairs. Jim could tell she had been crying. "Honey, what is wrong?"

She looked up at him with a glare. She didn't for one moment buy Josh's story. She was sure it was Jim who had been hitting him. No two people can look that much alike.

Jim was stunned. Lilly hadn't ever glared at him, even after what he had done yesterday. "Honey, did I do something wrong?"

Lilly growled at him. "As if you didn't know." She stepped right up to him. She wanted to slap him as hard as he had Josh, but she knew she couldn't. "How could you?"

Jim shook his head. "Hon, I am sorry I am late getting home. I saw that I wasn't going to make it before the court house closed, so I stopped off at Luke and Annie's, on the way home, and asked them to join us tonight for supper. I got to visiting a little and it took me longer than I thought. I am sorry. I sent you a message when I knew I was going to be late. My phone died after that or I would have at least sent you a message to let you know I was on my way home. I had a woman in labor come in just as I was getting ready to leave. I am sorry, but that is how it works some days. I tried to – I will just have to hope Josh understands. I will try to make it tomorrow. I am sorry I wasn't home in time. Or really," he glanced at the clock, "I am sorry I wasn't really even home early."

Lilly frowned at him. "You were home in plenty of time and you know it. How dare you treat him like this! What is your problem? How dare you let your anger take control of you like that! Especially when you acted like it hurt you so much last night."

Jim was even more stunned and confused. He took a step back. "What?"

"You heard me," she was almost yelling. "You won't raise a hand to my children, but you beat yours almost to death. How dare you. Then you have the nerve to come back home after you storm off, and act like you don't know anything about it." As her temper was rising so was her voice. "How dare you be so cruel!" She burst into tears. "How could you? After all the things you said and promised wouldn't ever happen again."

Jim froze. "What? Who has been beating Joshua?" his voice rumbled like thunder. He turned to Jared. "Where are your brothers?"

Jared bit his lip. "Um- they will be down in a few minutes." Jim heard the hesitancy in Jared. Instantly he knew the boy was hiding something. He was going to find out what it was, but first he had to make sure Lilly believed him. His heart ached. What had his brother done?

It was his fault for keeping his twin's existence a secret from her. More lies and more deception, just because he hadn't talked. Had John whipped Josh at school? He had to find out.

He sighed. He had to fix this, first with Lilly, then with Joshua, then with Jared and Jordan.

Jim turned back to Lilly. He moved slowly, afraid that John had made a move on her and he would frighten her. He reached out and placed his hands gently on her arms. "Honey, please believe me. I haven't hit him today. I didn't want to last night, but I had to. I don't know why you think I have toady. Well, I guess I spanked all of them last night, and a few other times, but that is all it was. I haven't just hit him to hit him. I promise." He kissed her lightly. "Hon, please believe me. I haven't beat him today. Last night is the first time, since I got out of prison. And I pray to God it is the last time I ever strike him."

Lilly felt the tears still running down her cheeks. Could she believe him? Did she dare?

He turned and started up the stairs. "Jim, where are you going?" she demanded.

Jim turned back to her in surprise. "I am going to find out

what is going on. I am going to have a talk with our boys. Jared stay here with your mother and if John comes back, holler as loud as you can."

Jared paled. Josh hadn't wanted his dad to see what the principal had done to him. He thought Josh's story more likely to be true now that he had seen his dad acting like he didn't know anything about it. He knew he should try and stop his dad, but he couldn't. His dad needed to know what was going on. This had to be stopped, and Dad was the only one who was going to be able to stop it.

Jim walked up the stairs. As he neared the boy's room he heard Josh cry out. He slowed and peaked in. The sight he saw made him want to throw up, but also brought tears to his eyes.

Josh grunted in pain again. "Pull it just a little tighter. Okay there, now wrap it."

Jordan slowly made another roll around his brother. "I wish I could kill him. Between him and Johnathan you are lucky to be alive. Do you know if Mom is going to buy your story?"

Josh bit his lip. "It's not a story, Jordan. It's true." He grunted again in pain, but shook his head slightly. "Jordan, you have to keep it tight."

Jordan frowned. He had noticed that the principal and his dad looked a lot alike. But for the principal to come in here pretending to be his dad didn't really seem like it could be true. "Is he really Dad's twin?"

"He really is. It probably wouldn't have gotten so bad here, but when he saw I knew who he was-" Josh stopped and gripped the edge of the dresser in pain as Jordan wrapped the bandage around him again.

"How do you know it was him. It looked just like Dad?"

Josh shook his head. "Not, just like him. Uncle John has a small mole on his neck that Dad doesn't have. It is the only difference in them that I have found, but I saw it when he was yelling at me downstairs. I knew then, that I was in for it.

"Just don't say anything to Dad, please. He doesn't need to know what happened or that I was in a fight or that Johnathan planted his robbery on me." He stopped to gasp in a breath. "Do you think Jared will tell on me? Ow. Jordan." Josh put his arm around his ribs and groaned.

Jordan shrugged even though he was standing behind Josh and

knew Josh couldn't see him. "I'm sorry, Josh." His back was to the door, but he suddenly felt a hand on his as he started to wrap another round around Josh. He froze. It was his dad.

Jim quietly took the bandage from his son and motioned for him to keep quiet about it.

Jordan nodded then said to Josh, "Is that too tight."

"No," Josh moaned. "It has to be tight." He dropped his head. "Just try and tell her again. We don't want Dad to know what is going on. It will get way worse if he does. Please don't tell on me, Jordan, and try to get Jared to be quiet. You saw last night so you know what will happen if Dad finds out that there was porn magazines in my locker at school. Even if I didn't put them there, he isn't going to believe me. He will beat me anyway." Josh bit his lip again as he felt the bandage tighten, then tighten again.

"Ow," he grunted trying to keep from crying out. "Come on, Jordan, that hurts. I know I told you to keep it tight, but loosen it up just a little. I need to be able to bre-" As Josh reached back to get the bandage, his hand brushed another hand and he froze. It wasn't Jordan. He felt his heart sink. How long had his dad been there?

He jerked and would have spun around, but couldn't.

Jim's anger rose as he saw the state of his son's back. But he pushed down his anger. "Who did this to you, son?" his voice was quiet, but Josh heard the anger in it loud and clear. As Jim spoke he motioned for Jordan to leave so he could talk to Josh in private.

Josh hung his head as he waited for his dad to hit him. He heard the door close and he started to tremble.

Jim waited to hear the answer. He hoped that Josh would trust him enough to talk to him.

Josh bit his lip. He didn't dare cross his dad, not now. "Uncle John," he muttered.

Jim nodded slightly as he unwrapped the bandage slowly. "I was afraid he might try something like this. But I had hoped you would tell me if he was. Why haven't you? Your back says today wasn't a first."

Josh trembled even more. "No, sir."

Jim slowly unwound the bandages the rest of the way. He shook his head in disgust. "He really ruffed you up, didn't he, son?"

Josh dropped his head. "Yes, sir." Suddenly he cried out as his dad touched his back.

Jim sighed. "Turn around so I can see the rest of you."

Josh trembled, but slowly turned around. He kept his head down, afraid his dad would see the hand prints on his neck, that he knew would be bruised tomorrow.

Jim shook his head. His anger grew even more. He wasn't sure who he was madder with, Josh or John. "Let's get you cleaned up." He muttered.

Josh trembled in fear, but let his dad touch him. He cried out again as his dad felt his ribs.

Jim frowned more, but slowly examined his son. Finally he looked up at him. "Why weren't you going to tell me?"

Josh trembled, but answered honestly. "He said I wouldn't live to regret it if I told."

Jim nodded slightly. "How much has he hit you?"

Josh bit his lip. He was still unsure if it was his dad or his uncle who beat him at night. "Every day at least once."

Jim's frown deepened. "Why?"

Josh shrugged. "A variety of reasons."

Jim nodded again as though thinking. Carefully he wrapped the boy's ribs up in the bandage. "Since school started?"

Josh hung his head even more. "Yes, sir." He grunted in pain as his father pulled tighter on the bandage.

Jim sighed. "Son, why didn't you tell me? I wish you would have. Did you think I really wouldn't care?"

Josh shuttered. As his dad pulled the bandage tighter. He gasped and jerked his head back trying to guard against the pain. As he did Jim saw the hand prints on his son's neck.

He released the bandage and grabbed Josh's arms. "What is that?"

Josh whimpered, but slowly lowered his gaze to meet his father's. "It's a reminder."

Jim felt his blood heat up even more. "He has been hurting you like this since the start of school and you say nothing! He threatens to kill you and still you were not going to say anything!"

Josh bit his lip, but kept his gaze locked with his dad's. "Yes, sir. This was the first time for this though."

Jim gripped Josh's arms tighter. "Why? Why did you let him do this to you?"

Josh trembled even more. "I had to, Dad."

Jim nodded slowly. He didn't understand it all, but he did understand that Josh had been trying to protect the others. "He isn't going to do this again. If he even comes close to touching you, you had better find a way to let me know. Is that understood?"

Josh bit his lip as Jim picked up the bandage and started to wrap his ribs again but didn't answer.

Jim looked up at him, "Joshua, I said is that clear. I want your word that you aren't going to let him hurt you again without telling me about it."

Josh hung his head. He couldn't give his dad that promise. He knew Uncle John would beat him tomorrow, and whoever it was at night would beat him again tonight.

Jim released the bandage once more and gripped Josh's arms, turning him to face him. "What is it, Joshua?

Josh looked up at his dad. "Yes, sir," he knew he was going to regret it, but his brothers were right, he needed to talk to his dad, but his fear held him back. He just couldn't make himself talk to his dad heart to heart.

As Jim finished with the bandages, he frowned. "We are going to make it through this, son. I will do what I can." He looked his son over again, then sighed. "There, that should help. Now let's get going. Get your shirt on. We are meeting with Luke and Annie and their kids, and going out to supper. I am sorry I wasn't here earlier. Now I am really upset with myself for letting my schedule get messed up. I wanted to take you to get your license today. I suppose Mom told you that."

Jim felt his anger rise even more as he looked at his son, but Josh refused to look up at him. "I am sorry, son. If I was here I could have put a stopped to this." He stopped again. He felt his blood freeze as he reached out to his son and lifted his chin. "Joshua, what happened? I mean, what really happened?"

Josh tried to turn away. They had already talked about this, but he understood his dad was trying to get him to talk more. "It's nothing."

Jim frowned. "It isn't nothing. What did he do to you? Was this a threat?"

Josh slowly nodded.

Jim gripped his arm. "Was it more?"

Josh looked away. "Yes, sir."

Jim sighed again. "I am sorry, Joshua. Maybe someday I will be a good dad to you. It kind of seems like right now, all I am good at is messing it up."

Josh shook his head. "It's okay." He didn't know what to say, but for the first time in his life he wanted to make his dad feel better.

Jim smiled slightly. "No, Joshua, it really isn't okay, I shouldn't have gotten so mad before, because if I wouldn't have been so mad last night I would have seen your back before I hit it and known that someone was hitting you. I never should have beat you like I did, son. I should have let you talk, but thanks. And hopefully this won't happen again."

Josh turned away.

Jim frowned. "What?"

Josh bit his lip. Did he dare tell his dad about the nighttime beatings? He trembled. He still wasn't sure it wasn't his dad doing it, but in his heart he knew. He just wasn't willing to accept it yet. He turned away with a shrug.

Jim watched him for several seconds then, with a sigh, motioned for him to lead the way. If Josh wasn't going to tell him, he was going to find out for himself. But he was sure there was even more than Josh was telling. He looked at his son again, and felt the anger rise in him. He could still see his brother's hand prints on his son's neck, and he knew that the man would try and get to him again tomorrow.

As he followed Josh down the stairs a plan began to form in his mind. A plan formed for helping Josh and catching his brother, but also to find out who panted the porn in his locker and if someone planted it here at the house or if it was him.

A sickening thought came to him. If it wasn't Josh who brought it into the house it had to be either Jared or Jordan. Both boys had watched him beat Josh mercilessly last night and not said a thing. His anger mounted. They were in serious trouble if it was them.

Josh trembled, but walked in front of his dad out to the hall where Jared and Jordan were waiting.

300

30

At dinner Luke watched Josh. He was worried about him. He had seemed to be in pain earlier today. What was happening in his life? He wished he could get him alone long enough to talk. He wished the boy would come to him and tell him if his dad was whipping him again, but he was sure if that was happening that Josh wouldn't say a thing.

Josh sat at the table with the others and thanked them for the gifts and for coming. He tried to join in the conversation, but he was in too much pain. He felt sick. He didn't want to eat. He didn't want to be around people.

Jim sensed that his son was uncomfortable, and was sure he was in pain. He looked at him and sighed. Josh hadn't touched his food and it was obvious to him that he was in too much pain to eat. Just then his ears perked up. What had Luke just said?

Luke smiled at Josh. "Joy told me you got the acceptance letter back a few months ago. When do you plan to go to college?"

Josh's head jerked up. Fear sparkled in his eyes.

Luke saw and quickly changed the subject, but Jim didn't forget the look on his son's face. What was he hiding now?

Josh sat in misery. He wanted to go home. He hoped his dad would forget what Luke had said. He didn't want to explain anything. He just wanted to be able to let his dream go, but he couldn't. How could he, when he had been so sure that was God's will for him? Why were all these things happening if God willed something else?

I know the plans I have for you. Came the soft whisper to his heart. He hung his head.

Please forgive me for doubting, God. I know you have plans in store for me to prosper me and not to harm me, but right now it is really hard to understand what you are doing. Please help me to believe in you. Help my faith not to waiver as it has been. Please.

He looked up at his dad and saw that he was looking at him. He wondered if he had been spoken to, but Jim turned the other way and said something to Luke.

He sighed. He didn't want to be involved in the conversation right now. He just wanted it to be over so he could go home.

At last the party was over and everyone rose to leave.

"I can take the boys to school tomorrow, Jim. It's not a problem. I am going right by there about that time anyway. No sense in them having to walk." Luke smiled warmly as he spoke.

Jim returned the smile. "Thanks, Luke. I don't want to leave early, but this time it can't be helped."

Luke smiled again. "No problem." He turned to the boys. "Be ready to go by seven forty-five. Is that okay?"

All three nodded their agreement.

Josh turned away. If they were at school early, was he going to get a whipping then too? He shivered.

Jordan looked at his brother and knew instantly what he feared. He feared it too. What was he suppose to do about it? He wanted to tell his dad, but he was afraid it would get Josh in more trouble. Finally he decided he would talk to Mom when they got home. Maybe she could talk to Dad. Yes, he decided, that is what he would do.

Julia and Jimmy were asleep by the time they got home. Jordan picked up Julia and followed his mom to the house. She was carrying Jimmy.

Lilly smiled at her son. "Thank you, Jordan."

Jordan shrugged. As he lay Julia down he turned to her, "Mom?"

She looked worried at the look in his eye. "Yes, son."

"Mom I need to talk to you about something that is important, but I don't know how to exactly."

She smiled. "Just say it. That is usually the best way."

He nodded and walked out into the hall. Softly he shut Julia's door. "It's about Josh."

Lilly raised an eyebrow, but waited patiently and quietly for him to go on.

"Mom, the principal is beating him. Like bad beating him. He busted him up really bad just yesterday, but it happens every day. I don't know what to do. Josh never does anything to deserve it and he won't say anything, because he is afraid Dad will whip him too. I told him he won't but Josh doesn't believe me."

Lilly looked thoughtful. "Thank you for telling me, Jordan. I will see what I can do. I am afraid from what we saw earlier today, Josh may be right. I have never seen your dad that way."

Jordan nodded. "Mom, the principal at our school really does look identical to dad. I never put two and two together, but it really and truly could have been him and not Dad. It's just not like Dad at all. I don't believe it was him. I am afraid the principal is going to kill him. I want to tell Dad. I know he would put a stop to it, but -"

Lilly looked Jordan in the eye. "Do you really believe that it wasn't your dad here earlier this after noon? Do you really think he has a twin brother?"

Jordan hesitated. "He has a twin for sure, whether it is by blood or not I don't know, but the principal at school, Mr. John Peterson looks exactly like Dad, like I just said. I have thought it was him a few times. There is like no differences. I have looked. Josh might have come up with one, but I haven't." He stopped. Josh had said something that was different, but he couldn't remember what it was.

Lilly looked thoughtful. "And you say it is the principal who is beating him?"

Jordan nodded. "Yes, ma'am."

Lilly nodded. "Thank you, Jordan. That is a big help to me."

Just then Jim called from the top of the stairs, "All three of you boys to your room. It's time for bed and I want to talk to all of you now."

Jordan looked at his mom, and she shrugged. "I'll be in in a little bit to say good night, son. Go on."

Jordan nodded and hurried to his room. He saw Jared coming up the stairs, but he didn't see Josh anywhere. Both boys hurried to their room. They stopped in the doorway, surprised to see Josh already there.

Jim looked up at them. "Come on in, boys. I need to talk to all of you."

Jared and Jordan slowly walked in and perched on Josh's bed on either side of him.

Jim looked at each one of them. "I want all of you to know that I am tired of all this jealousy. I am tired of you trying to get each other in trouble. I am tired of having to get after all of you. Do you understand?"

All three nodded their heads, glad that they had already talked about this.

Jim nodded. "Good, now for what I really wanted to talk about," he looked at Josh.

Josh saw the look and he dropped his gaze. He was afraid his dad was going to make this more painful than it already was.

"I don't want any more problems at school. I don't want any fighting. None." He looked straight at Josh.

Josh bit his lip and dropped his head. How could he explain to his dad that he didn't ever start it, he was just always blamed for it?

Jared felt his temper spark. "We don't!"

Jim frowned at him and he snapped his mouth closed.

Josh and Jordan both looked from one to the other in surprise. Jared hadn't shut his mouth that fast in forever.

Jim sighed. "I have to head in early in the morning. I don't want to hear a thing negative about school, is that understood?"

All the boys nodded, even though Josh knew, and the others were pretty sure, that that wasn't going to happen.

Jim nodded. Just then Lilly walked in. He smiled at her. "Just in time. Lets pray with them and get them in bed."

Lilly nodded. But her stomach tightened slightly. She had to talk to her husband tonight, and let him know what Jordan had told her. If it was the principal who had come here pretending to be Jim, and beaten Josh how much worse did he hit him when no one was around?

304

The next morning as Luke dropped the boys off for Jim, he watched Josh and was surprised to see the boy holding back as though he was afraid to walk into school. Luke frowned. Why would Josh not want to go into the school. He watched as the three of them congregated in the front yard, away from the building. Just what was going on?

31

Josh moaned as his Uncle John once again jerked him to his feet. "I told you not to pick a fight any more!" he screamed.

Josh fell to the floor as his uncle hit him again. *God, help me!* He didn't really have time to say it, but the prayer whispered up in his heart at that moment was a desperate one. His ribs were throbbing. He felt sick.

John grabbed his arms and hauled him to his feet again. He grabbed the boy's shirt and jerked it off of him. His eyes landed on the bandage rapped around Josh's chest. "You told." His voice was a low growl.

Josh fell back, his hand and arm over the bandage.

"How dare you." John raised his belt to strike him.

Josh crumbled to the floor. "No, please. I didn't tell, please don't."

"Liar!"

"Ah!" Josh's cry seemed to be almost jerked out of him.

John grabbed both his arms and slammed him into the wall. Angrily he gripped the bandage and jerked it off of him.

Josh stared at his uncle in fear, but grimmest in pain.

John gripped a fiberglass pole in one hand as he gripped Josh with the other hand. "You got anything you want to say, boy." He growled, "Cause I can tell you right now, if you do, you better say it, because when I am through with you, you won't be squealing any more."

Josh tried to pull away. Fear gripped him. *God! Help!*

Jim pulled up to the school and quietly snuck in. He knew his brother didn't expect to see him, but that was what he was counting on. He had to get the evidence he needed, and this was the only way. He crept up to the office. He heard Josh cry out and the snap of something, but he couldn't distinguish the sound.

He pulled out his phone to record it, then slowly he tried to sneak in. He had no idea what would work. He just knew he had to stop it. He saw Josh fall to the floor. Then the principal jerked him back up

Jim felt his anger rise. He knew he had to let the man hit his son a few times to get his recording, but it was stopping as soon as he had the evidence he need.

He recorded for fifteen minutes and it was horrible. Finally he could stand it no more. He burst into the office. "What is going on!"

Josh moaned as his head dropped to the floor. His breathing was labored, and pain wracked his body. Now what was going to happen to him? This had to be worse than being a slave, like they had been studying in history.

John looked at his brother in anger. "You should have raised him better, Jim. All he wants to do is steal and pick a fight or look at pornography."

Jim looked at him and his anger flashed in his eyes like fire. "The only thing he did, was what you made up. He didn't do anything and even if he did, I don't see you hitting any other kids around.

John scowled and threw a magazine on the desk. "You think I am making it up, do you? Well, here is the evidence. This was found in the boy's locker this morning."

Jim knelt beside his son. His heart throbbed. He didn't know whether John was lying about the magazine or not, but he did know that after the beating he had given Josh over it, the boy had better not have gotten more and tried to hide it at school. He looked down at Josh and gently touched his back.

Josh lay on the floor face down.

Jim slowly rolled Josh unto his side. He looked at the marks on his son, then he looked at his brother.

Josh moaned again. Then coughed. He felt his dad touch him, but he couldn't force himself to open his eyes for fear that the whipping would start again. In stead a pitiful whine escaped his throat as he pulled away from him and tried to shield himself from the next strike.

Jim slowly and gently helped him to sit up. He waited for Josh to open his eyes, then he helped him stand. He looked at John again. "Good bye, brother. I am taking my children home.

"I should have listened to my wife from the beginning and had them at home. And that is what we are doing. He will not be back and you will not be sneaking into my house, or around it, to hurt him again. Now, go back to your desk. And don't you ever lay a hand or anything else on him or even come close to him again."

Jim felt Josh crumple and he gently helped him back to his feet. "Come on, son. Let's go home." He felt Josh's knees buckle again.

Josh looked at his dad in surprise. *Thank you, God. Thank you for Dad. Please help it to not be him who is hitting me. Please help. And thank you for sending him to help me. Amen.* Josh felt his stomach turn in pain. Then his legs gave out and he fell to the floor.

Jim felt himself grow even more worried about his son. What all had his brother done to him. He reached down and gently and carefully picked him up. He was surprised at how light the boy felt. He hadn't noticed that the boy seemed to be losing weight here lately, though now that he thought about it, it had been a while since he had seen him really eat much of anything.

Josh groaned in pain.

Jim tried to keep from moving him more then necessary. "Hold on, Josh. I will have you home soon," he whispered. He walked out of the office and down the hall. He pushed open the door to the class room in which Jordan and Jared were.

The teacher looked up in surprise.

Jim cleared his throat. "I have come for my boys." He turned to them. "Jared, Jordan, get your things. We are leaving. And you won't be coming back."

The boys looked at their dad for a moment then jumped to their feet and hurriedly grab their things. When they saw Josh it made them even more afraid, but also curious.

Jim turned and led them all out to the car. Gently he laid Josh down in the middle seat. But even though he tried his best to keep from hurting him, he heard Josh's low moan. He looked at Jordan. "Keep him as still as you can," he ordered. Then looking at Jared he continued. "You help also."

Both boys nodded. They were terrified. They had never seen their dad look so scared for one, and for the other, they had never seen anyone look so beaten as Josh did at that moment.

Jim tried to be careful, but he was in a hurry. When they got home he quickly and carefully carried Josh in to the living-room and laid him on the couch. Then he walked to the kitchen to get some bandages and on the way called the police.

After explaining what had happened, he headed back to the living room.

Josh looked up as his dad walked in.

Jim saw fear flash in his eyes, and it puzzled him. "What's the matter, Joshua?"

"Nothing." He looked away quickly. He didn't want his dad to see how afraid he was. Would that make him whip him worse at night. Would his dad hit him again for porn, or was he going to have him hit him, and them whip him much worse? Again he trembled and bit his lip to keep back the whimper that was in his throat.

Jim sighed.

Jared and Jordan stood in the doorway watching. Jim turned to them. "Do you two know anything about this?"

Jared glanced at his brother. Neither one of them knew if they should tell what they knew. Would it just get Josh into even more trouble?

Jim saw the look. "Okay, out with it. What are all three of you trying to hide from me. Come on spill."

Josh bit his lip, but he was the one who responded. "Johnathan said I stole his knife. He said I took it then dropped it on the ground when he started to beat me up for it."

Jim nodded. "Any truth to it, son?"

Josh shuttered as his dad slowly and gently rubbed some salve on the cuts on his chest. "No, sir. I didn't take anything from him. Why would I?" He grunted in pain and jerked a little when his dad's hand touched him.

Jim looked Josh in the eye. "I hope you never will, son. But if you do, you better be honest about it."

Jordan saw Josh flinch again, and he knew he was scared that his dad wasn't believing him. He silently prayed that Dad would believe Josh and not hit him any more. He prayed that if it was Dad hitting him at night that would stop too, but he was afraid it wasn't his dad. Should he tell Dad about it?

Jared saw Josh stiffen, and he felt his anger rise. He knew he had tried to frame him for a lot that he hadn't done since he had moved here, but this was different. Josh hadn't done anything. And ever since school started all the principal did was hit him. He looked at Josh and his dad again, and felt his anger rise even more. Josh hadn't ever given Dad a reason not to believe him, yet Dad was all but accusing him of lying.

"Josh didn't do any thing. We hadn't even been there for five minutes," Jared cried out. "He just wanted an excuse to hit him, so he said he hadn't hit him enough yesterday for stealing the knife. And he was yelling about finding stuff in his locker."

Jim glanced at Jared then back to Josh. Pain ripped through his heart.

If that was true, had John been hitting him since before school had started. "How long did he hit you, son?" He kept his voice quiet, so the other two wouldn't hear everything.

Josh looked away not wanting to give his dad the truth.

Jim rested his hand on his son's shoulder and felt the tremor that ran through him. "Answer the question, Joshua."

Josh felt tears sting his eyes. "Before school."

Jim clenched his fist. Why had he waited so long to get to school, and why had he waited to get proof before he stepped in to make it stop? "I'm sorry, son," he whispered. The words seemed so small and insignificant.

Josh bit his lip harder and looked away.

Jim saw the look, "Josh, does he hit you more than just at school?"

Josh looked up at him, surprise in his eyes. Slowly he nodded.

Jim felt his blood boil. Anger raged inside of him till he wanted to beat his brother to a pulp. *God, help me with my anger. Repaying evil for evil isn't your way. Help me to trust you with this.*

"When does he hit you, son? How long has this been going on?"

Josh trembled even more.

Jim saw, but he waited knowing that Josh would answer, if for no other reason, than to keep from getting a whipping again for not answering. Knowing that stung his conscience.

Josh sighed. He knew he had to answer and risk it being his dad at night, because if he didn't it would be worse. He took a deep breath. "Since before school started, at night."

Jim looked him in the eye. "Where?"

Josh looked away, ashamed. "In the garage, mostly."

Jim stood and walked over to the window. His anger raged.

The knock on the door startled them all.

Jared went to answer it, and came back with a tall brood shouldered cop, who appeared to be in his late twenties. "We got the call. I was sent to get the evidence we need for a warrant."

Jim motioned the man into the living room. The officer stopped and looked down at Josh. He cleared his throat as though he wasn't sure what to say.

Jim held up his hand to stop the man before he started talking. Slowly he reached down and helped Josh roll over.

Josh grunted in pain as his father touched him and moved him.

The officer's eyes widened. He looked at Jim in surprise. "Do you have any evidence as to who did this to him.

Jim nodded. "I saw part of it today, but I didn't know it had been going on since before school even started. That man has been coming here, the boys just told me."

The officer looked down at Josh. "Well, boy, what do you have to say about all this? Who has been hitting you?"

Josh trembled, but looked up at his dad.

Jim smiled and nodded, trying to make Josh less afraid. "It's okay, son. Just tell him the truth."

Jared and Jordan stepped forward.

The officer looked at them. "Sir, we are his brothers and we know it was the principal at our school. We saw him multiple times. We didn't know what to do. Josh always begged us not to tell, because he would be in worse trouble. So we didn't tell, but yesterday it just got too bad and the principal, I guess he is Dad's twin, but we didn't know that, anyway, he came in here pretending to be Dad. I think he did it so Josh wouldn't talk. He came in here and started whipping him, it was awful. When he left and we discovered it wasn't Dad, we knew we had to tell. That is why Dad went to the school today. He

311

wanted to catch the man red handed, and boy, did he ever.

The officer looked down at Josh as though asking if this was all true.

Josh slowly nodded. "Yes, sir. It's all true." He gasped in pain as he tried to talk. "It's not just school though. He does it at night here too. He hates me for some reason. I don't really know why, but he just wants to hurt me. I think he enjoys it."

The officer nodded. "I hate to ask, cause I am sure you don't want me to, but I need to take some pictures of you."

Josh slowly nodded. "Okay."

Jim motioned for Jared and Jordan to leave.

The boys quietly slipped out of the living room.

As the boys left, the officer looked at Josh and then at Jim. "Joshua, has this man ever hurt you more than just like this?"

Josh looked up at him confused a moment, then he realized what he was asking. He gasped. "No!"

The officer nodded. "Good. I am sorry, but I had to ask." He looked over at Jim, "If you would remove the boys shirt and then stay in here to help me roll him over in a few moments."

Jim nodded, but fear and pain stung him as he saw how much pain Josh was in. Why had he not said anything? Why had none of them said a word? Anger burned in him. He wanted to beat his brother to a pulp and throw away the pieces.

God, you are going to have to help me with my anger. Help me to remember it is only because of your grace that I am not the one who did this. It is only because of you that I am changed and I need to be a light not a hindrance to others. But God, help me to be here the next time to protect him. Please don't let him get hurt more. Please God..

Josh moaned as they rolled him over. Then cried out in pain. "Dad, stop, please!"

Jim froze. He looked down at him in shock.

Josh groaned again. "Please, don't! Just let me back down, please!"

Jim nodded as he slowly lowered him back down to the couch.

The officer nodded. "It's okay. I think we have enough any way. I will let you know when every thing is going to happen."

Jim nodded again.

When the officer left and it was back to being just them, Jim called his family together. "We have some things to talk about." He looked at all three of the boys, then at Lilly. He smiled at Julia who was sprawled on the floor showing the baby one of her dollies.

"Your mom and I have talked, boys, and we have decided that you are not going back to the school. Even if John is arrested, that is no guarantee that all will be well. And based on your previous behavior, I am sure if something were to happen, I wouldn't know about it. So You are going to be doing school here at home. Mom is going to be your teacher.

"It's going to be a while before you get the books, probably a few weeks, so you are going to have a bit of a break, but that doesn't mean that you will be without things to do. So starting tomorrow, school will be at home. You will listen to you mom and you will obey and respect her. If you do not, you will be punished. Do you understand?"

"Yes, sir," all three answered in unison.

Josh felt his pulse race, but at the same time he felt that sinking feeling in his stomach. He still wouldn't be allowed to graduate early, he knew.

Jim looked at Josh, then at the others. "We are going over to Luke and Annie's tonight so she can help us figure out what all we need. She said she already had your books Josh, and that she would be glad to have you using them, so we are getting them tonight as well. We will figure this all out, it just may take some time."

Josh nodded slightly. He wished he could tell his dad what his hope was, but he didn't dare. It wasn't worth a beating, just to talk to his dad. Even if it wasn't his dad beating him, it wasn't worth a chance.

Jordan and Jared grinned. "So Josh has to do school tomorrow and we don't till we have books. Hot dog! This is awesome."

Lilly smiled sweetly at her boys, but Josh saw the ornery sparkle in them. "You two boys will be working on a book report and a research paper on a subject which I will let you choose, and a written report on a president. I think that will keep you occupied for this week anyway."

"Aw, Mom!" they both cried loudly.

Jim cleared his throat and they both snapped their mouths shut, but Jared scowled. "No fair," he muttered under his breath.

That night as Luke and Annie talked with Jim and Lilly the older kids: Joshua, Jordan, Jared, and Joy, played a very lengthy game of monopoly, while the younger kids sat in the living-room and played with toys.

Annie was showing Lilly what would be good to order for the boys when Luke sat back with a smile. He looked over at Jim and saw him watching the women with a smile in his eyes.

"Well, I guess maybe Josh will get to go to college in the spring after all. I am glad he took his acceptance letter instead of having Joy throw it out, like he asked her to."

Jim was startled, as was Lilly. They both looked at him in shock, but it was Jim who found his voice first. "What?"

Luke looked at them both in shock. "He hasn't told you?"

Jim shook his head. "Told us what, Pastor? As far as I knew he was a senior this year. He wouldn't be able to go to college till after he graduates. That would mean college next fall not in the spring."

Luke looked over at Annie.

Annie cleared her throat softly. "He was working hard at getting ahead more last year. He had hoped to graduate in December and head to college in January. I can't believe he didn't show you the letter. He had been hoping and praying for weeks, months, that it would come. I figured he would be so excited when he got it that even if he had to wait a semester he would be telling you about it.

Jim cleared his throat. I guess there are still some things my boy needs to talk to me about."

Lilly looked over at him and bit her lip. She hoped this wasn't going to cause a problem , but she had a feeling it just had. Why was Josh trying to keep things from them? Was he just not telling them because he had been in school and he knew he wouldn't be able to go in the start of the second semester, or was it more then that? What was he so afraid of?

Jim cleared his throat. "Maybe he just didn't want us to think that he was trying to rush off."

Lilly tried to smile. "I am sure that is possible."

Annie pulled out a pile of books. "These are the books that he started working on last year and the ones that I had ordered for him to finish out his high school classes. Why don't you take them with you. Then he can go ahead and keep working. It will probably be a couple of weeks before your other boy's books come though."

Lilly cleared her throat as she looked at Jim.

He nodded. "We will take them. I think we are going to have the other boys work on some reports and things to keep them busy while they are waiting for their books."

Annie nodded. "That is a really good idea. They need something to do, I am sure."

Lilly smiled, "If for no other reason than to keep them out of trouble."

Jim laughed. "They are boys. They are going to keep her busy anyway, whether they are kept busy or not."

Annie smiled. "I know what you mean." She looked down at the kids playing on the floor .

Luke looked at them also and a smile lighted up his face. "I know you are all nervous about this, but it is going to work out just fine."

Lilly looked at him nervously. "I hope so, Pastor. I really hope so."

When they got home later Jim turned to Jared and Jordan. "You two boys, head on up to bed. Joshua, I need to talk to you."

Josh felt his pulse leap. He saw anger in his dad's eyes and he trembled even more.

Jared and Jordan looked at each other, then headed up the stairs. Lilly waited till her boys were out of sight before motioning Jim and Josh into the living room. "Come in here, the others don't need to hear.

Josh felt himself grow pale. He wanted to ask what he had done, but he didn't dare.

Jim gripped Josh's arm and stood before him with anger flashing in his eyes.

Josh trembled even more. What had he done?

"Is there something you need to tell me, son?" He finally asked. He was glad he was able to keep his voice steady.

Josh trembled, but frantically searched his mind for what he had done. "No." his voice sounded as hesitant as he felt. Jim gripped his arm tighter and he bit his lip to keep back a moan. What had he done?

Lilly could see how scared Josh was and her heart went out to him. "Jim," she softly laid her hand on his arm. "You don't need to be upset with him. In a way this is our fault too."

Josh trembled visibly. "What did I do?" he didn't want to ask, but if he was going to get belted over it he wanted to know."

Jim gripped his arms hard. "Why didn't you tell us you were wanting to go to college in the spring? Why didn't you show us the acceptance letter?"

Josh felt the color drain from his face. He glanced at Lilly.

Lilly smiled. "Josh, it's okay. We just wish you would have told us. We want to be a family. We want to share in your hopes and dreams. We don't want you to feel like you have to keep things from us."

Josh looked up at his dad. He turned his head slightly as though expecting his dad to strike him. His whole body shook.

Jim sighed. "It's not just this, Josh. What other things are you hiding from us? If you won't talk to us about this, how many other things are you keeping secret?"

Josh dropped his head. Tears came to his eyes, but he refused to let them fall. How could Luke have told on him?

Lilly looked at Jim and he looked at her. Finally Jim gripped Josh's arms again and waited for his son to look at him. "Josh, do not keep things from us. Big or little. Understood? We want to be a part of your life. Can you let us try?"

Josh slowly nodded, but looked away.

Jim sighed again. "Go on and get ready for bed, Josh. We will be up in a few."

Josh nodded and headed for the stairs. He trembled even more with fear. What was his dad going to do to him now that he was home all the time. Was he the one who had been beating him at night, or was it someone else. He shrugged. He would find out soon.

Over the next couple of weeks things seemed to go great. The boys got along better then they had been, and Josh finally started to come out of his shell a little bit. He was more ready to smile and laugh. Jim and Lilly both enjoyed watching the change in him as he seemed to warm up to the family.

Then one night everything changed again.

Josh had gone outside for something for his dad and when he came back in Lilly noticed that he seemed nervous. "Josh, is everything okay?"

He jumped a little. "Fine, just fine." He wouldn't look her in the eye. But instead looked away.

Jared and Jordan looked at each other. Had something happened to Josh again?

Jim walked up behind him and Josh jumped again as his dad put his hand on his shoulder. "What's the matter, son?"

Josh trembled as he turned to look at his dad. His stomach turned, but he didn't let it show. As if his dad didn't have a clue what was wrong with him? Tears burned the backs of his eyes. He had hoped his dad really had changed, but he was wrong. He knew he shouldn't have been so trusting, but he had wanted to believe that his dad was changed and everything that happened was his uncle and not his dad. But he was wrong. He stepped away. "Nothing, Dad. It's nothing. I'm going to head on up to bed."

Jim frowned. "Son, what is going on?"

Josh bit his lip and looked down.

Jared and Jordan looked at each other again. They weren't sure what to think, but they were pretty sure that something had happened to him.

Josh slipped up the stairs. When he was alone in the room he pulled off his shirt and groaned. Just then the door opened.

Josh jumped and spun around.

Jordan flushed. "Sorry, Josh," he whispered, "It's just me."

Josh looked down. "Why are you up here?"

Jordan looked guilty. "I guess I wanted to see if something really did happen. Who was it?" He grimmest as he saw Josh's back. It looked like he had been whipped then drug across concrete.

Josh shook his head. "I was wrong to think he had changed. I guess it wasn't all Uncle John."

Jordan looked at him confused. "What do you mean?"

317

Josh scowled at his brother. "Just don't cross Dad. I didn't realize I had, but I guess I did."

Jordan felt the color drain from his face. "Did he get mad about what happened in school earlier today? I didn't think Mom told him."

Josh shrugged. "I really don't know what started it. But he is not happy. Just don't cross him. Tell Jared too."

Jordan bit his lip. "But Josh, why did he hit you?"

Josh looked away. "Because I'm his, and he can."

Jordan felt sick at heart. "I thought that Dad wasn't going to show differences in us from now on."

Josh kept his head down. "Well, you thought wrong. Just drop it and don't do anything to aggravate him, please."

Jordan nodded. "I'll tell Jared."

Josh nodded again. "Thanks. And don't say anything when I have to go out in the night. And, Jordan," he looked up at his brother with pain in his eyes. "Please don't say anything to dad. Don't let him know that you know."

Jordan felt uneasy. This just couldn't be his dad. It just couldn't be. He nodded, but felt his stomach tighten. Could he keep his word. "Okay, Josh. I won't."

Josh dropped onto the bed and pulled his shirt off again. He groaned moved.

Jordan felt sick as he saw Josh's back. Slowly he turned and walked out of the room. What should he do?

Lilly noticed the change in Josh almost immediately. He stopped eating and he sat ridged during school. He was angry. She could see it in his eyes and in the way he held his body. She wasn't sure what was happening, but she knew it wasn't good. She let it go for a few days, but she knew she was going to have to tell Jim soon, if Josh didn't get back to his old self. She just hoped and prayed the boy would tell them what the problem was without being forced to.

"Please, God," she whispered. "Please help him to trust us."

After a few days of his withdrawing attitude she noticed that his grades were dropping and she started catching him sleeping in school. Her mind told her she needed to talk to Jim, but she kept putting it off hoping to avoid the conflict.

One evening a few nights later, Josh pulled on his jacket and headed for the door. "See you later," he called.

Jim stopped him before he got out the door. "Where are you going, son?"

Josh trembled slightly. "I am taking Joy out for supper. That's all. I'll be back home before ten."

Jim frowned. "I don't recall telling you you could go out tonight, son?"

Josh trembled. He had taken the beating from his dad more than willingly last night so he could go out with Joy tonight. He had paid the price. How could his dad say he didn't remember? His jaw tightened.

Lilly saw the anger flash in Josh's eyes. She stepped up to them. "Jim, it's okay. Have a good night, Josh. We will see you when you get back home. Just ask permission next time. Okay?"

Josh glanced at his dad again. "Yes, ma'am." His voice was hard and Jim was surprised that Josh was so angry.

Jim nodded. "Go on, son. Just get permission next time, and a few days ahead so we know."

Josh scowled at him and walked out the door. Jim was more than surprised that his son acted that way. He had raised him to show more respect then that.

Joy smiled as Josh pulled up in front of the house. "Thanks for dinner, Josh. I really enjoyed the time together. It gets kind of crazy when Jared and Jordan are always around too."

Josh smiled at her. "I know. Thanks for going out with me. I wasn't sure your dad would like the idea. You know, with us having been brother and sister and all. I just didn't know how he would feel about me dating his baby girl."

Joy laughed. "You could definitely tell I was the first one of his kids to go on a date. He was so worried about me, even though I was going out with you."

Josh loved to hear Joy laugh. He loved the way her eyes sparkled in the moon light. "Maybe we can do it again next Friday?"

Joy flushed. Was Josh wanting a more serious relationship than she had thought? "I would like that, Josh, but -" she stopped unsure what to say.

Josh looked at her. "What?"

Joy shrugged. "I guess I was just wondering, are we doing this for fun, or are you being serious?"

Josh flushed, "Is it okay if I tell you I don't know yet?" he whispered.

Joy smiled. "It's fine. I just didn't know what you expected."

Josh grinned. "Just going with you. I don't want you to feel pressured. If you are uncomfortable at any time, just tell me. I don't want to push you, and if I do something you don't want me to do, please just tell me. Okay?"

Joy nodded. "I will, Josh. Thank you."

Josh nodded, "Well, I better get you back in the house, before you are late for your curfew and your dad has my hide."

Joy laughed again as Josh chuckled. "I am sure that is going to happen."

Josh winked at her. "You never know."

Josh walked her to the door, then waited till she was safely inside. He then turned and walked back to his car.

As he drove up in front of his dad's garage, he felt uneasy. His night with Joy had been so nice. He wished his dad would just accept the fact that he was growing up. He sighed and opened the door, but as he stepped out of the car he felt someone grab him from behind. A hand went over his mouth and a fist hit him square in the stomach turning his scream into a muffled grunt.

He fell to the ground and gasped for breath, but someone kicked him in the side before he could pull enough air in his lungs to breathe. He tried to pull away, but again the foot kicked him. He felt someone grab him and pull him back to his feet. He groaned as he looked up at his dad. Slowly he let the fight drain out of him, and let his dad pull him into the garage to beat him. Pain laced his body and mind. Was this ever going to stop?

Jim paced the hall. Anger surged through him. What was Josh doing out with Joy this late? Darkness had long since cloaked the house. He glanced at the clock. Eleven. He started for the door, then turned and walked back toward the kitchen. Then turned and started for the door again.

Lilly looked up at him and shook her head as she rocked little Jimmy to sleep and fed him.

He looked down at the small bundle in her arms and smiled. Jimmy's dark lashes rested on his chubby cheeks. His breathing was deep and even.

Lilly slowly stood. "I think I am going to put him to bed," she whispered.

Jim nodded and stepped aside so she could go up stairs. Once she was gone, he started pacing again.

Why was Josh so late? Was he doing things he shouldn't be, or was he just having a good time with Joy? Maybe they were just over at Luke and Annie's playing a game or something. Yeah, that must be it. There wasn't anywhere to be in town at this late in the evening. Maybe he should just call and have Josh head home.

He sighed and shook his head. He needed to have a talk with his son about what time was appropriate to be out with a girl. And He was going to set a firm curfew. He should have done it already, and he would have, if he had known that Josh was interested in dating. But not knowing had kind of thrown a wrench in the gears.

He sat down on the couch. He thought about Josh's strange reaction to him earlier this evening. Why had Josh gotten so upset when Jim had asked him why he hadn't told them he was going out? It really didn't make sense. He shrugged. He would talk with him as soon as he got home. It was time for some answers.

Jared let out a whoop from upstairs followed by Jordan and he knew that he had something more important to tend to at the moment than Josh. Slowly he stood and started up the stairs.

Josh bit back a groan as Jordan pulled him through the window. "Why didn't you just come in through the door?" he cried.

Josh fell to the floor with a grunt and a groan.

Jared and Jordan stared at their brother in shock.

Josh rolled over and groaned again. Pain wracked his body. He didn't even think he could speak. But he knew he had to try. "Just don't tell Dad I'm here," he whispered. Pain sounded in his voice and he thought that even that much effort was going to make him sick. He knew his dad would be downstairs waiting on him to get home. He had stormed out of the garage when he had finally got done beating him up, and Josh knew it was so he could act like he didn't know why the boy was late, so he could beat him again. So he knew that he would have to find a different way into the house, so his dad wouldn't see him.

Jared's eyes widened. "What did you do to Joy, to end up looking like this?"

Josh glared at him. Then coughed as he tasted blood in his throat.

Jordan felt his eyes grow round. "Did you do something to her?"

Josh turned his head. "Help me sit up, will you?" his voice rasped with pain.

Jordan reached down and slowly helped his brother to a seated position. "Josh, come on, really, what happened to you?" He tried to be careful not to touch Josh's back. "Who did it?"

Josh shrugged. "I guess Dad didn't like the idea of me going on a date. This is his reminder to never do it again."

Jared let out a whoop and then a laugh, Jordan laughed also.

Josh flinched. "Be quiet, would you?"

Jared and Jordan both looked at him. "Come on, Josh. Do you really expect us to believe that? Dad didn't do anything to you. He has been here pacing the floors most of the night worrying about you, but he didn't beat you because you went out with Joy. Did he?" Jared cried.

322

Josh looked away. "Do I look like I'm kidding?"

Jordan bit his lip. "I'm sorry, Josh. I thought you were just covering for something. I really didn't think Dad would do it."

Josh shrugged. "Help me up. I need to get cleaned up before Mom sees, but Dad told me not to come into the house tonight, so just help me make sure he doesn't see me, please."

Jordan looked at him questioningly. "Why didn't Dad want you in the house tonight?"

Josh shrugged. "I don't know, Jordan, but that is what he said. He-"

A knock sounded at the door and the three boys froze. In horror they turned to look at the door.

Jim heard the boys talking and frowned when they didn't answer. "Boys, what is going on in there?" He pushed open the door.

Josh gasped as his dad stepped into the room and Jared and Jordan stepped between him and his dad. He shrank back wishing he could disappear.

Jim stared in shock at Joshua. "What is going on here?"

Jared and Jordan stood frozen, unsure of how to answer.

Jim stepped closer to the three of them, then in two quick steps crossed the room and gripped Josh's arm and pulled him to his feet.

"Ahh." Josh cried out, before he thought. Then he snapped his mouth shut and shrank away from his dad.

Jim stood almost frozen in horror. What had happened to his son? Surly he hadn't done something to Joy, and Luke had given him the what for. He took a deep breath to control his fast rising temper. "What happened to you, Joshua?"

Josh shivered. What was he suppose to answer?

Jared and Jordan exchanged looks.

Jim looked at them. "Do you two know what is going on?"

They both shook their heads and looked at Josh.

Josh shuttered as he stood facing his dad. He really didn't get how his dad could act like he had no idea what was going on, or what he had just done.

Lilly stepped into the room a frown creasing her brow. "What is going on in here? Jim, what are you doing?"

Jim turned to her. "I am trying to figure out what our son is doing up here and how long he has been here and what in the world happened to him tonight."

Lilly stepped closer and gasped. "Joshua, what in the world is going on!"

Josh looked at his dad with anger in his eye.

Jim raised his eyebrows in surprise. His son hadn't looked at him like that in a long time. He waited for him to answer.

Lilly turned to Jared and Jordan. "You two go to the living-room. I will speak to you in a little bit. Just go read a book or something."

Jared and Jordan both groaned, but obeyed.

As they left, Jim gave Lilly a grateful look, then turned back to Josh. "Son, I want you to tell me the truth right now. What is going on?"

Josh looked at him with pain in his eyes. "Like you don't know." he growled.

"Josh, what is that suppose to mean?" Lilly's voice was soft, but held more of a question.

Josh shrugged but his dad wouldn't let it go.

Jim gripped his son's arms and shook him slightly. "Son, you had better tell me who whipped you unless you want a whipping to match it."

Josh jerked away from him. "And what? Would you enjoy it just as much this time, or would you enjoy it more? What reason would you come up with this time? Dad, I am sixteen years old. I am old enough to date. And I really don't care whether you like it or not. I took the beating for it last night, so what was tonight for, huh? Why can't you see that I am growing up and get over it? I am not a child anymore. Beat me if you want, but it's not going to change anything!" He winced in pain as he put his arm around his stomach.

Jim stared at him. He had to fight himself to keep from slapping is son on the mouth for the way he was talking, but he couldn't believe what the boy was saying either.

Lilly cleared her throat. "Josh, are you telling me that your dad beat you like this. He did this to you?"

Josh glared at his dad. "Yes, that is what I am saying."

Lilly looked at Jim in shock. "When?"

Josh trembled but looked at her. "What do you mean when? Just now. He started when I got home from being with Joy, over three hours ago, and he quit a few minutes ago."

Lilly shook her head. "Has he been doing this a lot here the

324

last few days?"

Josh shuttered, but as he glanced at his dad, he saw Jim nod for him to answer. "Yes, ma'am."

Lilly looked at Jim. Surprise registered in her eyes. "I guess this explains why you have been pulling into yourself the last few weeks, and why you have stopped eating again then doesn't it? Did he threaten you that he would beat you if you ate?"

Josh trembled even more. He glanced at his dad again, and again Jim nodded for him to answer. "Tell your mother the truth, son."

Josh forced back a whimper. "Yes, ma'am," he muttered. He wanted to jerk away and guard himself, but he knew it would be useless.

Jim motioned to Josh and the boy slowly turned his back to his dad, knowing he didn't have a choice.

Lilly gasped.

Jim felt his anger rise even more. His son's bloody back was definitely proof that his brother was back. "Son, I didn't hit you tonight, or last night. I have been here in the house with your mother since before you left this evening."

Josh trembled. He wanted to believe his dad, but if he did, that meant that someone else was after him.

Jim looked him in the eye. "I am sure you don't want to believe me, son, but I have been here with Lilly all evening. I promise you. But now I understand, why you were so mad earlier, if you thought I had beat you for going out then still wasn't going to allow you to go. I am sorry. But I wish you would have said something so we would have known."

Josh looked down.

Lilly gently touched his cheek.

Jim wasn't surprised to see the boy flinch and pull away slightly.

"Don't worry, Josh," Lilly whispered as softly. "It's going to be okay. We will get this worked out, but I wish you would have said something when it started happening. Then we could have got it worked out from there. Instead you have had to live with it for how long now? Son, you need to talk to us. Please. Don't just suffer."

Josh nodded.

Jim frowned. "Where did he beat you at, Joshua."

325

Josh shivered as he looked up at his dad.

"Where, Joshua?" Jim's voice was hard and stern.

He swallowed hard. "The garage."

Jim nodded. "Makes sense." He motioned to Josh, "Show me."

Josh bit his lip to keep back the groan, as he forced himself to move.

Jim saw his son's pain, and anger once again ripped through him. He was going to take his brother apart if he ever got the chance. Suddenly there was a knock at the door.

Jim looked at it in annoyance. Slowly he went to answer it with Josh leading the way.

John stood at the door and smiled menacingly at Josh.

Josh shuttered and stumbled back a few steps.

Jim saw his brother and his anger boiled over. "John, what are you doing here?"

John laughed. "Just came to see how you were doing. But by the looks of your boy, I would say you are back to your old self." He looked at Josh and laughed again. "What did you do, boy, to make your old man whip up on you like that?"

Josh looked away.

Jim felt his temper rise even more. Suddenly he swung at his brother and knocked him backward. "John, I licked you more times than I can count in my life, and I will do it again if I have to. Don't you dare touch my son again. You want to beat someone, beat your own child. I am sure he needs it. Now get away from here. And don't you ever come back here pretending to be me. Do I make myself clear?"

Josh stared at his dad in shock.

John shook his head to clear it. He looked up at his brother in shock.

Jim saw the anger in his brother's eyes and he leveled another punch to his jaw, knocking him to the porch floor. "I asked you a question, John. You got an answer for me? Or, even better, maybe you can tell me why you pretended to be me tonight and beat my son, or last night or any other night this week."

John frowned deeper. "The boy needs to be taught, and you aren't doing it."

Jim threw another punch and busted his brother's lip open.

John ducked down to dodge the next punch. Jim followed him. John stepped back.

Jim swung one fist and then the other catching him off guard and down John went again. "Get out of here! Do not touch him again. I have already called the authorities. They should be here to get you any time. You want to try and touch him now?"

John looked down. He had taken it too far hoping his brother wasn't home tonight. He should have just let the last beating he gave Josh do, but he wanted to hit him more before the night was over. He sighed.

Josh jumped when he saw the lights pull in the drive.

John turned to his brother. "You were serious?"

Jim's eyes blazed. "Yes, I was serious. I knew something was up, but I wasn't quite sure what it was. Then I saw him tonight, and I knew it was you. Who else would pretend to be me and be able to fool him?"

John sighed as the cops walked up. This was it. He was going back to jail, and this time there wouldn't be an out. But what surprised him was his brother's protection to his son. Maybe God really had changed his brother. Maybe it was time he listened to him. Maybe there was hope for a future more than just to die in this world.

Josh stared at his dad as the cops came in the house. He couldn't believe his dad was protecting him. He saw his dad's jaw tighten as the cops cuffed John and led him out.

Jim turned back to Josh. He was breathing hard, but his eyes looked scared and concerned.

Josh looked at his dad with a new respect. "Thanks, Dad. I never thought you would do that for me." He choked on a sob.

Jim reached up and placed his hand on Josh's shoulder. "Don't ever be afraid to tell me if he touches you again. Please, son, don't hide from me."

Josh dropped his gaze to hide the fresh tears that had welled up in his eyes. "Yes, sir."

Jim nodded. "I need to go upstairs and check on you mom and the baby."

Josh nodded. "Thanks, Dad."

Jim smiled at him. "I love you, son."

Josh felt stunned at his dad's words. He didn't remember his dad ever telling him that before. He watched in silence as Jim walked out of the room. Did his dad really love him?

He shook his head. He wasn't sure, but his actions tonight were definitely different than ever before.

32

Josh turned to Jared and Jordan as they followed him up the stairs. "I told you guys I am not talking about this."

Jared frowned. "Come on, Josh. We don't want you to go. College is a long ways off. You shouldn't be going to college for at least like two years. Why do you think you have to go now?"

Jordan sighed. "Josh, come on. How hard did you have to work to get out of school early? Do you think I could, at least, get out next year instead of the next?"

Josh shrugged. "If you work at it, maybe. But it takes a lot of work and some long hours with the school books. You don't get a break just cause you want to get done early. You still have to do all the work. I don't know why you are so worried about it now anyway. I am not leaving for college for another month. And that is, only if I get the rest of my school work done."

"Yeah," Jared sighed, "But Dad did give you the okay. It's not fair. I want to go to college now. I don't want to have to be in high school for another two years. And what if Dad makes us go back to public school when you are gone? Then I won't even get the chance to get out early.

Josh shrugged. "I don't think he is going to put you back in public school, but that is between you and him. I am not asking for you."

Jared sighed again. "Fine."

Jordan smiled and his eyes twinkled, "You aren't going to mind if I take Joy out on a few dates while you are gone, are you?"

Josh's eyes snapped. "Yes, I do mind. You leave her alone. I am staking my claim right now. Don't either one of you even try it."

Jared laughed as Jordan scowled. "If you still lived with them one of us would be taking her out as soon as we have our birthday. But just cause you are older, you get first dibs. It's not fair."

Josh shrugged. "I don't care if you think it's fair or not. That is how it is. She is my girl, and you leave her alone."

Jordan frowned. "On one condition."

Josh eyed him warily. "What?"

"When you find a different girl in college you will let me know before Jared so I can take her out."

Josh laughed. "Find your own date."

Jared and Jordan both sighed. "Fine."

Josh laughed again as he pulled his jacket out of the closet. "I am sure you will find a girl that you like. If you haven't met her yet, you will. I got to go. See you."

Both brothers waved to him then flopped down on their beds as Josh ran out the door.

"I can't believe he won't even let us date her." Jordan sighed. "She is the prettiest girl in the whole church, and just because he turned sixteen two months before we do, he gets her. It is just not fair."

Jared smiled. "He doesn't have to know we asked her out on a date. What he doesn't know won't hurt him." His eyes sparkled with mischief.

Jordan smiled too. "Hey, yeah, that is true. How about once he is gone we will split it up. I can take her out the first week and you can the second."

Jared frowned. "No, I get to take her out the first week and you can the second."

Jordan eyed his brother with anger. "Maybe we will just ask her and see who she agrees to go out with."

Jared shrugged looking smug. "No problem. It will be me."

Jordan sat up straight and looked his brother in the eye. The fight in him was growing. "It will not!"

Jared scowled. "So too!"

Jordan swung.

Jared ducked and the blow fell short, but as Jared stood a connecting blow knocked him to the floor. In anger he slammed into Jordan and knocked him to the floor as well. In absolutely no time the boys were in a knock down drag out fight.

Josh took a deep breath as he knocked on the door at Luke and Annie's. He and Joy had been going out steadily for about a month now and he was looking forward to the next month before he had to leave. He hoped she was too. He didn't want to be leading her on, and he wanted to know if she was being serious or if it was all in fun for her, so he had decided to ask her tonight. He was nervous to hear her answer.

Joy answered the knock, and with a smile and a small laugh, she invited him in. "Mom is getting some stuff down from the attic. She needed me to watch the little ones. When she is done, we can go. Sorry."

"That's fine." He smiled and watched her as she walked back to the living-room. How had he missed how much she captivated his mind when he lived here? Was it just that they were not brother and sister now? Is that why he seemed to see her with different eyes?

"Josh?"

He looked up surprised.

She laughed again. "What are you thinking about?"

Josh flushed. He didn't even want to look at her, afraid that she could read his thoughts and see exactly what he had been thinking about."

Luke walked into the house at that moment, and Josh felt himself grow uncomfortable. He hadn't been thinking things he shouldn't, but he hadn't said that and now he was worried that Joy may think he was.

Luke smiled at him and Joy. "You two going out again? My goodness! This is like the fifth time in five weeks. You better be careful, Joshua, or people may start thinking you two are getting serious."

Josh glanced at Joy wondering what she was thinking. She just smiled at him.

Josh turned to Luke. "Is it a problem, sir, if I am getting serious?"

Luke looked at him in surprise. "I thought you were heading off to college in a few weeks. Don't you think you are a little on the young side to be getting too serious?"

Josh shrugged. "So I can't be serious, just because I am heading off to college?"

Luke shook his head. "That's not what I meant. I just didn't think you would be ready for a serious relationship till that was all over with, or at least for a couple of years. You know, till you had a year or two of college under your belt."

Josh shrugged again. "I'm not really sure what all will come of this, sir. But I assure you, I don't want to break her heart."

Joy flushed.

Luke smiled. "Good. I am glad. You two run along. I will watch the kids. I don't want you back too late."

Joy smiled. "Okay, Daddy. Thanks." She gave her dad a quick kiss on the cheek and a quick hug, then walked out with Josh.

Josh smiled a tight lipped smile before walking out. Maybe he was feeling too serious about their relationship, but he couldn't help it. He loved her. And he was determined to find out if she felt the same.

Joy noticed all through the evening Josh was quiet. He seemed to be deep in thought, but he also seemed bothered about something. She waited hoping he was going to share what he was thinking, but he never did.

As they were driving home she decided she had waited long enough for him to talk. If she didn't say something he probably wasn't going to tell her what was wrong. Was it what her dad had said to him? She shrugged to herself there was only one way to find out. She took a deep breath and turned to Josh with a smile. "Josh, you have been really quiet. What is going on. Are you bothered by what Daddy said to you before we left tonight?"

Josh shrugged. "Not really bothered by it, maybe just thinking about it."

Joy felt her pulse race. "What are you thinking about?"

Josh shrugged. "Joy, I want this to be more serious. Are you interested in that? Do you want us to be more serious, or would you rather not since I am leaving?"

Joy found her breath caught in her throat. She knew without a shadow of a doubt that she loved him, more than a brother, but she hadn't thought that he was serious. She had prayed and prayed that if he wasn't God would show her. But she had felt God telling her to just hold on. That he had a plan in store for her and Josh. She hoped she was right and not just going by what she was feeling. "What exactly are you asking me, Josh?"

Josh bit his lip and looked away. He sighed as he pulled into the driveway at her home. He put the car in park and turned to her. "Joy, I want a relationship with you. I want to go out, I don't just mean a few dates. I mean seriously. I want to date you. I know we are young, but I want to date you with the plan of marrying you someday."

Joy gasped. She had no idea Josh was that serious. "Are you serious?"

Josh looked deep into her eyes. His voice was raspy when he said, "Yes, Joy, I am that serious. I don't want to pressure you, but I do want you to know what I am feeling." He reached over and took her hand. "I am not asking you to marry me now, but would you date me with that as a thought? Would you be willing to go out with me and see what happens to us in the future?"

Joy looked into his eyes and smile. "I would love to, Josh." Her heart was singing. She closed her eyes and silently thanked God for answering her prayer. "And I hope this means, you won't forget me when you go off to college." She looked up at him with a smile. "It would be nice to hear from you once in a while. And if we are dating more seriously, Dad won't care, I am sure, if you call me once in a while."

Josh smiled. "I couldn't ever forget you, Joy. You know that. But if you are asking if I plan to date anyone else at school, the answer is no. I only want to date you. Do you feel that way? If you don't feel this serious about me and want to date some one else just tell me."

A smile broke all over her face. "Definitely. I only want to be with you, Josh."

Josh relaxed. "Good, because I have a feeling that as soon as I am gone my brothers are going to try everything in their power to date you."

Joy laughed, "Don't worry, Josh. I will just have them talk to Dad first. He can tell them no."

Josh chuckled. "I love you, Joy."

Joy felt a warm feeling all over her. "I love you too, Josh. Thank you for telling me what you were feeling. It helps me. I wanted to know what you were thinking about us, but I was afraid to ask. I was afraid I would scare you away."

He smiled. "If you ever wonder what I am thinking, just ask."

"Okay." Her smile reached her eyes in a teasing light. "Are you sure?"

Josh laughed out loud. "I am sure, Joy. Don't worry. I want to know what you are thinking too."

She blushed and looked away.

Josh smiled. He squeezed her hand and she looked up at him. "Can I hug you?"

She smiled and nodded slightly. "I would like that, Josh."

Josh lovingly wrapper her in his arms and held her tightly for a few moments. He then pulled back and smiled into her eyes. He wanted to kiss her, but knew that he shouldn't push too far. "Come on. Time to get you back in the house, before we are in trouble."

Joy nodded and waited for him to open her door. Her heart soared. He loved her. It was as she had hoped. Now she just had to pray that God would help her to be patient. She didn't want to rush God's timing. It was perfect and she needed to be sure not to get in front of God. But she couldn't stand the thought of waiting four years or more till he was out of college to get married.

33

Josh sighed as he closed the door to his room. His head ached and he was pretty sure he was running a fever, but he didn't want to miss classes. He lay down on his bed, telling himself he would only rest for a few minutes. He glanced at the clock. He had an hour before supper, then it was time for P.E. He felt his stomach turn as he lay there.

He closed his eyes and tried to get the world to stop spinning. He hadn't felt great for the last two weeks, but this was the worst. In all truth he really hadn't felt great since he had gotten here, but today it was the worst.

He rolled on to his side and shut his eyes willing his stomach to settle.

"Josh!" his roommate called as he hurried into the room.

Josh moaned and opened his eyes. "What?"

Lucas frowned. "What's wrong with you?"

Josh tried to sit up, but as soon as he moved the room tilted and spun. He groaned and lay back on the bed.

Lucas looked at him worriedly. "Your Dad is on the phone. Said he wants to talk to you. Can you make it or do I bring in the cordless?"

Josh opened his mouth to talk, but quickly closed it. Lucas grabbed a garbage can and handed it to him. Once he had emptied his stomach, he groaned again. "Just bring me the cordless, Lucas. And please don't say anything about me being sick."

Lucas nodded. He hurried out. He would bring Josh the cordless, then go let the dorm Dad know he was sick. He knew Josh didn't want him to, but he also knew that someone needed to know. He looked awful.

Josh tried to move again, but the world spun making him even sicker. He hadn't felt this bad in a long, long time.

Lucas walked back in and handed him the phone. "Do you need anything, Josh?"

Josh shook his head. "I'm okay. Thanks."

Lucas shrugged and walked out.

Josh put the phone up to his head, but with his head throbbing the way it was he didn't want to listen to it. "Hello." His voice was raspy and he knew he sounded almost as bad as he felt.

Jim was surprised to hear his son sounding so exhausted. "Josh, what's going on? You sound exhausted."

Josh groaned. He didn't want to worry his family. "It's nothing, Dad. What's up?"

Jim could tell Josh was lying. "Joshua, are you lying to me? What is going on?"

Josh bit his lip. He knew he wouldn't be able to lie to his dad. He shouldn't have even tried. "I just got the flu. It's nothing. I am sure I will be fine by morning."

Jim frowned. "I hope so. Aside from that, is everything going good for you?"

Josh bit his lip. "Yeah, fine, Dad. How is everything there?"

Jim hesitated. "Josh, you knew that Luke resigned at the church didn't you?"

Josh felt his blood freeze. "No, when?"

"Last week. They are leaving in about three weeks. He has a new church somewhere back east."

Josh felt his stomach turn again. Joy hadn't said anything about it when they talked two day's ago. Nor had she mentioned it in the last letter. "Why?"

"He didn't really say. Just thought that it was time to move on. God seemed to be calling him elsewhere."

Josh was quiet. He didn't dare try and talk. Every muscle in his digestive system seemed to be trying to work backwards.

336

Jim sighed. "Son, are you sure you are okay and this is just the flu. How long have you been sick?"

Josh shuttered. He didn't dare tell his dad how long he hadn't felt well. His dad would get after him for not saying anything sooner. He didn't want to worry them. This had to just be some kind of a bug, and he wasn't getting over it because he wasn't getting enough sleep. "It's fine, Dad. I just got sick today. I am sure I will be fine by morning."

Jim muttered something Josh couldn't hear then spoke louder. "I'll call you tomorrow and hope you are better."

Josh swallowed before he answered. "Okay, Dad. Talk to you then."

"Bye, son. Get some rest."

"Okay." Josh hung up the phone and rested his head back into his pillow. He was miserable.

After a week of almost solid sleep and still not getting any better, his family came to the college. Jim walked into the room, took one look at his son, and immediately proclaimed that he was taking him home.

Josh looked up at him in surprise. "Dad, no please. It's just a cold or something. That is all. Please, don't take me home. I am still keeping up with my classes. I can do this."

Jim shook his head. "Son, you are going home. If you get better you may come back next semester, but I am going to guess that it will take you at least a year to get better."

Josh looked at him in surprise. "What do you mean?"

Jim shook his head. "I will run the blood work on you when we get home, son. Just to be sure, but you don't need to be here. Your body isn't going to keep up with the work you need to do this year."

Josh sighed. He didn't understand why God would bring him here just to send him home. "Okay, Dad, what ever you say," he muttered. He was too exhausted to fight about it.

Jim nodded. "He called out into the hall for Jared and Jordan.

Josh vaguely saw them put his stuff in boxes and was aware that his dad went out for a while and came back with someone, but he

337

really didn't know who. Exhaustion captured him again, and while his family packed his stuff, he slept.

When they had the van loaded Jim turned to the dorm dad. "Sorry it has to be like this."

The dorm dad shrugged. "I am just sorry we didn't call you sooner. I just kept thinking that surly he would be better in the morning, but it just never happened. So you think it is serious?"

Jim nodded. "It's okay. Serious, yes. Contagious, not highly, but it can spread. We will get him home where he can get rest and hope for the best."

The dorm dad nodded.

Jim turned back to Josh, "Come on, son. I'll help you down to the car."

Josh turned his head slightly and looked at his dad. His head ached more then ever, but he slowly pushed himself to a seated position, then stood. His legs gave way beneath him as he stood and Jim grab him and held him up. He slid under his son's arm and they made there way to the van slowly.

Once in the van Josh lay his head against the back of the seat and was back to sleep. He slept all the way home, eight hours. Once they got there Jordan and Jared helped their dad carry him up to his bed.

Josh moaned as they laid him back down.

Jim frowned. The moan was a moan of pain, and not just sick pain. He pulled the covers down from his son and rolled him up on his side. Gently he pushed on his son's back.

Josh cried out in pain, then lay still. Fear gripped him anew, but he was too exhausted to fight.

Jim slowly pulled up his son's shirt. Very fresh welts covered his son's back. Anger turned in him. Who had been hitting him? And why?

He wanted to question him, but knew that now wasn't the time. Yet, He needed to find out what was going on.

Jared and Jordan came in carrying stuff. "What's wrong with him, Dad?" Jordan asked concerned, as he saw his father lower Josh's shirt.

Jim turned to both his boys. "Did Josh ever give any indication that someone was hitting him?"

Jared and Jordan both looked at there dad in shock. "What do you mean?" Jordan asked weakly.

Jim turned back to the bed and pulled up Josh's shirt.

Jared and Jordan stared in shock at his back. Then they looked at each other.

Jim saw the look. "Who was it boys? You know something about this."

Jordan shrugged. "Josh just told me that he likes the college, but one of the boys there is really mean."

Jared nodded. "He said the there was a fight in the dorm a few weeks ago and he bested one of the big guys and made him really mad. He said the dorm dad broke up the fight, but the big kid swore he was going to get even.

Jim nodded. "Looks like he did if this is his work."

Josh groaned as he rolled over. He looked up at his dad with fear in his eyes.

"Who was it, Josh?" Jim's voice was full of pain.

Josh looked away. "One of the guys got mad at me. I guess I was an easy target when I was the only one in the dorm cause I was sick.

Jim felt his anger rise even more. "He did this to you when you were sick!"

Josh nodded. "I would have bested him again if I wasn't sick, Dad. You should know that." He gave him a weak smile.

Jim sighed. "I don't know what to do about this, Josh."

Josh shrugged. "It doesn't matter any more, Dad. I'm gone. He can't hurt me here. Just let it go."

Jim nodded. "I guess you are right."

Josh closed his eyes again too exhausted to even talk.

Jim bit his lip. He was worried about his son, but he knew the main thing he needed was sleep. That was the best thing he could do right now. He motioned to Jared and Jordan and they all three quietly left the room.

Jim turned to the boys. "Any kind of suspicious activity and you had better tell me. I mean it. If he starts sneaking out at night, if you see that he is being hit. I want to know anything that shouldn't be going on. Do I make myself clear. No more hiding anything. No secrets. His life may depend on it."

Both boys silently nodded. "Okay, Dad," Jordan answered. "We will."

Jim smiled and nodded to both of them. "Now the main thing we need to worry about is getting him well. It is going to be a long road, and he is going to sleep through most of it. You boys need to let him sleep as much as he can."

Again they both nodded. "Okay, Dad. We will."

Jim nodded. "Thanks, boys. Let's pray for him right now. I know God has a reason for this." He bowed his head, "Dear God, please take care of Josh. Make him well. Your will be done, Father. Amen."

Again both boys looked at their dad and smiled. They all felt sure that God was going to answer. There was no doubt. God was in control of this situation. And he had a reason to let it all happen. Quietly they headed downstairs, leaving Josh to sleep.

34

It was seven moths before Josh was really back up and around. He spent most of that time sleeping. His family worried about him, but he really didn't have much memory of those months.

When he finally got up and around he was surprised at how much effort it was for him to do anything. He told his dad he felt like he was a new born foal.

Jim laughed. "Well, I am sure that, just like a new born foal, you will be back to your old self soon."

Josh smiled. "I don't want to lay around any more."

Jim smiled. "It's good to see you up and around, son. But I want you to take it easy for a while. I don't want you having a set back."

Jared and Jordan were both trying to get done with their last two years of school in one year so a lot of their time was spent in study. Josh found it hard not having anything to do. He missed Joy. He wondered where she was. He hadn't heard from her at all since he had been sick, and his dad said they hadn't heard from her family either. They seemed to have vanished.

Josh was worried about her. But that only added to his missing her.

He got a job at the local hardware store and started saving up to go back to college, but he wasn't sure now what God wanted him to do.

His dad warned him about getting too tired and that he should take it easy for a while. He followed that advice, but still tried to keep himself busy enough he didn't think about Joy.

He wanted to write to her, but had no idea where they had gone. Not even a town to put on the envelope, or even a state. Finally he decided to get in touch with some of the family that he knew and see if they had any idea where they were.

He wrote a letter to Luke's brother and anxiously waited for the answer. After a month and no answer he tried again. Finally the answer came that they knew Luke and Annie had moved back east, but they had no idea where. They would try to find out and let him know.

More waiting followed. He wondered why she never wrote. Was she mad at him?

Finally, a little over a year after Josh had first got sick, an answer came from the cousin that they had moved to upstate New York, but he didn't know any more than that. He had no address, nothing. He wasn't sure how to try to find the information. All he had been able to learn was that they had taken a small church and they weren't wanting people to know where they were.

Josh's concern grew. Fear ate at him. His loneliness grew even more. Why didn't she at least let him know she was okay? He sighed. This wasn't how his life was suppose to go.

God, I was trying to follow your will for me. Did I mess up? What did I do wrong? Where is Joy, God? Why can't I find her? Why did my life fall apart like this?

He sighed, but then in his heart he heard the whispered words, "We know that all things work together for good to them that love God, to them that are called according to his propose." Romans 6:28. A smile crossed his lips.

Well, God, I love you. And I know I was called by you. So I will trust you to show me just what you want me to do. Just help me to keep trusting, and, God, if it be your will, please bring Joy and me back together. If she isn't the one you have for me, then please, show me that as well.

He sighed again. He knew he had to trust, but he was struggling. "Help me, God," he whispered.

One night a few weeks later, Jared came into the room. "Josh, what do you think?"

Josh looked up at him confused. "What do I think about what?"

Jared rolled his eyes. "Look at me."

Josh looked his brother over and guessed that he had a date, by the way his hair was slicked back and plastered to his head. He tried to control his laughter, but his smile sounded in his voice. "You look like you stuck your head in a frying pan."

Jared sighed. "Oh, Josh, come on. You have been on more dates than I have been. Help me."

Josh sighed and stood. He grabbed a comb and went to work on his brother's hair. "Who is it?"

Jared's smile almost split his face. "Lexi, from Church."

Josh smiled, glad to see his brother had a little bit of good taste anyway, "Nice girl. Good luck."

Jared grinned. "Thanks. We have liked each other for a long time, but her dad wouldn't let her date till she was seventeen, and that happened yesterday."

Josh grinned. "Not waiting any, are you?"

Jared laughed lightly. "I can't let some other fellow hoan in on her. I got to stake my claim, just like you did with Joy."

Josh flinched.

Jared stopped short. "I'm sorry, Josh. I shouldn't have said that. I am sure there is a good reason why she hasn't let you know where she is. Maybe she will soon."

Josh nodded. "It's just not – I don't know."

Jared nodded.

Josh shrugged again. "Never mind. Have fun on your date."

Jared smiled again. "I will. If all goes well any way."

Two weeks more passed and summer was drawing to a close. Jim sat the boys down in the living-room one night and talked with all of them. "Boys, it will soon be time to be starting school again. I

343

know Jared and Jordan, you both finished last spring. You boys need to be figuring out what you are going to do this semester. Are you getting jobs or going to school? Josh, are you staying at your job or are you going to school? It's time to think about this, boys."

The boys exchanged glances. Jordan spoke first. "I have thought about it, Dad. I know I should have talked to you first, but I wasn't sure if I could make it in, and I wanted to do it on my own, I applied at med school, and I hope to start the end of next month, I just haven't heard back from them yet."

Jim looked at him in surprise. "I am proud of you, son. I hope you hear back from them soon." He turned to the other two.

Jared looked his dad in the eye. "Dad, I don't want to disappoint you, but I really think I am going to get a job. And as soon as Lexi turns eighteen next year, I think her and I are going to settle down with a place of our own. We have been talking about it, and we both know what we want. But we can't till she is eighteen, so we are waiting."

Jim nodded his approval. "I am not disappointed, son. I am glad you are thinking about it. Where are you planning on working?"

Jared shrugged, "I have been looking, Dad, but I haven't found the right job yet. I guess, I will keep trying."

Jim nodded. "Okay, son. I will let it go at that for now, but by the end of the month, you will have a job, got it?" Jared nodded.

"Josh," he turned to his son. "What are you thinking?"

Josh looked his dad in the eye. His world had been turned upside down ever since he had gotten sick. He wasn't sure what was suppose to happen with his life. He wanted to do what God wanted, but he wasn't sure what that was anymore.

"I really don't have an answer for you, Dad. I don't know what I want. I don't know what God wants of me. I am really not sure what I am suppose to do. I have been praying, I just can't find any answers."

Jim nodded. "I will be praying God shows you soon, son. I am glad to know what you are all hoping for. Now I hope you all have sought God's will in this."

All three boys nodded.

Jim smiled again. "Good. Well, at least now we have an idea of what the next few months, or years may hold."

35

Three years passed. The kids all grew and changed, but Josh couldn't settle down to anything. He couldn't seem to feel God telling him anything. He sought and sought God's will for his life, but he just couldn't get clear. He considered going back to college, but didn't feel clear in doing so. He got a good job working for a building contractor, and really loved the job, but he didn't feel that was what God wanted him to do forever.

He continued to pray for answers and one night as Jordan was packing up to go back to college after summer break, his answer finally came.

Jordan looked at Josh as he put some of his clothes in the suitcase. "Why didn't you go back if you were so sure it was what God wanted for you?"

Josh shrugged. "I really don't know why I haven't felt clear to go back, Jordan. I wish I had, but I haven't. I just keep waiting for God, but I don't think he hears me."

Jordan looked Josh in the eye for a moment as a serious expression crossed his face. "You told me that God always hears."

Josh nodded. "I know. I just feel really discouraged. And I feel like I am disappointing Dad. I don't think he wants me sticking around here forever, and believe me I really don't want to. I am twenty years old. I am ready to be out on my own."

Jordan shrugged. "Maybe you just need to take a step and then God will tell you what to do next."

Josh sighed. "I don't know which way to go, Jordan. I am seriously thinking of the mission field, but I don't know where."

Jordan jumped. "Hey, that reminds me. We got this in the mail yesterday. I was going to show it to you. It sounds like a great opportunity, but I can't go. I have to go to college that week." He held out a brochure to him.

Josh reached out and took the brochure. It was a mission trip opportunity to the orphanages in New York City. Josh immediately felt his pulse leap. This was actually what he wanted to do. "Thanks for showing it to me, Jordan. I will pray about it."

Jordan smiled hearing the excitement in Josh's voice. "Good. Maybe it will help you get out of this depression you have been feeling."

Josh nodded. "I hope so, Jordan. I really hope so."

A few weeks later Josh was boarding a plane headed for New York City. His excitement was mounting with each moment. He couldn't wait. Not only was he sure that this was God's will for him, but he was so excited to finally feel clear on something. He couldn't be more sure that this was what God's will was for him.

Jared waved to him at security. "See you in a few weeks, Josh, if you decide to come home." He laughed, "Just don't be gone too long." He put his arm around his very pregnant wife.

Lexi smiled at Jared then at Josh. "After all we wouldn't want you to miss the baby being born."

Josh laughed too, but he wasn't doing it to be funny. Jared had no idea what kind of an impact his words had on Josh. He really wasn't sure he was going to come home either. He had to just take it one step at a time, but in his heart he knew this was where he was suppose to be for now. Knowing that for sure, sent thrills through him.

"Thank you, God, I am so blessed." He turned to his dad.

Jim smiled and gave his son a hug. "Take care, son. I am glad to see that sparkle back in your eyes. It's been a long time."

Josh nodded. "It has been a long time since I have felt like I am doing what God wants of me, Dad. Thanks for your approval in this."

Jim nodded again then turned and took Jimmy from Lilly so she could tell Josh goodbye.

Lilly had tears in her eyes as she hugged Josh. "You be careful now, you hear. New York is a long ways away. We will see you in a few weeks."

Josh nodded as he hugged her back. "It's going to be fine, Mom. I will see you when I come back."

He knelt down and gave nine year old Julia a hug. "See you when I get back."

Julia hugged him tight. "Bye, Josh. See you in a few weeks."

Josh stood and turned back to his dad.

Jim smiled and nodded.

He turned and headed through security. As he passed through he turned around and waved. His excitement bubbled over as he saw his family wave back. Then he turned and headed to his gate.

Thank you, God, for giving me peace about this. Thank you for showing me what you wanted me to do. Help me to be sensitive to your calling God. And if this is where you want me to stay, help me to know that.

36

Josh's heart broke as he saw all the orphans in the orphanage. The place was packed. There were way too many kids crowded into the rooms. As the supervisor showed him and the handful of other volunteers around, he explained certain things about how they worked and how many children had come to be there.

Finally the tour came to an end. "This is our nurses station. We have two nurse on staff, but one is just in training, so legally she can't be the only one here. We have another nurse or two who fill in on the weekends till our girl that is training can pass her testing. Well, that wraps it up for the tour. You may all go to your rooms and refresh. Supper is at five, and tomorrow we will be putting you all to work." He smiled warmly. "And let me just say to all of you, thank you so much for coming and helping us out."

Josh smiled at the way the director put it.

The rest of the group retired to their rooms, but as Josh was walking down the hall he saw a group of boys punching each other. He snuck up behind them to see what was going on.

One boy had his hands over his face and was obviously crying as one of the other boys repeatedly slugged him in the stomach and face. "That's what you get for being where you aren't suppose to be you little twerp!" Snarled the bigger boy. "You may not know your way around yet, but you better learn fast or I will hurt you worse."

Josh felt his anger rise. He walked up behind the bigger boy as the boy turned to leave. The boy froze as he looked up. "Who are you?" he asked shakily.

Josh frowned down at him. "I think I could ask you that question. So you like to beat up on little ones do you? Do you think it would be very nice if I punched you?"

The boy glared up at him. "What do you care? Go away."

Josh frowned deeper. He gripped the boy's arm. "I will. But I think you get to go with me. First, we are going to take your friend to the nurse, then you are going to the office.

Adam paled. "Look mister I don't know who you are, but I don't think I need to go to the office."

Josh looked at him. "No, well we will see what Mr. Bundy has to say about it. Who is your friend?"

Adam scowled. "That's Daren. He is new here. Just got here yesterday."

Josh nodded. "I see. Well, come on both of you. We are going to get this settled now."

He picked up Daren and carried him to the office with Adam walking beside him.

Mr. Bundy was just coming out of his office when he saw them. "What in the world is going on?" He cried as he saw the five year old in Josh's arms and the smug looking twelve year old beside Josh.

Josh carefully set Daren on the floor and gave Adam a pointed look.

Adam dropped his head. "I was beating up Daren, and this guy caught me."

Mr. Bundy frowned. "What in the world are we going to do with you, Adam? You know better than this. You get in my office. We are going to have a talk."

He looked at Daren. "You better go over to the nurse and let her get you cleaned up. You may need some stitches on that cut above your eye."

Daren trembled and leaned back against Josh.

Josh place his hand on the little boy's shoulder. He could tell the boy was scared, and his heart went out to him. "I'll take him over there, sir. Then I will make sure he gets down to supper with no problems.

Mr. Bundy nodded his thanks. "That is very nice of you, Joshua. Thanks. We will see you at supper." He motioned to the office. "Get inside, Adam. You and I are going to have a nice long talk."

Josh nodded as he picked up Daren and headed across the hall to the nurses station.

He knocked on the door, but when there was no reply he opened it anyway and carried Daren in. Carefully he placed him on the bed and walked over to the medicine counter and picked up some ointment and bandages. He turned and smiled at Daren. "Now, let's get you cleaned up."

Daren backed away. "Are you sure you know what you are doing. Maybe we should just wait for the nurse." He hiccuped as he tried not to cry.

Josh smiled. "My dad is a doctor, I learned enough to take care of you. It will be okay."

Daren slowly relaxed.

Josh reached over and stared cleaning the boy's cuts. He wondered where the nurse was. It seemed odd that she wasn't here. He shrugged off the thought. This was something minor that he could fix.

Suddenly he heard a door shut. He figured it was the nurse so even though his back was to the door he started talking. "We just had a bit of a problem in the hall. We didn't find you in here, so I thought I would help you out. I think he will need your hand on this one above his eye though. Looks like it's going to take a couple of stitches."

"Thank you." The nurse replied as she stepped up behind him and looked at Daren's eye. "I think you are right. I can take it from here."

The soft voice startled him and he spun around quickly. His breath froze in him. "Joy!" he whispered. He couldn't believe it. Was he dreaming?

Joy gasped as she looked at him. Her heart skipped a beat. She never imagined that she would see him again. Tears sprang to her eyes. "Josh!"

Josh set the bottle down on the bed. "I can't believe it."

Daren watched in awe.

Josh slowly reached out and touched her cheek. "I can't believe it's you," he whispered. "After all this time. Why didn't you

350

ever tell me where you were?"

Tears suddenly filled her eyes and she turned away. "I have to get this little one taken care of, Josh. Thank you for bringing him in."

Josh felt like someone had kicked him. What was wrong with Joy? Fear ate at him. Had she found someone else. She was eighteen now. Was she mad at him because he had never found her.

Once she had Daren cleaned up she turned back to Josh, but her eyes were not filled with light and laughter as they use to be. Instead they were filled with pain and anger. They were hard and resentful. "What are you doing here, Josh?" Her voice was like ice.

Josh felt numb. Why was she mad at him? "I came for the mission trip. I had no idea you were here. How long have you been here?"

Joy turned away. "It doesn't matter any more, Josh. It's too late for us. Just please go away. You do your mission work, but stay away from me, and don't come back to the nurses station."

Josh stared at her. His heart broke. He didn't even know what to say. "I told Mr. Bundy, I would walk Daren down to supper. I need to wait here for you to get done."

Joy gave him a cool look then turned to Daren. Quickly she stitched up his eye and made sure that all his cuts had quit bleeding. She stepped back and looked at Daren. She didn't even turn her head to see Josh. "Looks like they beat you up pretty good. You better stay away from them. Be careful of that cut. I want you back in my office next week Daren and I will look at your stitches again."

She started cleaning up, but could feel Josh watching her. "Make sure someone else brings him in here next week," she said coldly.

Josh felt as if the world around him was falling. Slowly he turned and walked out of the room with Daren beside him. He felt numb with shock. What had happened to Joy? Why was she mad at him?

"Do you know her?" Daren asked quietly.

Josh nodded. "Yeah, I do. But it was a long time ago."

Daren nodded as if he understood. "Oh."

The two silently walked down the hall toward supper.

As soon as he was gone Joy burst into sobs. Why did this have to happen? Why did any of it have to happen? This wasn't suppose to be happening.

In her heart she heard the whispered words. "Trust in the Lord with all your heart, and he will direct your paths." She smiled. She knew the Bible verse well. "Thanks, God," she whispered. "Please help him to forgive me. I know I shouldn't have treated him like that. I have been praying for so long for him to find me, then when I see him I behave that way. I am sorry, God. Give me another chance. Please."

Josh sat at the table that night with a flock of boys and told them stories while they ate. The boys laughed. Josh smiled. He loved it here, but he couldn't shake the feeling that something was wrong with Joy. Fear ate at him all through the meal.

As soon as the meal was over he went back to her office. She was sitting at the desk doing paper work.

He walked in with out a knock.

"You never did respect a girls privacy did you, Joshua?" her voice was hard as stone and cold as ice.

Josh froze. "What?"

Joy looked up at him. "I asked you to leave me alone, Joshua. Please respect my decision." She tried to shield her heart from the hurt that she knew there would be when Josh learned the truth about her. He would leave her forever and there would never be even a dream of him again.

Josh stood in the middle of the room for a moment. "If that is really what you want, Joy, I will. But I want an explanation first. You told me you would tell me what you were thinking, but you haven't. What is going on? Why are you here? What happened to you? Why did you leave and never write to me or call me so I could find you?"

Joy looked up at him. Tears stood in her sad eyes. "I couldn't, Josh. It was all too fast and too hard. I'm sorry. It's too late for you and I. I messed it all up. Just let it go, please. I think it would be best if you don't come in here while you are visiting unless you have to." She kept her eyes on her papers, refusing to look at him. "Please leave. I have a lot to do."

Josh frowned, but turned without another word and left.

Again Joy burst into a fountain of tears.

352

Josh was confused by the coldness in Joy's eyes. Had she not known that he had left college because he was sick. Surely his dad had told them. He tried to think back to that time, but he knew it was not good. He had no memories of that time except that he slept. If something happened in that time that caused her coldness toward him, he wouldn't ever remember it.

He had to talk to her again. He promised himself he would find a way. He wasn't sure how, but he knew he would.

The rest of the week was very busy for Josh. He helped fix things around the orphanage and built four sets of triple bunks for one of the boy's rooms. On Friday him and three others were assigned fixing the roof. The shingles had come and they were carrying them up the ladder when one of the men noticed that Josh seemed pale. "You doing okay?"

Josh looked up at him and felt the world spin. He thought for a minute he was going to be sick, but finally the spinning stopped. "I'm fine." he grunted as he laid the bundle of shingles on the roof. But he knew he wasn't fine. His body was rejecting all the long hours. He needed to get more sleep. He promised himself he would soon, and knew if he didn't he would end up in the hospital.

As they got started, things went quickly, but about halfway through one of the men hollered.

Josh turned quickly to see what had caused the problem and saw a section of the roof collapse into the building. He jumped up to help and at the same moment was hit by another dizzy spell. He felt the world spin. He didn't wait for his head to clear before he ran toward the portion of roof that had fallen in. He heard one of the men yell, but it was too late. The roof where he was standing collapsed and he fell to the floor beneath. Instincts kicked in as he landed and he rolled to the side and covered his head as shingles and wood collapsed around him. For a moment he felt the pain, then his world turned dark.

37

"I am pretty sure he will be fine. I really don't know why he hasn't regained conscientiousness. He should have by now. I can't see where anything hit him in the head, but maybe it did."

Josh heard Joy's voice as he slowly came to, in the nurses office. Pain ripped through him as he tried to move and a groan escaped his lips before he realized it.

Joy was overjoyed when she heard Josh make a sound, but she knew in her heart that she couldn't let him know. She couldn't let him know she cared about him. That would only make the pain worse when he left. And it would only cause more pain when he found out about her. She shook her head quickly and turned to him. Tears sprang to her eyes. They had so many dreams when they were young. Why did it all have to change? It didn't seem fair that life could take so many wrong turns, through decisions that weren't even hers or his.

She shook her head to clear her thoughts as she walked over to him.

Josh watched her approach him, but didn't say anything. He wasn't sure if she was going to be mad at him, or what was going to happen. He tried to move again, but stopped as another groan escaped his lips.

Joy stopped beside the bed, but didn't touch him. "It's probably best if you don't move, Joshua. You took quite the fall. Just had to find some excuse to get in here, huh? You could have found a safer way. When I said I didn't want you in here unless you had to be I didn't mean to try and kill yourself."

Josh's head spun. He wasn't sure if it was from falling or from whatever it was that had been making him dizzy before he fell. He thought about saying something, but decided against the effort.

Joy looked down at him. "You took quiet a fall. It's best if you just rest for a while."

Josh looked at her silently. Then he saw the fear in her eyes. Fear that she tried to keep hidden. Fear for him. He smiled slightly. She did still care, but for some reason she was trying to hide it. He wondered why.

"Was anyone else hurt?" he whispered.

Mr. Bundy stepped forward. "No, you are the only one. Thank the Lord we had told the kids to stay off the third floor today, otherwise it could have been disastrous. I had no idea that ceiling was so rotten. I am sorry.

"We will have to replace everything. Even some of the rafters are rotten. But then I guess the building has been here for over two hundred years. It has a right to be rotten in a few spots. I just wish I would have known the leaks were that bad long before this."

Josh shrugged. "At least no one was hurt and the problems have all been found so they can be solved."

Mr. Bundy nodded. "Well, I need to go to the lumber yard and see about the materials for the roof. I will leave you in the hands of our very capable nurse."

Josh smiled and nodded. "I am sure she is that."

Joy frowned as Mr. Bundy left.

Josh turned to Joy. "Are you mad at me?" He winced at the effort it took to talk, and the pain caused by it. But he was determined to find out what was going on. Now my be his only chance, and he was going to take it. He had to know what happened.

She frowned. "No, why do you think that?"

He heard the sarcasm in her voice and wondered again, what he had done to her to make her hate him.

"Can we talk?" his eyes searched hers till she turned away. Pain shot through his heart and made it hurt worse than his body.

She shrugged. "I guess."

Josh tried to move a little to get more comfortable and she

stepped up and helped him sit a little, pushing another pillow behind his back. "Thanks." He groaned as he coughed. The pain caused by the little bit of movement was nothing compared to the cough.

Joy shook her head. "I am pretty sure that you won't be much help here the rest of the week that you are suppose to be here. Three broken ribs are nothing to try and work with."

Josh nodded. "Probably won't be much help to them then. But I don't think I can fly home yet either."

Joy nodded. "I guess you are right," she sighed.

Josh looked at her and his eyes widened in surprise. "Are you trying to get rid of me, Joy Dawson?"

Joy flushed.

He stared at her. "You are trying to get rid of me! Why? What happened to you that made you hate me so much? Why didn't you ever write and tell me? If I did something to make you hate me and want to leave the least you could have done was tell me what it was. Why did you just leave and never tell me anything?"

Joy looked at him, and he saw the pain in her eyes. "Daddy wouldn't let me tell you. We had to leave, and he didn't want anyone to know where we were."

Josh nodded. "He succeeded in that. I tried and tried to find you once I was well enough to. I wanted to tell you why I hadn't been writing you. But I couldn't find even a trace of where you all went."

"When you got well enough? What do you mean?" the confusion and pain Joy felt echoed in her voice.

Josh looked into her eyes. "I guess I better start at the beginning. I got sick at school. I didn't know what it was, but all I wanted to do was sleep. And all I could do was sleep and get sick. After a week or two of it, Mom and Dad came to school, and when they saw how sick I was, took me home. I really don't have much memory of the next few months. I don't even know for sure how many months it was. All I did was sleep and sleep and sleep some more.

When I finally got better, Dad told me that you and your family had moved away before I came home, that your dad had taken a new church back east, but he didn't know where. I tried to find you. I contacted DHS, I got in touch with some of your family, but no one knew where to find you. All anyone would say was back east. I found out from DHS that there was some kind of trouble, and the ones of the

357

kids who hadn't been adopted were in other homes now, but that was all they would say. They wouldn't' tell me anything else.

"What happen, Joy? What happened to the family? What happened to you?"

Joy burst into tears. She felt her anger at him start to melt away. No wonder he never called. "I tried to write to you and call you just before we moved. I called the college, but someone said you weren't there. They didn't say you had left or that you were sick. I wanted to tell you, but Daddy said no. He was very angry. He didn't want me talking to you or anyone else. He said that it wouldn't change anything. That you wouldn't care about me if you knew."

"Knew what?" his voice was raspy. It hurt to talk, but he was determined to find out what was going on.

Tears ran down her cheeks. "They didn't just take the foster kids away. They took all of the kids away, the ones who had been adopted and the ones who hadn't. I was the only one they left, because of the whole situation."

Josh wanted to reach out and hold her, but he didn't think he could handle the pain, and he didn't have the strength to put forth that much effort. "What are you talking about, Joy?"

Joy took a deep breath. "After you left for college, we got another placement, a teenage boy about seventeen. Daddy thought it would be great, but it wasn't."

Josh feared he heard what she wasn't saying, but remained silent hoping she would keep talking.

"He got into some trouble, told some lies on Dad and got him into trouble. They lost their license and all of the kids were removed. There was some other stuff that happened, but its not worth talking about right now. Dad was hurt and angry. He moved us away so no one would find out-" she stopped.

Josh turned his head to look at her. "I'm sorry." he whispered, wishing there was more he could say. He wished Joy would tell him the whole story. He could see in her eyes that she was hiding something.

Joy just shook her head. "It's over now. We have a new life here, and we are moving on with it. We aren't stuck in the past, like we would be if we had stayed there.

Josh nodded. He wasn't sure that he understood it all, but he knew that things were bad, or had been. "So what did I do to make you hate me, Joy? Just cause I didn't find you, or was it more? Is it because I didn't call or write to you?"

Joy shook her head. "You never did anything to me, Joshua. I was just mad. I let what Daddy kept saying to me finally make me bitter to you. I'm sorry."

Josh shook his head. "If I didn't do anything to make you mad, why don't you call me Josh, like you use to? You keep calling me Joshua, it reminds me of my dad," he grinned. "Kind of creeps me out."

Joy tried to smile. All the hurt of the past few years seemed to fade away. "Josh, you don't understand. Things are different now."

He smiled. "Are they that different?"

She looked at him her eyes full of questions. "What do you mean?"

"I still have feelings for you, Joy. Do you feel anything toward me besides annoyance and anger? Now that I have found you, will you at least let me see you a few times before I leave. Please don't hate me, Joy. I tried to find you. I just couldn't. I still love you. I have for a long time."

Joy shook her head. "Please don't, Josh. You don't know what you are saying. You don't know what all happened to me. You don't love me. You love who I was when we were kids."

Josh nodded slightly. "You may be right, but I can't get to know you again if you won't let me."

Joy sighed. "You are persistent as ever. Fine. I will let you at least talk to me."

Josh grinned. He felt a little of her defense slipping down. "When I can get around, will you go out with me?"

Joy shook her head, "One thing at a time,Josh. One thing at a time."

Josh shook his head. "Can't you tell me what I did wrong?"

Joy shook her head too. "You didn't do anything, Josh. It was all just a lot of stuff that happened and shouldn't have. We had to get away from everyone and everything. We had to start over. I know you don't understand, but that is how it is. Please don't hate me, and please don't ask."

Josh nodded. "It's okay." He felt his head start to throb again.

Joy saw the pain shadow his eyes again. She slowly stood and handed him some medicine. "You are going to want to take this every four hours, for the next couple of days. Even if you don't feel like you need it at that time, take it anyway."

Josh took it without even looking and popped it in his mouth. He took the glass of water she offered and quickly swallowed the pills. "Thanks," he whispered. When he was done he slowly laid back down.

She nodded then watched as he lay his head back on the pillow and closed his eyes. She knew in moments he would be asleep. Her head spun as she watched him laying there. What was she suppose to do now? She couldn't tell him all that had happened; he wouldn't ever want to see her again. But wasn't that what she wanted? She shook her head again. She couldn't even answer that question to herself.

38

Over the next few days Joy and Josh talked often. She seemed to be letting down her guard, and he felt a little better about it. He hoped she would tell him what had happened, but she didn't. He was finally able to get up and around a little. The boys begged him for stories as he lay around, and he was grateful to have something to occupy his mind and time.

As the second week neared an end and the work team started packing up to head home, he struggled with what to do. He wasn't ready to leave. He wanted to stay here. He loved the kids, but more than that he wanted to be close to Joy, if she would let him. He wanted to see Luke and Annie again, and the rest of the family. He still wondered what happened to them.

Two days before he was suppose to head home he slowly walked back to Joy's office. Though he was getting better it still hurt just to move. He knew it was just one of those things that take time, but it was frustrating.

Joy looked up as he came in and sighed. "Hi, Josh. You don't give up do you?"

Josh grinned as he saw the flash of annoyance in her eyes, but also a sparkle of laughter. He hadn't seen that sparkle in so long. "Not if it means seeing you."

"Well, you may as well come in and tell me what you want to say. I know you are going to pester me till I listen to you anyway."

Josh chuckled. "You do know me, don't you?"

Joy laughed slightly.

Josh moved into her office and stood in front of her. "Joy, I have tried to be patent, but I just can't wait any more. I need to know what you are feeling, or feel toward me. Can't you tell me what happened?"

Joy sighed. "Josh, I didn't want it to come to this. I -" she stopped unable to go on. She choked on her tears.

Josh reached out his work roughened hand and slowly tilted her chin up till she was looking into his eyes. He removed his finger from under her chin and just stood looking into her eyes and waiting for her to talk. Seeing the tears in her eyes sent a chill up his back bone, but still he waited.

The silence stretched long between them.

Joy wanted to look away, but she couldn't. Seeing the love in his eyes took her breath away and made her light headed. She loved him so much, yet she wasn't able to tell him. All she wanted was to be with him, but because of something that happened to her, and her dad being upset at the wrong person it wouldn't ever be able to be.

She felt tears pool in her eyes again. Then, slowly start to run down her cheeks.

Josh blinked in surprise. What happened to make her cry! "Joy?" he whispered. His concern grew even more as she looked quickly away. He wanted to pull her to him, but he wasn't sure if he should.

"Josh, I am sorry. I can't do this. Things have changed so much. You don't even know me. If you did you wouldn't want to be with me. You have no idea what all has happened. You just don't understand."

"Make me understand, Joy. I can't understand if you won't let me. I can't help, if you don't tell me what is wrong. I can't fix it, if you don't tell me what I did wrong. Please, Joy. I love you. I have ever since we were little, but it is more now. It is more than it was back when we were dating. I love you. I want to understand. Please help me to understand, or at least tell me what I did so wrong that you don't want to be with me. Is there someone else in your life now, Joy?"

Joy felt her heart constrict. "No, Josh," she answered, her voice soft and broken. "There is no one else and there never has been.

I loved you. I still do, but you love who I was. You don't know who I am now."

Josh shook his head in surprise. "I know how you are with the kids. I have watched you. I know you still have a compassionate heart, but you are right, I don't really know you any more. I want to get to know you better. Would you give me a chance to do that?"

Joy shook her head. "I can't, Josh. Dad won't go for it."

Josh felt even more confused. "Why? He was fine with us being together before. Why doesn't he want me around you? Is it because of him that you never contacted me, never let me know where you were, just stayed hidden away?"

Joy nodded slightly. "Josh, you don't understand."

"Make me understand!" he cried.

Joy stepped back as there was a rap on the door. "I can't, Josh," she whispered as the door opened.

Mr. Bundy opened the door and stuck his head in. "Is everything okay in here. I could hear you out in the hall?"

Josh stiffened as he turned around.

Joy smiled sweetly. "Everything is fine."

Mr. Bundy looked at Josh and nodded as though understanding something. "Joy, you have been working so hard lately, when was the last time you had the night off, a little early?"

Joy didn't follow where this was going, but she answered a little hesitantly. "A long time, sir, why?"

Mr. Bundy nodded thoughtfully. "I understand that you and Josh use to be brother and sister, and he hadn't seen you all in a long time. You haven't had time to take him out to see your parents since he has been here, and I am sure he would like to see them. How about, you take the rest of the day off and take him out to your place to see the family. I am sure they will be happy to see him."

Joy frowned at him. "Mr. Bundy-"

"Joy, I am not really making this a request," he answered curtly.

Josh looked at him gratefully.

The man nodded. "I think it will be good for all of you to be together for a while."

Joy frowned again. "Fine," she answered sharply. "Josh, come on. Let's go." She grabbed her jacket from the hook on the wall and picked her purse up off the desk. Angrily she stormed out of the room.

363

Josh nodded to Mr. Bundy. "Thanks," he whispered.

Mr. Bundy smiled. "If you can get a sparkle back in her eyes. We would love to see it. Just figure out what God's will is for the both of you. That is all the thanks I need."

Josh nodded. "I will do my best."

Joy felt guilty as she drove Josh to her home. She should at least warn him about how things were, and how her dad felt about him, shouldn't she? It was all just so complicated. She wasn't sure where to begin. She wanted him to understand. She wished it wouldn't change everything when he knew, but she knew it would.

Josh sensed Joy's uneasiness. He silently prayer for her and for whatever the situation was that made her so sad. He wished he knew, but he didn't feel right about questioning her. Silently he watched the town fade away as she drove him out of town into a quaint countryside, then up to a nice two story, white house.

Joy took a deep breath as she pulled up to the house.

Josh smiled to see a young girl who looked exactly like Joy sitting in the yard. Her bright blond curls clung to her face and he knew she had to have been playing out side for some time. He was surprised. Joy hadn't said anything about having a little sister. She looked to be around four years old.

As they emerged from the vehicle the child's face lighted up. "Mommy, Mommy! She cried as she ran into Joy's arms.

Josh was stunned into silence as he watched Joy kneel down and embrace the little girl. "Hi, sweet baby. Where are Grandma and Grandpa."

The child's dark eyes looked at him with questions in them. Then she turned her gaze back on her mother. "Inside. Grandpa just got home a little bit ago."

Joy smiled as she kissed the child's forehead, but Josh saw the sadness in her eyes and felt even more confused.

"Why don't you run on and play, okay, Janie. Mommy brought home a friend, and he wants to see Grandma and Grandpa."

Janie's whole face lighted up as she raced for the house calling, "Grandma! Grandpa! Mommy is home! And she brought a friend!"

Joy slowly rose to her feet and looked Josh in the eye.

He stared at her, unsure of what to say or think. "Mommy?" he choked. His throat seemed to constrict and he couldn't say more.

She cleared her throat. "I'm sorry, Josh," she whispered. Slowly she turned and walked toward the house. She knew he deserved an explanation, but she didn't want to give him one right now.

He wanted to stop her and ask her more questions, but he felt too confused. He quietly followed in stunned silence.

As they entered the front door, the good smells of baked bread and apple pie greeted them. Joy glanced at Josh out of the corner of her eye. Not for the first time did she wonder what was going to happen when he and her father saw each other. She just wished now she had warned him.

"Come on. I am sure Mom will be glad to see you." Joy lead the way into the warm kitchen where Janie was seated at the table with a glass of milk and a cookie.

Annie was at the stove stirring something in a large pot that smelled delicious.

"Mom," Joy smiled as she saw her mom turn around slightly. Her eyes grew round, and she dropped the spoon she held. She turned quickly the rest of the way around.

"Am I seeing things? Joshua, is that really you?" she hurried over to him and embraced him. "Oh, how I have missed you. I can't believe it's you. How in this world did you ever find us here?" Tears streamed down her cheeks as she hugged him.

Josh felt the warmth of her love as he embraced her back. "Hi, Mom." He felt emotion choke him. "It's really me."

Annie turned as Luke walked into the room. "Luke, honey, look who's come to visit."

Josh turned to Luke and was surprised to see his eyes darken in rage.

Luke felt his temper rise when he saw Josh standing by his daughter. Anger surged through him like he had only felt once before. He glared at the boy for half a moment then swung a fist at him and knocked him to the floor.

Josh felt the fist connect with the side of his head, but didn't even have time to respond. He fell to the floor with a hard thud. He moaned as the pain jolted his body from his broken ribs. He lay

365

stunned for a moment, too surprised to move. In all the time he had lived with them Luke had never struck him even when he had needed it. Why in the world would he now?

Joy gasped as she saw her father strike Josh and saw him go down. She knew it had to hurt him as hard as he fell, but for a moment she was to stunned to know what to do.

Janie started to scream in fear.

Annie went to her and picked her up. The child clung to her and sobbed. Annie quietly left the room with an angry glare at her husband.

Hearing Janie scream helped to clear the fog out of Josh's head. Slowly he started to move then stopped. He looked up at Luke. The man's eyes still blazed with anger.

As he stood Luke stepped up to him and gripped his arm.

Josh felt himself retreat inside, and resented that old feeling of fear he looked at Luke with surprise.

Luke felt his anger rise again. He looked Josh in the eye. "How dare you dare to show your face here after what you did," he growled.

Joy burst into tears. "Daddy, stop it!" she screamed as he slammed his fist into Josh's stomach.

Josh groaned again as he sank to the floor.

Joy knelt beside him. "I told you along time ago, Josh didn't do anything. Why don't you believe me?"

Luke glared down at Josh. "You dare to hurt my little girl and think I won't know. You think your sins will not find you out? Well they did. How dare you. I trusted you. You ruined her life and now you think you can just show up and get what you want. You show up at my house like you haven't done anything."

Josh glanced up at him, but didn't dare to make a move. "What are you talking about?" His voice was angry, yet laced with pain.

Luke slammed a foot into Josh's side. "Oh, like you don't know." He reached down to jerk him up, but Joy stepped between them.

"Daddy, stop it. I told you, he never hurt me. We never did anything. This happened because of that boy that was in our house for a few days. Janie just came early. Why don't you ever believe me. It wasn't anyone's fault, but his. It happened. It's time to let it go! Leave Josh alone. You are hurting him."

Luke glared at her. "I'll kill him, if he dares to touch you again!"

Josh's head was a fog of pain, but he heard what was being said and slowly it registered. He looked up at Luke. "If you thought I was the one who got her pregnant, why did you move away? Did you think I wouldn't take responsibility? Didn't you think you raised me better than that. You thought you would just move away and hide your family so I would never find out?"

Luke felt his hard heart suddenly crumble as he realized Josh was right. Everything he had done to try and protect his daughter had only served to hurt her more. He turned quickly and hurried out of the room.

Joy turned to him. "I'm sorry, Josh. I should have warned you." She knelt beside him and put her hand on his back. "Where all does it hurt."

Josh slowly pulled himself up. He felt shaky as he stood. "I'm all right, Joy. It just took me be surprise."

Joy nodded. "I get that." Suddenly she sniffed and jumped up to remove the pot from the burner that her mom had left there.

Josh came to stand beside her. "Will you talk to me now?"

Joy burst into sobs, but nodded. "Josh, I am so sorry."

Josh shook his head as he pulled her into his embrace. "Just tell me what happened," he whispered. "Please."

Joy nodded again. Slowly the two sat at the table. "Shortly after you went to college, Mom and Dad got another foster placement. It only lasted for about three days but that was three days too long. The first night he was there he snuck into my room," she paused, "at night." She looked up at him to see if he understood what she was saying. She could tell by the anger that flashed in his eyes that he did. Slowly she nodded, when he looked at her with a question in his eyes.

Josh felt his anger heighten. He tightened his jaw and determined not to say anything till she was done.

Joy took a deep breath. "He threatened me that if I told anyone he would kill me. I believed him. He was mean." Joy shivered again. Tears ran down her cheeks. "On the third night, Dad must of heard something, because he came into my room and saw what was happening." A soft smile lightened her lips. "He only meant to protect me, but his anger was great. He beat that boy almost to death. Then he called the cops on him. They arrested Dad for battery, since he was suppose to be the foster father. It was a couple of crazy days, then all of the sudden, Dad was out of jail and we were moving away. Dad told me I wasn't allowed to write to you or let anyone know where we were.

"When I found out that I was pregnant I didn't know what to do, but I couldn't hide it for very long. Mom was my support, but Dad was even angrier. I wanted to get rid of it, but I knew they wouldn't let me. So I didn't even mention it.

"Janie came right at thirty-six weeks. When that happened Dad was even more angry and started blaming you. It was like something in side him snapped. He told me I was never to see you again. And that if he ever saw you again he would kill you for what you had done to me. I tried to tell him we hadn't done anything, but he wouldn't believe me. I kept trying and trying. It didn't matter. Finally he told me if I ever mentioned your name again he would whip me.

"I knew it was time to let God take care of it. But I was so scared that I would never see you again. I didn't know what to do. I just didn't know what to do." Tears ran down her cheeks. "I also knew in my heart that it didn't matter if I ever did see you again. If I did you wouldn't want anything to do with me, and Daddy wouldn't let you near me anyway." She sighed.

Josh sat in stunned silence for a few minutes. Finally he reached out and took Joy in his arms and held her. She broke down and sobbed, like he was sure she hadn't let herself do since the other boy's hands first touched her. He held her as she cried. Finally he felt her relax against him.

Joy sat up and wiped her eyes. "Thank you, Josh. Thank you for caring and not hating me."

Josh leaned forward and rested his arms on his knees. "Will you let me try to care more?"

"What do you mean?" She looked up with tears and fear in her red swollen eyes.

"Let me love you, Joy. Let us get to know each other again. Will you even consider marrying me?"

Joy shook her head in amazement. "How could you still want someone like me?"

Josh felt his heart breaking. He reached out and brushed his hand across her face. "Joy, I still love you. I haven't ever loved anyone else. I want to spend the rest of my life with you. What happened to you was not your fault. You have held the blame on you for far too long. It wasn't your fault what he did to you. It wasn't your fault that you got pregnant. You are still a special child of God. And I still love you."

Joy shook her head. "It's different now, Josh. It's all so different from before. I am no longer just me. It's me and Janie. I can't ask you to take responsibility for someone else."

Josh looked into her eyes as he knelt down on the floor in front of her, despite the pain from his ribs. "Joy, you know that is not fair. If you are afraid that I don't love you any more or that I couldn't grow to love Janie then just say so. If you have that little faith in me, you are right, it will not work. Maybe you have changed your mind about me. Fine, but I haven't changed my mind about you. I am not just saying the words, Joy. Will you marry me?"

Joy looked into his eyes. "Let's just take it slow. One step at a time. I am not holding you to anything. If we see each other for a while and you decide you can't do it, just tell me. Okay."

Josh stood and embraced her. "Joy, the moment I saw you, I was so overjoyed to finally find you, I can't imagine loosing you again. Don't be afraid."

Joy smiled feeling all her hesitancy fading away. "Okay, Josh." She embraced him as well. "I love you too. And I am willing to give it a go."

Josh looked into her eyes, he wanted to kiss her, but he knew he should bide his time. He had already pushed her a long ways today.

Joy felt his struggle and knew he wanted to kiss her. Her heart hammered. She wanted him to kiss her. It had been so long since she had wanted to be loved and held and cared for that it took her by surprise. She knew he wouldn't kiss her without her permission, but she wasn't sure how to give it to him. Slowly she reached up and brushed his lips with her finger tips.

Josh felt his struggle increase. He looked into her eyes and saw the hope she was holding in them. Hoping he wasn't misreading the message he slowly bent his head down to hers. Lightly his lips brushed hers.

Joy felt the flutter in her stomach and her breath caught in her throat. She leaned into him.

Josh smiled as he pulled her to him and kissed her soundly.

Luke was standing in the doorway and his anger increased, but he tried to stop it. He knew he had been wrong. He had been wrong to keep the two young people apart. He had only hurt his daughter more. And he had hurt Janie, by keeping her from having a daddy. Why had he blamed Josh, then kept them apart? He should have known Josh would take responsibility. The boy was even willing to take a responsibility that wasn't his.

He felt ashamed. It wasn't just with what he had done with Josh, it was more than that. He had been running from God. Blaming God for all that had happened to his little girl. He had blamed himself for not being there, blamed God for letting it happen, and grown bitter and hard because of it.

Tears burned the backs of his eyes. Something inside him started to cave. *God, forgive me. I am sorry for what I have done. I am sorry for blaming you. Please forgive me. Let me have a clean heart and a fresh start.* He felt something inside him crumble, and the anger and bitterness he held inside finally seeped out of is heart.

His heart hammered as he felt the fresh hope in his heart. He turned back to the two young people. How was he going to tell them? He wasn't sure, but he knew he needed to. He needed to tell them and Annie. She had put up with a lot over the last few years and yet she had stuck by him.

Joy smiled looking into Josh's eyes. "I can't believe I forgot what it feels like to love you. All this time I have been fighting against it. It feels so good to just love you."

Josh smiled and pulled her into his embrace. "I am so glad to hear that. Now I want to keep hearing it."

Joy laughed. "Okay. But I think it's time to get supper on the table. I want you to meet Janie."

Josh smiled as he looked down once more into her eyes. "Don't worry, Love, it's going to be just fine."

Joy smiled a little apprehensively. "I am not worried about Janie, I am worried about you. She will probably cling to you like a leach. She is hungry for a daddy." Joy looked away quickly, wishing she hadn't said the last part. It sounded like she was being pushy.

Josh smiled. "Good, maybe she can convince you to move things along quickly." he chuckled slightly.

Joy felt her apprehension fade quickly. She laughed and turned to the stove to finish fixing supper.

370

In about ten minutes the rest of the family came in.

When Janie came in she ran to her mommy. "I missed you, Mommy."

Joy picked her up and held her tight. "Mommy knows you miss Mommy, but Mommy has to work, baby."

Janie's dark eyes fastened on Josh. She didn't say anything, but her inquisitive little eyes were wide with question.

Josh smiled at her and a faint smiled crossed her lips.

Joy hugged her again. "Janie, this is mommy's friend. His name is Joshua."

Janie frowned. "Why is his lip bloody?"

Joy looked at her dad with anger in her eyes, but it was Josh who answered. "I just ran into something. Next time you see me it won't be this way, okay."

Annie smiled at Josh in appreciation.

He nodded slightly.

Annie motioned to the table. "Please, everyone, sit down we will have the food on in a few minutes."

Janie sat by her mom with Josh on the other side of Joy, but she kept looking over at him. Josh saw the hope in the little girl's eyes and his heart went out to her. Joy was right. She was hungry for a daddy.

39

Josh and Joy wrote letters back and forth for the next five weeks, in each letter Josh included a little note to Janie. Joy felt touched each time she read his notes to her little girl. In each letter they missed each other more. In each note that was read, Janie liked Josh more and more and wished that he would marry her mommy so she could have a daddy.

Finally, Josh could take it no more. He arranged with the orphanage director for him to come and work there for a few months. This would give him and Joy the time they needed to decide if it was right to become a family. He didn't tell Joy of his plan and on the night he arrived he drove out to her place hoping to surprise her.

The knock on the door as she was sitting down to read Janie a bed time story surprised her. Joy slowly stood wondering who in the world would be here at this hour. Janie followed her mommy to the door eagerly.

Joy cracked the door open and peeked out. She gasped when she saw him there.

Josh smiled at the surprise in her eyes, but also the light that filled them. "Hello, beautiful. How are you this evening?"

"Josh," she whispered still not daring to believe it. "I can't believe you are here. What are you doing here?"

Janie squealed with delight as the door swung open and she saw Josh standing there.

Josh smiled down at her. "Hello, Janie. Do you have a big hug for me since your mommy doesn't seem to want to give me one?"

Janie giggled and clung to his neck as he swung her up in a big hug. She laughed with delight when he spun her around. "We missed you," she cried. "What took you so long to come back?"

Josh grinned at her. "I don't know why it took me so long, because I have missed you too." He planted a kiss on the little girls cheek, then set her down on the floor and handed her a small package. "This is for you."

Janie squealed again and looked up at her mommy. "Can I open it, Mommy?"

Joy smiled down at her daughter, but frowned slightly at Josh. "You are going to spoil her."

Josh shrugged. "She needs a little spoiling."

Joy shook her head. "Go ahead, Janie."

The little girl ripped off the paper and gave another glad cry. She picked up the baby doll and squeezed it tight. "Thank you, Mr. Josh. I love it. She is beautiful."

Josh smiled at her as she gave him another hug. "Just like you are, sweet heart."

Janie looked up at her mom again. "Can I go show my doll to Grandma?"

Joy nodded. "That is fine. And you may play with her for ten minutes, but then it is off to bed."

Janie bounced up and down. "Okay!" She spun around and ran back into the house calling, "Grandma, Grandpa, look what Mr. Josh gave me."

Joy shook her head again as she turned back to Josh, but her eyes were filled with tears. "You didn't need to do that, Josh. She already loves you to pieces. You didn't need to get her a gift."

Josh shrugged. He felt a little awkward, but he didn't know why. "I wanted to." He looked away then looked back at her. "She isn't the only one around here that needs spoiled a little."

Joy blushed.

Josh stepped up to her and ran a hand down her cheek. She

looked up into his eyes, and he saw the hope that lay there. But she was too afraid to let him know she felt it, he knew.

He pulled her to him and hugged her close. He felt her body relax against him, and he wondered how long it had been since she had felt safe, really safe.

Joy felt his strong arms circle her and she relaxed into his embrace for the first time, since he had left. She didn't want to cry, but for some reason the tears came running down her cheeks. She suddenly found herself sobbing.

Josh heard her sob and held her closer. "Baby, what's wrong?" he whispered. "I didn't mean to make you upset. What is the matter?"

Joy shook her head. "Nothing, I don't know why I am crying, but I can't help it. I missed you so much. I was just so afraid, maybe it was all a dream."

Josh squeezed her again. They just stood there for a few minutes and he let her cry. When her sobs finally ceased and she drew a long shuttering breath, he let her go.

She pulled back from him and gave him a shaky smile. "I'm sorry. I didn't mean to do that."

Josh shrugged. "It's okay, really. I am glad you feel comfortable enough with me to cry." He squatted down and picked up something he had hidden outside the door. "Now I have something for you."

Joy grinned. Then gasped as he handed her a bouquet of roses. "Oh, Josh."

Josh smiled as he saw the joy and delight brighten up her face.

"Thank you," she whispered. She looked up into his eyes and then kissed his cheek.

Josh pulled her to him and kissed her lightly on the lips.

Joy felt the sensation run through her as she kissed him back.

When he pulled away she smiled up at him. "I still can't believe you are here."

Josh ran finger over her lips. "Do I need to convince you more?" he asked his voice husky.

She nodded slightly and he pulled her to him for another kiss. When they parted this time she saw the light in his eyes. "You better come on in. I was just putting Janie to bed. I probably should go ahead and do that, if you don't mind. Do you want a cup of coffee?"

He shook his head. "No thanks, don't care for coffee."

She smiled at him. "That's good to know."

He nodded. "Yes, it is, because I really don't even care for the smell of the stuff."

She grinned. "Then I am glad that I don't like it either. Because if I did, you would just have to get use to smelling it."

"I think I could do that for you," he grinned. "But only for you."

Joy shook her head. "I really need to get Janie to bed. Do you mind?"

He shook his head and followed her into the living-room, where Annie and Luke were sitting. Janie sat on the floor, playing with her new doll.

Luke stood as the two young people walked in. "Joshua," he shook his hand. "I wasn't aware that you were coming back so soon."

Josh shook Luke's hand and smiled. "I wasn't either, but I am back to work at the orphanage for a few more months."

Luke nodded. "And what after that?"

Annie cleared her throat, "Luke, that's enough." her voice was soft, but embarrassed. She looked at Josh and smiled a warm smile. "It is good to see you again."

Josh nodded, but wondered at the coolness in Luke's eyes and voice. Did he think that Josh was only here to lead his daughter on? Or was he just afraid that Josh and Joy would decide they weren't meant to be together? Or was he worried about Josh taking Joy away from him?

Luke gave Josh a hard look. "How did you get into working at the orphanage?"

Josh shrugged. "When I was here before it was on a mission trip, but I really fell in love with the kids at the orphanage. I love it there. I felt like it was where God wanted me to be. When I got hurt and had to go home it was hard enough, but the whole time I was home I haven't felt at home. I got a message from the man who runs the place asking if I would be interested in coming back to work for a few months and maybe more. I jumped at the opportunity to be where, I believe, God is calling me to be."

Luke gave a grunt. "That's all you wanted to be here for?"

Josh shook his head. He felt himself blush slightly. "No, sir, that isn't all I wanted to be here for, but that is why I am back now. It is definitely a benefit that Joy and Janie are here. I am hoping to get to know them better too," he glanced at Joy.

She smiled at him and gave a slight nod.

He cleared his throat nervously. "This opportunity will give Joy and Janie and I the chance to see if it is in God's will for us to be a family."

Again Luke grunted. "Shouldn't you have thought of that before you fathered her?" He glared at Josh. He knew he had prayed for God to help him with his anger, but he still felt angry when he thought about Josh lying to him. He had trusted Josh and Joy both, and Josh had broken that trust. Yes, it was Luke's fault that Josh hadn't known about Janie sooner, but now he was acting like he had a choice in the matter of taking care of his child.

Josh felt his temper rise. Would Luke ever believe him and Joy? "Luke, I didn't hurt your daughter. Don't you think you raised me better than that? Not to mention my dad raising me better than that. Is that all the confidence you have in yourself?"

Luke glowered at him. "I don't believe you, Joshua. That is all there is to it. The evidence is there, clear as day."

Josh looked him in the eye. "When did I ever lie to you, Luke? What reason did I ever give you not to trust me?"

Luke looked into Josh's cool gaze and he knew the boy was right. He also felt the conviction on his heart. He knew he was in the wrong. He needed to do the right thing and forgive himself for letting his daughter get hurt and stop blaming Joshua for it, but he just couldn't. He still felt sure that Janie was Josh's fault.

Joy cleared her throat, hoping to break the tension. "Janie, it's time for bed. Tell Grandpa and Grandma good night."

Janie looked at her mom and smiled. "Okay, Mommy." The little girl stood and hugged her grandparents in turn, then smiled and said good night to them. She then turned to Josh, "Mr. Josh are you going to be here when I get up in the morning?"

Josh saw the hope in the little girls eyes and felt his heart skip. He was already loving this little girl. He couldn't imagine his life without her or her mom. He placed his hand on her head and smiled at her. "No, Janie, I won't be here in the morning, but if it is okay with your mommy I will come back to see you tomorrow afternoon."

Janie looked at her mom with hopeful eyes. Joy smiled at her little girl. "We will worry about that tomorrow. Now say good night."

Janie reached up her arms to Josh for a hug.

Josh knelt on the floor and hugged the little girl tight. He felt his heart lost to her. "Good night, Janie."

She squeezed his neck. "Good night, Mr. Josh." She let him go and skipped happily beside her mother off to bed, the new doll held tightly in her arms.

Annie smiled at Josh as Joy left the room with her daughter. "You seem quiet taken by our granddaughter."

Josh felt an odd feeling ripple through him. "I guess I am. She is quite a gal, just like her mommy."

Luke smiled for the first time. "That she is. So you better not break her heart." His lat comment was cool and hard and Josh heard the hatefulness in his voice.

Josh looked him squarely in the eye. "I don't plan to, but I wasn't the one who did in the first place."

Luke gave him an icy glare. Josh returned the look without fear. An anger had replaced the old fear he would have felt. He was upset, extremely so, that he and Joy had lost so much time because her dad had moved her away to hide her, as if it was her fault that Janie had come along. He wished again that he would have known what was happening. Why had he gotten so sick and forgotten so much of his life at that time? It didn't seem fair. He knew God had a plan for it all, but it still didn't seem fair.

God, help me to trust you. I know you have everything planned, and nothing takes you by surprise. I know you love Joy and Janie, even more than I do. Please help me to trust you.

Joy walked back into the room and smiled at him.

He stood and smiled back.

Joy looked at her mom and dad. "We are going for a walk. Janie is sound asleep."

Annie nodded. "You two have a lovely time.

Both young people bid her parents good night and walked out into the cool evening. As they walked along the path, Josh reached over and took her hand. "Joy, I know you are not ready to hear this, but please don't shut me out. I love you and Janie. I know you think I don't really know her that well yet, but, baby, how could I not love her when she is so much like her mommy?"

Joy blushed and was glad it was dark, so he couldn't see. "Josh, you don't-"

He squeezed her hand to stop her. "Let me finish, please. Joy," he stopped and so did she. He turned her to face him. In the dim moonlight she could see his eyes, though they were shadowed. "I told you once that I loved you and wanted to spend the rest of my life with you. I still do, to both. We've lost so much time, Joy. I don't want to lose any more."

He pulled her close and kissed her. "Joy, I want us to be a family. You, me, and Janie. I want to show you how much I love you. Is it to soon for you?"

Joy shook her head. "No, Josh, it's not too soon for me. I love you too. I never stopped. When you left last time it felt like my heart was broken all over again. I don't want to go through that again."

Josh smiled. "Give me enough time to find us a house and get settled into my job. When I have a place for us, will you marry me?"

Joy gave a glad cry. "You bet I will." She smiled as he pulled her to him again and held her tightly. "Are you sure?" she whispered. "Are you sure you want the responsibility of a wife and a daughter so soon?"

Josh held her back from him only enough to look into her eyes. The darkness shadowed most of her face but still he could see the fear in her face. "Joy, I have never been more sure of anything in my life. I can't imagine my life without you and Janie. I don't want to."

She smiled and hugged him.

He turned and walked her back toward the house. "I want to take you and Janie out for supper tomorrow night. Is that okay?"

"Okay. I'll let Mom know so she doesn't fix supper for us."

Josh squeezed her hand.

Joy looked up at him. He glanced toward the house, then back at her. "I love you, Joy," he whispered as he pulled her to him and kissed her again.

Joy flushed. "I love you too, Joshua." She smiled as he pulled back slightly.

"Don't call me that, okay. Josh is fine," His voice was tight and had an angry, sharp edge. "Just, please, don't call me Joshua."

She nodded slightly surprised.

He brushed his hand over her cheek. "Sorry if I sounded harsh, I just don't like to remember who I use to be. Joshua is my dad's name for me, and brings back a lot of times I would rather not remember."

Joy nodded. "I understand. I love you, Josh. I am glad you felt like you could talk to me about it." She smiled into his eyes, "I had better get inside and you had better get back and get some sleep. You will have a big day tomorrow I am sure."

Josh smiled and nodded. "I am sure too. See you in the morning."

Joy smiled and nodded. "In the morning."

They kissed again then she went into the house, and he headed back to the orphanage.

The next morning and day was busy for Josh. He worked in the orphanage repairing and fixing things long since neglected. He saw Joy in passing, but they were both busy with little time to talk.

As the day drew to an end Mr. Bundy asked Josh into his office. "You did a good work today, son. I just have a question for you." He said as Josh entered and closed the door behind him.

Josh felt slightly hesitant. "Yes, sir?"

"Is there something wrong between you and Nurse Joy?"

Josh quickly shook his head. "No, sir. Why?

He shook his head quickly. "I have just seen you two pass each other many times today, but you've hardly spoken a word to her."

Josh shrugged. "No, there is nothing wrong with us. We are just busy, I guess."

"Okay, Josh, as long as you are sure."

Josh nodded. "I am sure. I am actually better than great, and things are better then great between us. I asked her to marry me last night and she said yes. As soon as I can find us a place we will set a date."

Mr. Bundy smiled. "I am glad to hear it, but I hope this doesn't mean you will be leaving us soon. Or taking her away from us."

Josh shook his head. "No, sir. I plan to stay on here for a while if I can. I really feel like this is where God wants me to be."

Mr. Bundy smiled again. "It does get in your blood. God is amazing. He has everything worked out so wonderfully."

Josh nodded.

That evening he drove out and picked up Joy and Janie and took them to a restaurant. As they ate he got a kick out of Janie. She was a live wire. She couldn't sit still for anything, and no matter how many times Joy told her not to stare she was constantly looking at other people and questioning her mom about them.

Josh chuckled and received a scowl from Joy. This made him want to laugh, but he quickly looked away and hid his laughter.

When the meal was over Josh handed Janie something under the table. "Hey, beautiful, is it okay with you if I give this to your mom?"

Janie looked at the small box in her hand and looked up at him with a puzzled frown.

Josh smiled and opened it. Slowly he pulled out a beautiful diamond ring. Janie smiled and Joy gasped.

Josh looked up at her with a hint of mischief in his eyes. "Joy, I wasn't joking when I said I wanted to spend the rest of my life with you. Will you marry me?"

Joy choked on tears and nodded her head, unable to get a noise to come out of her mouth. Josh slowly slid the ring on her finger. Then he turned to Janie. He knelt down in front of the little girl. "Janie, would you be my little girl and let me be your daddy?"

Janie gasped in surprise. "You mean it really? You love me and want to be my daddy?"

Josh smiled. "You bet I do, beautiful. What do you say? Do you love me enough to let that happen?"

Janie nodded her head with excitement. "Yes!" She flung her arms around his neck and squeezed him tight.

Josh held the little girl close. His love for both Janie and Joy was already so big he couldn't imagine it getting even bigger, but he knew it would with each new day as they became a family. He held her tighter. "I love you, Janie."

Janie squeezed his neck tighter. "I love you. Can I call you Daddy?"

He looked up at Joy and saw her wiping tears from her eyes. She smiled at him when she saw him watching her, and gave a slight nod to his silent question. Josh looked at Janie and kissed her cheek. "I would love to have you call me Daddy. You don't have to wait."

Janie squealed. She hugged him again. "I love you, Daddy."

Josh blinked back tears as he hugged Janie again. *Thank you, God. For so long I thought you didn't care about me. For so long I thought you hated me, because of what happened to me. Forgive me for doubting your goodness. Thank you for bringing me to this point in my life.*

40

Three weeks later, Josh was working in the orphanage late one afternoon when his phone rang. He glanced at it and saw that it was Lilly. He was surprised. His dad had called him a few times in the past few weeks but Lilly hadn't called in a while. He wondered what was going on.

"Hello." He knew he sounded hesitant, but he couldn't help it.

"Josh, it's Lilly. You need to come home." Lilly's voice was frantic and broken.

He was startled. "What's going on?" He asked in surprise. Even the franticness in Lilly's voice was out of character for her. As he listened to the voice on the other end for a few minutes, tears came into his eyes. "Okay, Mom. I'll catch the first flight out of here."

There was a pause while she answered him.

"No, Mom. It's okay. I'll be there as soon as I can. It's going to be okay. We are going to get through this. No, Mom, I am glad you called." He paused again. "Okay see you in a few hours." He hung up and glanced up at Joy who had come to tell him good bye before she headed home for the day.

"Is everything okay?"She saw the fear in his eyes. Her stomach twisted.

Josh shook his head. "No, Joy, it's not. My dad is in the hospital. They think – I mean -" he shook his head as he looked away then looked back into her eyes. "He's dying, Joy." Saying the words made it all become reality and he fought to keep his composure.

Joy stared at him in shock for a few minutes. Then she reached out and held him. She stepped back and looked into his eyes. "You need to go."

He nodded numbly. "Come with me?" he whispered.

She looked at him in shock. "Josh, I can't-"

"Please, Joy, come with me. We can stop by your place and pick up Janie on the way."

"But, Josh-" she stopped. She saw the fear in his eyes, but also the pain. What ever it was that had happened had to be serious. How could he know his dad was dying? He hadn't said they thought he was dying or something like that. He had said he was dying. She didn't want him to leave her, but how could they go together and not cause a problem or look bad.

He looked at her with pleading eyes. "We can have your dad marry us before we fly and we'll have a real wedding when we get back. Please come with me."

Joy smiled at him. "I don't need a real wedding." She touched his face. "Josh, it's not that. It's-"

He looked into her eyes. "Will you come? Please?"

She nodded. "I will, if you are sure that is what you want."

Josh pulled her close. "Thank you. I will make it up to you. I promise. You can plan the wedding of your dreams when we get back."

She shook her head. "Just being your wife, finally, is all that I want." She smiled at him. "It's going to be okay, Josh." She took his hand. "Come on, we need to go."

He nodded. As they drove out to her place he called and checked the flight schedule. After talking for a few minutes he hung up and turned to her. "We are booked on the next flight. It leaves in three hours. So we are going to have to hurry."

Joy nodded. "Let me throw some stuff in a bag for Janie."

When they got to her place she ran in ahead of him and quickly packed a bag while Josh explained the situation to Luke and Annie. When Joy came back out with two suitcases and a small bag of toys to keep Janie occupied on the plane, she smiled at her parents. "Please be okay with this. We don't want a big wedding anyway and this way it won't look bad, us all traveling together I mean."

Luke nodded. "It is a wise choice, and of course you should be there too." He had the two young people stand before them and say their vows. He then prayed over them and also asked God to spare Jim is he saw fit.

In less than half and hour they were on their way to the airport. And less than an hour later they where boarding a plane headed for home.

41

When the plane touched down, Josh was on edge. After a delay at the desk, they rented a car and drove as fast as he dared to the hospital. When he arrived he saw that his siblings were already there.

Jared and Jordan looked up as they entered the room. Lilly was seated by the bed holding her husbands hand. Josh absently passed Janie to Joy and stepped up to the bed.

Joy held back unsure of what to do.

Lilly looked up as Josh stepped up beside her. "How is he?" he whispered.

Lilly shook her head. "He slipped into a coma just after I called you. Your brothers got here just a few minutes ago. Their families are waiting in the waiting room. He hasn't woke up since I talked to you. He was asking for you just before that."

Josh nodded.

Lilly wiped at her tears.

"What happened, Mom?"

Lilly shook her head. "The little bit he told me before he slipped into sleep is that a man came into his office claiming to have a hurt arm. He told the man to remove his coat so he could look at it and as he turned away he heard the click of a gun, he turned back just as the man fired."

She broke down. "That was all he said about that. Then he asked for you. That was the last thing he has said."

Josh nodded and motioned toward the door. "Mom, this is Joy, I am sure you remember her."

Lilly nodded.

Josh smiled. "Joy and I got married a few hours ago, just before we headed this way."

Lilly gasped. "That was fast."

Josh smiled, "Not really. But it worked out better to come married. This is our little girl Janie."

Lilly smiled at both girls.

Joy smiled back as she walked over to Lilly and gave her a hug. She then turned to Josh. "I think I need to leave you and your family alone for a few minutes. I will just take Janie down to the waiting room."

Josh nodded slightly. "Are you sure? I can walk you."

Joy shook her head. "No, Josh. If he was asking for you, you need to stay here by him. If he wakes up, he needs to see you."

Josh nodded, "Thanks."

When Joy and Janie had left, Lilly once again place a hand on her husband's hand. "The doc said the bullet just missed his heart." she whispered through her tears. "I don't know what I am going to do if-" she broke down.

All three of the older boys put their arms around their mom. "I am sure it is all going to be okay," Jared whispered.

Jimmy sat wide eyed looking at all that was happening, but not really comprehending it. Julia, sat in silence with tears in her eyes.

Josh nodded slightly

Lilly watched him for a few minutes wondering what he was thinking. It had always been hard for her and Josh to communicate. She was never sure if he really believed she loved him like a son. She hoped he knew that, but what if he didn't. If his dad died would he feel like he wasn't wanted in the family any more.

Tears steamed down her cheeks. She didn't even want to think that. She took a deep breath, "Josh, I am going to give you a few minutes with your dad alone. Just call if there is any change."

Josh nodded again, and as Lilly and the others walked out, he slowly stepped up to the bed where she had just been standing. "What did you need to tell me, Dad? Who was the man in your office? What did he have against you?" As he spoke he was surprised to see his dad open his eyes and look his way.

"Josh?" came the whispered words.

Josh leaned in, "Dad? What is it?"

Jim smiled. "I asked Lilly to get you here before it was to late. I asked God to keep me here so I could talk to you before I go. I am glad he answered."

Josh smiled. "She did, Dad. And God did, but don't say that. You are going to be fine."

Jim shook his head slightly. "No, Son. I know I don't have much time, that is why I have been holding on for you. Josh, forgive me."

Josh felt his tears start to fall. In all the years of growing up that he wanted his dad to love him and never knew if he did, now he was asking for forgiveness. "Dad, i-"

Jim gasp for breath. "Son, I wasn't the dad to you I should have been. I was horrible. I know those first seven years of you life were a nightmare for you. And I am sorry. I know I told your mom that I would love you like you were mine, but I didn't. Every time I looked at you I saw the man that your mom had been with before me. I hated her and I took it out on you. When she left shortly after you were born, I told you she had died. All these years I have kept up that lie to you. She really is dead now, she died about ten years ago, but I didn't want you to know what she had done.

"I thought I could keep you from knowing what a bad husband I am and a horrible dad. But you already know I am a horrible dad. I am sorry, son. I wish I would have done the test sooner. If I would have known -"

He coughed then started again. "You are my son. Even if it wouldn't have shown up in the blood test I should have known. I should have treated you better. I know that it didn't get better for you after you moved back in with me as a teen. I should have been easier on you. I was just afraid that if I was, you would end up like your mom. Forgive me, please."

Josh nodded. "I do forgive you, Dad. Please hold on. Please don't go, Dad."

Jim shook his head. "Keep your family safe, son." Jim place his hand over his son's hand. "Take care of all of them. I love you." His words ended in a whisper as his last breath eased out of his body.

Josh bit his lip as his dad's body fell limp. "No, Dad. Don't go yet. There are still unanswered questions. Who was it, Dad? Who shot you. Did you know him? Did he have something against you?" His head dropped forward as he let his tears finally fall. After a few minutes he sensed a presence behind him and turned to see the doctor standing there, shaking his head.

"I'm sorry, I wish there would have been more that I could have done," he whispered mournfully.

Josh shook his head. "It's okay. You did what you could."

The doctor smiled at him, but it was a sad smile. "I really can't believe that he stayed alive long enough to see you. He was more dead than alive when he got here."

Josh nodded. "He just had some unfinished business to take care of. I guess in times like that God grants the grace to complete it."

The doctor nodded in understanding.

Josh slowly stepped away from the bed. "I need to go and tell my family. I think we will need a few minutes alone with him, before-" his voice broke and he couldn't go on.

The doctor nodded. "Take as long as you all need. I will be back in a while."

Josh nodded, then slowly walked out of the room, heading for the waiting-room to break the news to the rest of the family. He bit his lip as he thought of his dad's final words. Why was his dad asking him to take care of Lilly, Jimmy, and Julia? He knew they would need it, but why was it laid on his shoulders? Yet at the same time as he was questioning, he knew why. His dad trusted him. He was the oldest and he wanted to know that he was leaving his family in dependable hands. For, though Jared was married and had a little boy and another one on the way, he had already been through three jobs and was currently working as a janitor in the school. Jordan was more reliable than his brother, but he and his wife were expecting triplets in a few more months and would be very busy with that. Josh also knew that would be good for Lilly. It would help her, to be able to help them. It would keep her mind busy.

They all looked at him expectantly as he walked into the room. Joy saw the shadow in his eyes and knew his dad was gone. Lilly saw it too, and burst into sobs. Josh reached out to her and held her close. He reached out to little Jimmy and held him close too. The rest of the family gathered in the hug and all clung to each other for moral support.

Finally, when the tears were drying, Lilly looked at her

388

children. "Thank you all for being here. I know things are going to be ruff for a while, but with us all together they will be okay."

Josh felt his stomach tighten. He knew in that moment that he couldn't return to New York. Not yet any way. He would have to help Lilly through the next few months till she could handle life again. He looked up at Joy and knew she saw the pain in his eyes.

"It will be okay," she mouthed. "God will work it all out."

About a week after the funeral Lilly walked into the living room with and envelope in her hand. She had a small smile on her lips.

Josh looked up at her curiously. "You look like the cat that got the mouse. What do you have there?"

Lilly laughed lightly. "I was going through a few of Jim's -" her voice broke slightly. "I was going through some of Jim's things and I found a letter in his draw addressed to you. It was dated just two days before he was shot." Her voice broke again and Josh jumped up and wrapped his mom in his arms.

She cried hard, pressing her head into his shoulder. She had never dreamed that this was going to happen. How was she going to make it without Jim. He had been her support for so long. She felt so lost without him.

Josh felt Lilly trembling as she sobbed. Silently he prayer for God's help. He prayed that God would, also, heal her hurt and help her to move on.

Finally Lilly stopped crying and pulled away from Josh.

He looked at her curiously again. "So, what is in the letter?"

Lilly shrugged as she held it out to him. "There where few things that your dad didn't tell me, but when it came to you and the life he lived before prison, there was a lot I never knew. I only glanced at the first few lines, and decided it really wasn't my business to be reading. So I thought I would just give it to you and if you wanted to share you could."

Josh slowly reached out and took the envelope. Now he was nervous. He opened the envelope and his eyes went to the date on the top right hand corner. Lilly was right it was just two days before his dad was shot. Why hadn't his dad mailed it?

He bit his lip and let his eyes roam the paper for a few minutes before he started to read. Tears sprang to his eyes as he saw his dads smooth even writing. For being a doctor his penmanship was amazing.

He looked up at Lilly and Joy and tears were streaming down his cheeks. "I don't know if I can read it," he whispered, tears sounding in his voice.

He took a deep breath again and slowly started to read. But tears quickly ran down his cheeks and dropped onto the paper. He stopped took a deep breath and wiped his eyes. Silently he prayed for God to help him. With another shuttering breath he started to read again.

Dear Son,

I know I haven't been the best father in the world. I don't even come close. I have some things I need to talk to you about. I know that you are doing as you feel God wants you to just now, and I am grateful, but I do wish we could see you more often. Since I don't know when the next time will be that I will see you, I am going to write what I need to say. It is all very fresh on my mind and on my heart just now, so this way maybe I won't forget anything. Also, this way, if I lose my nerve to talk to you, it is all written down and I can just give you the letter instead.

As you know, your mother and I were very young when we got married. I was just out of med school and she was just out of high school. Yeah a lot of people told me I was robbing the cradle, but I didn't care. I loved her and I was sure she loved me and would be a great wife.

We hadn't been married a month, when I learned that she was posing for porn magazines. It hurt me deeply and I begged her to stop, but she refused. She wanted to be free, she said. Then she told me if I couldn't satisfy her she would go to someone who could.

Her words hurt me deeply, but not so deeply as a month later when we learned that she was with child. She swore up and down that it was mine, but I wouldn't believe her. I was angry about all that she was doing, and I refused to believe that the baby was mine.

I let a hate start to grow in me, but I kept it quiet. I never let her know that I didn't believe her. I acted happy about the baby being born. I acted like I was fine with it and happy in our marriage.

Eight months later you were born. The moment I saw you, I hated you because of her. Once again, I hid it. I acted like the happy father that everyone expected me to be, but I was miserable. My hate was eating me up.

I started to take my anger out on her. When we were alone I would hit her and yell at her. Finally when you were about two weeks old, she had enough. She looked me in the eyes, and I will never forget her words to me. She said, "Jim, you wanted a baby and I gave you one. I don't care whether you believe he is yours or not. I didn't want a child and I was happy with who I was before. You and I are through. This is your child and I don't want him or you. Don't try to find me. I will kill you."

I yelled back at her that if she was any kind of a fit mother she wouldn't be doing porn shoots or being in their movies, but she just laughed at me.

She told me I wouldn't ever be a good father because I was more of a failure as a husband then she was as a wife; and if I couldn't be a husband, how was I suppose to be a dad?

Again I swore to her that I could and would love you even though you weren't mine.

She shook her head. "Jim, the baby is yours, but I see that you will never believe me. We can't have this kind of marriage, and I can't live this way. Good bye." She turned and walked out the door and I never saw her again.

I was left with a two week old baby all alone.

I had made a promise that I was going to

love you and I tried hard to keep that promise, but it seemed impossible to me. Every time I looked at you, all I saw was the men she was with. The man she was in bed with the night I came home and learned all that she was involved in. It made me sick just to see you.

I tried to get over it, but I just couldn't let it go. I married again about a year later, and in another year another baby was on the way. This time I was excited, but the baby came too early and then in less then a year we were expecting again. This time you know what happened, mama and baby died, because I wasn't there in time to help them.

I know you probably will think that is not true, but to myself all these years that is how I felt.

You were three then. I knew I needed to get you into a church, but since your mom had left I had no interest in church. Still I knew for you I needed to. I didn't want you to be like your mom.

My hate toward you grew. It wasn't your fault and it was nothing you did. It was me. I hated me, and that made me hate you. I am so sorry son. I never meant to start beating you like I did, but my anger and hate were blinding me to what I was doing. I guess part of it was thinking if I beat you hard enough you wouldn't end up like her and the other part was taking out my anger at her on you.

Shortly before I went to prison, I had sent off DNA samples. I just had to know if you were my son. I had trier to let it go and just tell myself that I could except the fact that you weren't mine and I would just act like you were. But it was eating me up inside and causing the anger and hate I had in me to grow even bigger.

After I was in prison, I got the results. I know I shouldn't have ever let it change anything, son. You are my son and you would have been no matter what the DNA samples said.

When I saw the results and that they were positive that you were indeed my child something broke in me. All those years of anger and hate. All that I had let grow in me. It was my fault. I was the one who had hurt you and your mom. I was the one who was wrong.

It started an ache in me that only Jesus could heal. And he did heal it, once I gave it to him.

I am sorry I was so hard on you son. Even

when you moved back in with me and Lilly and I promised you I wouldn't hit you. I know that I didn't keep that promise.

The night I whipped you so bad about having the porn I know I said some things that hurt you and probably made you wonder what was going on. I don't know what happened it just started a huge fear in me.

I saw that stuff and suddenly all I saw was your mom. I didn't want you to be like her and I was determined if I beat you hard enough you wouldn't be. It hurt me inside, but it was more than that. I hurt you the same way I hurt your mom. It was her I was trying to get back at. I am so sorry, son.

I hope that some day you can find it in your heart to forgive me. I love you. I am sorry for all those years that I hated you, and then all those years that you more than likely hated me. I don't blame you one bit, son.

I am proud of you, son. You have grown into a fine young man. Know that I love you with all that is in me. You are my son, and I do love you. I am sorry for all the years that I didn't, and I am sorry for all the times I hurt you, those before prison and those after prison.

I hope that someday you can find it in

your heart to forgive me. I love you, my son. I am sorry it has taken me this long to say it. I know that as a child you longed to hear it, but I never told you. Again I am sorry.

Always keep your hand in the hand of the Lord. That is the best place you can be. If I wouldn't have left his hand I never would have ended up like I did and I wouldn't have all the scars of the past and neither would you.

Don't ever let Satan trick you, son. He is a liar. I love you more than I can ever tell you and I am sorry for all the times that I didn't tell you that, and I the times that I didn't love you.

Let God hold your future, son. He won't ever let you down. Don't try to hold it yourself. Take it from one who knows. All you will do if you try to hold your future is wreck it.

Once again, I love you, son.

I know you must be wondering about your mom. So I will tell you, I learned about two years ago that she died of cancer. By that time she had been married seventeen times and no, she hadn't had any other children.

If you want to know her name ask me, but I think it best to just let it be. She is gone and there is nothing we can do about it. So until *we talk face to face I will just keep that to me.*

I hope you understand why I never told you any of this. And I hope that some how you can find it in your heart to forgive me. I can't wait to see you again son and talk to you about all of this. God bless and keep you.

Dad

Josh looked up from the letter with tears streaming down his cheeks. "I never knew," he choked. "I never knew why he hated me like he did. I just knew that he hated me. I can't believe it. All this time."

Joy reached out to him and wrapped her arms around him. "Honey, it's okay."

Josh nodded and looked up at Lilly. "Did you know?"

Lilly shook her head. "I only knew that he had beaten you as a child. I knew he hated himself for it, but I never did learn why he did it. He told me repeatedly after you moved in with us that he was afraid he was going to go back to the man he was, because that was all he saw in himself when he looked at you."

Josh shook his head in shock.

Lilly smiled faintly. "The night that he beat you so badly because of the magazines. He left this room and bawled. He had never wanted to hit you again, but he said he just couldn't let this one go." Lilly sighed. "He said he hadn't finished and he had to whip you as much as he said he was going to. That was why he went back in there. Do you remember?"

Josh nodded. "I will never forget. That was the time he made me hit him. That was worse than being hit myself."

Lilly nodded. "I think it will stick with you."

Josh nodded. "It will. Thanks for giving this to me."

Lilly smiled. "I am glad I decided to go through some stuff and found it."

Josh nodded.

Lilly and walked out of the room.

Joy smiled at Josh. "You know what your dad said is right. We need to let God hold our future. We keep making plans and they keep getting messed up. We need to trust our future to his hands and ask him more what he wants from us."

Josh nodded. "I agree. Let's pray about it. Dad is right, God is the one who hold the future. I know we have sought his will with big decisions, but we need to do better with letting him have all the future, not just the big part."

Joy smiled. "Let's talk to him right now and let go of our future and let him hold it."

Josh smiled. "Okay."

Together they knelt by the couch and committed their lives into God's hands and their future into his will. They asked him to lead them and show them the way, each knowing how hard it would be to wait on God to answer. Yet as they said amen, an overwhelming peace flooded them. The kind of peace that only God can give, when he holds your life in his hands.

Josh smiled into Joy's eyes. "Now, my love, we wait and see what the Lord has in store."

Three months passed and life was adjusting as well as could be expected. Lilly was getting along. She had insisted on getting a job, so she could support herself and Jimmy and Julia, though Jim had left enough for her to live comfortably for the rest of her life. The kids all understood that she needed something to do.

Jimmy would be in school the next year and Julia was in school. She needed something to keep her busy. She needed to feel like she was doing what she needed to for her family. It was almost back to a place where things were normal.

Joy smiled as she thought about how much Josh had help his mom settle into a new life. She loved being with him. She loved being loved by him. She watched as Janie and Jimmy chased each other in the back yard.

It would be hard on Jimmy when they left, but she knew it was going to happen and soon. Jimmy and Janie had been inseparable since they had been here. But the time had come to move on. She and Josh had discussed it at length a few nights back.

He felt that his time at home was over. He had done all he could to help his mom. She was on her feet again. God was moving them on to other things. She felt it too.

Once they got his mom over the major hurtles in life, which they seemed to have done, they were heading back to New York. But this time to start a new work with the kids on the streets and a ministry to the gangs that lived in New York City. Some of the work would still involve the orphanage, but they both felt their calling was something more. They weren't sure what, but they did know that God would lead them as they followed him.

Joy smiled again as she heard Josh coming up the front steps. She rested her hand on her stomach. There would be one more surprise that awaited him when they got ready to move, and she couldn't wait to tell him. God had so richly blessed them both. She thought back over the last several years, the years since Josh had moved back in with his dad. How things had changed! But God had always been there. He did control their lives.

Josh smiled as he walked up the front steps of the house. He was so blessed. "God, thank you. You promised me a long time ago that you had plans to prosper me and not to harm me. I trusted in you, and you blessed even more than I could have imagined."

"Thank you for taking the time to love someone like me. Thank you for all your blessings. And thank you for your keeping. You have truly blessed beyond my wildest dreams."

He saw Joy wave to him from the front window and his smile widened. If he wasn't mistaken his wife was keeping a secret from him, and he was pretty sure he knew what it was. "Thank you, God, again. I am so overwhelmed. You are in control and I am trusting you to stay there."

He smiled as he reached for the door. "You are the Lord of my life, God. Thank you for loving me. You have truly given back all the years that were lost and more. Guide us on the next steps in this journey, and help us to keep our hand in yours as we do our best to follow your will. Please help us to remember that you are the only one who is capable of holding the future and help us to leave our future in your very capable hands. Amen."

Made in the USA
Monee, IL
17 March 2020